ILLUSION - *of* - SPLENDOR

J.D. EASLEY

Waterton Publishing Company

Waterton Publishing Company

www.watertonpublishing.com

Published simultaneously worldwide.

Library of Congress Control Number: 2012947104

ISBN 978-0-615-68604-2

In Memory of Rain Walsh

1994 – 2011

*"Teach us that wealth is not elegance,
that profusion is not magnificence,
that splendor is not beauty."*

Benjamin Disraeli

I REVENGE

On the Atlantic coast of northern Morocco a bearded man wrapped in a long white cotton shawl stands alone on the side of a hill. It is not yet dawn and gazing down into the distance he can barely make out a few dim lights believed to be houses or fishing boats moored in a harbor. He lowers to a rounded boulder and rests a sandaled foot on an adjacent rock and an elbow on a knee, takes a drag from his cigarette, waits, and watches; before long the starless night sky gives way to slate gray with streaks of burgundy highlighting low-hanging clouds. As he waits, the color fades, and so too the windows' glow as square pale buildings take shape scattered among indistinct date palm and eucalyptus trees. The lone man on the hillside remains motionless, thinking, wishing he had come to this tranquil village for a different reason.

Sawahi is a pastoral community – life passes gradually the way it has for centuries. On this January morning, like most this time of year, a thick layer of clouds hangs over the coast creating a surrealistic haze beyond which palm fronds rustle, roosters crow, and songbirds sing. From out of the mist emerge children on their way to school, shopkeepers on their way to stores, and fishermen on their way to boats. Most of the men make their living casting and trolling in the open ocean from small wooden skiffs with benches and outboard motors and large trawlers with cabins and woven nets draping from poles like heron wings rising from their decks. Others catch their family's evening meal from a stone breakwater that begins where a boardwalk ends to the north.

Boulders pile adjacent the road for a dozen or so meters until jutting more than fifty meters into the Atlantic as a rampart against the pounding waves. Fishermen jam cork handles of long stout poles into stone crevices; translucent lines dangle from tips, flutter in the breeze, and disappear in ripples below the water's glassy surface. The sea washes crystal clear over a long stretch of fine white sand beyond the breakwater. After school, children will splash in the surf, run down the beach, chase crabs and pick up empty shells and other objects deposited by the retreating breakers. Later, some of the villagers may build fires in stone pits sheltered by post and thatch huts.

Hills and ravines enclose the village on three sides so it remains an isolated oasis of white on a green and blue background from which just one narrow dusty spur accesses paved thoroughfares many kilometers distant and, eventually, highways, towns, and cities such as Tangier and Casablanca. There are few visitors to the village. Most are vendors bringing food, water, and dry goods by truck to resupply local merchants; tourists from the south fishing for perch, billfish, and tuna; families arriving by car or boat to meet friends or relatives; or passengers on vessels bound elsewhere in Morocco, across the Atlantic to Spain or Portugal, or through the Strait to countries of the Mediterranean.

It took Alwar almost three days to reach the dirt road and hillside overlooking Sawahi from his home in Libreville, Gabon. Driving through Cameroon, Nigeria, Niger, Algeria, and most of Morocco, he traveled as early as possible to avoid the midday heat but never early enough it seemed to avoid the congestion of people and livestock plodding the rural thoroughfares. His life-changing journey began with a simple instruction delivered by a red-haired American wearing round tortoise shell glasses, a white short-sleeve shirt stained gray around the armpits, and a bright yellow tie. The out-of-place foreigner pretended to be in the market for sea bass while making his way around the docks in Libreville. Eventually, he stopped at Alwar's small sailboat, the Jubilet.

The American stooped down, picked a fresh anchovy out of a bucket on the dock, and whispered to Alwar that he must sail the next day to a point a kilometer or so off the coast where the Gulf of Guinea meets the Gabon Estuary. There, at the periphery of a prominent sandbar well known in the area for very poor fishing, he would meet with a British Secret Intelligence Service officer from Port-Gentile. "Sail out by no later than six-thirty" advised the American, "then drop anchor, cast a fishing line and wait until at least eight for Michael Crane to arrive." He handed Alwar a dollar bill and Alwar wrapped the tiny fish in newspaper.

Jubilet's anchor plunged through kelp near the sandbar and a red warning buoy early the next morning. The weather was perfect; warm, clear but for a few white wisps, just a slight southerly breeze. Upright on deck, Alwar soon spotted what he believed to be a cabin cruiser motoring from the east. The vessel appeared and disappeared under the sun and swell as he tried with difficulty to keep track of its whereabouts through binocular lenses shielded by polarized sunglass. When the boat became larger than the waves, Alwar could see that it was navigating a steady course toward him and, when it was ten or so meters away, a nameless red and yellow wooden cabin cruiser slowed and a dark boy wearing a Red Sox cap hung two white bumpers over the side.

"Alwar!" the boy's overly-enthusiastic loud greeting apparently a misguided attempt to mislead eavesdroppers – despite there being no other boats within view – followed more reserved by the boy asking if he was indeed addressing Alwar: "Êtes-vous Alwar; comment allez-vous?"

"Bien, oui, mon nom est Alwar, êtes-vous?" Cautious was the tone of Alwar's welcome as he dropped the sponge grip of a black fishing rod into a steel tube bolted to the hull. Line ran taught from the pole tip to the water's surface as the Jubilet rocked casually side to side with a squid tentacle enveloping a hook less than a meter under keel.

"Je suis bon;" answered the boy, "monsieur Crane est ici!"

Alwar silently examined the boy wondering why he had not asked if Alwar was alone, and, after a few seconds, twisted, leaned far over the side of the Jubilet and rubbed the palms of his hands briskly in seawater to hide the residue and smell of squid should Michael Crane wish to shake his hand. Once again standing, Alwar shook his hands, reached down to retrieve a dirty blue towel from the deck, dried, dropped the towel on a nearby bench, turned both palms up, and shrugged his shoulders in an obvious quizzical gesture to the boy. The boy's muted response was simply to stand straight with feet apart, gaze at Alwar with eyes wide, and point in the direction of the yellow cabin.

The red and yellow cruiser drifted and recoiled as the two foam bumpers grinded and squeaked between the chipped paint of sealed hardwood slats. Alwar took a bow line tossed by the boy and looped it around a cleat, lifted the vinyl cushion of a bench in the back of the Jubilet, and removed binoculars. Walking along the railing he studied the horizon, vigilantly circling the deck twice searching for any sign of a possible intruder, anybody, in a position to see the two boats.

"It's okay, there is only one boat and it is at least two kilometers away" proclaimed Alwar while pointing to the north.

In one leap the boy stood atop the yellow cabin, eyes shaded with his right hand he squinted and focused on the distant north, rotating his head very deliberately as the tiny outline of what appeared to be a fishing trawler popped in and out of view. He knelt and pounded on top of the cabin, "Il est vrai, monsieur Crane, il n'y a qu'un seul bateau."

The old teak door of the small cabin creaked and soon a dark brown head appeared followed by chiseled hands grasping both sides of the doorframe. Michael Crane ascended cautiously from the cramped compartment; a lean and tall man, at least one hundred ninety-five centimeters, he crouched low, bending at the neck and waist to clear the top of the entry and twisting in obvious pain to straighten. His right hand held the brim of a tan straw hat supporting a red and blue rolled bandana, his left, a pair of gold wire aviator sunglasses.

Michael Crane was born Chiwetel Otaphi in a small Nigerian oil town where the bathwater smelled of tar and gas fumes flared night and day. His father died in a rig explosion when Michael was five, and he and his mother moved to Lagos, where she found a job washing dishes in a Mediterranean restaurant. Michael spent days in the streets running with the other children and nights in the restaurant playing with the owner's son, eating kabobs, listening to Persian music, and watching scantily-clad belly dancers writhe through dimly lit tables.

When Michael was eight, his mother contracted malaria while visiting his father's gravesite near the oil field, and was bed-ridden for nine weeks before dying. The owner of the Mediterranean restaurant took Michael in, but there was very little space in their two-room apartment – with six other people – and he left after three weeks. Michael wandered the streets of Lagos for nine months, surviving on handouts from the restaurant and sleeping under a bridge on Ozumba Mbadiwe Street near the bay. Sisters from the Streets of Eternity Orphanage found Michael digging in a trash pile one sweltering August night and he spent the next two-and-a-half years studying Catholicism and speaking English.

A British schoolteacher and his wife, volunteers at the orphanage, adopted Michael when he was eleven and moved him to their house in central London. There, he attended parochial school, played football on the school team, and fell in love with a blonde violinist. She moved away with her family to Paris when Michael was seventeen and, in an act born of remorse, he enlisted in the Royal Air Force by convincing the recruiter he was eighteen. Michael learned young how to shoot and parachute from airplanes and kill people in close quarters using knives, small arms, and guerilla tactics; he wanted to be a pilot but his height made the cockpits of smaller jets confining and a football injury to the left ear had caused an almost total loss of hearing. So instead, he became a soldier, a very good soldier.

Michael served two tours in the Bosnian War operating radar aboard troop transport planes. During one campaign in early 1993, while flying in a blinding snowstorm, his plane made an emergency landing near a village in Eastern Bosnia and he wandered the town and saw the snow-enshroud graves of Muslim men, women, and children killed by Serb forces. A woman appearing about forty approached Michael and tried to talk with him in Bosnian. He responded in French and English. The woman understood when Michael said in English that he too was a follower of Islam and she bent down, raised her billowing black skirt, and showed him deep purple scars around both ankles.

Michael applied with the British Secret Intelligent Service, MI6, after the war, became an Intelligence Officer, and was, after training and taking first in his class, assigned to a Lagos field office. It was 1995 and his cover was a cacao and palm oil export company on a noisy Victoria Island side street next to a sewage canal. Michael spent days monitoring monotonous telephone communications, following local news reports of questionable veracity, and conducting generally meaningless surveillance, and evenings in the Peacock Café across from the Radisson Hotel, plying locals with dirty gin martinis and befriending bartenders and prostitutes.

Members of the Alliance for Democracy broke into Michael's office in March 1998, in a well-planned effort to discover the names of companies buying palm oil – to organize a boycott – and stumbled upon a file at the bottom of an unlocked wooden cabinet. Pinned to the cover was a photograph of Michael in his RAF uniform; inside were other photographs of Michael, papers on RAF letterhead, and a handwritten note from Air Marshal Peter H. Wiggens. One of the burglars later told a friend about the file during a birthday party on a sightseeing ferry in Lagos Harbor.

The following week, on an overcast Wednesday mid-afternoon, two black men in khaki pants and bright dashiki shirts appeared at the export company entrance. They glanced up inconspicuously searching for security cameras and, finding none, the taller man casually rang the buzzer. Michael's partner, Kender Frederickson, set down his teacup, rose from a chair behind his desk in the front office, descended one flight of tattered carpet stairs and peeked out through the wrought iron bars of a very small one-way glass window encased in double-ply laminated and sealed iroko wood.

"Who is it?" he inquired in a loud voice.

One of the men, the shorter of the two, responded "Hello! My friend and I, we have a palm plantation in Kenya. We are looking for someone to sell our oil."

Kender studied the men through the small window, his eyes moving slowly up and down each, darting from the shorter man to the taller man and back again; he surveyed the men to make out the style of shoes and looked closely for signs of nervousness or any bulges in the shirts.

"Please step back away from the door" Kender requested, demanded, again in a loud voice and one clearly conveying suspicion. The men stepped backward in unison and Kender could see that both wore clean, probably brand new, Adidas or Nike running shoes.

"I'm sorry" Kender said, again loudly, even more resolute, "we're not taking any new orders at this time. Why don't you try a block down on the other side of the road, the Pyramid Trading Company? By the way, how did you hear about us?"

The same man, the shorter, responded "Okay, thank you, yes, we will," but neither man answered Kender's second question.

The two suspicious visitors turned their backs to the door. Kender leaned closer to the window, his nose pushed against the glass, watching curiously as the men scrutinized both directions up and down the street until walking briskly between passing cars in the direction of the Pyramid Trading Company. The orange and blue rubber soles of their shoes began flashing fast, and faster, becoming smaller and smaller as the men sprinted out of view.

Kender turned from the door. His mind was racing, something was wrong, but what? Wanting quickly to compare what he remembered of the men, faces, sizes, clothes, voices, with those in a database, wanting hastily to file a report and telephone the Pyramid Trading Company and warn Michael their cover was blown, he started to move. "Wait, but I'm safe inside" he thought, nothing happened, maybe there was no danger, maybe the visitors were indeed just selling palm oil.

As happens in the end, control relinquished to circumstance. Everything around Kender seemed to slow down; legs became paralyzed, unable to respond to commands, comprehend the exigency – the top of the stairs, his desk, so far away. A left foot settles upon the damp fibers of a stair, a right hand touches the smeared paint of a handrail, and a splintered remnant severs the quadriceps of a right leg; life smothered, family, friends, irrevocably damaged, all by a small package wrapped in a white cloth once lying at the foot of an impenetrable door.

Michael was at that terrible instant upstairs in the back office. The bomb shivered the concrete building, shattering windows, tossing him like a ragdoll from his chair behind a steel desk. Michael's head slammed the concrete wall and he blacked-out briefly, and, in a daze, found that he lie propped against the wall under holes where a few minutes ago were windows. His body was torn and twisted, arms dangled, legs crumpled. It felt like a dream. Moving his arms, legs, one at a time, just a little, bending at the joints, Michael tried to leverage his elbows against the floor for support but felt stabbing pain. He slumped, and felt the warm fluid streaming down his forearms, pooling in shards and slivers of glass.

"Kender?" there was no response to Michael's faint plea; "Kender, are you OK?" he knew the answer, "Kender!"

Michael spent three days in Lagos General Hospital for a concussion, ruptured cervical disc, and lacerations on his arms and back. On the fourth day an MI6 section chief in Libreville chartered a Cessna, flew to Lagos, took a taxi to the hospital, and escorted Michael from the hospital back to Gabon. After a week in Libreville, recovering and awaiting his new assignment, Michael received word to report to an outpost in Freetown, Sierra Leone, and assume the title Head of Operations. It was January 1999.

Over the next four years Michael Crane directed security service operations for Sierra Leone, Guinea, Guinea-Bissau, and Liberia; his officers infiltrated low-level rebel factions and helped Liberians United for Reconciliation and Democracy in their battle to dethrone President Charles Taylor. Michael rarely took direct part in covert operations, however, because of constant pain in his neck and numbness and tingling in his right arm. He was also addicted to fentanyl, injecting the potent narcotic in his numb right arm twice a day, and double-shot Bacardi dark rum and espresso cocktails, which he imbibed every afternoon at a vibrant outdoor café overlooking Susan's Bay.

It was at this café two months after arriving in Freetown that Michael arranged for the assassination of the men responsible for Kender Frederickson's death. He learned their identities while hospitalized in Lagos, after paying a private operative five-hundred dollars. The operative made contact with a young fruit-cart vendor, Alliance for Democracy junior officer, occasional paid informant for Western intelligence services.

The informant agreed to reveal the bombers' names only after being paid, told the reason, and on condition that the operative's principal make the request in person. Following some finagling the operative late one night escorted the fruit vendor to Michael's hospital room where the prospective informant handed Michael his five hundred dollars and agreed to provide the names in exchange for a "promise you will remember me." Michael promised.

After settling in Freetown, Michael called a friend in Frankfurt, Klaus Adalbrecht, a "specialist" under occasional contract with MI6 and the CIA. Klaus boarded a flight to Freetown the next day. Michael met Klaus at Lungi International, drove him to the café, and slipped a two-thousand Euros deposit – cash from a special fund – under a napkin.

It was a sunny day, clearer than usual and not too humid, and the two sat outside at a table closest to the railing next to banana trees and a shack so as to admire the bay. Klaus discreetly slid the white napkin from the table, crumpled it in his hand to conceal the bills, transferred the napkin to his lap, removed the money with his right hand and with the other removed a nylon pouch held by a belt under his pants and stuffed the money into the pouch. He and Michael spent the next hour drinking double gin and tonics and laughing as each recalled lighter moments during training for the foreign intelligence services.

As fond memories faded, and laughter ebbed, Michael leaned forward after having surreptitiously surveyed the patio; smile gone, voice hushed, he stared intensely at Klaus until revealing something that had for weeks inside him percolated rage: "Kender bled to death in pieces." Michael wanted to say more but choked upon hearing the words; holding back tears long overdue he at last blurted, "I want these bastards *exterminated*." The word lingered as somehow improper – even evil – an uncomfortable violence daring to disturb tranquility.

"That's what you paid me to do, Michael," Klaus replied in compelled casualness too late. Wanting to release the tension and ease Michael's discomfort, Klaus uncrossed his legs and shuffled to the edge of the chair, crossed his forearms on the tabletop, looked into Michael's eyes, and explained serenely, "It is what I am trained to do, you know, exterminate," followed up by a long sip of gin and tonic.

"Yes." Michael paused, looked down at the table and up at Klaus, "I have the package for you; it's in the trunk of the Ford, everything you asked for. Contact me with your expenses, the usual, Midland and Brookfield, if you get in a pinch, and I'll arrange payment to your Cayman account."

"That's fine;" Klaus took a sip, "how do you want confirmation?"

"Your word is good with me Klaus, but if you can get a photo without risk, that would be great. I'd like to see...." Michael did not finish the sentence. This was not about prevention; it was about vengeance, pure and simple, revenge.

Klaus understood; "I'm sure an image will be no problem."

"Your flight is at seven-thirty, I suppose we should get going." The two men raised their drinking glasses dripping condensation in an unspoken, understood toast; ice cubes rattling, they took one last long drink, pushed back their chairs, and stood. Michael went to meet the waiter as Klaus stayed behind, hands in his pockets, contemplating the bay and the shanties lining the hillside. "What a picturesque slum" he thought, and slowly walked to a path leading from the patio through a grove of mango and banana trees to a dirt parking area. Michael joined him and they strolled without speaking to the Ford.

Michael arranged for Klaus to hitch a US Army cargo plane from Freetown to Lagos and drove past the Lungi International terminal along a chain-link fence half a kilometer to a closed gate. A large sign mounted on a pole at the center of the gate cautioned passersby, in English and French, against stopping or loitering. Behind the gate, two Military Police Corp officers with M4 carbines stood a silent vigil.

Holding his left arm straight out the window, consular identification card in hand, Michael slowed the car to a stop. The gate barely opened and an MP squeezed through and carefully approached the car with both hands on a carbine low and to the side. The other MP stood behind the gate, carbine low and center, finger on the trigger. Klaus placed his hands on top of the dash and cocked his head for a view out the driver's window.

Michael spoke first: "Michael Crane, British intelligence, with a passenger for the seven-thirty transport to Lagos, cleared by

Colonel Firston." The MP lowered his chin to the left and whispered into his collar; remaining focused on Michael and Klaus he reached and took hold of the identification card, stepped back, and studied the card. After several minutes he lowered the carbine and walked back to the car, handed Michael his card, and said "You're clear, stop at the hangar" while the gate swung open.

Michael drove a short distance down the dusty road, turned right, and proceeded until passing through gaping sliding doors into a cavernous metal hangar empty but for a few pallets loaded with cardboard boxes. He and Klaus stepped out of the Ford, lingered for a moment surveying the vast structure, and walked out into the sunlight toward a dark green C-12 Huron sitting on the runway. A gray-haired man in fatigues stood in an open rear door of the airplane. He waived at Michael and Klaus as they approached, disappeared, reappeared in a door toward the nose of the plane, and quickly descended a rolling staircase to meet them.

"You must be Michael Crane," the man looked directly at Michael, obviously aware that he was Nigerian, and in a friendly voice approached and held out his hand, "I'm Johnny Firston."

"Colonel," Michael grasped the Colonel's hand, "it's a pleasure, this is Klaus Adalbrecht," and nodded toward Klaus who reached out with his right hand.

"Good to meet you, Klaus, you ready for a ride?"

"Yes sir," replied Klaus with his German accent and confident smile, "as long as the stewardess is serving cocktails."

"I'll get the rest of your things, Klaus," exclaimed Michael, turned, and jogged to the hangar; after unlocking the Ford trunk he delicately pulled out a black satchel and black canvas scuba duffel, slipped his right hand through the strap of each, hung the bags from his shoulder, walked briskly back and handed them to Klaus. The men talked a few minutes longer and said goodbye. Klaus and the Colonel ascended the stairs as Michael leisurely returned to the hangar.

About three and a half hours later, Colonel Firston drove Klaus to a hotel in upscale Ikoyi on Lagos Island. Klaus did not necessarily want the attention of riding in an Army M1117 Armored Security Vehicle, but no other transportation was available from the isolated corner of Murtala Muhammad International Airport where the C-12 landed and, if dropped at the airport taxi stand, cab drivers would suspect he was with the United States military. He figured cab drivers were infinitely more talkative and troublesome than bellmen.

After settling in his room Klaus drew the curtains, placed the satchel and duffel on the bed, sat down on the bed, opened the satchel, and carefully removed two thick manila folders. One folder he placed on a nightstand next to a clock radio. The other, identified by a Nigerian name he tried to pronounce but could not, followed by the words "Shorter Man," he opened.

The first set of documents consisted of twelve color photographs all presumed to be of the Shorter Man, wearing different clothes, taken in different settings, and including different people; he walked along a sidewalk, ate in a restaurant, talked to another man on the street, opened a door, talked to two women on the street, stood alone at a bus stop, pushed a two-wheeled wood cart, and drank beer out of a bottle with one man and two men at the same outdoor café. Behind the last photograph was a three-page typed dossier fastened to the folder with metal prongs and, under the last page of the dossier taped to the inside cover, a color photograph of Kender Frederickson's mutilated corpse laying in the remains of a drab stairwell.

Klaus stared at the photograph. He had seen hundreds such photographs – crime and combat scenes – but each he found agonizing, and this one, especially so. He knew Kender, not as well as Michael, but had socialized and worked with him on three or four occasions and found him a pleasant and likeable person undeserving of such cruelty. Klaus set the folder gently on the bed, next to the duffel, and picked up and thumbed through the other, also identified by a Nigerian name, the subject referenced also by his relative height, "Taller Man." The same type of documents held the same order. He placed that folder back on the nightstand, reclined, and gazed at the ceiling.

"Each of the bombers will have to die alone because catching the men together will be next to impossible" Klaus thought, meaning the kills would have to be very close in time, otherwise, his chance of escaping Lagos alive was very slim.

Eyelids drifted together for a moment. Klaus leaned forward and sat with his hands on the edge of the bed, yawned, stood and turned, quietly contemplating the zipped black duffel. He remained next to the bed for a long time, walked to the bathroom and bent over the sink to splash cold water on his face, grabbed a hand towel from a rod, dried, and stared solemnly into the mirror while clinging to the white cloth. Eyes met in the reflection. Looking down at the sink, sighing, Klaus tossed the towel on the counter and returned to the black duffel.

Inside, seven soft packages wrapped in brown fish paper and sealed with clear strapping tape. Firmly, but delicately, Klaus grasped the largest package with both hands. Long and narrow, about the length of his arm, he raised it from the duffel, set the widest end on the bed so that he could hold the narrow end with one hand, and reached in his pocket with the other to pull out a silver folding knife about the length of a credit card, push a steel button, and draw a razor-sharp edge under the tape. He tossed the knife on the bed and methodically turned the narrow end of the package with one hand, gathering fish paper with the other, to reveal a black plastic stock and steel gun barrel each cocooned in bubble wrap. Klaus recognized the parts at once as belonging to a Heckler & Koch PSG 1 semi-automatic sniper rifle.

Laying the stock and barrel next to the duffel, Klaus unrolled bubble wrap from each, dropped the wrap on the carpet next to the fish paper, and carried the cold black sections around the bed for alignment neatly atop the soft beige bed cover. He walked back around the bed and lifted a second brown package from the duffel, slit the strapping tape, and unfolded the paper and bubble wrap to unveil a Glock 27 forty-caliber pistol. This, he had also requested. Klaus held the gun, twisting and pivoting his wrist to appreciate the feel while working the safety and magazine releases, after which setting it gently next to the H&K.

The next four packages contained two magazines filled with Smith & Wesson hollow-point cartridges and a plastic pistol grip,

Hendsoldt telescopic sight, and twenty-round NATO magazine for the H&K. Klaus thoughtfully positioned these items around the rifle and pistol. Last of the wrapping at the bottom of the duffel bag turned out to cushion a hand-held paper shredder and assortment of currency outlet converters; Klaus plugged the shredder into a converted outlet over the washroom basin and set it on the counter.

Back at the bed Klaus grabbed the satchel and removed a large plain brown envelope, went to an outside corner of the room where he turned on a floor lamp next to a reclining chair and fell back into the cushions. Inside the envelope he found a Lufthansa airline ticket sleeve and fifty twenty-dollar bills, which he removed, thumbed through, counted, and stuffed back into the envelope. Unfolding the ticket sleeve he removed the ticket: business class one-way travel to Frankfurt at eleven the next night. A glance to the clock radio and some quick math confirmed thirty-two hours to find two men in a strange city, terminate both, most likely in public, ditch guns, destroy documents, and check-in.

"Not much time" thought Klaus. He inserted the ticket into the sleeve and slid the sleeve into the envelope, which he returned to the satchel, and picked up the two manila folders. Lying back in the cushioned chair next to the lamp he carefully read each dossier stopping only occasionally to study a photograph or write illegibly on the back of a folder. When through, he stood and pulled back the curtain to expose a bright tropical late afternoon landscape filled with ordinary people going about their ordinary lives. He watched for several minutes before lifting his leather carryon bag from the floor next to a round table on the other side of the room. Inside was a notebook computer – after a few minutes he was comparing Lagos driving routes with the folder notes.

The Shorter Man was not married and lived alone, visited the same outdoor café almost every afternoon at around four-thirty, sat at a table near the street and drank a bottled beer, usually with one or two men, sometimes with the Taller Man, sometimes alone, for an hour or so. The Taller Man was married and had one child; he lived close to the same café in a ground floor flat and bought cigarettes and coffee each morning at a nearby market. Klaus jotted cryptic letters and numbers on a hotel writing pad as he studied the folders and maps.

The airport was about fifteen minutes driving time – assuming moderate traffic and no construction or accidents – from the café. It was about twenty-five minutes from the ground floor flat. Four-thirty at the café, to the flat, and to the airport by nine was possible under the best of circumstances. Klaus smiled; the shorter man worked near the café but lived in a fifth floor apartment on the other side of the lagoon at least forty-five minutes from the airport.

It was six-thirty when Klaus finished considering possible strategies for completing his assignment. He powered off the computer and slipped it back in the leather bag and turned on the television. Tuning to CNN he adjusted the volume to a high, almost unpleasant, level. The folders and scuba duffel he carried to the washroom where he ripped out documents and shredded all but one photograph of each man. The narrow strips of paper floated into the duffel.

Klaus placed each of the folders – empty but for one photograph – back in the satchel, scooped fish paper and bubble wrap from the floor, stuffed it all into the duffel, added two large bath towels and an ice bucket, and toted the billowing bag to a plastic trashcan next to an icemaker at the end of the corridor outside his room. Once satisfied nobody else was in the hallway or perhaps peering out a cracked door, and that no cameras overlooked the trashcan, he quietly unzipped the duffel. Raising and holding the lid with one hand Klaus shoveled wads of firearm cushion and shreds of assassination orders into the open can, replaced the lid, pulled out the ice bucket, fluffed the towels still in the duffel, zipped closed the duffel, filled the bucket with ice, and strolled back to room conspicuously carrying the full bucket.

The ice bucket and towels Klaus set next to the sink, laid the empty duffel on the bed, neatly positioned the fully assembled and loaded H&K and Glock inside the duffel, pushed the bag under the center of the bed, and brushed his teeth. Grabbing the shredder, satchel, and the notepad and pen, and pulling a full-size Nikon thirty-five millimeter digital camera from the leather bag and hanging it around his neck, he felt for the money belt under his pants, hung a do-not-disturb sign on the outside doorknob, walked to the end of the hallway and descended one flight of stairs. At the second floor, Klaus found another plastic trashcan next to an icemaker, where he discreetly deposited the shredder and subsequently resumed his descent to the lobby.

The bellman hailed a waiting cab. Klaus glanced at his watch, scribbled on the pad, and stepped outside. It was still very warm and humid. He slipped on sunglasses and waited three minutes. The taxi door opened. Tipping the bellman two dollars, Klaus scribbled again, took a seat in the back, examined the driver's photograph taped to the dash, and rolled down a window. The old Dodge smelled of cigarettes and sweat.

"The Radisson," Klaus said politely while again glancing at his watch and writing. The Radisson was a few blocks from the café. The driver tapped a meter and slowly pulled away from the bellman; Klaus focused intently on the passing surroundings when not looking down as he sporadically did – seemingly without reason – to make notes.

"In heavy rush-hour traffic without any delays arrived at the Radisson thirty-seven minutes after leaving the hotel" – Klaus memorialized his thoughts in a cryptic entry. He handed the driver a twenty-dollar bill, exited from the backseat slowly, and looked around while flipping pages of the notepad. "The café should be three blocks on the right" he surmised; and, turning to the street, jotted a reminder about the hotel-front cameras, "3 candy – red licorice 10, 12, 2," and set off for the café.

The street was busy with traffic and the carbon monoxide from old American and Japanese cars permeated the humid air so completely that it felt as though poison was seeping into his pores. Klaus tramped along in the dirt and dust of a narrow path adjacent to the oncoming cars and trucks, stopping every so often to snap a photograph of the road in both directions interspersed with a photograph of some building or object he believed tourists found of interest. Ahead on his right, across the street perhaps a hundred or so meters from an intersection, he could see an outdoor patio with tables around which people sat. It was the same café as in pictures once attached to the manila folders in his satchel.

Klaus stopped to survey the side of the road to the intersection, trying to find an inconspicuous place to photograph the café above the flow of cars and trucks. There was a knoll covered by trash-laden scrub and two tall palms, a bus stop with a bench a few meters beyond, and a bland white three-story building with windows, probably apartments, behind the stop. "The knoll and bench would be too noticeable," Klaus thought, maybe he could see the café from a second or third floor hallway window in the white building.

He walked briskly along the road, past the knoll, and behind the bus stop, where he paused to search for some evidence of the white building's purpose. He found none. Neither were there a porch or front door – merely a tan dirt walkway leading to an opening where once, it appeared, hung a door. It was also clear to Klaus that some of what he thought were windows were instead empty frames where glass at one time shattered.

Klaus stood at the doorway of the abandoned tenement, turned, and again surveyed the area; knowing the building was likely home to vagrants, perhaps worse, he evaluated the preparatory value of any photographs when considering possible loss of the satchel dangling from his shoulder and the expensive camera around his neck. It was one thing to take pictures, he concluded, but keeping them may be a problem. A quick pat to his right trouser pocket confirmed with some satisfaction the small folding knife brandished in impromptu self-defense on several previous occasions; "I knew I should have brought the Glock" he muttered.

Looking around again, Klaus raised the wire-embedded strap of the satchel over his head and positioned it on his left shoulder to prevent the case sliding from his arm. He stepped back and considered the windowless rectangles in the wall above; deciding quickly, for no empirical reason, the benefit was worth the risk, he cautiously stepped forward over a threshold of dirt-filled cement block into the building.

A narrow space of shadows masking chipped concrete led to

wood stairs adjacent to a wall and a dark hallway beyond. Klaus stopped at the base of the stairs, leaned slightly, and examined – listened really – down the dim corridor for any sign of life. There was none. His tense upper body straightened, ears strained for sounds and squinted eyes sought anything at the stair's zenith but a stream of sunlight illuminating a graffiti-laden cinderblock wall. Onto the first stair, the second, keen to every sound, Klaus cautiously made his way up into the shadows.

Standing on the last stair at the second floor – and the sun's welcome glow – Klaus paused, and quietly pressed against the wall to peer around the corner. The sun shone from an opening across the hall, a doorway; low enough on the horizon was the sun that through a window, or a cavity, it cast light across the vacant room into the hall and onto the wall. Nothing moved. Still, Klaus waited, and listened. Faint sounds soon emanated from deep within the hall, pounding, scratching, perhaps an animal, perhaps not. Klaus leaned back slowly from the corner and focused his attention down the stairs. With his right hand reaching in a pocket he pulled out the knife, felt the handle, placed his thumb on the round steel button, pressed, and held the springing blade firmly against his belt to let it arch and lock quietly.

In an advance of experience and expertise, quick and smooth, Klaus crossed the hall and through the doorway; in his right hand, the knife, close to his side, blade at forty-five degrees turned inward just slightly. He hesitated and surveyed the space. "This is fortunate" he thought, one vacant room with two window frames, no glass, one of which overlooked the intersection.

The entire café patio was easily visible across the street a short distance from the intersection. Klaus set the knife on a window base the width of a concrete block, raised the camera, and looking through the viewfinder adjusted the zoom and shot several photographs of the busy patio. Next, he adjusted the power higher and began photographing people's faces; pausing, he adjusted the zoom to a higher power while looking through the eyepiece. It was the Shorter Man – he was sure.

Klaus lowered the camera. He had not expected to see the Shorter Man; it was past six-thirty and background surveillance described in the dossier suggested the man never stayed at the café past five-thirty. Klaus raised his camera and again found the man in the viewfinder. Moving his head slowly, he began studying each person at the table under the lens' highest power; four men equally positioned at the table, all drinking coffee, perhaps tea, out of cups resting on saucers, none laughing, all leaning forward, arms on the table, hands almost touching. The conversation appeared quite serious. Klaus continued staring through the viewfinder at one man whose face he could not see and who, he hoped, would soon turn.

A loud thump from the hallway startled Klaus, though, and his body twitched and he instantly let the camera drop to his chest, grabbed the knife, and pivoted. The sound was like that of a muffled collision, "like a head striking carpet" he thought, but no carpet in the hall. Maybe it was nothing, maybe something. He moved closer to the wall and, facing the room, sidestepped hurriedly toward a dark corner with a view down another wall to the doorway still bathed in sunlight and the door hinged from the other side. Klaus considered his options: no door exit, two window exits, one of which about three-meters above hard packed soil, no diversions, no hiding places, no gun, hand-to-hand combat training and a small knife.

The decision took about two seconds: he would jump out a window.

Klaus with a cautious but strong gate proceeded as his shoulder rubbing the concrete wall guided him toward the window, all the while keeping keenly observant of the doorway; midway to the window and hearing a different sound however, those of footsteps and talking, a group not just two or three people, his pace quickened and his eyes focused solely on the window and he thought of nothing but escape.

A gruff angry voice loudly demanded to know "What are you doing?" Klaus turned in a flash and saw two men enter the room and a third and a fourth; in the sun's waning rays high against the wall and through the doorway he saw only dark bearded men scowling "Stop!" quickly vanishing in the dark, and he heard running, and he ran.

Still clutching the silver knife in his right hand, with his left, Klaus threw the camera over the right shoulder and the strap went taught against his neck as it fell to his back. No time to hang from the ledge – he had to jump. First very briefly studying the ground he gave the knife a slight toss and next, placing both hands on the concrete, threw his legs over the ledge. Knees buckled as feet touched the ground. He rolled to one side on packed dirt with the camera and satchel bouncing around his neck and quickly to feet scoured the dirt under nearby bushes until the knife was firmly in grasp.

Above, two angry men yelled and shook their fists; "Damn lucky" Klaus ventured aloud, they had no guns.

"Somebody had to have seen me jump or at least heard the commotion" thought Klaus. He moved quickly toward the road and folded the knife, dropped it in a pants pocket, positioned the camera at his chest and the satchel to his side, and brushed fine brown dirt from his clothes. Nearing the empty bench his pace slowed and he passed cautiously and surveyed the street in both directions; nobody seemed to be paying any attention to him or the white building in the background. Turning once more and finding the window frame empty, Klaus inspected the camera, stepped leisurely to the intersection, and paused to consider the next – hopefully less hazardous – twenty-eight hours.

The choice was simple; either try to take the men that evening without the usual tools, which also meant trying to locate the Taller Man, and take an early flight, or wait as planned until the next afternoon. "A bird in the hand" Klaus thought, if, the Shorter Man was still at the café, no certainty now but also no certainty tomorrow. He decided to walk past the patio.

It was dusk, traffic lights turned, cars and trucks stopped, and bicyclists bolted through the intersection. Klaus looked, walked across the road between bicycles, looked again, waited for the light to change, and crossed toward the café. He went through a parking lot, down a dirt path, and suddenly was next to the low chain-link fence enclosing the patio.

Four people with arms outstretched encircled the same round table near the fence. Klaus glimpsed two of the men's faces as he walked by; they sat together on the far side of the table only a few meters distant. The man to their left, Klaus had identified, through the camera lens. The man to their right sat with his back to the fence. Klaus pretended to look past the patio into the café, passing the table looked ahead, and followed the fence to the café entrance. In position to see the fourth man's face – but not daring to turn and look – he opened a glass door, slipped on his black sunglasses, and stepped inside the café. Hoping still to go unnoticed, he weaved through a row of tables and stood at the edge of the patio, as might a German tourist searching for the perfect table from which to enjoy a cocktail at dusk.

The unseen man was the Taller Man; almost sure, Klaus' eyes locked on the man for brief intervals while pretending to survey the patio, head pivoting slowly, thinking about the photograph but certainly not wanting to unzip the satchel in the restaurant and pull out a manila folder to make the comparison, he discreetly kept the men in view. They talked close together seemingly at once; voices low they leaned toward the center and faces intense their eyes darted from person to person.

"Sit anywhere!" a young woman's pleasant voice broke Klaus' concentration.

"Oh, yes, thank you, I'm waiting for my wife," Klaus smiled, started to back into the café away from the patio, but too late.

"Here, you can sit here," a woman spoke as she stood from a chair at a nearby table; "Yes, please, we are leaving," it was her male companion in a black fedora standing from his chair and motioning with his arm.

"No, thank you, no, I'm waiting for someone," Klaus smiled and gestured with his palms facing the couple, fingers up, as if to say "It's not necessary."

Klaus glanced at the men around the table trying not to move his head, peering instead from the green edges of his sunglass lenses. The two facing Klaus, the Taller Man and another, had stopped talking and were sitting straight and studying him. Klaus kept smiling at the couple as he stepped back, pivoted, and entered the café. Walking in deliberate leisure toward the exit, squeezing at times between chairs sideways facing the patio, he saw that the two other men had their heads turned and all four were closely monitoring his departure.

Nonchalant as a foreign tour-group sightseer intentionally but carelessly straying from the pack, Klaus pushed the glass and strolled through the doorway down a concrete walkway to the road. He did not look in the direction of the patio. At the road he stopped and turned away from the café, paused, and raised his camera. Peering through the viewfinder he adjusted power and slowly turned his head to take in the cityscape. What must have to others been meaningless vistas gray in the looming night – speckled only by headlights, lampposts, signs, and windows – Klaus captured, and began a brisk exodus from the café. There appeared to be a hotel in just five or six blocks, which almost assuredly meant a cab and a safe retreat back to his hotel.

Making his away along the busy street toward the hotel, horns, diesel engines and brakes, choking fumes, crossing one narrow street at a roundabout Klaus took a path barely visible in the imploding darkness and meandered through a vacant lot overgrown with vegetation. Thereafter a bus stop, another roundabout, a gas station, and another treed strip of land; he stopped on the asphalt and stood at the edge of the forest. It was a dark and foreboding place illuminated just slightly by the pumps and a neon petrol station sign to his back. A trail barely visible led through dense undergrowth. "No, no," he thought, this was too much, better to follow the road and try to hail a cab, no telling where the trail led; he hurried along the forest edge toward the welcoming lights and sounds of a busy thoroughfare.

Peering down the road toward his destination and witnessing the loud rush of cars and trucks coming and going, Klaus realized, there was no place for a pedestrian to walk or run. Large palms and leafy trees grew to the edge of the pavement, towering and hanging over the traffic, with smaller trees, bushes, and grasses making up part of a thick barrier in the dark impenetrable undergrowth. He decided to stay put and try forcing the attention of a passing cabbie in need of a fare.

Facing oncoming traffic, Klaus leaned with his right arm

stretched out waving up and down so close to the flashing metal and glass that occasionally his hand reflexively jerked back. Within a short time an old white Ford sedan jetted from the stream of lights, came to rest abruptly between him and the neon sign, and disgorged four occupants before Klaus realized the vehicle was not a cab. The men, he recognized instantly even in the faint light, and slipped the fingers of his right hand down a pant pocket to cradle the small silver knife.

The driver and the man behind the driver, one of the very men Klaus was under contract to assassinate, the Taller Man, took positions slightly apart in front of Klaus while the other two including the Shorter Man stood on the opposite side of the car, one facing the street, the other, gas pumps. In one smooth action, Klaus moved his right hand concealing the knife from the pant pocket and, palm inward, fingers together, thumb pressing the cold steel handle a millimeter from the steel button, lowered the hidden knife to his side.

"What do you want?" the inquiry a subdued trembling deceit as Klaus, raising his left hand, palm out, fingers slightly spread, gestured "Stop, please, I don't want any trouble."

"We want your camera" the Taller Man demanded confidently, "and your sunglasses. Give us your wallet, that bag and your money belt, *now*, or we'll take them!" The two men's hands curled into fists and they stepped closer to Klaus, close enough to strike.

Klaus quickly responded, again, displaying timidity, "Okay, okay, you can have them."

Raising his quivering right hand, Klaus reached into a shirt pocket, carefully pinched the black plastic sunglasses with his thumb and forefinger and, still concealing the knife, held the sunglasses with his elbow slightly bent in front of the Taller Man. The man's left hand lurched and his fingers seized a lens just as Klaus' thumb slid from the plastic frame over the steel button and pushed just slightly; the blade flashed and locked; a right hand twisted and wrenched as dark red blood spewed from the Taller Man's left wrist. There was a scream. Klaus lunged. He grabbed the man's head with his left hand and with his right plunged the small blade through the carotid artery and out the back of the neck. The man with eyes wide in disbelief crumpled to the asphalt.

The driver turned to run but Klaus pivoted and leapt; another scream; the driver's legs buckled under Klaus' weight and he fell to the asphalt. The blade red with blood lay against the man's throat for just an instant until with his other hand Klaus slammed the man's head against the hard surface, raised it, and slammed again. This assailant would live to remember a German tourist who turned out to be a very poor choice for robbery.

Toward Klaus from behind ran another, not the Shorter Man, this attacker shrieked a war cry while in his right hand clenching a long machete raised high to wield a decapitating blow. Klaus jumped to his feet, flipped the knife, caught the blade with the thumb and two fingers of his right hand and jettisoned it twirling toward the man's face. The blade struck its target in less than a second – penetrating the mouth and sinking deep into the tongue and throat. The war cry turned to gurgle.

Still in possession of the machete the man stumbled backward just long enough for Klaus to jump and, with his left hand, hold off the blade and, with his right, pull the silver knife from the man's mouth and jam the blade deep into his neck. The man tumbled backward. Klaus fell forward crashing onto his writhing body all the while pulling and jamming the blade until the writhing ceased and the machete released. Klaus lay on the man and into vacant eyes seeing death gasped for oxygen; shaking, sweat and blood dripped from his face.

"Just one more thing to do" he thought, finish the assignment – the Shorter Man – no salvation for either prey or predator.

The Shorter Man, Klaus instinctively knew, fled deep into the jungle to escape the carnage; vanishing into the terrible darkness down a narrow trail the terminus of which Klaus could not possibly know. Rising painfully, Klaus stood over his victim, in his right hand a small silver knife, in his left, a machete. Khaki pants and floral shirt earlier that day new emblazed in dark wet red as was the scored nylon satchel pressing against his stomach. Sunglass and camera lay strewn in fragments on the asphalt.

Klaus was unsure of the time, unsure of how much time had elapsed, unsure of how many people knew what brutality had befallen five people there under a faint neon glimmer. The Ford was empty but the engine rumbled and the headlamps illuminated the forest wall until succumbing eventually to the awesome black.

Standing for just a few seconds considering what would be in all likelihood his final moments, Klaus' thoughts were not of self-pity, but of finishing a job and protecting his client. "Soon, passersby will find lifeless bodies by the car, police will comb the area, sunglasses and camera will provide evidence linking me to the scene. Self-defense, I could argue, perhaps, but tomorrow while I'm still at the police station a hotel housekeeper will find the computer and cache of precision firearms. Not an option, anyway, the Shorter Man has to die. In a few days someone will find the Shorter Man's body somewhere distant from this place and sometime later they may find my body. With it will be no documents or identification. The authorities will piece together part of the puzzle, know it was an execution with at least two intentionally killed, but that is all, no motive, no connection to Michael."

Drawing a deep breath as if about to submerse in a dark pool, Klaus lowered his head under a tree branch visible under the headlamps and, holding the machete and knife at ready, entered the menacing maze. He walked cautiously at first, getting used to feeling his way along the trail, managing fear, occasionally colliding with a tree branch or stumbling on a root or a rock, while insects buzzed all around drawn by the blood. After a short distance he began sprinting with his head down and the machete held in his left hand, high out in front like a battering ram, thrusting the long blade, striking, cutting, jolting at times to recoil against his head or shoulder leaving gaping wounds, stopping, listening, jogging, walking, sprinting, heart racing. After a while Klaus began to feel as one with the jungle, an animal, a predator pursuing his prey, invulnerable to fear or pain, finally accepting of his mortality.

There came a time when the machete was still, branches and leaves did not rustle, and the sensation against arms and shoulders subsided; after a few steps, Klaus perceived the change and stopped. He stood and listened, tried to see, anything, and could; ahead was a dim narrow glow visible through the trunks and leaves. His feet in soft rhythm motions glided in the direction of the light while the muscles in his arms and shoulders rippled, sinew tight, blades, appendages of his anatomy, positioned to slice.

The distant glow evolved into a bright point of shedding radiance in the distance. Klaus moved even more deliberately, quietly, one shoulder, the right, jutting forward, in his right hand the machete poised to thrash, his body crouched to pounce. The bright point expanded to a ball, a dancing spire, a fire, a bonfire; people stood around, perhaps ten, perhaps more. Klaus lingered in the dark and considered the scene as might a lone wolf or hyena. It would be impossible to approach unnoticed – retreat his only alternative.

Years of meticulous preparation and unwavering experience, however, steadied impulse and Klaus reconsidered; too far, too much lost to go back. Sighing in recognition of the challenge in store, he rested the machetc handle at the base of a palm, folded the knife and slipped it into a pant pocket, and unzipped the satchel, withdrew and folded the documents and stuffed them in his pockets. Once again grasping the knife in his right hand, around it making a fist, he began to move in large purposeful strides toward the gathering.

As Klaus drew closer the people became clearer, men and women, old, young, children, all dark, some laughing, others drinking, smoking. A few meters from the fire he was noticed, by one, by a few, until by all; heads turned one by one, talk and laughter silenced, the crackling torment of a large fire the only sound. No slowing in stride or trying to appear harmless Klaus determined; no time; eyes focused on the group, on each man, waiting for one to bolt, the straggler, wounded and afraid.

Then it happened. A man broke from the human circle in front of Klaus, dashing close to the burning branches and pushing through a wall of people on the other side, in a scrambling panic to find darkness. Klaus accelerated and running hard grazed those unable to step out of his way or simply immobilized by the sight of frenzied bloody death. Crashing through the undergrowth, glow soon gave way and, arms flailing, Klaus ran, crouched low, head down, while ahead the Shorter Man stood in the dark holding high a heavy tree limb.

First absorbing the club's force was Klaus' right hand and the knife went flying; a blow to the head, above the right ear, Klaus tumbled to the ground. Dazed – but conscious – both hands reflexively cradling his head, Klaus squirmed in the dirt as a beached fish squirms in the sand desperately for water. The club struck his left arm. Klaus pushed in the dirt with his hands, trying to crawl, the left arm and shoulder, battered, down again on his belly, stabbing pain, more squirming, another blow to his back on the left side. Klaus rolled to his right in the blinding dark until his torso pressed against the man's legs. The club pounded his low back, once more, and again. Wrapping his arms around the man's ankles and calves, Klaus pushed with his legs, and the attacker tilted like a timbered tree.

Resembling a terrible parasite, Klaus slowly inched up the legs of the Shorter Man screaming desperately for help and wriggling in vain to break free all the while bludgeoning Klaus with the heavy wood. Klaus held firm despite the relentless battery, pulling his body up the Shorter Man's legs, driving, until the infected host finally accepted an incurable malaise and succumbed to the cool soil. Klaus pummeled the man's stomach with fists in an anger borne of pain, the man's chest, his face, and finally, lying atop the dying man, wrapped fingers around his flaccid neck and wringed out the remaining life.

A silent crowd formed close around Klaus and his unfortunate prey. Out of the haze of his rage and fear, the cloud of his numbing pain, Klaus lifted his eyes and saw light, legs and feet, and, head turning just slightly, realized there was no escape. Releasing his grip from around the man's neck and arching his chest and stomach, knees in the dirt, pausing, raising one knee and planting one foot, pausing, the other foot, very slowly Klaus reared with his feet on either side of the motionless body. Confronting this torn and bloody monster the crowd stepped back. No person spoke. Klaus thought of running but did not have the strength and solemnly lowered his head.

A big man on Klaus' left spoke first, forcefully, "That man dead?" and bobbed his head once. Klaus at first did not respond but soon moved his head up and down, just slightly, eyes fixed on the Shorter Man's corpse between his legs.

"Why you kill him?" the big man demanded. Klaus did not respond.

Others in the crowd shouted out "Why, what has that man done to you?"

Klaus raised his head and stared vacantly into the distance, "Because, he tried to kill me."

The crowd rumbled and the big man raged, "That man running from you! He is much smaller than you. How this man try to kill you?"

"With that" Klaus replied wearily while raising his hand just enough to motion in the direction of the thick tree branch lying in the dirt next to the dead man's right hand.

The rumbling more pronounced, whispers, talking, short bursts of angry words, feet shuffling, and the big man took two steps forward, reached down, put a left hand around the broad end of the tree limb and held it with both hands close to his face, inspecting the weapon under the dull white glimmer of a kerosene lantern. He turned the bough slowly, examining it carefully, until, relaxing the fingers of his left hand, rotating the wrist slowly to consider his palm and fingers sticky with blood. His gaze fixed on Klaus.

"He tried to rob me" Klaus muttered.

"What's that?" the big man shouted.

"He tried to rob me" Klaus raised his head and looked in the big man's eyes, "He tried to rob me."

"What do you mean, tried?" the big man grew angrier, his voice louder, "You mean he tried to rob you and then you chase him, you kill him?" The rumble turned to roar – hyenas yapping around a lion wounded in the hunt, excited by the prospect of finally taking down the ferocious carnivore.

Klaus thought of his knife somewhere in the dirt, likely under a foot, concealed from view; he would play his last card. "I have money," the words were clear and yielding, "at the car, you can have it."

"Quiet!" the big man roared at the crowd and with both hands raised the club above his head as though an ax soon to split a log.

They fell silent.

The big man turned; the weapon that had caused Klaus so much pain, poised, in much stronger arms, to strike again. "How much money, where is your car?" he demanded.

Resolve and strength renewing, adrenaline rushing, Klaus replied "Back that way, at the station, but the money is hidden, there is two-thousand American dollars in twenty dollar bills, you can have it, but let me go when it's in your hands, promise me that." He calculated the Ford was by that time crawling with police and spectators.

The big man grinned wide with yellowed and missing teeth visible even under the lantern's faint glow, "We will let you go, if you give us the money, if no money, no freedom, and you die."

The crowd restless closed in on Klaus, each man and woman, each child, anxious, wanting not to be last, to be left wanting in the illicit bounty. They pushed against the dead man and Klaus like a crashing wave pushes against driftwood until it comes to rest high on the beach. Klaus turned and ran, the crowd closed in behind, and several of the faster men and women with the lantern took the lead down the narrow path ahead of Klaus, past embers once flame, past the machete leaning against a palm, through the heavy brush and low branches until they could see the neon sign above the growth.

Those in front of Klaus slowed to let the big man pass but once in the lead he came to a stop, turned, and motioned for everyone to stop. They did. The big man conferenced with those standing between him and Klaus, after which, the big man and one other man proceeded down the trail cautiously, quietly, alone in the dark toward the crime scene.

"What now to do?" Klaus' mind raced. Soon, his kidnappers would know their reward his ploy; trapped, no way past the two in front and, even if there were, the trail's end was for him certain doom. Cash, credit cards, and passport still bound concealed to his waist. Any chance of survival whatsoever required a very quick escape from his captors and Nigeria; meaning a change of clothes and either a car or an international flight from the airport.

Klaus turned away from the petrol station sign and began shuffling slowly back through the crowd, thinking only of the machete some distance down the trail. One by one he passed close to each person. First, cautiously but confidently stepping aside a tall thin man, looking in his eyes, Klaus muttered "I have to take a piss." Pressing past a woman strong of build; "Excuse me." The first two unresponsive, watching, another woman, "Excuse me, I need to go" apologetically, a boy, a man, a girl, they all observed in silence. Squeezing by the last, a woman, and taking a few short steps, Klaus turned and touched the zipper of his trousers with his left hand; "I'm just going there." He pointed toward a patch of partial darkness just a few steps away.

Placing each foot very gingerly, instilling trust, turning frequently to assure his pensive audience, Klaus proceeded; certain of standing in the dark, barely visible to onlookers, Klaus stopped; facing away from the lantern's glow, feet shoulder width apart, Klaus unzipped; tugging the nylon pouch, feeling for the zipper, unzipping the pouch, feeling the contents, removing several bills, zipping the pouch, separating the bills, Klaus relieved himself; twenty-dollar bills fluttering one by one to the ground, eyes closing in silent prayer, Klaus sprinted.

The hungry crowd's wrath erupted. Klaus heard their fomenting furor, felt their disastrous desire and ran as fast as he could, crashing into obstacles, through branches and twigs and leaves, stumbling, searching in fear for embers' glow. The commotion behind soon subsided though, as the raging assemblage devolved to a conglomerate of opportunists, each novice kidnapper becoming simply a beggar scratching urine-soaked soil for money. A glimmer appeared and Klaus slowed, concerned only of the machete he combed trail walls, remaining instinctively cognizant of the closing danger.

Grasping the handle in his sweating hand, accelerating, gulping air, past a pile of orange coals Klaus ran, his heart racing; don't give out now he beseeched heart and legs – can't be much farther. There indeed was the Shorter Man lifeless in the dirt. Klaus paused, kicking furiously in the muck for a glimpse of his knife, but nothing. More running, listening, swinging the machete, scared, gasping, and suddenly, he was upon light and civilization.

The trail widened and through the forest canyon cars and trucks with brilliant headlamp beacons from left and right and across the road streetlights and buildings with windows through which incandescent lights glimmered. Klaus laughed loud. Bursting from desolation and despair to civility and hope he traversed the two-lane road between cars, jumped to a sidewalk, and turned to see if the mob pursued. The trailhead chasm appeared a hideous orifice ready to vomit certain death at any moment yet he waited – no sign of his captors – caught a glimpse of his right hand brown with dried blood, other, same, shirt, ripped and soiled beyond recognition.

"Must keep moving and find some clothes" he thought; still much survival to do.

To Klaus' right as he faced the road and forest, an intersection, which, he concluded, meant that he stood on a side street with the hotel taxis probably two or three blocks behind him down the crossroad; that road, however, too busy and a cab too risky given his appearance. Klaus analyzed further. To the right he knew, an intersection, to the left, a building, beyond which an open door and people lingering on the sidewalk; maybe a bar or a nightclub. Moving closer it became clear.

Slipping through a small crowd and an open door, Klaus entered a room where loud music filled his head and dancers under flashing lights raised his spirits. Calypso, a smooth vibrant rhythm, people swayed shoulder to shoulder. Klaus relaxed, smiling, twisting and turning, he approached a bar jammed with customers and beside it an exposed washroom from which trailed a long line of men and women. He took his place, hands in pockets, and reveled in the conviction he was still alive.

Leaving the washroom with hands and face wiped clean and two twenty dollar bills tucked into a shirt pocket, Klaus again stood in line, this time at the bar to order a double-shot gin and bottle of Budweiser. Leaning against the wet sticky surface, he promptly depleted the gin and, mounting an elbow on the bar, sipped beer, watched, and waited, until a man of his approximate height wearing a shirt appearing new or at least very recently laundered paused at the bar.

"Excuse me" Klaus said to the man, "I like your shirt."

The man looked down at his shirt, "Oh yes, I just bought it, thank you" and started to order a drink when Klaus interrupted, "I will give you twenty dollars American for it," displaying the folded bill between two fingers of his left hand.

The man laughed, "Okay. How much will you give me to take your shirt?"

Klaus laughed, "It's on the house!"

The man laughed again and reached for the bill. Klaus moved his hand, smiled, and pointed at the man's shirt; the man shook his head in affirmation and he and Klaus exchanged shirts and possession of the twenty-dollar bill at the bar. The man donning a damp filthy rag nonetheless proudly beckoned the bartender with his well-bartered currency as Klaus took one last long drink from the beer bottle and maneuvered through the throbbing mass to catch a cab.

A taxi pulled alongside the curb after a few minutes and Klaus lowered with relief onto the old orange beach towel covering what was left of a cushion behind the front passenger seat; "I need to get to the airport and on the way an internet café."

"No problem;" the cabbie sped away from the curb, turned right at the intersection, and weaved between cars past the hotel from which Klaus first intended to depart. After a short distance the old Dodge made a left turn, went a block, and came to rest in front of a storefront bearing the sign "West Africa Coffee and Internet."

"Wait here, I'll only be a few minutes" Klaus said, handing the driver a twenty-dollar bill; "No problem."

Folding tables with chairs and dirty numbered computers close together lined both sides of a narrow room where people silently stared at screens and typed. Klaus scanned the tables on his way to the glass display counter and seeing a vacant seat ordered a double-shot espresso and questioned the young man behind the counter, "How much for the coffee and internet?"

"The espresso is a hundred twenty naira and the internet is a hundred naira for fifteen minutes, how long do you need it?" the man replied.

"Fifteen minutes is fine;" Klaus pulled two dollar-bills from a thick fold and handed them to the man who responded "Thanks; change?" Klaus in turn replied "Thanks; I'm okay."

"Take number four," the man motioned and Klaus strolled with his cup and saucer to the assigned computer. After setting the swirly blue and white porcelain close to the keyboard, he slid a chair from the table between a man and a girl, neither of whom paid him any attention, and, sitting comfortably, took a sip of the strong Kenyan coffee and typed "classifieds" into the web search bar. Next, he clicked on "usa," "south dakota," "midland," and "post to classifieds, for sale, sporting"; under "posting title," typing "Used Fishing Poles 4 Sale," followed by an imaginary email address and a brief description. "For sale, two poles, one short, one tall, both in very bad condition, would include tackle but all stolen, police report filed, have decided to give up fishing and retire south, price $17,473 for both, wire only."

While sipping espresso Klaus reread the message, clicked "submit," exited the site, deleted the browsing history, and enjoyed the calm for a few moments longer until leaving the café and, what he hoped soon, Nigeria and Africa. It would take the police several hours to complete an investigation of the crime scene determined Klaus; his camera and sunglasses would provide little immediate evidentiary value, the man he left alive would undergo interrogation sometime later at a hospital, and his hotel room would remain undisturbed for another eight hours or so – ample time to catch a flight out of the country.

"Which airline?" asked the cabbie glancing in the mirror and slowly turning the cab onto Airport Road; "Arik" replied Klaus. The car slowed to a baggage stand in front of an Arik Air sign.

Klaus settled with the driver, entered the terminal, found flight monitors and studied them carefully, waited in the Arik ticket line without any bags and bought a one-way ticket to Johannesburg – the soonest flight to a suitable destination that he could purchase. Three days later, in Johannesburg, Klaus purchased a one-way ticket to Buenos Aires and, from there, Caracas; from Venezuela he caught a freighter to Belize City, bought an old Toyota Corolla from a shrewd American expat staying in the same hotel, and drove to his cottage a few blocks from the beach in Dangriga.

After resting for a couple of days, satellite internet service again active, Klaus opened a bottle of Warsteiner beer and sat down at his desktop computer. First confirming a deposit into his Cayman Islands account he pulled up the online classified site; the "USA, Missouri, Brookfield" – an avenue in London that Michael remembered fondly from his childhood – "lost and found" message read "Two Fishing Poles Lost, one short, one tall, paid $17,473, never caught a fish but lost a friend, my heartfelt thanks to the man who took them."

Klaus smiled.

II PRIVACY

Robert Downing lowered his head while appearing to reflectively fixate on the light gray speckled vinyl tile floor, hands in dark gray wool trouser pockets, jacket unbuttoned, pacing in front of and under a ten by seven foot photograph of a surveillance camera mounted on a pole directly below a billowing American flag. He stopped, turned, took two steps toward the bleachers filled with students, raised his head, gazed at the back row far above where he stood and spoke in a low voice.

"What is privacy?" a rhetorical question he nevertheless hesitated.

"Is it an act born of free will, or is it the existence of a condition, or both?" Professor Downing paused again. "If you want privacy, how do you achieve it – by sitting in the very back?" A short burst of laughter from the audience, to the speaker signifying at least some attentiveness.

"What if somebody, or something, invades your privacy, as I am doing now?" – cutting short another burst: "How do you protect your privacy, are there privacy laws, are there privacy police?"

The professor gazed around the room at wide-eyed closed-mouth faces staring at him and the photograph of a flag-enshroud camera.

He glanced down again and scanned the front row, speaking authoritatively, "The concept of privacy is not easy to comprehend, and it is what we are going to spend the rest of today's class, as well as the short remainder of the term discussing. It clearly means more than just the opposite of publicity. In its most basic form, seclusion, privacy at some level is an absolute necessity for every living thing.

"Conceived through both conscious rationalization and unconscious behavior, rising to the level of instinct, privacy is the initial and easiest method of protecting the individual and the family. The concept of privacy relates to those of personality and vulnerability. To reveal the private is to accept the consequences of vulnerability."

The background image slowly transformed into a brown and white wolf, beautiful blue eyes focused keenly on the class, two small puppies huddled under her taught frame. All that could be heard from the audience was the isolated crackle and squeak of chairs.

Professor Downing's voice projected louder as he moved to the podium and lectured into the microphone: "Privacy is a fundamental human need, indeed, a need for all living things, and at some level, a matter of survival. In a cave surrounded by enemies, or predators, the location of food, the number, gender, and routine of inhabitants, these were facts undoubtedly kept secret as a matter of life and death."

He briefly stopped, looked up, and back down. "The same was undoubtedly later true in a hut, in a house, or in a castle. No authority had any right conferred by society at large to invade this right of privacy when survival was at issue.

"How do we reconcile privacy and survival with what the American writer Ayn Rand observed" queried Professor Downing to his students, "that 'Civilization is the progress toward a society of privacy. The savage's noble existence is public, ruled by the laws of the tribe. Civilization is the process of setting man free from men.'?"

The professor looked up, slipped off his frameless reading glasses – more for comfort and show than necessity – and held them in his right hand above the podium. He surveyed the entire class. "Do you believe privacy has been with us since the cave – that we as a society are losing our privacy; and, if we are indeed losing our privacy, are we becoming more or less civilized? Is Ayn Rand correct, that we are moving toward a society of privacy and therefore becoming more civilized?"

"Losing it!" a young man bellowed from the side of the room.

"Okay…" Professor Downing reacted, thereafter pausing to focus on all of his students, "does that mean we are becoming less civilized or more civilized?"

Just a few arms jutted above the crowd of faces and the professor pointed to one on the other side of the room; the hand lowered and a young woman raised a voice, "We are becoming more civilized."

"Why?"

"Because nobody can do anything uncivilized if they don't have any privacy!" A wave of faces turned to look at the woman and broke into smiles; Professor Downing smiled too, and considered the woman as she smiled in return, waiting for him to affirm the validity of her answer.

"And you are?" he asked as a prelude to looking down, fumbling with a roster, and pressing his right index finger on the bridge of his glasses.

"Rain Walker," the woman responded somewhat less confidently, "My name is Rain."

"Well, Rain, you have touched both sharp edges of the sword I'm afraid," Professor Downing slipped off his glasses, glanced at Rain, and addressed the audience, "because privacy is essential to each of us while it is, in practice, a hindrance to civilized society. The question is, just because we are becoming more technologically advanced, and are applying that technology to protect our society, are we also then becoming more civilized?"

"Rain?" the professor called and in response the young woman clasped her hands and leaned forward against her desk for security, "Well, I don't think so; it isn't really very civil to spy on one another."

"So, we are in fact becoming less civilized in an Orwellian attempt to provide security for our citizens;" the professor was standing next to the podium holding his glasses, "as we forsake privacy for security, we move back to a less civilized society, do you agree?" He examined the classroom full of people as the question hung in the air, "...And if this is true, that we are becoming less civilized, than aren't we in fact in more need of privacy, to protect ourselves and our families?"

The room was silent as young heads harboring minds enlightened or bewildered followed the instructor in front of the podium and under the grand image of the protective wolf mother guarding her young puppies.

He broke the silence, "If we are losing our privacy it is because it is being taken away from us, isn't that correct, by our government and our institutions! We as a society are sacrificing our privacy in the hope our government and institutions will protect us. Protection has become more important than civility. Now, doesn't that open just a huge can of worms?" and glanced around the room.

"Aren't we really turning over control of our lives to our government and our institutions – hoping that they are guided by our best interests?"

Professor Downing took another break to consider the audience, turned, moved slowly to the podium, pushed his glasses into place and crumpled his notes. "Is this civility? Let me read the quote from Ayn Rand again: 'Civilization is the progress toward a society of privacy. The *savage's* noble existence is *public*, ruled by the *laws of the tribe. Civilization* is the process of *setting man free from men.*' Rand doesn't seem to address the issue of setting people free from politicians and the people that make up governments.

"Let's see a show of hands; how many of you think Rand is right and that civilization is progress *toward* a society of privacy?" A few arms rose at first slow and cautious followed by those from others at first uncertain until there appeared a field of hands all sizes and colors.

"Okay; how many of you think Rand is *wrong* and that civilization is really progress *away* from a society of privacy and toward a public existence governed by laws?" The professor watched the students beginning at the wall to his left; just a few hands lifted hesitantly.

"Hmm, so most of you believe we are moving away from civility, or I suppose you may believe we are progressing toward a society of privacy and therefore civility.

"Let's see which it is." Professor Downing focused on the center of the class and removed his reading glasses, "Just those of you who raised your hands because you believe Ayn Rand correct, how many of *you* believe we are progressing toward a society of privacy?" He kept his head still and moved only his eyes, looking for reaction, but there was none.

"Now, everyone, how many believe we are progressing toward a society of privacy?" The students were still, not an arm in the air.

"And this is probably true of our society as a whole" he pronounced confidently into the microphone, "we do not believe our society is progressing toward privacy, we believe our society is progressing *away* from privacy."

"Let's draw some conclusions" lectured the professor, glasses low on his nose, reading from his notes, speaking methodically, glancing at the class above lenses between sentences, "based upon the fact we elect our representatives. First, the majority of our society now must believe security is more important than civility. Second, the majority of our society must trust our government and institutions, such as corporations. Third, these two conclusions lead to the inescapable conclusion that we, as a society, are willingly turning over control of our private lives to governments and institutions. And, fourth, if we as a society do not believe security is more important than civility, or if we do not trust our government or institutions, as a society, than we have lost control of our lives because we have lost control of our privacy."

Professor Downing lowered his head and spoke softly into the microphone. "I will tell you that I believe, as a society, we do want security more than civility, for reasons we shall discuss later, and we do not trust our government or institutions, and, therefore, we have lost control of our individual privacy, our individuality, our independence."

After allowing a moment for the class to absorb and reflect on his opinion, the professor lifted his head and changed tone. "These are the questions we will examine during the remainder of this class and next class. When and why did America choose security over civility; when and why did we, as a society, as a people, lose control of our private lives; and has our country slid irrevocably past the peak of civility so that we are now regressing as a civilization."

Many of the students glanced at their phones or the wall clock, thinking the class time over, as Professor Downing might have expected using time itself to reposition his reading glasses and review his notes.

With ten minutes left he went back to the microphone – in obvious dismay to some in attendance – postulating that "Privacy is still quite often the only bulwark against vulnerability, some of which may result in serious injury or death, depravation of freedom, or financial ruin. This is why its erosion, as a matter of public policy, has always been hard-fought; a balance struck between the individual's need for privacy and society's need to know the facts. In truth, however, it is never society which purports a need to know sufficient to supplant the individual's right to privacy."

The wolf and her pups became a large man wearing a uniform leaning down with his hands on the sides of a young girl, a child, patting her clothing – the scene obviously an airport security checkpoint.

A sense of unease descended on the room.

"It is government," he looked over his reading glasses directly at the students in the front row, paused, and looked down at the lectern, "government made up of people, people made up of objectives, objectives sometimes contrary to those of society, whether society knows it or not."

Professor Downing continued looking down at his notes, careful not to look up, to see the inquisitive faces and to hear the question – are you saying our government is corrupt?

"Privacy is an important component of individualism and independence; privacy from government oversight is liberty in its rawest form, freedom from government intrusion and, therefore, oppression, the freedom to carry on human activities without government knowledge or interference; privacy is the foundation of a democratic society, of a people free to elect their representatives without fear of reprisal; privacy is the essence of individualism bestowing upon each person the opportunity to make free choices and exercise free will; privacy is the hallmark of independent thought and independent action," his eyes moved to each of the students and he continued very slowly, "private thoughts...enable private decisions...that promote private action."

Professor Downing stopped speaking, glanced at the wall clock, and turned his head to study the image. A little blonde girl larger than life, holding open the lapels of her red wool coat by her tiny hands to expose only a white sweater with embroidered blue and red flowers; beside her, a large smiling man wearing a government uniform, representative of the most powerful, certainly one of the most civilized, societies the world has ever known, a stranger to this child, inspecting her clothing for a bomb. America feared this little girl wantonly or maybe unknowingly capable of causing the destruction of a commercial airliner and the lives of hundreds of people and the professor hoped – in silence – that what he found to be an irony would not be lost entirely on his students, that some aghast at the image may wonder in stunned introspection if their country had not lost perspective.

After some time, perhaps a time too long, in perhaps only a thinly veiled attempt to reinforce and promote his belief in the erosion of the right of personal privacy, the professor spoke softly into the microphone: "Ayn Rand said, the savage's noble existence is public, ruled by the laws of the tribe. Is this child a savage? Are we the tribe? Are we moving toward civility or toward security; are the two mutually exclusive?"

A waving hand in the middle of the second row caught Professor Downing's attention and he removed his glasses and pointed at the student. A young man lowered his hand and exclaimed quite certainly that "I, for one, would rather give up some privacy in exchange for safety, what's the alternative if terrorists are blowing up airplanes; you have to search people one way or another!"

Professor Downing nodded while looking at the roster, "You...must be," using his right index finger he counted seats from his right, "Cindy!" There was an eruption of laughter and the young man smiled bashfully and replied, "No, sorry, she's back where I usually sit, we traded places so she could sit with her boyfriend today, um, my name's Frank."

The professor expressed a slanted smile clearly signifying "What's the point of a seating chart...," glanced at his notes and responded, "So now Frank, we are back to Rain's double-edge sword, as well as the issue of consent. There is no doubt that privacy hinders a civilized legal system in pursuit of individual justice that depends for its legitimacy on an accurate discernment of the facts. Otherwise, the innocent are prosecuted and the guilty escape punishment. Absolute privacy is effectively a bar to absolute justice, without an accurate factual foundation law has no relevance and justice no application.

"What Frank is saying, I believe," Professor Downing took off his glasses and rotated again to review the PowerPoint image, "is that there has to be a balance between protecting the individual's privacy, by calling it a 'right,' and protecting society at large."

Returning his stance toward the audience, "Privacy is the first line of defense against vulnerability and therefore harm; publicity subjects us to potential harm from individuals and organizations. Disclosing information you hold private to people you don't know is fraught with danger. If you have to make such disclosure, for example to buy something online, the legal system is supposed to afford a second line of defense. If the legal system is ineffective, if there is no law or no immediate enforcement, privacy becomes more important than convenience. This goes back to our institutions and trust.

"Privacy invokes thorny issues. Reasonable expectation is the lynchpin of protected privacy in almost all judicial analysis, this evaluation intended objective, narrowed ever so precisely for the situation in which the unfortunate proponent finds his or herself. We have a reasonable expectation over our bodies while in the home, in the office, in a car, in a phone booth, walking down the sidewalk, and crossing the street. Whether our expectations are protected is a different matter altogether; the reasonableness standard inevitably produces hard and fast rules tossed out ever so readily by a judge exercising subjective reasoning. Is the murkiness of privacy clear yet?"

Professor Downing focused his gaze at the center of the second row; "Back to Frank's point, the government – our elected government – would argue the girl's parents consented to her search by trying to board a commercial flight and refusing to allow an x-ray scan. Is this coerced consent? Is there a right to fly commercially? Is there an alternative, ship travel for instance, to Europe? Is a person's home the last place left where the law may find a person enjoys a reasonable expectation of privacy?"

Looking directly at Frank he asked "Are you okay with that?"

Without any delay Frank responded "As long as there're wackos in the world, I'm okay with giving up a little privacy, but that girl is obviously not a wacko and there isn't any reason to search her!"

Several other students clapped faster than the professor could retort, "So you would give some Americans a right to privacy and not others? How would you make the call?" He immediately wished that he had not asked the question or had phrased it differently.

"I know how I would make the call" replied Frank, "I would only search people who look like they are from the Middle East."

"I assume by that you mean people who appear to be of one faith but was Timothy McVey a Muslim," Professor Downing carefully prodded Frank, "or the kids who shoot up schools, or the IRA, I mean, can't you think of extremist examples in any group of well-meaning people?" This was an argument the professor had lost in the past, a complex issue pitting his liberal, really libertarian beliefs against the most common of sense.

"None of those people," Frank's anticipated response did not surprise the prepared professor, "blew up airplanes."

Professor Downing took hold of the podium, leaned back, placed his left foot on the bottom of the stand out of view, stared at Frank and confirmed "Neither have ninety-nine point nine, nine, nine, and on and on percent of the world's almost two billion followers of Islam."

He hesitated for a couple of seconds while watching Frank and thereafter quietly perusing the room allowed his students a few moments for consideration and analysis before foreclosing additional discussion of the topic by announcing in an upbeat voice that "For next class, I want you to finish the assignment for today's class, and also be prepared to discuss the concepts of balance and consent within the context of government intrusion on individual privacy; a la prochain – until next time!" With those words the professor lifted a black leather shoulder bag from the floor and began packing his computer and notes.

The Washington of that late morning in early May reinvigorated Robert with cool air and billowing white clouds, a slight breeze, and yellow flowers blooming in reddish clay planters along a concrete walkway just few steps from large ornate doors leading from the Political Science Center. Reminders all, the semester would soon be ending. His hair, gray, full and over the lobes of his ears, tossed in the wind and a smile curved his lips imagining the summer ahead. Brisk his step, an athletic frame bounding at fifty along the flower-lined sidewalk dividing expanses of budding trees and green grass, intent on a quick salad at the commissary in advance of hordes of students and faculty.

Passing others along the way, coming, going, boys, girls, men and women, alone, together, some recognized but paying no heed, Robert pulled his Blackberry from a pocket inside the wool jacket and, finding a waiting voicemail, adjusted the ringer volume, pressed a key, and held the phone to his ear. It was his daughter. Robert heard the familiar "Hi Dad!" and pressed the speakerphone key, adjusted down the volume, held the phone close to his right ear, and straddled the sidewalk to avoid passersby and shimmering blades of grass thought to be damp.

Sandra's voice resonated with high-pitched cheerfulness well known to Robert as reserved for the most joyous of occasions, "...here, things are going great, hope things are good at home, but I've got something exciting to tell you! Call me! Love you!" Robert pressed the end key; the digital clock displayed eleven thirty-five, "Five thirty-five in Paris...time enough" he thought, for a quick lunch.

The Memorial Union cafeteria was abuzz as Robert handed the cashier a small plastic tub of lettuce, purple cabbage, black olives, artichokes and feta cheese covered by clear plastic wrap, and a credit card bearing the college emblem that he used as often as possible to enrich an airline frequent flier account. Then he heard the voice.

"Professor Downing?" the sound conveyed polite interruption founded in certainty that the man addressed was in fact Robert Downing.

Robert fumbled with his wallet, reinserting the credit card while holding the salad, focused quizzically on the young man standing in an adjacent cashier line, and wished at that instant to be someone else.

"Do you have a moment?" the man persisted.

Robert slipped his wallet into a trouser pocket, grasped the salad with unnecessary force to the sound of crumpling plastic, and moved toward the drink dispensary, all the while quietly contemplating his approaching inquisitor, a young man about Robert's height with dark hair cut close, fashionably unshaven, black rimmed glasses, a blue Under Armour sweatshirt and baggy torn jeans, guarding a sandwich in his left hand and an empty soda cup in his right.

"Frank, from class a few minutes ago, isn't that right?" Robert needlessly but cautiously queried with a smile.

"Yes, my name is Frank Caprizio; I'm in your Tuesday-Thursday Ethical Studies class, the one we just got out of." The man's firm enunciation suggested resilience combined with a certain satisfaction.

"I see" casually ventured Robert, "if you have a question, I have office hours, they're in your syllabus, right now I have short lunch, so if you'll excuse me," thereupon abruptly turning toward the drink machine, eyeing a paper water cup, hoping the dialogue was temporarily at an end but unable to take a step because the man responded, by moving closer, so close that Robert could feel warm moist air against his face.

"I just wanted to say that your liberal bullshit has no place in higher education" – the words rumbled, their sound expanding, the man's face straining under barely leashed emotion – "and this isn't about privacy, it's about war! My older brother died on Flight Five Eighty-Seven, you know, right after Nine-Eleven!"

Frank's right hand moved up with the empty soda cup and an index finger extending, pounding home a point several inches from Robert's face, "It was Islamic terrorists, I believe that and I don't care what anybody says, screw your privacy! These people need to die and I don't care how we do it!" The last word screamed. Robert knew instinctively there were other people all around, but the room fell into a silent vacuum, a cavernous silent vacuum.

Robert and an enraged young man he did not know stood as two boxers ready for a title fight, speechless, their faces not an arm's length apart; until the aggressor's right arm slowly lowered to his side and eyes once vacant took on a look of complete surprise, perhaps shock. Stepping backward, Frank looked briefly at the floor in obvious embarrassment, perhaps even shame. The sounds of other people began to rematerialize and Robert, knowing intuitively a security guard was fast approaching, turned to sight a large black man in a light blue uniform shirt pushing through a crowd of startled diners.

Reflexively stepping forward to meet the protector, Robert put his hands out in front and to the sides of his chest, fingers spread, pointing up, in body language pleading stop. With an air of calm he said to the ready guard, "It's okay, it's all over, just a misunderstanding, it's finished." The guard's momentum reduced to stillness close, very close, to Robert's outstretched arms and he stared at Frank. Robert maintained a defensive posture with his hands no more than an inch from the guard's massive chest.

"Are you sure?" quizzed the guard, his watchful glare intense, "'cause it sounded like it was going violent." The words rendered the subject limp, speechless, as spectators glided pensively all around, toting trays and plastic containers, drinks and wrapped cookies, ever attentive for erupting emotions, ever recalling recent publicized tragedies.

Robert noticed the guard's right hand on the grip of a holstered pistol and carefully chose words uttered in a most soothing tenor, "Yes, yes, I know this boy, Frank, it was a misunderstanding, I'm sure we both just want to finish our lunches."

A young woman's voice bellowed uninvited, "That man is dangerous!" to capture Robert's attention from behind and continued without hesitation; "He was yelling and pointing, threatening to kill all Muslims, he's dangerous!"

Robert turned his head to see the wide brown eyes of the brown-haired girl with whom he had conversed just a short while earlier; Rain stood a few feet from Frank, to his side, behind and right of Robert. She demanded of the big man in no uncertain manner, "You need to see if he has a gun!"

A motionless Frank Caprizio surveyed the cafeteria in agonizing confirmation he was at that moment, if for some inexplicable reason not sooner, the center of all attention and meekly attempted sounds incoherent to those around. Robert relaxed his arms in concession to the rationality of Rain's demand and the security guard brushed aside in a bolt suddenly finding Frank face down against cold tile, arms painfully pulled back, shackled wrists strapped in plastic strips, seeing only two plain black lace dress shoes and the scattered makings of a turkey sandwich. Three guards soon knelt over the helpless antagonist, ripping at his pockets, disgorging books and papers from his backpack until appeared a two-ounce canister of pepper spray.

Robert moved toward the fray and offered a wishful proposal, "If he's not armed, perhaps you could release him."

A portly guard with short blonde disheveled hair and a mustache tartly responded "No, he's coming with us for questioning, the DC police have been called," as two other guards lifted Frank by his armpits until erect. Blood dribbled down his chin.

Rain interjected in matter-of-fact rationality, "Professor Downing, you should let them do their job, people don't yell threats in cafeterias unless their demented, especially to their professor."

Robert ignored her and focused on the guard who had advised the police were called, "Perhaps I should come with you as a witness."

"And me" firmly exclaimed Rain, "I saw the whole thing!"

"Yes, yes, you both come," agreed the second guard quite apparently in charge, "the rest of you go back to eating or whatever it was you were doing." Directing instruction next to a cashier, "Can somebody mop up the floor here, there's blood...."

Robert and Rain followed the three guards escorting Frank without speaking, out of the cafeteria, through a long hall leading to an exit from the Memorial Union, across an employee parking lot, and into the Administration Building and a small office down an inconspicuous corridor on the first floor. There, the guards locked Frank in a tiny room empty but for a chair and visible only through a small chicken wire mesh window in a steel door. As the guards turned away a loud bang suggested a kick to the door and they chuckled in callous amusement.

"Why did you put him in there?" Rain suddenly demanded, continuing without giving the guards a chance to respond, "How long are you going to leave him?"

"Until the DC police get here" replied the guard first on the scene.

"When will that be?" Rain's dismay seethed.

"We're pretty low priority unless there's an emergency" answered the second guard with clearly audible annoyance, "probably later this afternoon or this evening."

"You're kidding!" Clearly incensed, hands on hips, passing Robert an exasperated glance Rain quickly continued, "He doesn't deserve that, he's in handcuffs for crying out loud! He just yelled! He didn't even have a weapon!"

Robert considered the irony of a valuable lesson thrust upon these two of his students with sublime intrigue as a scene not possibly enacted in class; and speculated from experience the unnecessarily onerous outcome. One he tried in vain to curtail. Frank Caprizio would remain imprisoned in the Administration Building well into the night, escorted by police officers in the back of a patrol car to a station, and booked and locked in a cell until appearing before a magistrate sometime the next day to be at that time formally charged with a hate crime. Rain would plead Frank's case to the security guards without success until surrendering to sleep and apathy; waking the next morning in the comfort of her own bed to champion a new cause. Eventually, they all may come together in a courtroom to compound the injustice.

"Rain," fatherly Robert's tone, "let the officers do their job and they may find it in their hearts to let Mr. Caprizio sit out here and have a cup of coffee waiting for the police. These situations are difficult for everyone, and their job isn't easy. So come on, let's go over here, give our statements, and go home...."

"Good idea!" proclaimed the second guard beckoning Rain with an outstretched arm to sit in a side chair at a desk across the room.

She complied and Robert followed.

It was three o'clock – nine in Paris – when Robert finally left the Administration Building. He walked to his green two-seat BMW convertible on the other side of campus, lowered into the driver's seat, closed the door, and dialed Sandra's cell phone number. After a delay and several rings came a voice over the loudspeaker: "Bonsoir" Sandra answered politely.

"Bonsoir mademoiselle," Robert's attempt at French aristocracy fell on ears practiced with his humor and overly cadenced French dialect, "êtes-vous la dame de la maison?"

"Non" Sandra played along, "je suis la femme de ménage, qui est ce?"

"Mon nom est Clouseau, Inspector Clouseau!" Robert did not know the French word for inspector.

Sandra giggled, "And I suppose, Inspector, you are looking for the Pink Panther? Dad, you really need to brush up on your French if you are coming to Paris!"

"Il est vrai I'm afraid" Robert conceded in Frenglish, "sorry to call late, Sandy, but it's probably not that late for you, how are things?"

"They're great!" she cheerfully replied, "And, I've got some exciting news; we, are going to the Grand Prix!"

Robert thought for a moment, "Which one?"

"Monte-Carlo, silly, and Cannes, we're going to the Grand Prix!" declared Sandra; "I have a friend, here in Paris, and he has three tickets, good tickets, to the race; and he's been invited on a yacht! I told him you were coming to visit and he said you are welcome to come along! I want you to go with us!"

"Hmm, you want dear old dad along to the party as a chaperone?" Robert rejoined sarcastically; "Slow down Sand...when is the race?"

"It's in about three weeks, the end of May, and the film festival is about the same time, so we can do both!"

"It sounds like fun," Robert hesitated, "...are you really sure you want me along?"

"Of course!" affirmed Sandra until inadvertently diminishing its value with "You'll be here anyway, what else would you do?"

Not wanting to dampen Sandra's enthusiasm, Robert proceeded delicately, "Sandy, it sounds like a good time, but who is this friend? Is he a boyfriend? How long have you known him?"

"Dad," Sandra muted her exuberance, "he is a friend, I mean, we've been dating, but it's not that serious, I think he's a player, but he's a nice guy."

"Well" Robert continued slowly, "if I wouldn't be in the way, and if you still want to go when I get there, I don't see why not, I mean, yea, it sounds like fun! My room for the seminar is already booked, and after that, I was going to stay with you and Rachel for three weeks, so I don't see a problem, or I could stay in your apartment while you're gone, but that doesn't sound like much fun. My lecture's on the twenty-second, so we could leave any time after that!"

"Good; then it's settled!" Sandra was accustomed to getting her own way with Robert; "I'll let Gilbert know you're going. Email me your flight information again, we'll pick you up."

"I will Sand, and I'll pack for the Riviera!" The sound of the words, teasing though they were, excited Robert; "Talk soon, love you."

After pressing the red key Robert continued holding the phone in his right hand, elbow on the console, staring out the windshield reminiscing about his last trip to the South of France. A well-planned holiday with Sandra's mother early in her pregnancy with Sandra, it was during a period in his life, their lives, marked in his memory by endless happiness and boundless hope for the future. Time, so fleeting, and always taking with it so much.

Sandra, twenty-four, had been living in France since January; unable to find a job out of college last June she went to Europe with a girlfriend to escape reality. Robert could not blame her. The loss of her mother to suicide a year earlier, the blindly foreseeable result of habitually overusing drugs and alcohol that Robert, if no one else, privately deemed suicide, how Sandra managed to cope let alone finish college he found remarkable.

The tragedy brought Sandra and Robert closer. He helped her to sell the family home, in which he had not resided for years, and she used the money to pay off a trifle of student loans, buy a new car, rent an apartment, and travel Europe for a year. Robert eventually accepted and finally came to encourage the sabbatical when apparent that a distressing inability to land a position teaching secondary French or Spanish foretold Sandra's mental ruination.

Talking with her that evening Robert realized, perhaps for the first time, the courage of his daughter and the value of his release.

The sound of a growling stomach quickly returned Robert to the need foremost at hand; lunch, he realized, did not occur, and the Greek salad inadvertently abandoned on the security guard's desk was by that time, he surmised, either soggy or no longer available. A brief stop at the Whole Foods near George Washington University followed by the drive home to his apartment in Georgetown, he strategized, to review assignments and refine his France itinerary.

Home by seven-thirty, Robert was within minutes at the computer logging onto his faculty account; six unread emails, all from students, one from Rain, "Professor Downing, Sorry I botched things today...guess I didn't realize how things work in campus security and maybe overreacted but Frank seemed like a terrorist talking about killing Muslims. I thought maybe he had a bomb or a gun. You know what happened at V Tech. It pays to be careful; but the guards didn't have to torture him by locking him in that little room. I hope he's okay. See you Tuesday. Best, Rain."

Robert contemplated the email, a myriad possible responses, instructional quips, lectures to be disregarded in lieu of a lifetime's experience, and typed a hasty response, "Rain, not your fault, Frank should not have lost composure – he's not really a terrorist, just lost a family member to an airplane crash that he believes was caused by a terrorist. Don't forget your assignment! PD" followed without much thought by clicking on each of the other student emails, opening hyperlinks, and downloaded finished assignments to individual student folders.

From work to personal email and an inbox comprised of eight new unread messages quickly reviewed by subject; two certainly spam one of which guarantying lasting penile erections, his younger brother with another unwanted quip of conservative humor, two female friends for reasons as yet unknown, the ACLU seeking another donation, a male faculty member likely confirming lunch for that Saturday, and Malik Said of the East-West Business Development Foundation; this last being the first email opened as Robert had been anticipating final details for the Paris lecture.

"Dear Professor Downing, It is with great pleasure that I welcome you to the first of hopefully many more lectures to come in the series, 'Islam within Christian Cultures, Seeking a Broader Understanding' presented by the East-West Business Development Foundation. Yours will be the third lecture in the May Paris seminar, the topic being religious freedom under American law, and you are scheduled for 1 ¼ hours on May 22 beginning at 1:00 p.m. It is anticipated you will speak for approximately fifty minutes and the remainder of your time will be allotted for questions and answers. English is acceptable, as is, of course, French. The audience will consist primarily of business people and representatives of non-governmental organizations. We will reimburse your airline ticket fare, business class, airport to hotel and hotel to seminar private transportation, and two nights' hotel accommodations and meals of your choosing not to exceed €300 per day. Your fee of €500 will be paid upon your arrival. The seminar will be at the Hotel Internationale on Boulevard Saint Germain near the Arab World Institute. I await your arrival with much enthusiasm. Respectfully, Malik"

Robert keyed a short reply, "Dear Malik, Thank you for your kind email. I am very much looking forward to this engagement and meeting you on May 22. I will call once in Paris. Best regards, Robert"; noted on a yellow sticky pad, "photocopy lecture materials and résumé," and reviewed his flight itinerary, online, Washington to Paris May 20 returning June 10. Reclining in his high-back leather office chair, stocking feet on the edge of his cherry roll top desk, eyes closed, Robert's thoughts were of the ten days prior to May 20: one more class and preparation, final assignments to be graded, the final exam, and finding someone to water his plants and feed Friskers, the large male Siamese cat on the couch, asleep on a pillow. Another thought and eyelids rose, "what if a subpoena arrives for Frank Caprizio's trial, if trial there were, could it possibly be that soon?" Deciding not, Robert left the chair for the kitchen and a glass of refrigerated day-old red wine.

Meanwhile, not far from Robert's apartment, in a very large room with concrete floors, backup generators, and expansive cooling ducts, a mainframe computer programmed to inspect millions of emails each minute initiated an algorithm based upon a combination of specific words in one exchange: "security, terrorist, Muslims, bomb, gun, V Tech, guards, torture, terrorist, airplane, crash, terrorist, assignment."

A second algorithm initiated within a few seconds, associating at least one of the email accounts triggering the initial hit, "east-west business development foundation, malik said, Arab world institute."

A third algorithm confirmed a relationship between the two email strings, and a fourth identified the senders and recipients by name, "Robert Downing, Malik Said, Rain Walker." A digital report with copies of the suspect emails arrived at the National Security

Agency's intake analyst section within seconds.

Glenda cherished two things: her morning tea, spiced ginger with a teaspoon of honey, and Heidi, the white and brown American Pit Bull Terrier rescued from a fighting ring when just a puppy. Glenda was a dispatcher for the Montgomery County Police Department seven years ago when late one Saturday a complaint of dog fighting came across her desk. The dispatch went to the patrol officer closest to the scene, William Bryant, an amiable young man with a community college Associates Degree in law enforcement and just six months out of the academy.

Officer Bryant responded to the call alone – his partner had gone home earlier that day complaining of the flu – and pulled his patrol car to the curb two blocks away from an old brick house on a treed acre in Wheaton. Confirming his arrival on the scene with Glenda, he agreed, reluctantly, to wait for backup before approaching the house. For a reason Glenda did not comprehend until holding Heidi for the first time, however, Officer Bryant did not wait.

The post-mortem investigation concluded he voluntarily abandoned his patrol car shortly after radioing Glenda and walked alone on the sidewalk past a row of tightly parked cars until close enough to the brick house that he could probably hear the sound of men yelling and cheering. Glenda believes he also heard barking, perhaps even, whimpering. Whatever the reason, Officer Bryant left the sidewalk for the grass instead of the driveway, walking in spongy leaves under towering oak and hickory trees toward a waist-high chain link fence adjacent to the garage, hoping perhaps to peer unnoticed into the backyard.

Not more than two steps from the chain link fence, Officer Bryant inadvertently touched a barely visible ankle-high makeshift electric fence consisting of just four wires several inches apart running from two electrical outlets the length of the front yard. The contraption was designed as a deadly obstacle for any dog clearing the chain link barrier. A shoe, a sock, a pant leg, William Bryant's ankle come into contact with the wires while stepping cautiously toward the fence, probably causing him to fall forward, screaming and reflexively grabbing at the links while two-hundred-twenty volts streamed through his body. The investigation was unclear as to when and why he drew his revolver, found in the tall grass a few feet from his body.

The brick house had been through foreclosure and vacant for over a year. Officers arriving later on the scene found no sign of people, just dogs, dogs locked in rooms, tied to trees, in cages, mothers and puppies, alive, malnourished, some with gaping infected wounds, others dead, still others buried. Glenda drove to the scene as soon as she heard of Officer Bryant's death and found animal control officers at the house loading live dogs in trucks for transport to animal hospitals and shelters.

Glenda walked around the back of the house and found Heidi, alone, huddled in the corner of a basement window-well where she had apparently fallen, near death from starvation. Tears spilling down her cheeks, Glenda stooped, reached, and with one hand pulled the quivering puppy from a certain coffin. Holding the tiny body to her face she whispered, "It's okay now, you'll be okay, I'm taking you home with me." A few days later, after attending the memorial service for William Bryant, Glenda named the puppy Heidi, after William Bryant's two-year old daughter.

Sitting at her kitchen table under the faint glow of an energy efficient bulb over an electric stove, Glenda sipped ginger tea and squinted to read a Washington Post front page article about the Supreme Court's acceptance of a Fourth Amendment search and seizure case. The FBI searched a computer hard drive without a warrant, resulting in a conviction for securities fraud. "Why," Glenda wondered, would the cops not have time to get a warrant to search the hard drive of a computer?

With a teaspoon she scooped more honey from a jar and swirled it into her cup, took another sip and held the paper closer, squinting even harder, reading with some difficulty that the defendant was an accountant for a hedge fund, that the hedge fund was under investigation by the Securities and Exchange Commission, and that the accountant was boarding a plane to Hong Kong carrying a notebook computer. Squinting until her eyelids were barely apart an inquisitive wrinkle crossed the bridge of Glenda's nose. "Why didn't they just detain the accountant at the airport" she pondered aloud, "and go get a warrant?" She swirled the honey and took another sip.

Waiting prone on oak flooring in a corner of the kitchen next to a food bowl and sliding glass door, Heidi's head sprung and tilted slightly above a pillow of paws attempting to discern any culinary intent behind Glenda's words. Glenda adjusted the paper to catch as much light as possible from the hood and read on: "Ah," certainly addressing Heidi, "he was a citizen of China and had a diplomatic passport; how does an accountant get a diplomatic passport?" Glenda let loose the newspaper and to paws went Heidi's head.

"The accountant's going to win old girl," Glenda shuffled to the sink and into it placed her empty cup, "because he's Chinese!" opened the door of a cabinet and removed a plastic tub. Heidi jumped to her feet.

Arriving at her station a little after eight, Glenda logged in as "Analyst 47335" to find waiting fourteen emails; she skimmed the subject lines, opened an intake folder and counted twenty-two analyst requests, computer generated queries related to email exchanges requiring further attention. Sighing in relief, "Thank God it's Friday," Glenda grabbed a Redskins sixteen ounce travel coffee mug, swiveled in her chair, stood, exited her work cubical, marched through other cubes uttering pleasant good mornings to all she passed, through a door and into a large break room to pour a cup of strong coffee from an old Bunn double carafe brewer. One cup was her daily allotment; savoring the aroma, she returned recharged to her computer and sat back in front of the screen.

About two hours later, ten-thirty, Glenda opened Analyst Intake number 1443994-879, "Robert Downing, Malik Said, Rain Walker;" reading Rain's email to Robert, Malik Said's email to Robert, Robert's email to Rain, and, finally, Robert's email to Malik Said. She pulled up a daily log report, typed the Intake number in a report field, pressed the tab button, and typed "appears to be of no significance but due to nature of incident will follow-up: run IAFIS and local searches, Robert Downing, Rain Walker, Frank Caprizio LNU DOI 04/26/12, IAFIS Interpol Malik Said, background Downing, Walker, Caprizio, Said, East-West Business

Development Foundation, Arab world institute." A subsequent flurry of keystrokes over a period of about eight minutes initiated searches of city, state, national, and international law enforcement records and the three primary credit bureaus related to persons named Robert Downing and Rain Walker living in the Washington, DC metropolitan area and a person named Malik Said residing in France.

Glenda shook the empty Redskins mug, swiveled, got up and walked back to the kitchen, filled the mug with hot coffee and, smiling somewhat deviously, returned to her cube. "Let's see" she muttered, sliding the mouse with her right hand and tapping the keyboard with the fingers of her left, "Google, Yahoo, Washington District College." A line started to form on the bridge of her nose; staring at the screen the mouse jiggled rapidly back and forth, no longer a smooth gliding motion, as the keyboard tap turned to a repetitive thump.

"But that's a strange email, malik dot said at encryptosecure dot ye," she said to herself, picked up her desk phone and dialed three numbers. After several rings, "Ricky, it's Glenda in intake with a quick question. I have an email address from an outfit called encryptosecure, the domain is a ye, I think its Yemini, are you familiar with them; can I get a history? Call me when you have a moment, thanks, Bye."

Lunch for Glenda was cherry pastry and coffee sitting with two coworkers in the base cafeteria; back at her desk in thirty minutes, digital responses to her earlier inquiries began trickling in from agencies around the world. She pulled up the log report, tabbed to a follow-up space, and entered information she considered material from each response:

"Robert Downing, 52, owns in Georgetown, drives a BMW, professor of law and international studies, WDC, ACLU, Greenpeace, Palestine Children's Relief Fund, lecturer Arab organizations, East-West Business Development Foundation, divorced, one daughter appears to be in Europe, listed as victim-witness DC case against Frank Caprizio charged with Islam hate crime assault, airline ticket to Paris in May."

She tabbed to another space: "Rain Walker, 20, student COTP, in Prof Downing's class, unemployed, student loans, witness to DC case re Frank Caprizio, no known adverse affiliations except perhaps Prof Downing."

Tab: "Frank Caprizio, 25, student at WDC, in Prof Downing class, employed at Carbone's Real Italian Pizzeria, brother killed in plane crash, investigated by FBI for sending letters to politicians demanding investigation of crash al-Qaeda link, arrested once before re assaulting an airline spokesman case dismissed, open DC case for hate crime assault, unpaid medical bills psych."

Tab: "Malik Said," Glenda stopped typing, re-read the response, and typed, "appears to be linked with EWBDF in Paris, no further information."

Glenda stood, arched back with hands on her hips to relieve a low back knot, and noticed pinned to the wall of her cubicle a photograph from two years earlier. Glenda was kneeling in green grass next to Heidi while in Annapolis visiting her nephew. She thought for a moment about Lucas sailing around the Pacific on an aircraft carrier and whispered to the photograph, "Something's not right with this one, old girl; fanatics, too many fanatics in the stew."

In the break room Glenda poured coffee from a Folgers canister into the used paper filter, poured water from a carafe into the reservoir, pushed the on button, and waited, staring at the coffee maker, still thinking about Malik Said. "Maybe a call to the French Central Directorate of Interior Intelligence would be worthwhile," she thought, but then again, there really was not any negative information about Said, just an absence of information.

"You won't make it work any faster, Glenda," Sharon startled the contemplative Glenda, "Did you just make it?"

"I did, and I'm giving it a little encouragement" Glenda replied in a tone of sarcastic frustration; "It seems like I make a lot of coffee around here."

"That's probably 'cause you drink most of it girl," Sharon smiled and opened the refrigerator.

Glenda continued upbeat, "Hey Sharon, have you talked to Ricky in email today?"

"Nope; why?" answered Sharon while bent over rummaging through a produce drawer.

"Oh, I put a call in to him this morning but haven't heard back," Glenda tipped her mug over the sink to be certain it was empty, removed the lid, pulled out the carafe in mid-brew, and poured a viscous dark liquid.

"Yea, sometimes he's kinda slow, he'll call," Sharon was upright holding a banana, "I still can't believe you can drink that stuff straight!"

"Creamers are for pussies, girl," Glenda smiled, adding as she was going through the break room door, "stop by later if you're in the neighborhood."

Sharon almost blew a mouthful of banana.

Standing outside Glenda's cubicle, Ricky was first to exclaim "There you are!"

"As I've been all day" Glenda replied with a smile; "you got my message?"

"That's what brings me to your fine abode; show me the email."

Glenda walked past Ricky into the small workspace and he followed; she set her coffee next to the keyboard, sat down, moved the mouse, clicked several times, and said "Here it is, an email from this guy named Malik Said, I think he lives in Paris, anyway, he's associated with an NGO called the East-West Business Development Foundation, they're on our do-not-support list, you can sit if you want." She stood, moved aside, and lifted her mug.

Ricky sat down and scrolled through the email; "Well, it wasn't encrypted, interesting."

"No, this is how it came in," Glenda's response conveyed intrigue.

"Hmm, well," Ricky paused while concentrating on the screen and soon rose from the chair, "this EncryptoSecure is a company out of Yemen, as you suspected, but we don't yet know where, and they use multi-layer email encryption, TLS, PKI, IBE, combinations, which means they're very hard to decode, and the company doesn't cooperate, obviously, if we don't even know where they are."

"So..." Glenda's questions developed slowly, "what kind of people use this company? I mean, do they advertise online, can anyone get their service?"

"Not that we know of; I will tell you that several higher-level Qaeda's used them, but there are probably others also, without any FTO affiliations."

"Why didn't he encrypt this email?" Glenda sought confirmation of her hypothesis.

"Because, probably, it would seem kind of strange to the college professor," Ricky promptly confirmed Glenda's initial conclusion, "who's going to Paris for a lecture, he would need the key, or a password, it would just seem too strange, nothing top secret, also maybe because the sender, this Said, knew the email was being sent to a Google account."

"Whereas," Glenda finished Ricky's thought, "if he is a bad guy, and sends an email to another bad guy, they would want big-time encryption."

"Yes; all we would receive is an email address – some fictitious name or pseudonym at EncryptoSecure; so, really, it's pretty cool you got his name."

Glenda reflected on the totality of her evidence after Ricky left by writing on a legal pad "liberal prof donates to Palestinian causes, speaks at watch-list ngo headed by man using FTO email account, accosted by rightwing radical upset over classroom lecture; malik said, probable FTO affiliation; rain walker, no apparent connection, no more action unless additional contact; frank caprizio, domestic threat level 1, fbi should talk with da."

She reread the words and thought for a moment about their implication and a prudent course, took a sip of lukewarm coffee, and accessed the interagency contact site. In a matter of minutes,

Glenda was advising an FBI liaison officer to begin surveillance of Robert Downing and communicate the importance of a psychological evaluation and tightly supervised probation to the prosecuting attorney in the Frank Caprizio case; her next call was to Paris and the French Central Directorate of Interior Intelligence.

Sandra Downing's and Gilbert Beaulieu's forks dipped from opposite ends of a small table into a warm crème brulée at Le Restaurant Blanc in Paris. Sandra laughed, "Are you afraid I'll eat the whole thing?" Gilbert, a mouthful of crème, smiled and again dipped his fork.

"S'il vous plaît monsieur," Gilbert waved his left hand slightly to the attention of a nearby server, "peut-on avoir deux Sauternes."

The server's head bobbed once and off he darted for a short bar next to the kitchen entrance.

"You have almost eaten the entire dessert!" Gilbert teasingly said of Sandra while exchanging the fork for a spoon, "I now present *la pelle!*" They both laughed. On the table, the server carefully placed glasses of wine, bowed slightly, and retreated in a well-rehearsed pivot.

"To Monaco," Gilbert held out his glass; "To Monaco!" the glasses chimed.

"I'm so glad my father's coming," Sandra's green eyes sparkled to a candle's flicker, "that was so nice of you to invite him; it would have totally been rude to leave him here, I mean, I just couldn't have."

The server quietly extracted the dessert dish. Gilbert waited until sure to be unheard by all but Sandra, sipped from his wine glass, and answered deeply, each syllable finely pronounced in a French accent, "It is with pleasure, Sandra, I'm anxious to meet this father you speak of so highly, and I am as excited as you we are going. It should be very enjoyable, with just very few of us on the yacht; it was fortunate I handled the account; there is just us and my boss and his family, from the bank."

"You'll have to help with my wardrobe" Sandra beamed, "I don't have all my clothes here in Paris."

"We'll go shopping," Gilbert smiled and sipped from the glass.

Sandra and Gilbert sat for another hour, concluded their romantic banter with espresso, and waited as the valet sprinted to a black Maserati Quattroporte parked several blocks away and returned the car slowly to the restaurant entrance, leaving open the driver's door, holding open the passenger door for Sandra. Gilbert handed five Euros out the window and accelerated into traffic on the boulevard. In silence, Sandra and Gilbert absorbed the muted lights of Paris through black tinted windows as the car glided fast and slow, stopping at an occasional light, coming to rest eventually under the glow of a streetlamp in front of Sandra and Rachel's apartment.

Once shifting into park, Gilbert pushed a button subduing the Maserati's rumbling purr, turned to smile at Sandra, opened the door, walked around the front of the car and opened the passenger door. Sandra gracefully slid from the dark maroon leather and they walked arm in arm along a short cobblestone walkway to a wrought iron and glass door. There, Gilbert placed his hands on Sandra's arms without saying a word. Gazing into her eyes, he moved his hands slowly up her arms, over shoulders bare but for narrow silver straps, along the sides of her neck to the sides of her head, holding the long blonde hair gently from her face he lowered his head to kiss her lips. For what seemed both an instant and an eternity, the two embraced, until Gilbert whispering "Bonne nuit" returned to the black sedan and drove away.

It was 8:30 a.m. in Washington when wiretaps activated on Robert Downing's home and cell telephones; FBI agents had been monitoring the townhome since the previous night via digital video cameras mounted inside a parked Mustang half a block away and on a telephone pole in back overlooking the garage. Two agents in a Dodge Charger pulled behind the Mustang at eight forty-five; on the passenger's lap was a notebook computer displaying split-screen video from both cameras.

"I hope he doesn't decide to stay home all day" said the driver – a middle age woman with auburn hair wearing sweatpants and a Georgetown sweatshirt – flatly to the passenger.

"Maybe's he's got an overnight lady friend" said the passenger

– a middle age man wearing Levy jeans, a Nike t-shirt, and a Nationals cap – in lighthearted response.

"Ha," the driver smiled; sardonically retorting "maybe that Rain girl."

The passenger pressed a button and the adjacent window descended; "Beautiful day" he exclaimed while unwrapping a stick of chewing gum. The driver did not acknowledge what she considered to be obvious and they sat silently looking out their respective windows. Boredom was a job detriment too well understood by both.

At shortly after eleven the passenger suddenly announced "The garage door is opening" while staring at the computer screen. His voice startled the driver and she turned the ignition key and moved the console lever to drive. "The car is backing out," the passenger's coolness to the driver conveyed a sense of urgency, "it's a green BMW convertible, I think a Z3 or something like that."

The driver made a hurried U-turn and pressed hard on the accelerator. "He's out, the door is closing, he's turning, going the other direction." The hemi roared and the Charger's front-end elevated with the soft rubber rear tires digging into pavement. "He's...out of view."

The brake pedal applied too firm, tires squealed, and the driver quietly uttered "Shit." The passenger clenched a handgrip above his door; the Charger leaned heavily to the driver's side, slid for several yards, straightened briefly, and slid again as the driver worked the brake and accelerator to maneuver into the alley well behind the BMW.

"He's turning left" advised the passenger with his right hand still tightly gripping the vinyl handle.

"I know...I can see" the driver tartly responded as she slowed the Charger; "I hope we didn't freak him out with the tires screeching and...."

"I'm just glad there weren't any other cars," the passenger's exclamation interrupted the driver's sentence; "Amen!"

The Charger turned left at the alley's end and onto a

residential two-lane road several car lengths behind the BMW cruising down a hill toward the river. The passenger reached back with his left arm and after feeling around the floorboard retrieved a small cardboard box, let go of the handgrip, and opened the lid. Inside was a small metal device, about the size and shape of a paper cup lid, one side covered by a plastic cap. The Charger followed the BMW to an intersection, turned right after several cars passed, and left as the BMW a block ahead pulled to the curb and stopped. The Charger continued slowly past. The passenger monitored the BMW in the rearview mirror outside his window until the Charger turned, slowed, and stopped.

"I'll bet he's going to Barnes & Noble" remarked the passenger, "That's just great, Saturday morning in downtown Georgetown, he couldn't have picked a busier place."

"Let's go, we'll pull the lost dollar gag, we've got to get this done." The driver was outside closing her door. A short brisk hike and the two paused a few feet from the BMW as shoppers strolled all around. The passenger reached in a jean pocket, pulled out several bills, selected a one dollar note, and replaced the others. They continued walking slower, passing the BMW, subtlety looking ahead and behind, stopping on a short bridge over a creek they talked for a minute until retracing their steps back to the BMW.

"Oh, did you see that, it flew right under that car!" the driver's boisterous line the result of previous rehearsal.

"I'll get it honey" replied the passenger with due inflection, glanced up and down the street, stepped off the curb, discreetly slid the metal object from a pant pocket under his t-shirt and pried off the plastic cap. He stooped, crawled, leaned and reached, until the object adhered magnetically to the BMW's frame well behind the back bumper, crawled out and proudly presented a dollar bill to the driver. She raved in response, "You're the best!" and kissed the passenger on the cheek as precise location information beamed to a surveillance computer.

As they walked back to the Charger, the driver quietly reminded the passenger, "Don't forget to call the city about that camera at the intersection, and make sure there were no others."

Robert returned to his car several hours later to find, of no surprise, the driver's side windshield wiper holding in place a parking ticket. He settled into the seat and lowered the convertible top; a circuitous route back home, a warm breeze under the sun, a tree-lined neighborhood of intermittent shade, all helped to sooth his disposition. An hour later the BMW entered the townhome garage and behind rolled closed the door.

At once to his desk and booting a notebook computer, Robert was within seconds typing commands and online; several keystrokes later an external display broke into four images divided by thin white lines. The top two images showed views from the front of the townhome, the bottom two, views from the back of the townhome. A tap with the right finger and the mouse maneuvered just slightly, causing the view in the top right corner of the screen to change as a digital video camera concealed in a Lady Palm next to an upstairs bedroom window panned and tilted on a tripod. Another tap, pressing keyboard arrow keys up or down, the view zoomed in or out on a blue Mustang parked a half block away.

Robert smiled. The lower left image clearly portrayed a video camera mounted on a telephone pole behind his home; the climbing of the pole and mounting of the camera were recorded digitally through infrared illumination the night before. Robert had watched that recording. He felt certain also there were taps on the phones, email intercepts, and monitoring of his whereabouts through GPS or human surveillance.

"The savage's noble existence is public" he thought, still smiling, ruled by the laws of the tribe. "We shall see."

"On Sunday, the BMW remained stationary on Thomas Jefferson Street near the Barnes & Noble for three hours and fifteen minutes, a Starbucks, Rock Creek Park, and a liquor store; Robert Downing did not have any visitors to his home, did not send or receive any email, and did not use the telephone."

"On Monday, the BMW remained stationary at Washington District College for four hours and thirty-two minutes, a Starbucks, a Whole Foods Market, and, for four hours and ten minutes beginning at six-thirty p.m., on Thomas Jefferson Street; Robert

Downing did not have any visitors to his home, did not send or receive any email, and did not use the telephone."

"On Tuesday, the BMW remained stationary at Washington District College for six hours and seventeen minutes and parked on Thomas Jefferson Street for two hours and thirty minutes; Robert Downing did not have any visitors to his home, did not send or receive any email, and did not use the telephone."

The surveillance reports concluded: "We must now assume Mr. Downing is aware of the surveillance and may be using public transportation, a different email account, and a different telephone."

Into the lecture hall from a door right of the podium on Tuesday afternoon strolled Robert Downing while addressing his students: "This being our last class, not of course counting the final exam on Thursday, and the subject being consent, and you of course having completed your assignments for today, I am hopeful you will engage me in some insightful discussion about the current role of privacy in America."

The professor's camel sport coat physique posed a dramatic lonely silhouette against the grand image behind and to his left – a video camera mounted on a telephone pole pointing directly at a residential townhouse not more than two car lengths distant.

Behind the podium, Professor Downing stopped in silence to survey the classroom, especially, but without being obvious, looking for Rain Walker and Frank Caprizio. Once satisfied both were in attendance and pleased in fact to find them seated adjacent one another, he slid black frame reading glasses over lowered eyes and spoke into the microphone:

"Ayn Rand, remember, believed that civilization is progress toward a society of privacy; the savage's noble existence, she said, is public, ruled by the laws of the tribe; civilization is therefore, she believed, the process of setting man free from men. Now tie this to the concept of consent, which implies freedom, freedom of choice; freedom implies knowledge, knowledge implies information, and information implies a meaningful decision, in this case whether or not to consent to an invasion of privacy.

"Remember the child being searched at the airport? Look at this photograph," he raised his left arm and extended the index finger without turning, "did the occupants of this home consent to what we may presume was an uninvited privacy invasion, a search, if you will? Are we setting men free from men, or are we creating a society in which the tribe or those strongest in the tribe impose their consent on the individuals, the savages, treated as savages? Does security trump privacy?"

For the next forty-five minutes, professor and students interacted, debating intensely the concept of privacy, of consent, of freedom, of security. Nearing the dialogue's end, Professor Downing pointed to a young man seated in the front row with his hand raised – "Yes?"

"What does all of this matter if you don't have anything to hide?"

The young man's question was framed exactly as Professor Downing had been hoping for; "Madhav, thank you for that question, it is, really, the underpinning of our entire discussion." Professor Downing hesitated in a gesture signifying importance. "Anything to hide – let's think about that concept; each of us has something to hide, do we not?" He raised his left hand above the left shoulder and again extended the index finger; "The man, the woman, the family in this townhome, do they have something to hide? Of course! Each one of them does! What you mean is 'What does all of this matter if you don't have anything *criminal* to hide.' That is the essential distinction.

"How much of your private life are you willing to sacrifice allowing the government to invade your privacy searching for something criminal? Madhav? Do you want to have a video camera pointed at your bedroom?" The students broke into laughter. "This is the entire rationale behind the Fourth Amendment, no warrants shall issue but upon probable cause, supported by oath or affirmation, describing the place to be searched and the specific thing to be searched for."

Professor Downing stepped from behind the podium and rested his left elbow against the edge. Holding the plastic reading glasses in his right hand his tone softened; "You all are inheriting a society of fear. Generations ago, President Franklin Roosevelt said that the only thing we have to fear is fear itself; he was addressing a country in considerable turmoil. Today, the tribe, we as a society, is afraid, afraid of threats from the outside, threats from the inside, and threats from above; and when the tribe is afraid, the rights of individuals become trampled.

"The requirement of a warrant as described in our constitution is one of the first things to go when the tribe is scared. It isn't that you don't have anything to hide; it's that, unless there is a warrant, it's none of the government's business whether or not you have something to hide. Ask yourself this: is it not a form of consent not to resist?"

A short silence was followed by "Good luck on the final!"

Professor Downing began gathering his teaching materials from a shelf low in the podium to a rejuvenation of ordinary sounds, people talking and moving, and soon voices recognized; "Hi Professor," it was Rain and Frank, "Hi Professor Downing."

"Well, it's good to see both of you in attendance," Professor Downing did not want to jinx the occasion by expressing his pleasure at seeing the two of them together; "Did you have a question?"

"No" replied Rain, "We, I, just wanted to say how much I've enjoyed your class."

"Both of us" added Frank, "and thanks for what you...."

"Forgotten" Professor Downing interrupted, "it's been a pleasure having you both in my class and I sincerely hope all goes well for both of you."

"Thanks!" Rain and Frank reacted simultaneously but Frank had a need to continue: "It looks like I'll get probation, maybe some anger counseling, some grief counseling, it's probably a good thing...."

"That's great!" Professor Downing was relieved at the direction of the conversation; "Let me know if there's anything I can do."

"I will," Frank started to turn and with a grin added, "You're not so bad for a liberal."

Robert smiled, waved, finished packing his teaching materials, and flipped off the lights on his way out of the classroom.

Wednesday morning found Robert reviewing digital video recordings and examining the area surrounding his townhome by way of the four digital video cameras. Focusing within minutes on a blue Dodge Charger parked behind the Mustang – "A new game" he thought; typed the information in a spreadsheet record and hurried to the shower.

The drive to his office on campus included frequent glances in the rearview mirror and stopping at Starbucks for a grandé half-decaf coffee and Wall Street Journal. Robert found an available window table with a view of the parking lot and the blue Charger, discreetly observing in restrained satisfaction as the passenger entered the coffee shop a few minutes later and placed an order for two. While casually reading the previous day's business news, global stock markets, downgrades, sales, mergers, and investigations, he came upon an announcement that $250,000,000 in DigiFouré Telecom shares had been privately placed by Worldwide Investment Bank's Paris and Dubai offices. Robert sipped what little coffee remained in the paper cup, re-read the announcement, folded the paper and placed it under his arm, disposed of the cup, and strolled past the Charger smiling at the clearly unhappy occupants.

Also unhappy was Timothy Baxter. "Glenda, I realize you're just an intake – I don't mean, of course, any disrespect – you're an intake specialist with the NSA and I understand you didn't do any follow-up, but I just want your opinion." As the FBI agent assigned to the Robert Downing investigation, Agent Baxter found himself in the unenviable position of wondering on the one hand why there was any investigation, whatsoever, and, on the other, why the subject appeared so unconcerned. "Professor Downing had a confrontation with a kook in a cafeteria and is scheduled to give a lecture for an NGO with possible terror links; I mean, what has he done?"

Glenda shifted in her chair and held the coffee mug in her lap with both hands as she spoke into the headset; "You've seen my referral. Downing is communicating with a man who uses highly encrypted email, he works for what looks like a terrorist funding organization, and he is assaulted by a right wing fanatic who thinks all Muslims should die; not to mention he donates to a Palestinian relief organization."

Realizing the vacuous implications of her summary, she added, "I just have a feeling something's not right."

Timothy Baxter rose from his chair and looking out a window down Pennsylvania Avenue toward the Capitol, hands in his pants pockets, conceded the point, "And I agree with your hunch, because, and only because, our suspect knew almost instantly that he was under surveillance and stopped communicating over the phone or by email – he also taunted Julie and Fred in front of a Starbucks."

Glenda's mouthful of coffee entered her nasal passages and she sniffled, coughed, and covered her mouth, but not fast enough to avoid exacerbating Agent Baxter's annoyance. "This guy's leaving for Europe in two days! I'm trying to figure out if we expend the resources on a tail, have him picked up in France, or drop this whole fiasco." Before Glenda could respond, he added, "Remember, Said didn't use encrypted email with Downing; we can't just tail a guy 'cause he's a known liberal!"

Recomposed, Glenda reflected temporarily, subsequently pleading her case: "Ricky, in email, told me that we were damn lucky to get Malik Said's name, he said the email company, EncryptoSecure, uses highly advanced encryption technology and does not cooperate with us, the Europeans, anybody; he certainly thinks there's a terrorist link. Also, don't you think it's kind of weird that the email wasn't encrypted? Downing put the airfare on his American Express for crying out loud! It almost looks like they want anybody listening to know what's going on."

Timothy Baxter stared out the window at a young woman in a short yellow dress hailing a cab across Pennsylvania Avenue without thinking about the scene, his thoughts solely of Glenda's statement, encrypted email, lucky to get Malik Said's name, want anybody listening to know he is giving a lecture at a terrorist NGO sponsored event in Paris. He turned abruptly and looked at the telephone speaker, "Are you telling me that Ricky thinks this email company only, *only*, works with criminals?"

"No...he thinks this company only works with people who have something to hide."

"You mean, of course, in a criminal sense?"

"Yes...of course."

After a lull, Timothy Baxter continued, "We haven't found anything on Said; it's puzzling; but the NGO is a do not sponsor; I'm sure Downing must realize that." Agent Baxter had made his decision. "Alright Glenda; thanks for your input, sorry to call you on such short notice, better refill that cup" he finished with a smirk and disconnected.

The decision was to discontinue surveillance on Robert Downing and instead advise Interpol and the French intelligence service of the FBI's concerns regarding Malik Said and the East-West Business Development Foundation. "A hunch just isn't sufficient" concluded Agent Baxter in his report, "and any suspicion regarding Robert Downing does not, at least at this point, rise to a level of reasonableness such as necessary to justify a continued intrusion."

Robert arrived home that Wednesday evening to find gone the Mustang, the Charger, and the digital video camera affixed only a short time earlier to the telephone pole behind his home. After using his cell phone to convey a last-minute dinner invitation to an assistant professor of political science who recently arrived from Brazil – she eagerly accepted the invitation – Robert opened a bottle of French cabernet sauvignon and set it on the counter, made sure he had everything necessary for pasta and salad, turned on his netbook computer, activated a USB wireless adaptor, and logged onto encryptosecure.ye.

III DEVOTION

Michael Crane's boss, Calvin Witherspoon, finally ordered Michael to rehabilitation at a London clinic where he spent three agonizing months withdrawing from the fentanyl, the first week vomiting almost constantly and shaking uncontrollably. The headaches eventually subsided – allowing him to sleep without the nightly low doses of Triazolam. The clinic brought in a physical therapist after a couple of months to strengthen Michael's neck muscles, which helped considerably, and he decided against surgery after talking with the surgeon.

Immediately upon his release from the clinic, Michael asked Assistant Chief Witherspoon to send him back to Africa, which he missed dearly, and received a gratuitous low-level assignment monitoring ship traffic in Port-Gentil, Gabon. His cover was again an export company, but this time a timber exporter. He no longer took pain medication, instead exercising his neck muscles using a rubber cord with one end nailed to the wall in his office and the other end wrapped around his head, which he moved from side to side and round and round, and no longer drank espresso with rum, just Castel beer out of short bottles.

Port-Gentil is a tranquil island town with white sand beaches fading into a light blue ocean. Michael found it a relaxing place to live, actually enjoyable, as his job consisted of walking the docks, making note of boats and ships, checking manifests under the guise of export necessity, and sending reports by fax to London. Once in a while, he would run across a boat carrying refugees for money from Sierra Leone or Guinea.

These vessels were usually easy to spot because they entered the harbor at night, fishing trawlers without any sign of fish lying low in the water, their crews staying aboard and talking under their breaths in Portuguese or Spanish. Michael would order surveillance and wait for the seasick and starving immigrants to emerge under cover of darkness. They would be whisked by MI6 contractors to a converted wood chip warehouse, separated from their belongings, photographed and questioned, staying in relative comfort for several days while their photographs were compared with those of known criminals and suspected terrorists.

Michael met and fell in love with the desk clerk at L'Hotel Gentil; Aurélie was twenty-two, from Port-Gentil, with soft brown skin and bright green eyes and a smile that made Michael's knees weak. He made a point of holding all of his business meetings in the lobby of the hotel, paying Aurélie in cash to bring them hot tea and butter wafer cookies after a few minutes, which she delicately placed on a silver tray and set on a side table next to the high-backed blue floral lobby chairs. Michael and Aurélie married after several months and moved into a small house overlooking the ocean on the south edge of town.

The first true peace Michael had ever known was short-lived. A check of refugee photographs from a schooner out of Conakry turned up a match with two suspected al-Qaeda bombers in North Africa. Michael emailed MI6 headquarters for further information and received confirmation the two dropped out of sight in Western Sahara a few months earlier; his orders were to tag their bags and release them under constant high-level surveillance.

Michael assigned an agent to hide miniature GPS devices in the lining or contents of each suspect's bags. Two days later, agents found the canvas bags packed with clothes – the GPS sensors intact – by the side of the road near Onjouendjo. Their first night out of captivity the men launched a small outboard filled with supplies and crossed the Nikomi Lagoon in darkness, vanishing into the dense interior of Gabon as the tailing agents tried in vain to secure a boat.

The thick leafy canopy made an air search futile and a ground search was impractical, bordering on impossible, because the men could have traveled in any direction through the dense foliage. Michael theorized al-Qaeda supporters met the men soon after entering the jungle, or when, as perhaps planned, they doubled back to Onjouendjo or returned to the lagoon, having traveled inland just long enough to lose the agents. He notified the Gendarmerie Nationale Gabonaise, but they were overwhelmed trying to quell anti-government protests aimed at overthrowing President Ali Bongo Odimba and instilling their candidate, Andre Mba Obame. Michael lost the terrorists.

During a June raid on a mid-level al-Qaeda training camp deep in the Wagadou forest of western Mali – an enormous expanse of wilderness – the Mauritanian Army captured three terrorists and recovered documents identifying others trained at the facility, including the two Port Gentile refugees who had escaped Michael's surveillance by crossing the Nikomi Lagoon. The army conducted a site interrogation of the three prisoners by having them kneel, tying their wrists at the shins, inserting a steel bar between their arms and knees, hanging them from the ceiling, and beating them with batons. All three provided the same vague, but disturbing, information: a handful of al-Qaeda trainees handpicked for a special mission required isolated training in an outlying part of the camp known as the "Tanière du Tigre" or "Lair of the Tiger." These men had abandoned the camp a few days earlier.

The Lair of the Tiger was a hundred meters from the main Wagadou al-Qaeda training facility. The Mauritanian Army commandant with six infantrymen scoured the area, a barren scene with a pond fed by a nearby stream and two lean-to barracks. There, in one of the barracks, they discovered an odd assortment of chemistry equipment and diving gear. Damming the stream and digging a drainage ditch, the mud remains of the pond revealed a propane bottle, hoses, and crude underwater welding torches. In the other barracks was a map of North Africa bearing incomprehensible Arab handwriting and "27" to the side – no information of immediate value.

Mauritanian authorities shared their initial information with Western intelligence services, including the CIA and MI6, and on a Monday morning, the first of July, Michael received an encrypted email from headquarters alerting him to the possibility his escapees had traveled from Gabon to an al-Qaeda training camp in the Wagadou forest of western Mali. Pausing part way through the email, Michael leaned back in his chair and gazed at a large map of Northern Africa taped to the otherwise barren white wall of his office.

"Why would al-Qaeda bombers leave on a schooner from Guinea" he posed aloud, just to travel to Port-Gentil, have an elaborate plan to escape surveillance and capture, and travel back north to the Wagadou forest of Mali, an eastern neighbor of Guinea? Trying to formulate some plausible answer, Michael leaned forward, tapped the mouse with his right index finger and continued reading the email, "...believe they may be part of a high-level mission, purpose of which as yet unknown." His question loomed puzzling.

Al-Qaeda in the Islamic Maghreb, operating in a region of Northwest Africa west of Egypt, launched a series of attacks shortly thereafter. On July 16, a suicide bomber detonated a car bomb in front of the central police station at Bordj-Menaiel, 70 kilometers east of Algiers, and a bomber drove his motorbike into a crowd near the town hall, killing a police officer, a local official, and sending fourteen people, mostly police and military, to the hospital. The following Wednesday, an explosion at an army base near Baghlia killed two soldiers and wounded six others.

The end of July, Michael received another encrypted email, "Items from June 24 raid in Mali lead analysts to conclusion multiple Qaeda and related factions planning large scale joint operation, location undetermined, with meeting on Moroccan coast about this time next year, advise as to possible strategy and covert operatives in your area."

"Understood," Michael typed in reply, "will make preparations and confirm."

The continuing violence in Northwest Africa absorbed much of Michael's time however, and, understandably to his superiors, delayed preparation for the Moroccan surveillance and infiltration. Terrorists were on the offensive throughout the region; monitoring and struggling to anticipate their activities required much of his branch office's resources.

In August, two suicide bombers attacked an Algerian military academy, the Académie Militaire Interarmes, at Cherchell, killing eighteen people. In mid-October, Mauritanian forces went on the offensive with the assistance of two French surveillance aircraft after al-Qaeda landmines in the Wagadou killed several people. A few days later, opposition forces killed deposed Libyan dictator Muammar Gaddafi and, in November, al-Qaeda's North Africa branch chief told a Mauritanian newspaper that his group acquired weapons from stockpiles left unguarded in Libya after the fall of Gaddafi.

By early January, a temporary lull in the regional violence returned Michael's thoughts to Morocco, a possible action the details of which were completely unknown, initiating from some locale within a two-thousand kilometer stretch of coastline. Sending an email to headquarters, "Need more specificity on the Morocco meeting date and location – town, area, anything would help," but not anticipating receipt of any information he could use – years with MI6 had led him to conclude the ball once received, not easily returned – the next morning he was pleasantly surprised. "Intel from source in Algiers provided new data that Morocco may be a stepping off point for a May operation in Europe, not just a meeting, suggesting the need for a town with dock facilities across from a similar point in Spain or Portugal."

"That helps considerably" thought Michael; unfortunately, however, the operation had become one of prevention as opposed to merely surveillance.

Flipping through an old Rolodex kept but rarely used in a bottom desk drawer, Michael came upon the card for Yassine Keddaoui, under "M," and pulled it from the deck. His notes from eight years prior read, "Transnational Security and Terrorism, Bohn, Morocco Direction de la Surveillance du Territoire, French, English," concluding with a telephone number and personal email address.

Michael picked up the phone and dialed; after a few rings a man's voice answered "Allo!"

"Allo, Yassine Keddaoui s'il vous plais, c'est Michael Crane."

"Ahh..." the response; "Yassine ne fonctionne pas ici, pas plus, Je suis désolé, puis-je aider?"

"No merci, où puis-je trouver monsieur Keddaoui?"

"Je ne sais pas."

"Okay, merci, chao." Michael wondered if Yassine was still alive as he typed an email address into the "to" field of his personal email account and wrote "Yassine, we met at a conference eight years ago, I need some help with a situation in your neck of the woods, please respond and include the name of the conference if you're able to be of assistance, thanks, hope you're well, Michael." It was a long shot; he would wait a day or two and if necessary pursue other channels.

When Michael returned from a lunch of leftover seafood bisque with Aurélie at home, he pulled up his personal email account to find a reply from Yassine. "Michael, good to hear from you, long time since the security and terrorism conference in Bohn. I now work for the police force in Casablanca, since after the café bombing. I would be happy to help – what do you need? Call me anytime...," the message concluded with a telephone number and three words in Arabic that Michael did not understand but believed meant "peace" and "family." This presented a dilemma requiring at a minimum some confirmation of Yassine's work status, concluded Michael, as well as approval for outside assistance from headquarters.

He sent an email to his boss and typed a reply to Yassine, "Very pleased to hear all is well, Yassine, I just need some demo and geographic legwork from somebody who knows well the Moroccan coastline. Since you're no longer with the security services, I need to run it by HQ. Is there a superior in the police department I can call for confirmation?" Pausing, Michael reconsidered his direction; Moroccan security and police should know what was going on – his people would be entering their country pursuing an active investigation. It made no sense to treat the Moroccan authorities as obstacles. Still, thought Michael, "Loyalties often transcended job titles...."

Leaving the email unfinished, Michael raised from his desk and walked across the office through the door into a large room with workstations, metal desks with computers, two large white erasable boards on easels, each scribbled with red and orange words and arrows, wall maps, and a blackboard with "Weekly Export" printed in chalk at the top and numbers associated with locations below. Occupying the far left corner of the room was a small counter with cupboards below, obliterated by paper towels, ceramic cups, a coffee canister, tea bags, and a dirty black Hamilton Beach drip coffee maker.

"How old's the coffee?" asked Michael, walking past an African woman wearing reading glasses and a bright yellow rolled scarf typing while staring at a computer screen.

"This morning, I think," the woman responded without looking up, her facial expression unchanged.

"No, I made a fresh pot after lunch" interjected a younger white man with an English accent seated opposite the aisle; "it's only a couple hours old."

"Excellent!" exclaimed Michael, reaching for the glass carafe and touching the side with the fingers of his left hand, "Damn, the warmer shut off, we need to figure out how to turn off the automatic shut-off."

"We've only had that coffee maker for a year," the woman's sarcasm highlighted by peering over the top of her glasses smiling.

Michael laughed for a second and carried the carafe through a door leading to a hallway and small room with a sink and toilet, poured the coffee in the sink, rinsed the carafe, filled it with water from a five-gallon cooler, returned, filled the plastic reservoir, and pushed a button, "Looks like it's tea time...Ruby, what have you found?"

"I wish you wouldn't call me that boss" replied the woman lightheartedly without lifting her eyes from the screen, "It can only be one of about a hundred possible locations."

"They all have docks?" Michael responded in surprise.

"Yep; some look like small docks, like in a river, some in coves, but we don't know the size of boat."

The Englishman intervened: "It has to be able to make it across the Strait, carrying five or six passengers, so it's got to be, say, ten meters?"

"It depends on whether it sails or has a motor, you know, draft, keel," Michael sounded exasperated, "How do they expect us to pin down a location without knowing anything about the vessel or the passengers? It could be anywhere!" He heard gurgling from behind and turned around to touch the carafe with two fingers.

"Where can you fuel?" asked the Englishman.

The woman looked up from the screen, the sound from her throat signifying a certain respect for the question, "That's a good point, boss; but we don't know that it's motorized."

"It has to have a motor!" Michael sounded encouraged to the point of elated. "Tom's hit on something; nobody would risk just a sail across the strait or Atlantic to Spain or Portugal, especially on a time-sensitive mission, an important mission that's been in planning for months, maybe years, there has to be fuel, and enough to get them across!" He lifted a black cup drying upside down on a paper towel, looked closely into it, pulled a wrapped tea bag from a box, tore open the wrapping and left it on the counter, hung the bag in the cup with the label dangling and filled the cup with hot water.

"Focus all your effort on places with fuel, dockside, just dockside."

Michael walked along a wall carrying the cup in his left hand like a professor soon to give a lecture, stopped at a topographic map of North Africa and Southern Europe hanging by thumbtacks in a wood rail and, with his right hand, pointed to the top of Morocco between elevation rings labeled "0." "Remember, just this area," his finger moved about eight centimeters, back over the paper, and back again over five hundred or so kilometers of coastline from east of Nador west to Kenitra, "just this area," the tip of his finger tapped the map, "just dockside fuel depots."

Timely ringing of the office phone curtailed repeated instruction and the Englishman, Thomas, answered "Freeland-Gabon Export Company, how may I help you?" and after several seconds' silence, "Hello Duncan, yes, yes, he's right here." Putting his hand over the mouthpiece, Thomas tried expressing by facial contortions what Michael knew.

"I'll take it in my office," Michael flipped the door closed behind him and sat at his desk.

"Duncan?" Michael was silent; "Yea, I met him at a conference years ago, but he's the only operative I knew in Morocco, the situation is getting close, everyone in the region's down on manpower with all the goings on so I thought he may be of help." More silence. "I don't know." Michael did not speak for several seconds, "Yes, there's five hundred kilometers of coastline if we narrow the region to account for the fastest crossing. We're also now limiting our search to places with fuel as we think they are going to need a motor, to be sure." The room was quiet for a minute. Michael spoke again, "I'll see what I can find out and let you know; you know, even with a local, we're only going to be able to position five or six agents." After another moment, "Okay, I will; bye for now." Once having placed the phone back on its base, Michael took a sip of lukewarm tea and jiggled the computer mouse until his email to Yassine reappeared onscreen.

In place of the words Michael typed "Very pleased to hear all is well, Yassine, I need some surveillance work, there may be an incident developing on your coastline. Can you help? Best, Michael," and leaned back from the keyboard, read the note, reached for the mouse and clicked "send." Next, he opened a spreadsheet and pulled a legal pad from the top drawer of his desk; "Let's see" he mumbled while scrolling down a long list of names in column, stopping, quickly penning a name to paper, drawing a line through it, slowly printing the same name, scrolling further, stopping, printing, until eight names appeared neatly on the page. A brief look of satisfaction transformed to concern and from the writing pad he tore the page and carried it together with his cup to the woman's desk in the front office.

"Could one of you please get me email and telephone for these folks – MI and CI?" Michael deposited the page on the woman's desk as he headed to the coffee maker; first feeling the carafe with two fingers he poured hot water into a cool reservoir barely covering the tea bag.

The woman snagged the paper with one hand as she continued moving a mouse with the other, "Tom, do you want to do this or do you want me? I'm at Nador."

"I'm almost to El Behara, there's not much in this area after

Kenitra, let me take a look;" Thomas got up from his chair, took the sheet of paper, and nodded, "I'll get on it."

Suddenly, the woman exclaimed "Flash!" in a loud but composed voice, and Michael and Thomas turned to watch her face as she continued, "...bomb in Abidjan, six dead, car bomb outside the Ministry of Justice."

"Out of our area" responded Michael in a tone conveying relief; "They really seem to want to keep us busy, though, everywhere but Morocco." He sipped, "Call local and see if they need any help," returned to his office, moved the door with a foot until it gently closed, walked over to a long string dangling next to dusty brown metal blinds, tugged until the blinds held in position, and gazed through a dirty window into the alley. Garbage pales overflowing with trash only seemed the more unsightly sitting next to the pristine white block building beyond.

It was a rather dreary scene made hopeful only by the sun's afternoon light suggesting a finer place beyond. Michael sipped tea and thought about Morocco and why two terrorists would travel south from Guinea to Gabon aboard ship, attracting considerable attention, just to go north again to a training camp in Mali. His eyes fixed on a white and gray seagull standing on the rim of a metal can, pecking in the trash until uncovering its reward, chewing, holding its beak up to swallow, and digging down again to search the filth. A white and brown bird landed on the same heap of stench and perched above the gray bird squawking in anger instead of filling its stomach. The gray bird fluttered toward the intruder until brown wings flapped and the invasive bird leaped to an adjacent and even larger heap of refuse – one on which it could have easily at first lighted. It was as if the brown bird's annoying trespass was simply to distract the gray bird.

Epiphany jolted Michael. He set the tea cup on a stack of papers, took a seat, and maneuvered the mouse with his right hand until intensely studying the screen and typing fast with both hands. "Where is it?" he demanded of the computer. Clicking on one folder and another he soon found what he was looking for: "Refugees from Conkary."

Opening that folder a list of documents appeared. The first, "Report of Investigation," click, Michael studied a summary and scrolled to a passenger table, there, the two known terrorists highlighted next to facial photographs among twenty-two other men, women, and children. He scrolled down the page analyzing each passenger's photograph, scrolled to the top of the table and down again, scrutinizing the investigating agent's itemization of personal or other items brought into the country by each passenger.

The two terrorists carried canvas duffel bags that tied at the top with drawstrings, one brown, one green, but of the same size and manufacturer. Each bag contained inconspicuous items such as clothing and toiletries, shaving cream, razors, toothbrushes, toothpaste, and bar soap.   Michael continued studying the personal items column. Many of the passengers had similar bags but only one other carried a "brown canvas duffel with a drawstring closure at one end" manufactured by the same company as those carried by the terrorists. It belonged to a woman from Mauretania traveling alone.

Michael examined the contents list for the woman's bag: several items of clothing, a toothbrush, a tube of toothpaste, and a bar of soap. He paused, wondering "What brand of toothpaste?" "Perfect Shine," he scrolled up the screen, brand of toothpaste, Perfect Shine, again, brand of toothpaste, Perfect Shine. Fingers of the right hand over the mouse delicately slid and clicked, a folder entitled "Photographs," click, a list of passengers, click, a photograph entitled "Personal Items," click. "Thank goodness for protocol" thought Michael. The photograph showed a full tube of Perfect Shine toothpaste positioned next to a toothbrush and bar of soap. He printed the photograph, and another, and another; all three Perfect Shine, all three untouched.

"Sitting at the bottom of the bay somewhere," Michael hypothesized rather proudly, are three partially used tubes of toothpaste.

Having established answers to his final questions, Michael returned to the investigative report and scrolled to the heading, "Explosives Detection" under the words "Property Inspections."

There, he read without surprise the phrase "dogs not available;" scrolling to the report's end read another heading, "Supplemental," followed by "May 23...both canvas duffel bags found roadside .2 kilometers north of Onjouendjo, GPS locators and contents intact..." but not itemized. The document concluded with "Report prepared by Melody Susskind." Michael accessed a spreadsheet on his computer, picked up the phone, and dialed the number for Lagos Worldwide Export Company.

Melody answered. "Melody, it's Michael Crane, how are you? ...good, hey, I'm going to put you on speaker, okay?" He pushed a button, placed the handset on the receiver, stood up and arched back with hands on his side, stretched, and leaned against the edge of his desk near the telephone speaker. "...in Gabon? Fine, fine, I don't want to keep you, just have a quick question, do you remember the suspected al-Qaeda refugees that came to Port-Gentil from Guinea in May?"

"Of course" replied Melody, suspicious, yet sounding cheerful, "how can I forget?"

"Yes, I know, you were on surveillance, right?"

"Yes, why?" becoming less cheerful.

"The bags," Michael hesitated for desired effect, "you found the bags near Onjouendjo after the two skipped across the lagoon, do you recall?"

"Yes...."

"Good, I need to know, this is very important, was there toothpaste in the bags?"

Melody thought for a moment formulating a cautious response, "Well, we searched the bags, I remember, but I don't remember what was in them, is it in the report?"

"No...what did you do with the bags?" inquired Michael.

"Protocol," Melody was in definite self-preservation mode having neglected to itemize the bag's contents as required per protocol, "put them in plastic bags in the storage room, tagged them, you know."

"Good!" exclaimed Michael; "I wanted to be sure before I sent someone to look."

"What's the matter?" Melody's concern concealed the real question she wanted to ask: "Did I somehow screw up?"

"Maybe nothing...maybe," Michael hesitated, "Let me first confirm a hunch, and then I'll call you back."

"Okay," although disappointed Melody politely added, "Please let me know if you need anything else."

"I will, thanks Melody, bye, and take care." Michael disengaged the speaker, turned, and walked briskly to his door where he took a deep breath, opened it slowly, placed one foot in the room, and coolly demanded "Could you both come in here please?"

The woman Michael called Ruby, and Thomas, sat on hard wooden chairs facing Michael's desk, legal pads and pens in hand and legs crossed as though having just arrived from the steno pool, while Michael reclined in his custom cushioned lumbar-support burgundy leather chair behind his desk, feet apart and hands cradling the chair's worn leather arms. He cleared his throat and in a bland monotone announced "I have reason to believe there is a sleeper in Port-Gentile; that she has been here since May; that she has the makings for a large bomb; and that she will be making her move between now and May." The words flowed as would any short rehearsed speech about a very serious problem thought to be long since neutered, or at least, transferred, a speech once finished leaving the room uncomfortably silent, all of the dazed and perhaps guilt-ridden participants gazing vacantly at one another.

The woman swallowed and responded first, "Do you have any other information?"

"Some, at this point though, conjecture," Michael leaned forward; "One final thing to confirm; anyway, the suspected al-Qaeda members from May last year, the two who got away, I have reason to believe there was another, that three tubes of explosive, toothpaste tubes, were left with this person, who remained here, waiting, for a signal."

"What," the word dribbled awkwardly from Thomas' lips, "How?"

Michael shifted in the chair, straightened his back, and set his arms on each side of a keyboard. "Here is what I think happened" he replied firmly, "we knew about two Qaeda, so we tagged two duffels, we were instructed to tail, but there was another duffel, one carried by a third person, unknown, someone we didn't suspect. All three duffels contained toothpaste tubes filled with explosive ingredients, maybe acetone, peroxide, sulfuric acid, stuff like that, maybe in a benign compound, I don't know."

He leaned back in the soft chair, "The tubes were probably resealed. The two tubes belonging to the suspects were somehow transferred to the duffel of the person staying behind. They probably did it right away. The two suspected bombers took off, knowing their bags were tagged, planning to ditch them. These two served two purposes. First, they acted as decoys, throwing us off any other scent. Second, they probably needed to carry three tubes, and any one duffel with more than one tube of toothpaste would have been too suspicious. There's no other reason for them to have come here from Guinea and then go back to Mali."

Reclining with elbows resting on the scuffed leather and fingers linked on his lap, a slight smile turned Michael's cheeks, "The brown bird, we squawked at the brown bird, we should have been paying attention to the entire pile of garbage."

Thomas and the woman glanced at one another but, knowing Michael well, the woman chose not to ask the obvious question and instead wanted to know "Do we have any idea who it is?"

"Yes, I think so, that is, we have a photograph, but first we need to confirm there is no toothpaste in the duffels we retrieved." Michael leaned forward again, glanced down, brushed a trace of dust from the top of his desk with his right hand, and raised his eyes back up to Thomas; "So, I need you to run over to the warehouse, find the duffels, and let me know what's inside. If there is any toothpaste; and, to be on the safe side, be careful, if there is toothpaste, leave it alone, go through the bags carefully; I don't think there will be, it would have gone off before, if it was active, but just to be safe...."

"Alright, I'm on my way" exclaimed Thomas as he stood up; but starting to leave the office he was stopped by Michael – "Take the Toyota" – from a drawer handing Thomas the keys with "and be careful."

The woman waited until Thomas left the room and asked "What do you want me to do?"

"Hold tight Ru...do" responded Michael with a grin, "if there isn't any toothpaste, we'll need to notify the local authorities and run an APB. For now, though, back to Morocco."

Rudo paused when she reached the door and turned toward Michael still seated behind the desk, "Aren't we really paying attention to that brown bird of yours, Michael, chasing toothpaste tubes and this possible third bomber instead of nailing down Morocco? I mean, couldn't it all be a second-stage ploy, another decoy, to keep us busy while the terrorists plan a big surprise in Morocco?"

Michael stared at Rudo without speaking and after what seemed a long silence responded in a quiet, conciliatory tone, "Yes, you're right of course; the third bomber, if there is one, is another brown bird." Hesitating again he leaned back far in the leather chair, "It seems Morocco must be that important to the terrorists, I guess it's possible they figured we'd eventually conclude there was a third terrorist on that boat and three tubes of possible explosive." Finally, after tapping the desk with an index finger, carefully planning his next words, Michael said "If there isn't any toothpaste, we'll turn it over to local and let them handle it, we'll concentrate on Morocco; that was a good catch Rudo."

Rudo smiled, turned, and closed the door behind her. Michael remained at his desk, motionless, reclining, chin resting on the knuckles of his left hand, elbow resting on the arm of the chair, eyes fixed on the wall map. After a while he stood up, walked across the office, opened the door, took a few steps and asked Rudo "Who's working on that list?"

"Thomas" she replied, "his area, he started south at Kenitra, there aren't as many harbors."

Michael found the list on a stack of paper next to Thomas' keyboard; "I'll work on this 'til he gets back," realizing the gratuitous disclosure's insignificance, adding, "in case he starts looking for it."

Rudo continued typing, eyes undistracted from her effort, and Michael returned to his office without closing the door. After sitting he at once typed a few strokes to access the secure MI6 personnel records, entered a name, jotted a telephone number and email address, and repeated the process for six agents on the list. He telephoned each, leaving messages for some while for others reciting a similar monologue, "Hello, this is Michael Crane, head of operations in Gabon, charged with organizing a surveillance team for Morocco in March, I thought you may be available." One agent said yes, another said yes, another called back and said she was assigned to a project, another said yes, two call-back no's, one vacation and one pre-assigned. That meant a team of at most five to cover five hundred kilometers of coastline.

In advance of contacting the CIA liaison Michael thought it best to find out how many fuel depots Rudo and Thomas had uncovered. The buzzer at the front door startled him, however, intensely considering what to do if more than five suitable docks needed monitoring. Rudo checked the camera from her monitor and clicked on the lock release button.

Thomas burst through the door and confirmed, almost joyfully, "No toothpaste!" Michael stood in his doorway; Rudo and Thomas looked at him for a reaction but Thomas first elaborated, "There wasn't any toothpaste or toothbrushes."

"They probably took the toothbrushes to make it seem less obvious" suggested Michael, "What about the soap?"

"All there" declared Thomas, "everything but the toothpaste and toothbrushes."

"Okay Ru" – an abbreviation that Michael occasionally quipped – "get on with our contacts in the local police force and military and I'll email you the suspect's photo."

Thomas sat at his desk as Michael explained "We're not going to follow-up on this, at least for the present; we need to focus on what's going down in Morocco. I think it's all tied together, though, but, as Rudo pointed out, the bombings elsewhere seem intended to divert our attention. So, I've found three of the six operatives we need, at a minimum, for Morocco. I want you to try and find three more; I've just gone through MI, not CI, so see what you can do. Update me as soon as possible. I know it's getting late, but I'd like to get this done before the day's out."

"Now," Michael looked around and mused "Where did I put my cup?" while ambling toward the counter.

At five-forty that afternoon, Michael received an instant message from Rudo, "forces alerted re toothpaste bomber, may contact you for additional details," to which he replied, "good, see if Thomas could use a hand," and gripping the handle of his cup walked to the window. The alley was unchanged but for the absence of birds, more garbage, and a long shadow following contours of the white building beyond. After a few minutes there was a knock to his door; he yelled "Come in" and turning from the window watched as Rudo and Thomas entered.

"I've – we've – found three others" Thomas announced; he and Rudo took two steps into Michael's office and stopped.

Michael remained by the window; "Good, anybody I know?"

"Perhaps" Thomas replied; "do you know Sean Strahorn, a CIA analyst in Libreville?"

"Hmm, doesn't sound familiar" Michael answered between slurps of lukewarm tea.

"His background includes work in Lagos" continued Thomas, "I thought you may know him."

"Must've been a different time; but, we've got six, good!" Michael turned to gaze again out the window and with his back to Rudo and Thomas sounded distant and reflective; "Try to get me Strahorn on the phone – and close the door on your way out."

"Sean Strahorn" – Michael pondered the name with eyes narrowed, fixed in glazed ambivalence on blowing paper and rolling plastic bottles in the alley. Maybe he did know the man; some memories of Lagos had faded, some had undoubtedly been repressed, still others were stolen by the explosion. Memory insecurity and the possibility of latent traumatic brain injury symptoms loomed a constant sensitive frailty for Michael.

Rudo did not reach Sean Strahorn until late the next morning. Over the phone Michael and Sean first exchanged pleasantries and small talk; Michael learning rather disquietingly that, while in Lagos, Sean followed local authorities investigating the violent deaths of several people at a petrol station. The victims included two suspected by American authorities of blowing up the British intelligence service field office in Lagos and killing Kender Frederickson. "Did you know anything about that, about them being killed?" This odd and inappropriate enquiry by Sean briefly rattled Michael.

"No, no I didn't, but, if they did it their deaths is good news," he replied, feigning lighthearted detachment, wondering about Klaus.

"It looked like a robbery or drug deal gone awry," Sean's response, honest, also intentionally serving to exculpate Michael, "pretty gruesome mess. One guy got away and claimed there was one killer, a tourist, maybe German or Swiss, and he took out two at least with a shiny pen knife. Must've been some pissed off tourist!" Let sleeping dogs lay the eventual unspoken conclusion of both men – for different reasons.

After Michael explained the reason for his call, Sean volunteered a fortuitous coincidence: "We have a mole in a loose knit group of al-Qaeda sympathizers here in Libreville, a good guy, his sister died in that mosque explosion in Maiduguri last month. They were close. A few days ago, he contacted one of our agents and said that a recruiter – he didn't know for what organization – wanted four men from this group, the best trained, to go to Morocco. That's all he knew. He didn't know who was recruiting or why."

Michael thought of myriad possible questions but posed only some in order of subjective importance:

"When?" Sean replied "Soon."

"Do you know the name of the town?" Sean did not.

"Where is your informer now, is he going?" Sean thought the informant was still in Libreville; he did not know whether the man had been selected for the mission.

"What's the man's name, can I talk with him?" Sean said the man's name was Alwar and a meeting near Libreville could be arranged.

"Anything else that caught your attention?" Sean thought for a moment, "The men must be good swimmers."

Later that day Sean sent an encrypted email to Michael: "Meeting possible Wednesday Jan 11 – meet me at 6 am at the port, pier 2, in Libreville."

Thomas arranged the flight and Rudo arranged for her fourteen-year-old nephew, Daniel, to accompany Michael on what was supposed to appear a father-and-son fishing trip. Michael tapped Daniel because he worked on a fishing boat in Port Gentile. The travelers packed clothes and fishing gear and flew one-hundred forty dark kilometers in a modified four-seat Cessna twin-prop to the Libreville Airport and, from there, took a cab to the port.

Waiting at the pier, Sean was barely visible in a blue-gray glaze; "Good day Michael!" he bellowed.

"It is indeed," Michael approached with his left hand on Daniel's shoulder, "I'd like you to meet my fishing pal, Daniel." Daniel smiled, somewhat, shyly.

Sean eased the boy's nerves with a smile and "And a good day to you, Daniel!"

From his seat on a twisted pile of rope and fishing net, Sean stood and stepped toward Michael, holding out his right hand, "Michael, you don't remember me, do you?"

Michael's eyelids narrowed. Clenching Sean's hand his eyebrows came together and his head cocked just slightly; but releasing the grip he was still unable, or unwilling, to answer. Sean kindly offered a reprieve: "It was a long time ago, in Bosnia, we spent the night in a bar in Sarajevo, you and me and your friends, Klaus and Kender, we drank all night, does this, do you, remember? It was right after the air strikes were suspended."

Michael's expression conveyed simple doubt and confusion yet inwardly it felt as though a bag of wet sand had dropped on his diaphragm.

Sean continued unabated; there was something he had to say. "I remember this night because your friend, Klaus, you must remember, there was a fight," Sean looked down at Daniel for just a second as if to apologize, "that Serb in the bar, a big burly Serb, he called Klaus a Nazi...." Sean's voice drifted away. Michael knew there was still a question to answer, but, for the life of him, he did not have an answer. The two looked into eyes in silence for just a brief moment, both remembering a faint noise, like a coin landing on travertine, followed by Klaus knocking the Serb to the floor with his fists and running a small silver blade across the man's trachea to prevent another sound.

Michael knew that Sean knew.

"The fastest man with a knife I ever saw; I thought he killed that Serb; I dropped my beer; that guy will never say that again!" With his next solemn words Sean tore deeper into Michael's conscience. "A bit too fast. I thought, that Klaus, he could kill three or four people with a knife within seconds if he had a reason." Sean's tone portrayed both remorse and forgiveness and, once sure Michael understood what he was saying, his eyes lowered and right hand gently touched the top of Daniel's head, "You're going fishing!"

Michael's ascent into welcoming sunshine and a warm sea breeze offset any temporary agony caused by exiting the red and yellow boat's cramped quarters. Donning his straw hat and aviator sunglasses, he looked across the deck at the Jubilet, and Alwar, and maneuvering in small steps to the railing asked "Alwar?"

Daniel jumped in, "Yes, Mr. Crane, that is Alwar."

First rubbing his palms against the front pockets of his blue cotton pants, Alwar offered an introduction and invited Michael to board the Jubilet, an invitation politely accepted by Michael uneasily straddling the rigging and finally taking Alwar's hand. Once aboard, Michael suggested the two speak quietly on the far side of the Jubilet and, because the sailboat's beam – width – was less than three meters, asked Daniel to wait in the yellow cabin. Michael and Alwar sat close together on overturned plastic buckets admiring the brilliant blue water.

Alwar explained that he was born in Libreville and knew just about everyone his age; some of his acquaintances, not close friends, sympathized with al-Qaeda and resented the British and American occupations in Iraq and Afghanistan, as well as their involvement in North and West Africa; these people made it known they were willing to carry out operations against Western targets and supporters; and they tried to lure Alwar to their fight.

"When terrorists killed my sister in Maiduguri, I knew that the cause, whatever cause, did not justify killing innocent people," there was silence until Alwar added, "Her name was Abeo – to bring joy."

Michael cleared his throat and responded softly, "I understand they want you to go to Morocco, when do they want you to leave?"

Alwar lowered his head and looked at the varnished teak deck, reached down, pinched a piece of squid lying at his feet and tossed it over the side, "The day after tomorrow."

Elbows on knees, Michael also gazed at the varnished teak, wondering about Alwar; "Why were you selected?"

"I was in the Nigerian Navy" replied Alwar, "the Special Boat Service," and looking out at the water spoke with a confidence borne of fact: "I am well trained."

Michael considered Alwar's answer, asking after a period of silence how Alwar intended to maintain communication while traveling with the terrorists. Alwar did not know. Nor did he know who initiated the mission, or why, or what would happen, or what he would have to do, or how he could ever return to his home in Gabon. All he knew was a driving sadness. He and Michael spent the next twenty minutes discussing strategy and logistics; when they were finished Michael returned to the small fishing boat, waved goodbye, and watched as Alwar sailed into the rising sun.

Looking down at Sawahi from his hillside perch, watching as sunlight breathed a new day of life into the village, Alwar could not help but wish he were there for another reason. Rubbing what was left of his cigarette into the ground he hiked down to the Mitsubishi parked at the edge of the slope a few hundred meters from the road. It was seven thirty and he knew the others, some from Libreville, would be waiting at the fourth house from the harbor on the road to the mosque.

Standing at the doorway, however, he recognized none of the four men in the room. One, like him, sub-Saharan African; two Arabs standing together in the kitchen conversing in low voices; and the fourth, "Berber most likely" thought Alwar, from Morocco. All of the strangers kept quiet as Alwar stepped slowly from the open outside doorway to a large ornate couch occupied on one end by the Moroccan – to whom he nodded a greeting answered in the same fashion – and slowly reclined into the soft cotton fabric cushion. There, he too remained silent for the next hour and a half until a fifth man entered the room.

"How many speak fluent English?" the man queried upon entering. "Perhaps he is Nigerian" thought Alwar, but his accent was English. All in the room responded in turn "Yes"; "Okay, than we will use English," the man waived the Arabs into the main room, "Please, join us."

The Arabs moved slowly to just inside the room and the man continued, "My name is Raymond; as you may have guessed, I am from the UK, London to be precise, but I was born in Nigeria. The first thing I want everybody to do is tell me your name, just one word, not your real name, not your family name, the name you want to be known by in the organization, where you are from, why you are here, and your code phrase, is that clear?"

All nodded; some said "Yes."

"Let's start with me, my name is Raymond, I was sent here to lead a team to southern Europe, my code phrase is 'the black rhino runs through the forest.' Now, how do we know that's really my code phrase? We know because I am carrying a list of names and code phrases that I will show you after we go around the room." Raymond held up a piece of paper for all to see; "Okay, let's start on this side of the room."

"My name is Ali, I was sent to this place; my code words are 'the prince dies with his sword'."

Raymond pointed to the next man, obviously nervous, "My name is Sharif, I was sent here, my code phrase is 'a lion sleeps only after making the kill'."

After glancing at the paper Raymond looked up at the black man seated in a wooden chair, who quickly and assuredly responded "My name is Qasim, I also was sent here; my code phrase is 'the martyr knows eternal peace'."

Alwar was next; code phrase, "The red hawk kills easily the dove."

The last man, the Moroccan, spoke carefully in broken English, "My name is Izem and I live here, in this house, 'the wind of change blows away the weak'."

Raymond studied the paper and addressed the group; "Yes, all is fine, there were some translation difficulties, but all seems fine. Here," he held the paper for Ali, "read this and pass it along. It is in English; does everyone read English?"

All replied "Yes" except for Ali and Izem.

"You will trust, I am sure, the others to verify the codes?" Once Raymond's question drew affirmative nods from both, he continued to the group, "I want to tell you some basic rules. You are all here because you have something special to offer. Don't talk with the others about your background. The less each knows about the others, the better for him, the better for all. I am taking only two with me to Europe; the rest will go home. The decision about who will go, and who will stay, will be made in two days. During that time, we will conduct some basic exercises outside of town, things you all should know how to do, fire a weapon, swim, hand-to-hand fighting with knives, basic explosives exercises. We will all stay here, in this house of Izem, until all leave. We will travel in the van parked outside. No one will leave this house without my approval; that means no one will go outside for any reason."

Raymond turned his head and through the open front doorway beckoned "Gatimu! Come in here please." A slender ebony man in a black t-shirt and khaki pants whose eyes were concealed under black plastic wraparound sunglasses stepped into the room; easily visible under his t-shirt was the imposing outline of a semi-automatic pistol positioned under a belt. "This is Gatimu" continued Raymond, "He is from Kenya and assists me. Please, show him due respect."

Alwar raised his left hand only slightly and asked "Does Gatimu have a code phrase?"

Gatimu covered the pistol grip with his right hand and said in a voice agitated and deep "*This* is my code phrase, man."

"I vouch for Gatimu" Raymond interceded, "but your question shows good thinking; we cannot be too careful." The eyes of Alwar and Gatimu remained locked until Raymond motioned with a hand and Gatimu turned and stepped back through the doorway.

"The final rule," Raymond hesitated and looked at Alwar, "is nobody speaks to Gatimu unless he speaks first to you. Now, I am sure you are all hungry, this house is well-stocked, let's assign cooking; tonight, Alwar and Ali, please see what you can do."

Six men sat down to a supper of freshly-caught black bass and saffron rice, after which they separated, some for prayer, others watching television or resting, eventually all finding space to lay blankets in the three room house. Gatimu remained outside throughout the evening and slept, if at all, in the yellow cargo van. Soon after sunrise the group traveled by van to a remote stretch of beach east of town, where Alwar and the other recruits first had to swim in the cold ocean until allowed back to shore by Raymond.

As each man came ashore trembling and breathing heavily, Gatimu handed him a sealed plastic bag of sand the size of a large watermelon; "Swim as fast as possible carrying the bag until I call you back in!" exclaimed Raymond. After a few minutes, one bag lost, two men treading water with heads submersing and reappearing, two men flailing exhausted strokes, only one man paddled forward holding the sandbag: Izem.

Glad to be back on land were all the recruits; bent over gasping for air were all the recruits except Alwar. Raymond waited and when the men had rested directed Alwar to "Tell me, what did you do with the bag of sand – the bomb you were carrying – what happened!"

"I am sorry Raymond, I am not a good swimmer, I thought I was going to drown, I released the bag," Alwar's head bowed, his eyes trained on the sand.

"So, you would rather live than complete your mission?" Raymond's indignation stirred the other men contemplating Alwar with contempt.

Alwar's demeanor changed abruptly and looking directly into Raymond's eyes a forceful reply issued: "I would rather live to complete a mission, than die with a bag of sand in my arms."

Raymond considered Alwar and his comment and, with an air of confidence, suggested "I think perhaps, that you are a better swimmer than you let on," followed by instructions for everyone to "dry off and return to the van, we go now to shoot!"

A few kilometers directly inland the van turned from a dirt road to proceed over an arid expanse of powder and shrub. The bouncing steel box tossed its human cargo against floor and wall, each impact a loud thump, until coming to rest after several minutes at the edge of a shallow sandy ravine. Raymond stepped out of the passenger compartment and slid open the side cargo door while Gatimu on the other side carefully removed items from a recessed storage compartment.

"Down there;" Raymond directed Gatimu into the ravine toward an embankment, "maybe two meters apart." Gatimu climbed down the sand and rock to a pale wash as emerald green geckos darted from under each foot, took twenty large strides in the sand, stopped, and sank the wood shafts of three shooting targets two strides apart. Each white paper target portrayed the life-size image of a black silhouetted man or woman divided by white rings concentric to a red spot over the middle chest.

Raymond scrutinized the targets, yelled "Good!" to Gatimu, and pulled a fully automatic Egyptian made AK-47 assault rifle and magazine from the soft brown case that Gatimu had leaned against the grill.   After inserting a magazine into the rifle, Raymond commanded "Follow me!" and bound sliding and leaping into the ravine. The recruits fell in line.

Standing in the sandy wash, Raymond, rifle held high with both hands over his head, commanded "You will each have a turn shooting the three targets as quickly as you can from a standing position; you may only use three rounds; the action is set on semi-automatic; I will yell 'go' and time each of you and compare both your time and your accuracy.   Does everyone understand?"   All nodded or mumbled confirmation. "We will go first with Izem, then Sharif, Qasim, Ali, and last, Alwar. Please, Izem."

Izem stepped forward; Raymond handed him the weapon and fell back.   At the edge of the ravine, halfway between the shooters and the targets, on a boulder sat Gatimu.   Izem carefully examined the rifle and flipped the safety; holding the butt pad firm to his right shoulder, head cocked, sighting the first target, he waited. "Go!"   Pop, pop, pop...it was over in three seconds and Izem lowered the rifle.   Gatimu tread through sand to the targets; one, he pointed and inserted a wad of white cotton into a hole, another, he pointed and inserted more cotton, the last, he pointed and stuffed another wad of cotton into the small round hole.   Raymond held his stopwatch. "Izem, you took three seconds and your shots landed three, six, and four, remember those numbers."

Sharif, Qasim, and Ali took their turns.   One of Sharif's shots landed in the red but he took eight seconds to fire three rounds; Qasim fired in three seconds with all rounds penetrating inside the fourth or fifth rings; and Ali, four seconds, one shot missing entirely the silhouette, piercing instead the white background.

Alwar stepped forward to receive the rifle from Ali.   Like the others, he examined the stock and recoil, grip, barrel, magazine, trigger assembly, and sights carefully.   Satisfied, he pressed the butt pad to his left shoulder and took aim at the black figure oozing puffs of white cotton. "Go!"   Pop.   Alwar gently pulled the trigger a second time but no response.   Instinctively, without thought, before Raymond could talk or Gatimu could move, Alwar dove behind a waist-high boulder and sitting in the sand with his back to the stone pulled the magazine, pressed the top round, opened the chamber, dislodged a round, reinserted the magazine, pivoted, positioned his right elbow on the boulder for stability and fired off two rounds. Stunned silence held all until Gatimu stood from the boulder and pointed to the rings – three, bulls-eye, and two.

Raymond studied the stopwatch with veiled amazement; Alwar had fired a shot, taken cover, cleared a jam, and fired two more rounds with more accuracy than the other shooters, in just seventeen seconds. "You were not supposed to fire from a resting position" Raymond reproved Alwar; "You seem to have a problem with the rules." Alwar remained silent; knowing his skill with the assault rifle went unmatched.

The recruits and Gatimu waited in the sandy ravine as Raymond climbed to the van, situated the rifle and magazine in its soft case, and retrieved two sheathed fixed-blade combat knives from under the passenger seat. Back in the wash Raymond provided instruction to the recruits. "You will pair up; because you are five, Alwar will pair with me. When it is your turn, I want you to leave the knife in the sheath and engage your partner as you would in a knife fight without ever releasing your knife. This is a contest; the winner will be the one who first puts his partner in a life-threatening position. Remember, the goal is not to wound your partner. When I yell 'Stop!' you must remain stationary. The goal is to show you would have won the fight by killing your opponent. The winners of the first round will then fight each other, and then the remaining contestants will fight.

"Alwar and I will go first; Alwar?"

Alwar stepped in front of the other recruits, took the handle of a sheathed knife in his left hand, and inquired of Raymond as to whether the exercise should include techniques of defense such as wrapping the other arm and hand with a shielding garment. Raymond responded in the negative, "This exercise assumes a combat situation in which you do not have time to prepare," and Alwar nodded understandingly. The two men an arm's length

apart faced one another; Raymond's feet shoulder width, crouched
at the waist, arms bent at the elbows, right hand holding the knife
beyond the left, left arm close to the chest in a defensive position.
Alwar assumed a slightly different stance with the knife in his left
hand – causing tips of the knives almost to touch – and his feet at
an angle giving the look of a fencing posture.

Raymond softly spoke, "You may start."

Alwar instantly pushed forward the knife causing Raymond at
first to withdraw his blade and slash at Alwar's exposed wrist,
moving just in time, the stance of each fighter growing wider they
pivoted around an imaginary point, darting in, leaping back, cheers
of the spectators unnoticed Raymond and Alwar stared eye to eye,
jousting the blades at times with thuds of colliding leather
supplanting the Medieval chime of iron, in a flash from his left
hand Alwar conveyed the knife to his right, all the while in contact
with the handle, and with his free left hand managed to grab hold
of Raymond's right wrist, and Raymond with his free left hand
grabbed Alwar's right wrist and the two locked for a split second in
a struggle undone by Raymond's bending knees toppling Alwar
sideways; Raymond, right leg thrown over Alwar's torso, thrust a
knee into Alwar's left cheek again and again, painfully bending
Alwar's left elbow each time; dazed, in agony, Alwar released his
grip and tried to roll but Raymond's sheathed blade found deep the
soft exposed back of Alwar's neck above the spine and the two
warriors suspended combat gasping for oxygen.

Gatimu standing nearby overheard Izem, Sharif, Qasim, and
Ali whispering to each other and stepping forward chastised the
four in a deep stern tone. "There is only one reason to fight with a
knife." Gatimu's black lens gaze turned to Raymond and Alwar on
their hands and knees in the sand; his vocal projection soft, his
cadence serious, the recruits paid him full attention. "It is because
you don't have a gun, or a spear, or a bow! You fight with a knife
because it is your only weapon. There is no such thing as a knife
fight – there is only a fight to the death and your most able weapon
a knife. In such a fight, you must use every available tactic to
disable your opponent, and then you must cut him deep in the
throat, not in the stomach or the back or the arm where he will be

wounded and more dangerous perhaps than ever, in the throat, you must cut his throat. If not, he will cut yours."

Alwar writhed to his feet wiping sand and blood from his black beard and sand from his clothes and in words laden heavy with deep breaths, "Gatimu speaks the truth...I just misunderstood...I thought we were to not cause injury...I will not misunderstand again."

Raymond on his feet wiped sand from his face and hair and while whisking sand from his white linen pants explained a demand, "Izem and Sharif, here, take the knives, do not cause serious injury, I want to see your technique, I want to know you know what to do; I used my knee against Alwar because he does not follow orders, go!"

Alone to the side of Raymond stood Alwar with a facial expression unrevealing of growing anger.

In no longer than ninety seconds, Izem, from atop, held the sheathed blade hard against Sharif's larynx as he lay paralyzed face-down in the sand. Izem had thrown both legs forward, fiercely kicking Sharif's shins and calves to topple him and from prone on his back pounced as would a cat to an unsuspecting mouse.

"Good!" cried Raymond, "Qasim and Ali take the knives and begin."

The new combatants faced off each toward the other thrusting and jabbing with a sheathed blade until Qasim to his peril attempted Izem's tactic. Ali was ready and Qasim was slow. Ali jumped on Qasim lying in the sand with his legs flailing desperately. Ali's left hand seized Qasim's right arm holding still the knife; Ali, a knife in his right hand, jammed the leather point in Qasim's neck at the jugular. Raymond declared Ali the winner and offered the combatants pause to quench their thirst with water from a gallon jug.

Izem and Ali, winners of the previous round, soon resumed the contest. Each fell into the other's grasp almost immediately and struggled in hand to hand combat, pushing, pulling, kicking, each unable to dislodge his opponent and, cognizant of Qasim's fate, unwilling to chance a fall to the sand. They remained locked for what seemed an eternity until Raymond yelled "Stop! Let me show you what to do when this happens." He counseled and the five students gathered close around; "Gatimu, please assist."

Raymond and Gatimu received the knives. Free hands clamped knife-wielding wrists, feet positioned apart, sinew rippling; the lesson was over almost as soon as begun. Raymond flipped his knife so the blade faced backward using the fingers of his right hand and, with the sheathed blade parallel to his forearm, flexed his wrist, pretending to pierce Gatimu's skin with the point until reflexively Gatimu's grip would loosen just slightly. This, "just the split second a defender needs" Raymond explained, "to pull his arm and then jutting forward run the blade in a slicing motion against the attacker's exposed wrist."

"If this technique does not work, you must fall backward and pull your opponent, then use your feet to propel him over your body like you see in the American movies," Gatimu was advising the recruits, demonstrating his lesson by falling backward, pulling Raymond, and at the same time positioning the center of Raymond's torso on the soles of his shoes careful not to hoist him into the air; "Remember, this is your life; you must think, and you must act!"

It was almost two in the afternoon and Raymond adjourned training so he and the others could return to the house for a midday meal. Qasim and Izem prepared a quick dish of lamb stew and brown rice which they scooped with khobz, Moroccan bread, while seated at the dining table. Ali and Sharif dined on the couch in the sitting room, Raymond and Gatimu took their plates outside and ate standing, and Alwar sat with a dish in his lap on an upholstered side chair in the corner of the sitting room. There, he had a clear view through the front window of Raymond and Gatimu's animated expressions reinforced by waving bits of skewered lamb and vegetable. After several minutes, Gatimu set his plate in the dirt and hurried out of Alwar's sight, soon to return carrying an object Alwar had seen many times.

"You all know what this is?" inquired Raymond aggressively, standing just inside the doorway and holding firm in a two-hand grasp four steel water pipes and wires bound by duct tape; "Is there anyone here who has never made or set a pipe bomb?"

Nobody responded.

"Good! So, you will have no trouble telling me what is wrong with this device – why it will not work! Ali, come with me." Carrying the improvised explosive device in both hands, Raymond led Ali to a back room; shortly, they returned, Ali sat, and Raymond led each of the other recruits to and from the back room, one by one, with Alwar last. Raymond consulted in a hushed voice with Gatimu as a prelude to addressing the recruits: "Only one of you knew the answer, what is wrong with this and why it will not explode; it is Ali; the rest of you did not know. Ali, please tell these experts why this bomb will kill only the user."

Embarrassed, Ali slouched in the couch and declared faintly "There is only ammonium nitrate in the pipes."

Raymond prodded: "And how, Ali, did you know that?"

Ali answered somewhat prideful, somewhat reluctant, "From the smell, you smell the fuses and all you can smell is the strong odor of ammonium."

"And why it will kill you," Raymond glanced at each recruit, "is because when the bomb fails to explode you will be captured by the enemy or you will be captured by me."

From his corner of the room Alwar sat in silence, as he had a few minutes earlier despite the fact he knew the device was defective almost as soon as Raymond placed the package in his hands; not only was the combustion mixture incapable of causing an adequate explosion, but the metallic caps did not properly seal and the electric fuse wires frayed at the cap heads. Alwar believed Raymond and Gatimu were suspicious; any greater expertise on his part would only serve to reinforce their suspicions, they would not select him for the mission regardless and perhaps because of that expertise, and the best possible outcome was at this point his life.

"I have now made the choice of who will go with me on this most important assignment" declared Raymond, "it is Ali and Izem. The rest of you are free to leave, but not together, we do not want to draw any further attention. Decide among you who will go first and the rest wait half an hour, and then another half hour. May God watch over you."

Qasim, Sharif, and Alwar exchanged glances until Sharif announced "I will go," went into a back room, returned with a Nike sport bag, and in a short hand wave and smile said goodbye.

Raymond called Ali and Izem to the dining table, which gave Qasim the opportunity to ask Alwar in a low voice, "May I go next or do you want to go?" Alwar congenially agreed with a nod that Qasim may leave next, got up from his chair, and strolled past the dining table – listening carefully – to the kitchen for a glass of water. Gatimu was standing next to the refrigerator tearing at a slice of fried bread.

"You are disappointed to be passed over?" chided Gatimu with a hunk of bread in his mouth.

"I'm sure there was good reason" Alwar replied while rinsing a clear drinking glass under a faucet; "Both Izem and Ali appear very capable. I would have come to the same decision."

Gatimu stared at Alwar through black lenses and gnawed the bread until water from the faucet stopped pouring; in his deep voice, deeper than usual, "No you wouldn't. Ali is quite handy, I think he just had a bad day with the rifle, but Izem, he can fight well and swim, but with the rifle and explosive he is not that good." He chewed some more.

Restraining any outward indication of puzzlement, Alwar leaned with his back against the sink, looking through the doorway into the main room and gulping water.

Gatimu stepped between Alwar and the doorway so as to receive undistracted attention, swallowed another tear of bread, and very discreetly announced "We need you for something more important."

Alwar took a long drink of the remaining water trying to see through the bottom of the glass and his reflection in Gatimu's sunglasses and, despite considerable curiosity, calmly asked, "And when were you and Raymond going to tell me?"

"When you were not the first weasel out the door!" an answer that Gatimu had clearly readied for the question.

The delivery if not the words somewhat stunned Alwar, who, regardless, quickly retorted "And if I was that first weasel?"

"You would be a dead weasel!" Never had Alwar seen Gatimu smile and his eyes could not help but focus on two large gold teeth beaming in the broad grin.

Gatimu motioned with a quick jolt of his head and he and Alwar strolled through the main room, out the front door, and into cool gray where a slight wind rustled the palm fronds above. Alwar paused to light a cigarette, Gatimu waited, and they resumed walking until in the center of the dirt road, stopped, and stood facing the harbor.

"Raymond and me, we are unsure about you Alwar," Gatimu moved very close to Alwar and spoke softly, "but we are going to take a chance that you do not have any loyalties above money."

After pausing to evaluate Alwar's facial response, Gatimu continued his throaty revelation: "We need some people who are very good, very well trained, for a most lucrative cause. We know that you have been through professional training, probably military, we can tell by your actions; we also know that you are hiding your talents; what we don't know, is why. Now, either you can go, leave this place now with our blessing and assurance that if you betray our blessing, the organization will hunt you down, you know what that means, or you can stay, tell us that you can be bought, and listen to what we have to say. If you stay...if you *stay*...you may not leave until after we complete our assignment, and you may not ever leave if you don't help us complete our assignment. You have the choice now, Alwar."

It was a strange unexpected development. Within a couple of heartbeats Alwar's thoughts mingled from sister, loss, promise, future, fear, an opportunity lost to a different sort of opportunity gained. Without clarity were words the speaking only dreamt over a life of meager subsistence: "How much money are we talking?"

Gold teeth flashed; "More money than you can imagine, twenty-five thousand American dollars once the job is finished!"

"And when is this job – how long will it take?"

"The job is in May and it will take no more than one week; until then, you will wait and train with me and the others." Gatimu's answer begged another question also preemptively answered, "And you will receive food, housing, and some money before the job. But you will not know the assignment until we are ready."

Nothing to lose and everything to gain – clarity – and Alwar accepted what little he knew of Gatimu's offer. The next day, Raymond, Ali, and Izem boarded a fishing boat bound for Lagos, Portugal, and Alwar and Gatimu headed off in the Mitsubishi for Mali and the Wagadou forest.

IV DESTINY

Outside terminal two customs, Aéroport Charles de Gaulle, Robert and Sandra embraced as two threads of a tapestry incomplete, bonded not only by love, but tragedy. "I missed you!" The words rang true for both father and daughter. "What a long flight," Robert lifted his carryon from the floor, "and a long wait in customs, that was nice of you to meet me here." He knew immediately it was a silly thing to say. Sandra put her arm around her father's waist and pulling a suitcase in shifts they walked and talked through the terminal to short-term parking, where they found Gilbert Beaulieu leaning on his Maserati smoking a cigarette.

"I thought you were going to give that up, Gilbert!" Robert could not tell if his daughter was serious or just teasing; "Put that away and come say bonjour to my father; Dad, Gilbert Beaulieu."

"It is a pleasure, sir," the sincerity heightened Gilbert's greeting; "welcome to Paris."

Their right hands extended and clasped, "Thank you, and please, my given name is Robert."

"And mine, Gilbert," he smiled. The trunk lid clicked and Gilbert wheeled Robert's black soft-side suitcase, recessed the handle, lifted with both hands and laid it gently in the carpeted trunk. "Do you also want that here?" Gilbert pointed to Robert's carryon and Robert replied "No, thank you." Gilbert tilted down the lid and opened the front and rear doors on the passenger side. Robert and Sandra walked around the car. Sandra insisted on the backseat, "You need to see as much of Paris as possible," and Robert acquiesced to the front with a smile, "Alright honey, I'm sure it has changed a great deal since my last trip to Paris, during the French revolution."

Gilbert gently secured both doors and once settled in the driver's seat asked Robert "Do you wish to see anything, stop anywhere before going to Sandy's apartment?"

Settling into the soft leather Robert graciously declined and remembering he was staying the first three nights in a hotel, said "I've actually got a reservation at the Hotel Internationale on

Boulevard Saint Germain for three nights – it's where I am speaking day after tomorrow and it seemed easier on all involved, besides, it's paid for." Sandra mounted a disingenuous protest to no avail; she had known for weeks the plan.

"What is it that you do, Gilbert?" asked Robert, gazing through smoked glass, making small but genuine conversation buoyed by the unduly ostentatious black sedan.

"Investment banking actually" replied Gilbert with pride, "I work for Worldwide Investment Bank."

Gilbert's answer drew Robert's attention from the passing scenes and more than a little surprised he studied Gilbert's profile and pursued the query, "Isn't that the firm that just placed two hundred fifty million dollars for a telecom company?"

"Yes," Gilbert smiled and glanced at Robert, "they are my client. I mean, there are several bankers involved – a consortium actually – and I am one of the advisers for Worldwide Investment Bank. I know DigiFouré's CEO personally. In fact, it is he who we are staying with in Monaco."

Even more surprised, Robert turned his attention to the street ahead and chose his next words carefully so as not to seem overly inquisitive, "That's terrific! That means you must work with a lot of equity funds and private investors?"

"Certainly, that is my specialty, private placements that is." Gilbert, luxuriating in a self-perception of recognized accomplishment, neither realized nor cared about the motive behind Robert's adulation.

Robert returned his focus to the fuzzy surroundings out the glass to his right, images appearing and disappearing, people, cars, elaborate and ornate structures. "If the bankers were invited" he reflected, than certainly the key private investors and fund managers were invited. What a strange coincidence, he smiled at the irony, what a strange – potentially disastrous – coincidence.

Malik Said – originally spelled "Sa'id" – was born in Istanbul sixty-six years before meeting Robert Downing. His father, an entrepreneur of sorts during the late nineteen fifties and throughout the nineteen sixties, controlled large poppy fields and manufactured and exported heroin.   In the early nineteen seventies, Turkey embraced a new multilateral capitalism, and with newfound prestige came a new philosophy.   No longer were the opium fields to be left to private enterprise with income limited only by petty graft, the government instead instituted oversight ostensibly confining sales to buyers advancing medicinal applications.

In the early nineteen-seventies, Kareem Sa'id moved his operation and his family to the frontier of Afghanistan, building his business into a multimillion dollar a year tax-free enterprise and becoming a powerful and influential local leader.   Malik Said worked the fields, learned the operation, ran the business and, in 1982 when his father was killed by a Soviet tank bomb, became a warlord.   His heroin operation generated revenue to buy weapons for resistance fighters waging war against the Soviets and he commanded a guerilla force of over five-hundred men, women, boys and girls.

By the end of the Soviet occupation Malik Said had amassed a fortune in excess of twenty million dollars maintained in Switzerland, the Azores, the Cayman Islands, and the United States.   Realizing the potentially volatile and impermanent nature of an illegal narcotics trade, combined with his burgeoning need for prestige, Mr. Said began moving money into legitimate investments such as stocks, bonds, mutual funds, and real estate.   Within ten years, he was worth over three hundred fifty million dollars, much of it as the result of lucrative short-term venture capital investments in booming United States dot com start-ups, and resided in Paris overseeing a multinational business conglomerate.

Shortly thereafter, Malik Said had his bank in the Cayman Islands establish a trust depository for the Cayman assets, with the bank as trustee and his newly-formed charitable organization based in Turkey as beneficiary.   He called the organization East-West Business Development Foundation.   The heroin enterprise on which his fortune built, in the hands of several itinerate franchisees depositing sizeable monthly sums into an Iranian bank account which, in turn, made quarterly deposits into the Cayman

Islands trust.

Attending a London private equity conference later that year, Malik Said was highly impressed by the one-hour lecture presented by a college professor from Washington, DC, Robert Downing. Professor Downing spoke on the diminution of the concept of private within the context of private equity, going into a bit of a rant on the general disintegration of privacy in western cultures following the Nine-Eleven tragedy. Privacy was Malik Said's rampart; he waited for the professor to leave the hall and approached him with flattery, a business card, and an invitation to dinner at a private club in Mayfair.

While dining at the club, Malik Said studied Robert, his appearance, voice, mannerisms, manners, his answers to abstract questions, and a few days later invited him to a private residence for dinner. Robert graciously declined as he was leaving for Washington that evening; but Mr. Said insisted that he offered a lucrative business proposition and would pay any expenses required of Robert staying an extra two days. The next night, a chauffeured Rolls Royce limousine whisked Robert from the Holiday Inn to a mansion in St. John's Wood.

Malik Said and a woman he referred to as a "close frien/ Geraldine, from Nice, reserved and much younger, and Rob ., dined on aged steaks and drank four hundred pound bottle of wine served by expressionless men and women in black dress and white gloves. Mr. Said explained that the estate belonged to an eccentric friend away on holiday with his family. It was during the second glass of wine taken in a library sitting room that Mr. Said told Robert that he wanted him to oversee his United States business interests. As Robert sat speechless, Mr. Said went on to explain that these interests involved holdings of securities, both private and public, bonds, real estate, and cash in various banks, and that he wanted it all moved to a trust in the Cayman Islands.

Responding that he was honored but inexperienced with such an endeavor, Robert suggested Mr. Said find somebody better qualified. Mr. Said would have nothing of it; he trusted Robert and believed in the similarity of their values – governments of the developed world, chief among them the United States, had become self-perpetuating goliaths unworthy of their citizens' respect. In fact, Mr. Said feared his US holdings soon would become immovable or, worse yet, attached. "All I want you to do" Mr. Said pleaded, "is act on my behalf in liquidating these assets and arranging transfer of the cash to the Cayman Islands." Receiving assurance that legal counsel would be involved in every step of the process, and more than satisfied with the proposed remuneration, Robert gratefully accepted the position.

Malik Said instructed Robert upon returning to the States to serve as Mr. Said's attorney-in-fact under a limited power of attorney enabling Robert to sign documents on Mr. Said's behalf; to serve as president and sole director of a new Delaware corporation, Said Holdings, which was to take ownership of all restricted securities; to open an escrow account for cash deposits with direct transfer to the Cayman Island trust; and to work with his attorneys in New York and George Town. Robert opened a bank account in the Bahamas for deposit of his consulting fee, knowing that he could never spend the money in the States without paying taxes, and without realizing the transfers would come from Iran.

Robert's devotion to privacy turned from obsession to necessity as it became clear there was no way out of his bargain with Malik Said. While vacationing the following year over spring break in the Bahamas – with a female linguistics professor nourishing only a passing sexual interest – Robert received a disturbing telephone call. A man with a thick German accent told Robert softly, but convincingly, that he represented Mr. Said's interests. The man warned – threatened – that he knew where Robert was and who he was with and that Robert needed to immediately return to Washington and arrange the sale of Mr. Said's remaining US assets or "there will be a most severe penalty."

Robert flew to Washington the next morning. Later, during a telephone conference, one of Mr. Said's attorneys in Grand Cayman told Robert there was recently a sizeable cash deposit to the trust from the Iranian bank as the result of "a very good crop in Helmand." It became apparent to Robert his employer was an international criminal.

Within a year most of Malik Said's US assets had been

liquidated with receipts transferred to the trust, but there were still a half-vacant office building in Colorado and Holiday Inn Express in Arizona unsold as a result of the general real estate collapse, as well as restricted securities in a Delaware biotech firm and a Reno casino, valued at close to fifteen million dollars. Robert's Bahamian trust meanwhile held just over one million four hundred thousand dollars in a Nassau bank and owned an ocean front condominium and thirty-four foot Sea Ray express cruiser on Paradise Island, neither of which Robert used often out of fear of drawing unwanted attention.

Malik Said sent an encrypted email to Robert, in October, with directions to arrange an off-the-books trade of the biotech and casino restricted stock for shares in a new French wireless telecommunications company, DigiFouré Telecom. Mr. Said had the approval of DigiFouré's CEO, Paul DuMorell. The transaction would go through Worldwide Investment Bank's Dubai branch. A wealthy American living in the Emirates would buy the biotech and casino shares at a steep discount, DigiFouré Telecom would receive the sales proceeds less transaction fees, and Malik Said would own shares in a growing company expecting within the year to undertake an initial public offering. Robert followed instructions, signing the restricted share certificates as president of Said Holdings and conveying the signed certificates to a banker, Stephen Waters, at Worldwide Investment Bank Dubai.

Then the US Securities and Exchange Commission audited the biotech firm's private securities transactions as part of an insider trading investigation of the controller, which led to a subpoena requiring Said Holdings to produce the original share certificates at a deposition. Robert consulted with Mr. Said's attorneys, who advised that he appear without the certificates and invoke his Fifth Amendment right against self-incrimination. Unfortunately, during the deposition, the government offered Robert blanket immunity in exchange for his testimony; thus removing any chance of incrimination. Robert had to testify.

The SEC found that Said Holdings had transferred restricted shares of the biotech company and the company, at the SEC's insistence, summarily voided the transfer and the shares. Left holding the bag, Robert, and the American expat who bought the worthless stock – the biotech firm's share value plummeted and Said Holdings dissolved.   The SEC continued its investigation with only Robert to hold accountable; Malik Said lived in France, was not an officer or director of Said Holdings, and owned shares in DigiFouré Telecom, a French company.

Walter Kragen had resided in the Emirates of Dubai for ten years and was extremely wealthy mostly as the result of a shipping business – and well connected.   His first course upon learning that he had lost twelve million dollars was to confront the president of the Dubai office of Worldwide Investment Bank, Stephen Waters, and demand the bank recompense his losses.   The bank initially refused but later agreed to cover half of the losses in exchange for a release of liability and confidentiality agreement; for his part, Mr. Kragen received six million dollars and the name of the person who benefited from the transaction.

In late December Walter Kragen's private investigators located Malik Said in Paris, and arranged a meeting the following week between Mr. Said and Mr. Kragen in the bar of the Ritz.   Messrs. Kragen and Said sat in stuffed chairs on opposite sides of a small table; in the lobby at least six private bodyguards paced uneasily for fifteen minutes until the meeting was over.   Cordiality between the two tycoons had quickly degraded to a battle of egos culminating with Mr. Said threatening to have Mr. Kragen's "balls ripped off and stuffed down your throat!" and Mr. Kragen yelling for all to hear that he would "ruin" Mr. Said and his family.   The room deathly silent, though filled with hotel patrons, the men left the table and walked through the bar into the lobby, where bodyguards took up defensive positions escorting them to waiting limousines. Truly, it could have been a scene out of *The Godfather*.

The SEC was still investigating the Said Holdings biotech transaction when Robert left for Paris five months later and, based upon Mr. Said's attorneys' counsel, fully expecting to be hit with a heavy fine and full restitution and have his financial condition carefully scrutinized by SEC investigators.   Prior to leaving for Paris, Robert exchanged what little cash he had in a Washington bank for traveler's checks, shipped some personal memorabilia to a mailbox company in Nassau, and left Friskers with an elderly neighbor who had a habit of shoving leftover fish under the fence separating their townhouses. "I'll be back in a few weeks" Robert lied; hugging Friskers he whispered, "I'll miss you." Of returning to the States Robert had no intention, planning instead to fly from London to the Bahamas and take up residence on Paradise Island.

Relaxing in Gilbert's Maserati, Robert made the impromptu decision to advise Malik Said of the invitation to Monaco, tell him the whole story, that his daughter's friend was a banker who worked on the DigiFouré Telecom securities placement and that Paul DuMorell invited the bankers and their families and close friends; and wait for Mr. Said to confirm he was also attending. Mr. Said had for some time known about the SEC investigation and knew that Robert had recently been under surveillance. Robert would also advise him that he was moving to the Bahamas. If Mr. Said did not want Robert in Monaco, he would not go.

A Persian bellman in a red uniform under the Hotel Internationale's rose-colored canvas awning opened Robert's and Sandra's door. Gilbert quickly exited the Maserati, opened the trunk lid, and wheeled Robert's suitcase to the bellman. Robert hugged Sandra, shook Gilbert's hand, and followed the bellman through the lobby to a reception counter, elevator, and room on the sixth floor overlooking the Boulevard. There, Robert unpacked a laptop computer, hung two suits and shirts in a black lacquer armoire, lay on the bed and fiddled with a television remote until settling in an oblivious trance on a French language soccer match between Cameroon and Belgium.

Most of the next day Robert spent preparing for his lecture on religious freedom in America; he reviewed his notes and rehearsed his monologue in the hotel room and only ventured out occasionally for lunch, tea, or an American café latte. The subject of religious freedom was not new to Robert, but he had never lectured to a predominantly Middle Eastern audience and devoted much of his preparation to distinguishing by Middle Eastern and Western cultures the concept. This required a certain amount of study undertaken in the Library of Congress before leaving Washington and revision to his lecture notes in Paris based upon the sound of the rehearsal. Robert wanted very much to impress his perceived benefactor, Malik Said, as well as his audience; and he decided it would be best to reveal his plans to Mr. Said after the lecture so as not to risk disrupting the presentation.

While dining in the hotel bar that evening, Robert received a Blackberry email from one of his attorneys; the email recited terms of a proposed settlement with the SEC that included twelve million dollars restitution, a one million dollar fine, and a requirement that Robert not serve as a director of any company issuing securities. It was an expected yet unsettling communication and, shaking his head in disappointment, Robert consumed half a glass of red wine in two mouthfuls, resuming with less enjoyment a Cajun spice blackened salmon and Ratatouille. A professor's salary, he surmised, would not even be able to pay the interest.

For the first time, Robert felt a ting of anger toward Malik Said. The SEC had previously been the sole focus of Robert's ire as he had irrationally rationalized that were it not for Mr. Said's generosity he would not be modestly wealthy. Seeing the numbers for the first time, however, the reality of the damage jolted Robert to the stark realization he was not wealthy at all, he was instead deeply in debt, facing prosecution, and forced by circumstances to flee his home and give up his profession, teaching, a vocation at which he excelled purely out of passion. The root cause of his inexorable predicament was, he deduced as dusk waned to night, Mr. Said's criminality, dishonesty, and ability to select a malleable accomplice. Of course, what this all meant was that Robert's own greed was actually the root cause of his predicament.

Reading the attorney email for a third time, Robert's anger coalesced to muttering under breath a favored sentence of all resolute deniers: "I'm not going to be the only one to take the fall." Blame nurtured by the influence of wine on mind, from breeze to full force gale, with foremost in contenders, Malik Said, followed closely by the attorneys and bankers who facilitated the illicit stock transaction. "I just followed orders," Robert spoke glumly into the wine glass at his lips, "and I'll be damned if I'm going to wind up the only asshole holding the bag." Only one problem, he acknowledged solemnly while swallowing more of the rich burgundy liquid, the possibility of an unpleasant premature death.

Robert determined by morning following a long sleepless night that he was not going to inform Malik Said of his plans; instead, he would return to the States from Paris after the Monaco event, hire his own attorneys, and try to negotiate a deal with the SEC and the Federal Bureau of Investigation that included exoneration and protection in exchange for cooperation. He would testify and provide documents against Mr. Said, the attorneys, and the bankers, if he could remain in a circumstance of relative freedom.

"The *very first* right set forth in the American Bill of Rights deals with religious freedom and these very *first* words in the *First* Amendment to the United States Constitution read 'Congress shall make no law respecting an establishment of religion, or prohibiting the free exercise thereof'," began Robert's lecture to over two hundred executives and professionals; "Citizens of the United States enjoy strong religious freedom and protection of that right. What we shall examine here today, is the application of this right and this protection to non-US citizens, foreign nationals, doing business in America."

At the conclusion of his presentation an hour later, after responding to a handful of questions from the audience, Robert received an envelope from the seminar moderator enclosing a note from Malik Said. "Please join me for dinner tonight at eight, Parisian Internationale, top floor Hotel Internationale – Malik." Robert attended the remainder of the afternoon session, listening from the hall's back row to speakers in English, French, and Arabic orating on a host of subjects ranging from differences in etiquette and apparel between Christianity and Islam to the nuances of contract negotiation between the two cultures and religions, and adjourned to his room for a brief nap, shower, and change of clothes to a sport coat and open collar dress shirt.

As it was early and the evening pleasantly warm, perfect for a short walk, Robert strolled from his hotel to the Institute du Monde Arab and once there boarded an elevator to the ninth floor, stepping out to a beautiful view of Paris, the Seine, and Notre Dame Cathedral. He approached the maître d' to request a Moroccan green tea; the steaming beverage arrived after a few minutes and Robert took the opportunity to relax whilst exhilarating in the sights. "The twists and turns of life" he thought, watching the sun recess behind dark buildings, remembering the words of Bartolomeo Vanzetti on death row: "If it had not been for this thing, I might have lived out my life talking at street corners to scorning men...."

Arriving at the Parisian Internationale a few minutes after seven was Malik Said in a black suit and yellow tie in the company of a tall athletic man with cropped gray-blonde hair wearing designer jeans, a red t-shirt and dark brown leather jacket, and a striking woman with long dark hair wearing a business blue dress.

Robert intercepted them near the host stand. "Monsieur Said, it is good to see you again," Robert's sentiment not altogether a ruse as there remained fondness, respect, and a certain appreciation for Malik Said.

"Robert," the intonation French with emphasis on the o and e; "I understand your presentation this afternoon was quite well received." Robert smiled and in gratitude bowed just slightly at the waist. Mr. Said continued, "I am accompanied by two people I thought you should meet. Mademoiselle Renoir, Robert Downing." Robert waited for a hand gently held and, as far as he was concerned, for all too briefly; "Robert, please also make the acquaintance of Klaus Adalbrecht."

Malik Said and Klaus met by chance in the upstairs lobby lounge at the Ritz-Carlton on Grand Cayman. It was mid-August, rain gushing, the airport closed, no flights in or out of the country, Hurricane Dean threatening to decimate the small island with winds of over one hundred fifty miles per hour. Mr. Said's visit to the island concerned establishing a trust. Klaus' visit to the island concerned long overdue rotator cuff surgery. Stranded by circumstance in abject luxury, they struck up a conversation which evolved to the subject of vocations. Both, it turned out, were entrepreneurs of sorts. Mr. Said was a farmer; Klaus was in pest control. It was the beginning of a fond symbiosis.

"Mr. Adalbrecht," Robert smiled congenially, reached, and as his right hand contorted in an overly firm grip heard the strong German accent, "Please, call me Klaus, and I will call you Robert."

At first trying to remember where he had heard the voice, or one similar, Robert replied "Good," but as Klaus released his hold, Robert thought of the phone call in the Bahamas and unconsciously flashed a grin from one side of his mouth that Klaus understood to mean the two had previously met. Of course, this, he knew.

A petite young woman with flawless timing wearing a strapless white taffeta dress announced to Malik Said that his table – certainly all others present must beckon only at his desire – was ready. The somewhat tense diners had not even time to unfold white serviettes or open menus as a bottle of 1989 Château Ausone was presented by a speechless waiter to Mr. Said. A glass tipped and twirled, the wine tasted, a gesture of approval, and soon all at the table were tipping glasses and settling in to peruse entrees. Robert found it difficult not also to absorb Michelle Renoir's face, as she in turn absorbed the list of Mediterranean and Northern French dishes, and doubted without care that his frequent glances went unnoticed.

Orders offered by each to the still speechless server, the atmosphere relaxed, and Malik Said presented a toast, "Health and happiness," to which chimes of glass signaled unanimous concurrence.

Mr. Said concentrated his gaze on Robert. "Mademoiselle Renoir and Monsieur Adalbrecht are in my employ, Robert; Michelle, well, I thought you may want a companion while in Monaco, and since Michelle has graciously agreed to serve in that capacity, I thought the two of you should meet; Klaus on the other hand, he is a solver of problems, that is, problems that can be solved by quick response and elimination, he will be accompanying us in Monaco, and should the need arise, he will I'm sure expedite a solution. You see, I have one problem already, with our host in Monaco, Monsieur Paul DuMorell, and I cannot have any other problems, do you understand?"

It was not the first time Malik Said's tact, or lack thereof, had unnerved Robert, but this time a coup de trump, the lion soon to be ensnared had instead trapped the trapper. Despite surprise and visible resentment, Robert maintained an exceptional degree of poise, perhaps due only to the close proximity of a woman he found stunningly beautiful, and his eyelids never blinked but he returned in kind the lion's stare until saying smoothly, with confidence, "I am sure this will be a wonderful vacation for all," to which Mr. Said smiled and nodded in approval and Klaus raised his glass in cheer.

The remainder of the engagement was uneventful to the eventual point of enjoyable. The four talked lightly about work and politics, family and religion, agreeing at times to disagree, disagreeing at times to agree. Michelle entranced Robert, though he maintained a certain remoteness given her calling, he the task, she the tool, still, it was hard for the lonely man in Paris not to lose himself in the beautiful woman's smile. Klaus had an easygoing style that Robert found relaxing, while finding it difficult at the same time to imagine such a man, so sophisticated and well-travelled, performing heinous acts at another's call. All too soon, a temporary farewell, Klaus driving Malik Said's black Audi A8L, with Mr. Said and Michelle in the backseat, as Robert returned to his room alone.

The muffled ring of his cell phone from a jacket pocket startled Robert awake the next morning. He blinked a few times and tried to gain a sense of his surroundings, jumped out of the bed, fumbled with the jacket draped over a cushion chair, and after four rings answered with a groggy "Hello."

"Good morning, Robert, how did you sleep?" again, the German accent.

"Good morning, Klaus, I apparently slept quite well," Robert's voice crackled, "what time is it?"

"Here in Paris – it is half past six. Malik wanted me to alert you that we fly to Nice this evening. Be at Le Bourget at eight p.m. Any taxi driver will be able to take you. Also, you may of course bring your daughter and her friend." Klaus paused, "Do you have any questions?"

There were so many that Robert knew not where to begin, "No, but I was planning on driving down, I really wanted to see the country and spend time with Sandy."

"You may, of course," the cadence of Klaus' words signaled

caution, "Do you wish me to tell Malik that you refuse his invitation?"

"No, no, of course not; but Sandy and Gilbert may have plans...."

Robert's words ejected faster than his thoughts coalesced and Klaus decided to stem the flow: "Yes, of course, I am sure Malik will not be too offended; we will look forward to seeing you all this evening for a pleasant hop to the Riviera. Good bye for now."

The line disconnected without Robert responding and he dropped the phone on his jacket, rubbed his eyes, and sprinted to the bathroom gloomily considering the ramifications of introducing his daughter to a heroin dealer and an assassin. Gilbert, well, he worked for a firm that participated in his demise, Gilbert could fend for himself; but Sandy, this was too much – Malik Said's tentacles wrapped so tight there would never be any escape. He could not bear to look in the mirror and head held low washed his hands and shuffled back to bed.

Alwar had by mid-May spent four months in a terrorist training camp somewhere in the interior of the Wagadou forest, constantly in the company of Gatimu and a band of self-proclaimed patriots fighting for the end of perceived western domination and imperialism. They engaged daily in combat exercises, patrols, study of the Qu'ran, and reverent discourse on the lives and deaths of famous freedom fighters such as Andreas Bernd Baader and Osama Bin Laden. Alwar attended such duties vigorously and with an appearance of enthusiasm, all the while remembering his cause: retribution for the death of his sister.

During these months it was impossible for Alwar to make contact with Michael, Sean, or anybody else not affiliated with the camp. On three occasions his cover required conduct repugnant at best, complicity in terror and murder at worst. He helped tape explosive to the legs of a twenty-one year old martyr from Sudan named Amsalu whose horrific death killed four and severely wounded six police officers in Barnako; drove Gatimu and two camp leaders to and from a recruiting mission in Monrovia; and stole an old Datsun pickup truck with a bed topper later packed with explosives and parked in front of a Christian church in Bongor. Alwar searched for ways to communicate with Michael or Sean each time he left camp, but never found an opportunity out of the company of Gatimu, who remained very close by his side.

The sixteenth of May, while concentrating on hand-to-hand combat using an Ngbandi knife, Alwar heard from behind a familiar voice, "Again you are too slow and expose sensitive areas around your fat stomach!" and twisted abruptly. Raymond smiled and Alwar's opponent seized the opportunity to jab a wrapped but nevertheless sharp curved blade tip against Alwar's exposed ribs.

"And you have no focus Alwar!" chided Raymond laughing loudly with Alwar's combat adversary after witnessing Alwar's reflexive sideways leap in reaction to the sting.

"You both are very funny" retorted Alwar regaining his composure; eyeing Raymond, "and I did not expect to see you again."

Raymond with a head gesture precipitated the other combatant's rapid exit and thereafter addressed Alwar: "Your expectations leave much to be desired; you should have known that I would return to lead our magnificent new mission."

As these words were spoken Gatimu appeared at Raymond's side, the two embraced, and Raymond's left hand remained on Gatimu's right shoulder; "Gatimu, you have not told our confused friend about our mission, have you?"

Gatimu grinned and flashing gold teeth taunted Alwar, "The newest lion to the pride must first prove his loyalty before running with the strongest and wisest hunters. This cub has only proved he can play with cubs; he has never brought meat to the table!"

Alwar realized his predicament – after four months knowing little more than of isolated violence and the camp's itinerate location he possessed no information about the January operation in Europe involving Raymond, Ali, and Izem, or the clandestine and important mission necessitating his continual grooming. "Perhaps I could escape the camp" he often thought, steal a car and help put an end to the terror; but he knew the forest, landmines, and sympathizers made the chance of success slim. Standing in front of Raymond and Gatimu, listening to Gatimu's words, he also knew the road had come to a fork; he would prove his loyalty by some vicious act soon to be mandated, or would have to escape, somehow, through the Wagadou.

Alwar's expression evinced dwindling options; "*This* lion has for four months proven his loyalty and ability – it is time for all to go on the hunt and stop playing the games of cubs!"

"We will see" countered Raymond after a short delay, "Gatimu, there is much to discuss." The two turned in conversation and laughter, the best of friends, strolling in camaraderie they entered a wooden shelter reserved for the leaders of a band of mercenaries waiting turns to die in glory killing people unsuspecting and, for the most part, innocent. Alwar, studying Raymond and Gatimu as they walked away, remained motionless except for a right hand massaging a tender rib. "I will be killing and maiming before the ordeal is over" concluded Alwar, longing instead for the quiet days fishing in clear waters off Jubilet.

"There is one thing I want you to do today," Raymond found Alwar early the next morning splashing water from a small tributary bound for the Senegal River on his head and arms; "Are you listening?"

Alwar drew a sleeved arm across his face, stood, and in a tone saturated with exasperation and irritation replied "Yes, of course, what is it that you wish?"

"You must kill Gatimu."

After wiping the sleeve across his forehead Alwar tilted and shook his head; Raymond, pelted by a shower of droplets, stepped back and grunted angrily, "Cub!" In a moment the shaking subsided and Alwar, hair wet and slicked back, head tilted just slightly to the side, eyes squinting, peered, very close to the breaking point, at Raymond – no longer riveted by the bizarre he contested with an icy "You kill Gatimu."

"I will if you can't" sneered Raymond, "and then I will kill you!"

Stepping toward Raymond, Alwar lowered his chin and said softly in almost a whisper, not as a dare but as a fact, "You cannot kill me, Raymond."

Raymond for a second speechless had to implicitly acknowledge the possible merit to Alwar's claim. "I do not have to kill you myself, cub, there are plenty of other cubs ready to perform the task at a snap of my fingers. That is how cubs kill, you know, in a pack they surround a wounded gazelle. Now, you will kill Gatimu, this day, or you will die this night, do I make myself clear?"

"And if I do this thing for you that you do not want to do," Alwar searched for some hope to a dismal situation, "what is it that I receive in return, besides my life? Why is it that you want to take Gatimu's life?"

"Is your life not enough, cub?" with a scowl Raymond berated Alwar, "The money, *money* is the answer to both of your questions! You will go with me on this assignment, you will be paid handsomely, more handsomely than if Gatimu goes. Besides, Gatimu would kill you before allowing you to share in the reward."

Alwar understood. Raymond simply wanted more money and the only way for him to have more money was to take it from Gatimu. This scheme required eliminating Gatimu's involvement in the operation, but Raymond needed talents possessed by Gatimu, so he needed first to find a cheaper replacement perhaps equally as capable. Alwar understood that sometimes a band of lions kills a trespassing nomad; and he understood unchecked greed knows no bound. With Raymond, he was no safer than with Gatimu.

"I will not do your dirty work, Raymond; I agreed to go on this mission for the money, a mission I still do not know, an amount of money I still do not know."

Raymond thought carefully. "Those of us on this assignment are to receive one hundred thousand dollars. That means if we are four, each receives twenty five thousand dollars, if we are three, thirty three thousand dollars, and if we are two, fifty thousand dollars. You are an outsider, invited to join; if it is you and me, I will take sixty thousand dollars and you will take forty thousand dollars."

Ever more puzzled, Alwar quizzed Raymond, "This mission, it does not matter how many go; it can be accomplished by two? What is this mission?"

"All you need to know is that the mission can be accomplished by two" – Raymond's eyes narrowed with each emphasized word – "*if* the two are strong and smart. Gatimu thinks we need at least three, that is why you were asked to join, but I do not, not after what I learned and after what I did to prepare over the past several months. I tried to convince him yesterday but he still believes three are required."

"These are not lions" thought Alwar, these are hyenas. "I will not kill Gatimu; if you want him eliminated, Raymond, you do it." It was by then clear to Alwar that murdering Gatimu held for him very few if any advantages and a slew of potentially devastating disadvantages, including foremost, there was no way to perform the act without drawing the wrath of all others in camp, other than by intentionally provoking Gatimu into a fight which Alwar believed he could very well lose.

A smile stretched Raymond's lips and creased his temples. "You have passed the test, cub, you may now hunt with the lions; we leave tomorrow morning at sunup. Today, you may rest, and pray." With that revelation he turned toward the hut.

With eyes focused on dirt Alwar's head shook in dismay, embracing the absurdity of life held teetering on the brink by madmen in the grip of perpetual paranoia. "Where is the cause?" he thought, the glorious cause that transcends human frailty, making unconscionable acts noble, ignoble men respectable. Freedom fighters or soldiers of fortune, Raymond and Gatimu were, in the end, simply capitalists selling their talents in a free market. They became the thing they most loathed. Worse yet, unrestrained by laws or norms of society they were rogues to whom eliminating an impediment to greater profit through the taking of life seemed no more dastardly than the lie told a prospective customer.

The next morning, Alwar, Raymond, and Gatimu left the Wagadou camp in Raymond's white circa 1980's Volkswagen Jetta. Once out of the forest they traveled Route Nationale One into

Senegal and northwest to the coast highway. In Mauritania, they filled four five-liter metal canisters with fuel, roped them to a rack on the roof of the Jetta, and taking turns driving continued north into Western Sahara.

Mid-afternoon on the third day of their journey, only several hours into the desert and for the most part isolated on a two-lane road, Gatimu, driving, saw in the distance what appeared to be a pickup truck parked across the road. He nudged Alwar, dozing with his head down and arms crossed in the passenger seat, pointed ahead, and proceeded cautiously, stopping only after Alwar confirmed the vague outlines of four people standing around the truck.

Gatimu twisted, leaned back, and with his right hand tapped Raymond's shoulder as he laid sleeping against a stack of duffels; "Hey, chief; wake up!" he said in a manner of urgency.

Raymond's eyelids opened wide and he jumped to the middle edge of the backseat for an unobstructed view through the windshield; "What? What is it?"

"Trouble" Gatimu calmly replied while reaching with his right hand under the seat, "maybe, or some fools out of petrol."

"Either way it's trouble" Alwar rightly corrected, reaching with his left hand for the holstered Beretta under his seat.

Raymond tapped Gatimu's right shoulder, "Flash the lights – give them the sign."

Gatimu leaned forward and with the fingers of his right hand twisted the headlamp switch to on, off, on...off, on, off, paused, on, off, on, paused, off. "Again!" yelled Raymond and Gatimu in the same cadence turned on and off the headlamps. The three waited in silence until Alwar softly affirmed what Raymond and Gatimu also knew, "They are too far away." Again, the headlamps flashed, again, silence. The three sat nervously, hoping for some favorable acknowledgment in the distance, evaluating a next move that in all likelihood would mean the difference between life and death.

A backdoor opened and within a few seconds Raymond stood adjacent the driver's window with the palm of his right hand up;

Gatimu turned off the engine and placed the car keys in Raymond's hand. Alwar opened his door and, standing between it and the torn seat, watched as Raymond unlocked the trunk, vanished below the lid, and reappeared holding a shoulder-fired RPG-7 rocket-propelled grenade launcher.

Knowing no rational argument against its use but feeling compelled nevertheless to convey mercy, Alwar asked, "What are you going to do?"

Raymond laid the launcher on the hood and darting back to connect a booster and warhead in the trunk, replied dryly, without looking at Alwar – the mere response itself an act of kindness, "You know what I am going to do, do you have a better idea?"

Alwar started to say something but Raymond interrupted, "We can't go any closer or they may blow *us* up! Do you know what weapons they have? We can't let that truck stay there and risk going around in the sand. We can't drive or walk down there to negotiate. It is a standoff. What do you want to do? Give me a better strategy."

Alwar leaned on the car door, gently massaged around his tired eyes, and turned to look down the highway; stepping away from the seat he closed the door, opened the backseat door, and patted each of the duffels. After securing a pair of binoculars and mounting his elbows on top of the open backseat door, he positioned the eyepiece lenses in front of his eyes and within several seconds declared "There are four...they seem to be looking in our direction, I think there is something, maybe a machine gun, mounted in the bed of the truck, covered by a tarp."

Gatimu demanded a turn at the binoculars by reaching into the backseat and snapping the fingers of his right hand. Alwar scanned once more around the truck and, by then, Raymond had finished assembling the missile and was loading the launcher. Gatimu opened his door, stood, peered through the lenses, and casually exclaimed "Yes, Alwar is correct, but now there is no tarp, there is only a fifty caliber machine gun being pointed in our direction."

With the loaded launcher pressed against his left shoulder,

Raymond sidestepped quickly from the passenger side of the Jetta and yelled for Gatimu to assemble another warhead. It was a task, however, which Alwar busy in the trunk had begun. Once about ten meters from the car, Raymond knelt in the sand, and directed the grenade launcher toward miniscule images far off down the road.

"They are getting ready to fire" proffered Gatimu; "it looks as though they may drive toward us."

"Cover!" yelled Raymond; neither Alwar nor Gatimu could place hands to ears in time to prevent the thunder of an explosion propelling a grenade-tipped missile from the launcher.

Gatimu immediately lifted the binoculars to view a plume of sand and smoke far from the road followed by a scene of the pickup truck moving in a half-circle to face the Jetta; "We have missed and the truck is soon to be speeding in our direction!" he announced with noticeably more urgency. Alwar in very long strides ran to Raymond, kneeling in the sand on the other side of the Jetta, and pushed a grenade into the launcher. "No!" shouted Gatimu with the binoculars at his side, "There is no time and we cannot afford to lose another grenade! We must *leave* – now!"

Without any rebuttal Alwar snatched the RPG launcher from Raymond's shoulder and the two plodded as fast as possible through the sand. After pushing Raymond and the loaded launcher into the back seat, Alwar sprinted back to slam down the trunk lid, leaped forward, and fell into the passenger seat as the Jetta lunged in reverse. Spinning the steering wheel, shifting to drive, reverse, drive, Gatimu was able finally to rest his foot hard on the accelerator pedal but not soon enough to prevent a tapping noise, like spring raindrops on sheet metal, ushering an ephemeral warning. The Jetta's back window shattered just after the occupants crouched low in their seats and Raymond let out a scream culminating with "...How far are they!"

By carefully tilting the rearview mirror Gatimu was able to advise that the pickup truck was less than fifty meters. From the backseat could be heard the sound of metal clanking; Raymond had hurriedly removed the projectile from the launcher and the grenade from the projectile and was instructing Gatimu to

"Slow...get them to ten meters! It is our only chance. I will throw the grenade and we must all pray that it explodes!" There was no time for Alwar or Gatimu to venture alternative scenarios or devise a safer strategy; Gatimu lifted his foot from the accelerator and pressed hard on the brake. The road between the Jetta and the pickup truck vanished almost instantly so that in the rearview mirror Gatimu able to see eyes of their enemy yelled, "Now!"

The machine gun's roar fused with a tumultuous blast of intense heat enveloping the Jetta. There had been an explosion, but traveling as fast as possible for at least a kilometer along the highway, nobody in the Jetta looked back to determine the result. Nobody said a word. Finally, hands squeezing the steering wheel, saturated in sweat, Gatimu glanced up at the mirror to find the Jetta intact and remains of the pickup truck scattered in the distance. The Jetta rolled to a stop.

Alwar quietly offered a prayer of thanks, turned, and saw Raymond lying partially concealed by duffel bags motionless between the front and back seats. "Raymond has been injured," Alwar jumped from his seat to open the backseat door, "help me to get him out!"

Gatimu also jumped out, opened the door behind his seat, tossed duffel bags to the asphalt, and delicately lifted Raymond's legs; "Let's get him on the seat."

With Alwar's hands under his arms and his head resting on Alwar's elbows, Raymond was gently lifted to the seat cushion and laid face up. Alwar removed his shirt on it wiping blood from his hands, rolled and propped the damp cloth under Raymond's head, and reaching down pressed two fingers against the carotid artery. The hand lurched back. "His neck is badly lacerated and he has lost a lot of blood" advised Alwar in a calm voice, "try a pulse at his wrist."

After holding Raymond's right wrist for what seemed an unnecessarily long period, Gatimu, without emotion, said "He is dead."

Alwar stood erect to behold the fiery scene of the explosion. After a moment he looked over the Jetta's roof at Gatimu who was also studying the destruction; "Do you want to drive down and evaluate our options or bury Raymond?" Upon saying the words Alwar did not need an answer; "He was your friend, I will drive down." They slid Raymond's body from the backseat, carefully carried it a short distance, and laid it gently in the warm sand. "Did he have faith, was he religious?" inquired Alwar of Gatimu; "Is there something you would like to say?"

A face of sadness, eyes staring blankly into the distant desert, Gatimu replied "No, I do not know, I never saw him pray, we never talked about it." There was silence for a minute as both men held their heads low, after which Gatimu elaborated "He has a sister in London, I know that, I don't think his parents are alive, I wouldn't know how to find her, but I will try when this is over."

Resentment and anger began to edge Gatimu's words: "We, him and I, we went on many assignments together, fighting the imperialists, we killed many and he never was injured. Now, we do this mission, for money, and he is dead before it begins; blood money; I didn't want to do it, but he said the money would help us buy weapons, train recruits. When your cause is wrong, the result, no matter what, is wrong."

Alwar was admirably surprised by Gatimu's words and gave him some time, thereafter suggesting "I better go see what we are up against" and trudging wearily toward the Jetta.

Nearing the explosion's outcome it became apparent there would be no driving over asphalt to traverse the wreckage. The pickup truck had flipped backward, landing upside down, tires ablaze, the entire engine compartment gone. One door lay a dozen meters down the road behind the chassis, smoldering blackened steel lay strewn over the road and nearby sand, and ripped crimson bodies and body parts otherwise obscured the surroundings in all directions. The grenade apparently struck the grill either directly or off a bounce. Alwar remained in the Jetta with the engine running as he absorbed the dreary landscape. "Who were these people?" wondered Alwar, why did they attack us? Of only one thing was he certain – he owed his life to Raymond.

Sitting in the sand, Gatimu, arms crossed on his knees, forehead resting on his arms, next to him the body of Raymond as overhead circled several large, almost black, lappet-faced vultures. Alwar approached Gatimu with prudent deliberation and announced "Gatimu?" There was no reply. "I will help."

"There is no need;" Gatimu lifted his head when Alwar's shadow shielded his eyes from the scorching sun, "the wind will soon blow away the sand for the scavengers. We should let them enjoy their gruesome supper and not waste time in a futile cause."

With his right hand Alwar shaded his eyes, turned to the sky, and counted seven hungry but patient birds. He stepped toward Gatimu, reached down, and with his right hand clasping a right wrist tugged Gatimu upright while proclaiming "We have a decision to make; do we proceed with the mission, if we can somehow get around the obstacle ahead, or do we return to our homes and families?"

Once Gatimu finished brushing sand from his green cotton pants he stared into Alwar's eyes and answered "Raymond said two could do the job, two who were strong, and smart; well, I am strong and you are smart!" Gatimu grinned. "Perhaps even smart enough to want half of one hundred fifty thousand dollars!" A barely noticeable smile formed on Alwar's face but not for the reason Gatimu thought; Alwar held no animosity toward Raymond and pictured as great his eternal reward.

As they neared the Jetta, Alwar told Gatimu that it was time he knew about the mission, and so digging into Raymond's duffel Gatimu secured a folded paper which once unfolded and placed on the hood revealed a map of Southern Europe. Alwar held down one edge of the map while Gatimu held down the other and described what he knew of the background and purpose for their contract:

"It was Raymond who was first contacted about this thing. He told me it started with an office worker in Dubai, a woman, she worked for a bank, and the bank had a client, a very rich American. Somehow, this American made it known to the woman's boss that he wanted to hire some people to carry out a job, not an ordinary job, of course, something you need special people for. So, the woman's boss, well, I guess she overheard the conversation somehow, probably snooping, anyway, this woman who worked in the bank told somebody that she knew, in the organization, and this person knew Raymond, and I guess the person in Dubai, that's where this person was stationed, wanted to, um, outsource the job."

A wind gust rippled the map. Alwar and Gatimu placed hands over each corner and Gatimu continued; "I know there are more involved in this job than just us. There is a team from the east, also, that we are supposed to meet, I don't know when or how many, or their specialty, but Raymond said he knew of the leader, Ty, and he was very capable. We are to proceed along this route." Gatimu's hand slid along the map, pressing it against the rusty metal, to a yellow highlighted line commencing in southern Portugal. His index finger slowly tracked the line through Spain, into France, and finally into Monaco.

"We are supposed to meet the other team in Nice. The rendezvous location is here, see?" Gatimu nodded to a patch of English handwriting, a name, date, and time next to a penned "X" on the map adjacent Nice. "At this place, we will meet another, who will give us details about the mission. All I know is that it involves taking a boat, actually, a ship, and it may involve, probably it does involve, hostages."

"We are to be kidnappers?" Alwar questioned in disbelief.

Shaking his head Gatimu answered "No, kidnappers take ransom; we get paid for taking the ship."

"I'm not sure I see the difference." Alwar's frustration stemmed from the word "hostages," an ugly word, especially in a world where hostages eventually, always, died.

Captive for months training to kill and die under an ideology that placed death above life, the future above the present, it was intended Alwar lose so much of his identity that he would trade for one heinous moment – for one displaced act of extreme violence – a lifetime of smiling faces, laughing children, and tender touches. A simple fisherman once content with tending his nets, happy for a meager catch and the sun's warmth on his brow, would become a deadly weapon in an illusory war with malleable objectives. But Alwar's puppeteers never met Abeo.

Alwar guarded his identity, shielded his soul, and freely addressed Gatimu's struggle to comprehend the difference between one intentional unconscionable act and another: "This is not the cause I trained for, I will go, but I will not take hostages, and I will not kill if I do not have to."

A single nod of Gatimu's head confirmed understanding.

Waving his arms like the wings of a goose taking flight and loudly barking unintelligible sounds, Alwar engaged a brief and futile effort to disrupt vultures alighting around Raymond's remains while Gatimu carefully folded the map. As respective tasks completed, two wary cohorts climbed into the Jetta with Alwar in the driver's seat and, in less than a minute, encountered the smoldering roadblock. Following a short interchange it was decided – primarily at Alwar's insistence – that Gatimu would navigate his way on foot through the debris to the dismembered truck door, drag the door back, and deposit it in the sand adjacent a small patch of exposed asphalt by the overturned truck.

This, Gatimu did, stomping to anchor the door, littering smaller metallic objects in the sand, and encouraging – with wild arm motions and gratuitous bouts of instruction – Alwar to maneuver the Jetta around the truck with left wheels on asphalt and right wheels straddling the makeshift bridge. When the right front tire rolled off pavement, the right front of the Jetta dipped as the door buried in the sand and Alwar instinctively pressed the accelerator pedal, which caused the right front tire to veer into the sand. He was able to maintain momentum with the left front tire, however, and, sand cascading high and far behind, the Jetta eventually crawled around the truck.

"God is with us!" exclaimed Gatimu.

Alwar quietly wished He had shown up sooner.

Once clear of the grisly site, Alwar stopped to refuel, leaving only three canisters remaining atop the car, and he and Gatimu enjoyed a quick supper of flat bread and canned chicken with water from one of two bottles in the trunk. They managed to maintain a good pace over the next two hours and never saw another vehicle. Near Cape Boujdour, they again stopped to refuel and add water to the radiator, so in town topped off both bottles; it was getting dark and after a long, trying day, and not wanting to risk travel through the desert at night, they decided to find a place to sleep and settled on a hotel of sorts.

They resumed the first leg of their journey with the rising sun and an hour and a half later, in El-Aaiún, found a café where they could order a breakfast of Bissara, bread, and sweet green tea and study a map of North Africa. "We still have a thousand kilometers to Sawahi," remarked Alwar, "we need to be there today."

"We will, we made it past the bandits, we will be in Sawahi today and on the boat tomorrow," Gatimu ripped off a piece of bread, dipped it in the Bissara, and with his mouth full added "Of course, we don't have any choice. The boat leaves tomorrow with or without us."

It was agreed Gatimu would take the first shift driving and they would rotate turns every hour so as not to wear down. After gas and water containers were topped off, and the engine fluids checked, they found the road clear for hundreds of kilometers. In Agadir, just after noon, supplies were again provisioned. Thereafter, driving through more populous and urban centers, including Marrakesh and Casablanca, automobile traffic and pedestrian congestion delayed their journey. It was almost eleven that night, therefore, when Alwar and Gatimu arrived exhausted at the fourth house from the harbor on the road to the mosque in Sawahi; within no time fast asleep on the couch and floor.

Awakened by a rooster far too early for his liking, Alwar found Gatimu awake, standing under a date palm in front of the house, sipping tea, monitoring the sun's rise. "When does the boat leave?" Alwar inquired, still wearing the white cotton pants and red dashiki shirt from the day before – the same clothes in which he had slept. Gatimu advised that they would have to be at the docks in about two hours, by eight, so Alwar returned to the house and heated a kettle of water on the stove.

Gatimu entered the kitchen just as steam began to whistle through the spout and implored Alwar, as he grasped the handle, "Pour me a little more water." Alwar filled his own cup and tilted the spout above Gatimu's over the sink. "Thanks;" Gatimu looked into his cup and after taking a sip of hot water said "You don't get seasick to you?"

"No! I am a fisherman!" Having spent the last four months together, Alwar was somewhat surprised by Gatimu's question.

"Yes...," Gatimu swirled his cup trying to extract some lingering flavor from the saturated tea leaves, "I know, but we will be going direct to Lagos, not following the coast, it is too dangerous."

Alwar gazed for a moment out a window, tasted his tea, and looked at Gatimu, "What kind of boat"?

Gatimu stood in front of the same window and casually replied "It will be a fishing boat, a wooden fishing boat with a motor and small cabin."

"It must be one hundred fifty kilometers to the Algarve," Alwar showed no emotion while looking out the window and sipping tea; "It will take us a day to get there, if the weather is good, the seas calm, and we don't run into the navy, or pirates. Of course," he turned to consider Gatimu's face, "if the weather is not good, the seas not calm, or we do get boarded, it could very well mean the end of our mission."

Gatimu did not immediately reply. Instead, after drinking what remained of the minimally-flavored lukewarm water he set his cup in the sink and parting the kitchen threshold, turned, looked at Alwar, and in a tone riddled with intrigue said "My friend, you are a pessimist, you need to believe, and for that you need faith."

Alwar smiled. Gazing out the window he leaned forward, twisted his neck, and reveled in a sky fading from orange to light blue separated only by several streaks of white clouds. "I am a product of my faith" he reminded himself; scrutiny and analysis my blessings.

Under shoulders full duffel bags, under shirts holstered handguns, Alwar and Gatimu strolled from Izem's house to the harbor and walked along a row of gray docks until arriving at a white and brown wooden boat named, in Arabic, "Swan." Seeing no one around, Gatimu yelled "Hey, anybody here!" From below deck arose a muffled affirmation, so Alwar and Gatimu stepped aboard. Very soon there appeared a bulky brown man with a black beard and long black hair weaved tightly into a ponytail; he wore a white sleeveless t-shirt, long plaid shorts, and round wire-rim glasses.

"You speak English..." the man mentioned while ascending from the cabin, "so English it will be. Which of you is Raymond?"

Alwar looked at Gatimu, who promptly responded "I am Raymond" and nodded with a grin at an uneasy Alwar, "and this is Gatimu."

"Fine," the big man also smiled and jutted a burly right hand toward Gatimu and Alwar, "I am called Swan!" Once he had inflicted a certain degree of pain on his guests, Swan directed an uncomfortable glare toward Gatimu until Gatimu recited "Find it in your heart to seek the truth." Swan's head tilted back and his lips developed a critical bend at the corners; he glanced toward Alwar and back to Gatimu until finally speaking in his gravelly voice: "The phrase is of course correct, but I was told that Gatimu has the gold teeth, not Raymond, and you...," a fat right arm unfolded and projected an accusatory finger toward Gatimu – "have teeth of gold!"

Alwar at that point interposed a stern reaction: "I...am Raymond. We do this test out of caution. Gatimu, is very loyal; if you were not who you say you are, he would be prepared, if it indeed was a setup to cause me harm. Now, pleasantries aside, we, need to move!"

It was a remark of such believability and force that Swan said no more on the subject but moved at once to release the bow and stern lines and throttle the boat from dock. Gatimu passed Alwar a thankful glance and the tense passengers settled on the foredeck to relax while the Swan meandered through a maze of other boats to the harbor mouth. Once beyond the stone breakwater, the small boat began to rock, and upon the open ocean to rock and rise in the bow, followed by precipitous falls, pounding with a splash over the crest of swells. Soon it became apparent to Alwar that he was aboard a boat of greater speed than reflective of her appearance, as the pounding gave way to a rumbling stability and white spray billowed from both sides of the bow.

After a short time they were beyond sight of land, rolling with the long Atlantic swells, catching an occasional glimpse of dolphins gliding through water and air alongside the Swan. Swan, the man, found time to tie the wheel and break out a loaf of French bread and bottle of Australian Muscat, both purchased in Rabat, both heartily enjoyed by Alwar and Gatimu tearing off chunks and taking swigs from the bottle when not in the captain's protective grasp.

All the while, Alwar remained cognizant of his fictitious identity, to the point of having to embellish tales of Raymond's escapades to satisfy Swan's incessant prodding and Gatimu's unwanted attempt at humor. Raymond was a legend it turned out, a man deeply respected by many self-proclaimed freedom fighters throughout North Africa, as evident from Swan boasting of Raymond's enlistment in the Afghan Mujahideen when only thirteen and within two weeks setting an explosive on the body of a Soviet armored personnel carrier.

Finally, with the bread devoured and the Muscat running low, Alwar managed to turn the conversation by asking Swan "Tell us about you, also of great repute, what brings you to this fight?"

Swan yanked the bottle from Gatimu's left hand, poured the remaining wine into his cavernous maw, tossed the bottle over the side, and explained his motivation. "I am from Beirut," he leaned back against the railing, "my family left during the civil war in my father's fishing boat. We went south and landed in Hiafa because we needed food and water. I was ten. The Jews impounded our boat, took what little money we had, and sent us to the West Bank in the back of a truck. I spent eight years there; during the Intifada, the first, the Israelis killed many of my friends. Over time I learned to hate the Jews and their protectors."

"How did you get out?" Gatimu casually asked.

"I went to Syria, then back to Lebanon, I walked a lot," the deepening pitch of Swan's voice predicated lingering mournful memories, "I never saw my parents or my brother again. I wanted to go back and get them, but...there was no way, so I stole a sailing boat, sailed to Benghazi, then along the coast, finally I made it to Morocco and settled in Al Hoceima. There was a Groupe Islamique Combattant Marocain cell there and I started hanging out with them and one day joined up. Since that day, I've been ferrying fighters between Africa and Spain and Portugal."

Alwar studied Swan's profile when he was addressing Gatimu and during a break asked if he predicted their voyage unremarkable. "No" Swan answered without hesitation, "we will have trouble; there is always trouble of some kind, it is the nature of this trade." The big man suddenly belted a high-pitched nasal squeal that seemed out of character and place and with a devilish grin exclaimed "Perhaps even the real Raymond will appear!"

Not completely taken by surprise, Alwar, at the rim of his vision perceiving Gatimu move a right hand surely to wield a loaded Beretta. A reaction to defuse the situation was not possible, or necessary, however, because Swan quickly explained, "I am aware that Raymond was killed in the Sahara, I have known since soon after; the word spread quickly." He roared, "You," looking toward Alwar, "tell a good story though!"

Gatimu steadied his right hand and inquired in a voice evocative more of a demand, "How did you know?"

Swan delivered a husky retort, "One of the murderers – one that you missed – survived by burying in the sand; after you left, he saw the birds; he walked and found Raymond's body."

Alwar and Gatimu exchanged the fleeting glances of confused men; Alwar sputtered "Who...who were they, how did you find out?"

Swan, still resting against the railing, both arms supported on knees chest level, smiled, "They were the men sent to kill you."

Alwar's and Gatimu's bewilderment prompted Alwar's continued insistent probing, "We are on a mission...who would know, who would want us dead, how did you find all this out?"

"It seems," Swan sighed as though bored of reciting worn facts, "that Raymond talked about this mission with a spy, one who called himself Ali." His knees lowered and he sat legs spread, arms stretched like beams to stable the bulky torso with palms planted securely on the deck, one sole of an enormous sandal visible to Alwar, the other to Gatimu. The attention of each man remained on Swan and his every word.

"It seems this is not an ordinary mission. You work against a formidable opponent. I do not know all of the details, but I do know that the men hired to stop you were professionals, and there may be more...."

Visibly and audibly agitated, such that his right hand returned precipitately close to the cloistered holster, Gatimu growled in objection to Swan's explanation: "How did you find out about Raymond?"

Swan, silent, staring at Gatimu, waited, replying coolly in his own time, "The man who I told you about, the one who escaped, made it out of the desert alive, somehow, and word spread through the network. I knew that Raymond had been killed, but I have already been paid, and it seems right that I fulfill my end of the agreement."

Gatimu looked to Alwar. The two locked eyes long enough to communicate mutual disbelief providing Gatimu the confidence to issue a forceful denial, "My friend Raymond, he would not have talked about this mission" followed by an angry clarification triggered by his own words, "about *any* mission!"

Desiring to quash Gatimu's impending, and surely untoward, act, Alwar added sternly "I agree, Raymond did not talk, so somebody else knew." Continuing to reflect on the possibilities aloud diverted the anticipated reactions of Gatimu and Swan: "Izem was not at his house in Sawahi when we were just there...," focusing on Swan, "Raymond, Ali, and a man named Izem went into Europe on a cause. Do you know, have you heard, what cause? What became of Izem?"

Swan's hands clasped with his fingers intertwined at the precipice of a keg-like belly and his head twisted and angled to the side, as if to clearly demonstrate industrious contemplation, with the result that surprisingly valuable information eventually passed his lips. "It is said that there were four altogether on the same mission as you now pursue. Raymond and the two you mention were on my boat in January. I was to take them to Lagos, but, as the Atlantic goes in January, we ran afoul of a nasty gale, actually not far from where we are now."

He stopped talking and looked toward the bow and beyond to the horizon, and Alwar's and Gatimu's eyes followed Swan's lead as they too imagined the peril. "I was holding the wheel, trying to keep her into the swell, against the waves, breaking over the bow, the three were in the cabin, I thought. I didn't think we'd make it. Water was pouring over the deck; I was standing in a pale-height of water. Finally, I tied the wheel and went below. There was only Raymond and Ali."

Swan hesitated, sighed, gazed again over the bow, and facing Alwar continued, "I asked them, 'Where's Izem?' Raymond was sitting, bent over, his head down with his hands over his head. Ali said, 'He's gone, he went over.' I was stunned, 'Why didn't you tell me? When did it happen?' He said Izem fell off the stern, he tried to reach him, but he went under, there was nothing he could do."

Grasping the bottom rail, the next, finally the top, Swan managed an upright stance in order to issue a well-rehearsed apology: "There was nothing I could do then, either, we couldn't see more than a meter in the rain and he'd gone overboard several minutes before and I couldn't turn the boat or we all would go down." The big man rotated with his back to Alwar and Gatimu and cried "Izem is now in Paradise, Allah be praised!" while on the pitched deck plodding toward four steps leading up to the wheelhouse.

Alwar gained his footing, shifted to the bow railing, and holding the top line securely in both hands considered the hopeless isolation of a man left to drown in open water; "Where is Ali?" he wondered aloud to the blue beyond.

But Gatimu answered, "He is at the end of our journey."

By two o'clock the temperature was a blistering thirty-two degrees and unrestrained sunshine bore down on the small boat floating all alone in a calm reflective pool. Alwar and Gatimu were by this time below deck laying either side of a table on cushioned benches. Swan stayed in the shaded wheelhouse, listening to the marine radio, studying the GPS, surveying the horizon, and monitoring the fuel, which to him appeared lower than expected at this point in their journey. He also had not seen another fishing boat in over two hours and felt uneasy, perhaps superstitious, about such unusual tranquility.

Tying the wheel, Swan descended the four steps and followed railing to the stern, where he peered through the wire rim glasses anxiously for any sign of activity. There was none. "Something's wrong" Swan muttered while shaking his head and concluding that it was too calm, too hot, and too quiet; "something's wrong." He followed the railing back to the steps and the cabin below, bent down low, and chimed in a serious pitch, "Hey, you two, wake up!"

Alwar and Gatimu jumped, with Gatimu striking his forehead on the edge of the table, and Swan bellowed "You awake down there? We got a problem up here!"

"Yes, yes" assured Alwar, "we're coming."

Moving quickly through the hatch onto the deck went Alwar and Gatimu – holding his bleeding head and expressing considerable displeasure as Alwar tried to determine the cause of the emergency. Swan motioned them both to the stern; "Look," he pointed at the sun, "look where it's at!" Peering through narrowed eyelids Alwar and Gatimu glanced briefly at the blinding glow and intently at Swan as he explained "It is not supposed to be there this time of day going this direction, the direction we are supposed to be going, toward the Algarve. It is too hot. I haven't seen a fishing boat for all afternoon!"

Apparent to Alwar and Gatimu was Swan's unusual intensity – genuine concern bordering on outright fear. Gatimu lowered his hand to check for blood and in a monotone saturated with irritation quizzed Swan, "Hold on, just wait, are you saying you don't know where we are? You have GPS, right, you have a map; so what's the matter?" He wiped wet blood on his pants. "You know, we don't have time for games."

"Games – you fool!" Swan's chest swelled an even greater girth and an angered rebuff targeted Gatimu: "This isn't a game! If we are lost, we are certainly lost! The GPS says we are where we should be, but the sun, the sea, they tell me different. That's all."

"Where do you think we are?" Alwar interrupted.

Swan shook his head, "There are no fishing boats; by this time we should have seen trawlers from Portugal. I need to go look again at the map and listen for any news. I need also to shut down the motor; if we are not on course, we need to conserve fuel. Keep a lookout until I get back. If we are in the shipping lanes...." With the muttering of those fearful words Swan rushed to the pilothouse, leaving Alwar and Gatimu on deck sweating in the hot sun deliberating the glimmering unknown.

V GLAMOUR

The rain plummeted in icy sheets as Raymond and Ali disembarked the Swan early one morning in January and made their way in the dark along docks and roads to a small hotel on a side street in Lagos, Portugal. After pounding the locked door for several minutes, a stubby gray-haired woman in a blue nightgown peeked out an adjacent window, opened the door just slightly, and between it and the doorframe demanded in Portuguese to know the men's purpose. "We need a room" was the reply in English and French. The old woman started to close the door when Raymond ventured the needed phase, "Swan sent us." She looked them both over and noisily unhooked the chain.

"Did you just arrive?" the woman asked harshly in English while hobbling toward a counter.

"Yes" answered Raymond, "from Morocco."

"Where's Swan?" she demanded.

"He stayed on his boat" replied Raymond.

The woman handed each man a small towel from behind the counter while explaining she had one room with two beds in the back on the first floor and that Raymond and Ali could stay until noon without charge. They expressed appreciation. The woman handed one key to Raymond, pulled another towel from beneath the counter, and, falling to her knees, began wiping the tile floor from the counter to the door. Raymond and Ali loping with saturated green duffels made their way down a hall from the counter to the last room on the right.

At nine the next morning, Raymond awoke for no apparent reason, leaped out of bed, and pushed aside a green flowery curtain hoping to see sunshine only to instead find a scene painted on red brick to resemble a view of the southern Portuguese countryside in summer. Not at all fond of walls, he slipped on his damp pants, which had been drying over a chair, and opened the door. The sound startled Ali awake and sitting upright he watched as Raymond disappeared around the doorframe only to reappear after a couple of minutes with two small round pastries. He presented one to Ali.

"This is the best breakfast" declared Raymond, "whenever I'm in Portugal, these are what I live on, *pastel de nata*. This is why I return plump!" The tart vanished from Raymond's hands in several large bites that left the corners of his mouth blotched in creamy custard. Ali quickly followed suit.

Both bathed in a rush with their small towels dipped in the bathroom sink and departed for the bus station. It was cold and gray, but the rain had stopped and for that, they were happy, slogging along the watery asphalt and concrete, around cars, down the hill, within minutes arriving at the bus terminal.

The plan was to catch a bus to Seville, and from there take the train to Madrid, on to Barcelona, and north to Nice. Raymond carried a UK passport; Ali did not have a passport so they would have to lay over in Seville for a day or two while an acquaintance of Raymond – a professional forger well known to terrorist watch-list vagabonds in Spain and France – manufactured the necessary document.

No passports required by the ticket agent in Lagos, as anticipated, Raymond and Ali carried their bags onboard the bus and tossed them on a metal rack over seats in the back, despite there being only a few seats in the front occupied by what appeared to be locals in route to Faro. "We may be stopped crossing into Spain," Raymond relayed in barely audible dialect to Ali as they sat, "are you sure you fully understand the plan?" Ali nodded affirmation. "Good" whispered Raymond, "wake me when we are near." With that, each stretched across a row of seats separated by the aisle.

Gazing out the window as the bus rolled through the Algarve, passing occasional cars and trucks and stopping only briefly in Faro, where most of the passengers disembarked and only very few boarded, Ali thought of his home and family back in Qatar. It had been months since speaking with his father or mother, or sister, and he wondered how they were and if they thought often of him. Ali's family was well to do by any standard. His father, a banker for thirty years and president of a small local bank, sent Ali's sister to study at Princeton and wanted very much for Ali to also attend college in America, so as to gain, what he termed, "a more objective worldly view."

This was not to be Ali's calling; instead, always championing causes, always in the thick of controversy. Almost two years earlier he joined a group of young men from affluent families bent on establishing economically fair societies in the Arab states. They held meetings, blogged, and recruited like-minded converts. After nearly two years of accomplishing very little, tired of what he considered a waste of time and resources and longing for action typified by an idealistically romantic view of revolution, Ali struck out on his own.

That was when he met Hamidah. She was in Qatar on business for Worldwide Investment Bank, meeting with local bankers to establish relationships, acting as Stephen Waters' emissary. Ali and Hamidah met in the lobby of his father's bank while seated in decorative, high, stiff-back chairs waiting to meet with Ali's father. After sitting in silence for ten minutes admiring the sultry yet reserved Hamidah, Ali, in Arabic, said hello, and from there they engaged an exciting discussion about the difference in banking regulations between the Emirates and Qatar. Finally, Ali confessed, the man both waited for was his father; they laughed and arranged to meet for lunch later that day.

Over the course of the afternoon, until leaving for Bahrain, Hamidah found out much about Ali, and he almost nothing of Hamidah. Two days later, she called his cell phone and invited him to visit in Dubai; when he arrived the next day she was waiting outside airline passenger pickup in the bank's Mercedes limousine and within a few minutes they were in the lobby of the Grand Hyatt drinking tea.

She asked him "How do you think you can make a difference, there in Qatar, the wealthiest country in the world?" This was a dilemma often confronted internally by Ali, but formulating a response, one that implied or expressed impending action, he found difficult. "I will work from within, like an antibody attacking the virus, making the body whole." Hamidah had to admire the poetry of what was otherwise no response at all; "The antibody must kill the virus, Ali, to save the body suffering," the words from her lips seemed foreign to the young idealist, "are you willing to kill the virus?"

"You understand, Hamidah, in this case, the virus is a system, it is not a man, you cannot save the body society by killing a man, you must kill the tainted system." Ali found solace in his reply, and leaned back, eyeing Hamidah carefully, as though their dialogue were a chess match and he having just declared "Check!"

"The system is run by men" bluntly replied Hamidah, slyly moving her rook to block the take; "you talk as though you're a politician. These men will never relinquish power, they will never change a system that made them enormously wealthy and powerful, that made them royalty. I understand you are not a fighter; the world needs politicians." It was a cold calculated move designed to taunt him into compliance, Ali later realized, a move that worked with stunning success.

Unable to control the swell of anger at hearing his manhood questioned, let alone by a woman, from Ali's lips thundered bravado and boast, provocation and promise, the very ingredients Hamidah needed to complete her recipe for his submission. "I am glad to hear these words from you Ali, I thought you a man from the moment we met, but I needed to be sure. Now, I see you are strong, but you need direction. Are you ready to take the next step, action?"

By that point well over the edge, Ali trumpeted his prowess with such enthusiasm that in two days he became not a soldier in the war on societal disparity, but a paid informant for an international heroin kingpin bent on outfoxing an American shipping magnate. Hamidah, buried deep within the leaching bowels of Malik Said, found a willing servant in Ali, who, in turn, was falsely introduced to a man whom Hamidah learned – from snooping through her boss's belongings and listening to his conversations – had been hired by Walter Kragen to extract a very potent revenge. This man was Raymond, and by early January Ali was in Sawahi and, shortly thereafter, in Raymond's confidence.

Sitting on the bus, however, all Ali knew was the name of a destination, Nice, and that the plan involved others; more information would be required if he were to please his beautiful handler and their deadly employer. Through the window passed an arid landscape of sporadic small towns and cotton fields. Reflecting on his errant path, Ali watched as dirt suddenly gave way to the Guadiana River and the bus glided over water between towering supports and cables past a fleeting sign: "Spain."

"Raymond," Ali reached across the aisle and shook Raymond's shoed foot – "wake up" he pleaded in a loud whisper; "Raymond, we are in Spain!"

Raymond's eyes opened and he leaned forward until seated facing the aisle and Ali; "How long?"

"Just a minute;" Ali's taut whisper the result of anxiety and fear-driven adrenaline spurts, "there are only five other people on the bus, will this work?"

Reacting as a professional Raymond calmly reassured his young apprentice, "Yes, yes, it will work; there probably won't even be a check. Now...," and reaching deep into his duffel felt for the small plastic vial filled with ipecac syrup. "Remember, if they come on board, as they are checking the last person, drink the whole bottle and then push the vial down your pants. Here," Raymond handed Ali the vial, a custard pastry wrapped in brown paper, and a British passport cover devoid of content, "now eat the pastry, and to be sure, don't miss the passport!"

Ali jettisoned the brown paper behind his seat, gobbled the pastry, and waited. The bus rolled along past predominantly pale brown scenery interspersed with tilled soil where rows of crops offered a green respite. Raymond rested against the back of the seat with his feet propped high on back of the empty seat in front, his window cracked open and eyes closed behind black wrap-around sunglasses, occasionally nodding off and waking with a jerk that each time startled Ali.

A half hour passed and Ali began to relax in the belief that he and Raymond would soon arrive in Seville without incident. This state of ease abruptly came to an end, however, when a tall man rearing toward the front of the bus removed his wool coat to reveal a dark green shirt with military or police insignias and emblems – Ali could not tell which. The man turned and began ambling down the aisle toward the rear of the rocking bus; a sight which caused Ali to squat in hiding behind a seatback, slide the cork from the vial still warm from over thirty minutes in his clenched fist, and pour the rancid liquid down his throat.

Raymond somehow became cognizant of a problem and bolted upright just in time to witness Ali pitch the passport cover and spasmodically spew streams of smelly yellow fluid until long after saturating the passport cover and the aisle floor. The fog of Raymond's half-asleep daze lifted after a moment to reveal reality: Ali ingested the ipecac syrup while the bus was still moving and no more distant than a meter from an excited soldier shouting in Spanish. Jumping to feet cradled in shoes immersed in used custard, Raymond grabbed hold of Ali while at the same time trying to alleviate the soldier's concern.

"Esta bien, it's okay, he's okay, mal, malo, infermo...he ate some bad food, a pastry" and with the fingers of his left hand Raymond pretended to convey imaginary food to his mouth while contorting a countenance befitting of extreme nausea; "He'll be okay...Carlos, Carlos!"

Ali remained bent over the aisle floor, grunting in between convulsive heaves in express confirmation of Raymond's illegible pronouncement.

The soldier meanwhile nodded in clearly disgusted understanding, pointed toward the rear of the bus, and muttered through the fingers of his right hand "el bano, por favor, pardon, pardon" as he squeezed by Raymond in furtherance of a necessary jaunt to the bathroom at the back of the bus.

It was not until the bus station in Seville that Raymond stopped laughing and Ali began to feel as though he may live. The bus driver pulled over after the soldier entered the toilet; Raymond also had to quell the driver's concerns with an added promise that Ali would sanitize the aisle floor and surrounding seats. Staying aboard the bus after all others had departed, Ali wiped the floor and seats with toilet paper until Raymond returned with a rag and disinfectant. After twenty minutes, and a nod of approval from the bus driver, Raymond and Ali entered the terminal and made their way to the taxi zone.

Stepping through the doorway they waited under a clear sky, not a cloud to be seen, on a cool but by no means cold mid-afternoon. After an elderly man and woman traveling together entered a cab, another pulled to the stand, and for the next half hour transported Raymond and Ali in bumper-to-bumper traffic to a second hand jewelry store in south Seville. There, at the far end of a small showroom, they found a middle-age man seated behind glass inlaid with wire mesh; looking up from tinkering, the man welcomed in Spanish the prospective customers or, as was sometimes the case, robbers.

"Hola, Senor, me llamo Raymond, y Carlos," with a tip of his head Raymond gestured to Ali, "Como se llama usted?" Raymond obviously had a very limited understanding of Spanish.

The proprietor's eyes narrowed inquisitively, "Me llamo Esteban; como...why do you ask?"

Raymond smiled and sighed in relief, "Good, English; Esteban, you remember me, Raymond, we met in Istanbul, you prepared a driver's permit for me, a Greek permit."

"Oh yes, yes, I remember now, you went to Greece on a ferry, yes." Esteban left his chair, stepped out of view, unlocked a door, and entered the room, "Raymond, it is good to see you again, a long time; what brings you to Seville, and to my shop?"

"My friend here, Carlos, he needs a passport." Raymond went on to explain that Ali needed a Spanish passport within two days. Esteban quoted a price reduced only slightly by a brief haggle, told the travelers they could stay in a room at the back of the shop until the document was ready, and led them out of the storefront down a short hall to a locked steel door. Raymond peered inside a rather small windowless dimly lit square room and graciously declined Esteban's offer: "No, thank you, we will get a hotel, Carlos snores."

"Fine; I will start with Carlos tonight after the shop has closed" instructed Esteban; "Be back here at eight, and Carlos, wear something bright, a bright shirt, and shave off that beard and cut your hair – we want the authorities to like you!" he said with a smile and a solid pat on Ali's right shoulder.

After walking a short distance from the jewelry store, Ali stopped Raymond to voice his concern, "We cannot get a hotel room, you know that, I don't have papers; where are we going to go?" Raymond smiled and replied "Follow me" as he knew a place where travel papers would not be necessary. Walking only a block farther, Raymond pointed across the street to an old brick building with a sign above the door that read "Hostel of Seville," nudged Ali in the ribs with his elbow, and with a laugh remarked "There, you see, refuge for the weary travelers!"

Climbing a rickety flight of stairs after paying a polite young man at the front desk twenty Euros, Raymond and Ali stepped into an open room where simple cots with white cotton linens lined walls to the right and left of the staircase. At the other end of the long room were two other smaller rooms with showers and toilets, one on each side, and between those another stairwell leading to a locked back alley exit.

They settled on two tightly covered mattresses barren of person, bag, or clothing, next to an open window where white chiffon drapes rippled in a cool breeze, stuffed their duffels under the cots, and lay down to relax for twenty minutes in anticipation of going back out to find food. Raymond had eaten three pastries on the bus but Ali was, of course, badly in need of nourishment. Around the block appeared a small market at which Raymond purchased processed meat slices in plastic wrap and a loaf of bread that in their entirety Ali promptly devoured, leaving Raymond to reenter the market and buy two dry apple pastries shelved in a glass case and a bottle of purified water.

For almost three hours the two rested on the cots until at a few minutes before eight returning to the jewelry store, Ali's face smooth, hair combed back and plastered with baby oil to his scalp, and sporting a barely-worn red and yellow stripe sweater his mother knitted him several years earlier. Esteban led Raymond and Ali back down the corridor to the locked room, removed the padlock, stepped inside and pulled a row of strings to render fluorescent bright the otherwise drab box.

"Here, stand against the wall, here," Esteban pointed across the room to a finely detailed depiction of a giant passport portrayed on a perfectly flat surface, blank white spaces reserved for the holder's new identity, a blank white square to capture the holder's pre-retouched image. "Stand with your head in the square"; Esteban waved his hands as though directing a theatrical scene and watched as Ali shuffled along the wall. "You're going to have to kneel down a little...there, okay...yes that will work; okay, you can stand while I make the camera ready." Esteban slid a tripod across the floor until the feet lined up perfectly within three small red squares painted on the tile. Lifting a black cloth at the apex of the tripod, Esteban with both hands carefully twisted knobs and pushed levers on a Hasselblad digital camera until once satisfied exclaimed "We're ready!"

The confined space made Raymond nervous and, without realizing, he paced a repetitive small oval while maintaining a constant vigil of the doorway. Finally, he asked as a matter of courtesy if his presence was required; Esteban said "No, you may certainly leave" and explained that the process of creating Carlos' passport would take some time and there was no need for Raymond to return until morning. As soon as Ali confirmed he could safely find his way to the hostel in the dark, Raymond bolted from the room, down the hall, through two other doors, and out into the chilly night air.

Esteban spent the next four hours photographing the mural and in front of it, Ali's head and shoulders. For each frame, Ali had to squat with his knees bent just slightly in a very uncomfortable position so that his head and shoulders centered precisely within the white square. After each series of three photographs, Esteban worked on a computer wired to the camera, returning after fifteen or twenty minutes to capture another series of images.

Ali finally left the store at just after one in the morning and though extremely tired made his way two blocks to the hostel, rang the buzzer, and, after the lock unlatched, tenaciously ascended the stairs and fell into his cot. Under the window's soft illumination Ali could see that Raymond's cot was empty; he wondered for a brief moment why, closed his eyes, and drifted to sleep. The rattling of his cot caused Ali a rude awakening at seven that morning.

"Wake up! Have you nothing better to do than sleep, Carlos?"

Raymond jested, "Come on, get ready, we need to be at the store at eight to catch the train at nine-thirty, hurry!"

Ali groaned, rolled over, sat up, and remained at the edge of the cot until mustering energy required of the new day's endeavor. "I'll wait for you downstairs," Raymond draped a duffel bag over his left shoulder, "hurry!" After no longer than ten minutes, Ali stepped quickly down the stairs carrying his green canvas bag and the two strolled leisurely to the store relishing the crisp air and sunshine. Ali thought about asking Raymond his whereabouts the previous night but decided, upon reflection, it was better not to ask such a question; if Raymond did not volunteer an explanation the answer would be, he concluded, either immaterial or immoral.

Esteban greeted Raymond and Ali with the enthusiasm befitting a proud craftsman soon to be handsomely compensated. Back at the windowless room, Raymond waited on the other side of the door, watching as Esteban immodestly presented his creation to Ali. "Carlos, may I offer...your ticket to freedom!" Feeling the dark red folder in his hands, Ali felt an unexpected, undeserving pride; "It's beautiful!" he exclaimed. "Only the best for my friends" pronounced a grinning Esteban.

Inconspicuously into the room slid Raymond during the impromptu ceremony and softly nudging the door behind him it closed tight. With the Beretta eye level in his extended right hand the back of Esteban's head in front of the muzzle hastened a sullen twitch of a finger on the trigger. The blast was deafening. The concussion shivered the tripod and fluorescent hanging lamps long after Esteban had collapsed dead on the floor. The only thing in the room not moving was Ali.

"Why did you do that?" he demanded in a fast high-pitched voice.

Raymond continued his slide across the tile with the Beretta pointed at Esteban's body, which lie face down, tapped the neck with the toe of his right shoe, bent down, examined the entrance wound and checked for a carotid pulse at the neck. There of course was none. "Last night I came back here, to the store, about an hour before you left," Raymond holstered the gun while tendering his short explanation to Ali; "I waited in the trees across the road. Not long after you left, two men drove up, knocked on the door, and Esteban let them in. They stayed for about fifteen minutes and then drove away." Raymond ushered Ali to the door while whispering in urgent refrain words that did not require saying.

"What got me suspicious was the way he offered us this room, with no windows and a heavy lock on the outside. Esteban knows I hate confinement, and he knew why; it seemed strange he would ask us to stay in what amounted to nothing more than a prison cell." Leading the way, Raymond proceeded cautiously into and slowly down the hallway to the storefront entrance, all the while continuing to enlighten Ali, "So, the men that came to meet with Esteban in the middle of the night, they were in a Fiat, a new one, they were dressed nice, short hair, athletic; cops, intelligence, nothing good, they knew right when you left, Esteban must have called them."

Raymond cracked the door and coursed slyly into the empty and dimly lit showroom with Ali close behind. The store not scheduled to open until nine, the front door locked, Raymond relaxed somewhat, stopped in the middle of the room, and from a very close distance stared into Ali's eyes ushering somber prose. "I figured they wouldn't try anything until after you had the passport. I also figure Esteban is supposed to be calling them right about now, telling them we have left on foot, walking to the train station. I believe the passport to be a good forgery – Esteban knew I could tell – but I am sure the bar code, the scanner, will not work. We cannot now go by train. We'll take a car. But first...."

He gestured toward a small black object above the door and pointed toward a similar small object above the protective glass – security cameras. "We have to find the computer, it's probably a wireless setup" Raymond told Ali.   They both scoured the showroom and back offices until Ali came upon a notebook computer, having used a stapler and letter opener to pry open a locked cabinet behind the glass.

"Here!" he whispered while holding up the black device.

Raymond ran over, glanced at the computer, and rummaged

through the cabinet; "We need to make sure there aren't any other drives" he explained and Ali understood. Once they were satisfied the notebook computer held the only video storage, Ali crammed it into his duffel bag while Raymond stood on Esteban's rolling oak desk chair, dislodging cameras from mounts and stuffing them into his duffel bag.

In a lingering state of shocked disbelief, Ali listened, as Raymond foretold their escape. "We are going to go out this door and *run* across the street, through the trees, through whatever we have to, to get to the next street; we have to be off of any street between here and the train station. Do you understand?" Ali nodded. "Have you ever lifted a car?" Ali's head shook. "Okay, pray that we find the right car; if not, we'll have to take one that's running, and you must know what that means."

Twist, click, the dead bolt retracted and Raymond and Ali were dodging cars to the shrubs and over a small fence, through an alley, over a larger fence and across a dirt parking lot to a broad main road. Suddenly halting and pivoting to re-examine the parking lot, Raymond announced they had found the right transportation, a well-preserved ten to fifteen year-old green Ford Escort vacated in their presence by a middle aged woman obviously in route to some dreary calling.

"Wait here!" With a brisk effort, but not so much as to cause alarm, Raymond intercepted the woman soon to pass through an employee entrance at the back of a building while a mystified Ali looked on.

Approaching the woman Raymond spoke in a polite tone; "Excuse me, pardon, habla usted Inglés o Francéss?" The woman looked ahead and kept walking. "Por favor, señora, quiero, um, darle el dinero para su coche...I want to give you money for your car...l'argent pour..." until finally he just held out a wad of bills.

The woman glanced back, saw the money, and stopped.

"Gracias señora – English?"

The woman nodded, "I speak some English, what you want?"

"I want to rent your car, that is all," Raymond separated two hundred-Euro bills from the fold and presented them, "I want to rent your car for two days, and I will give you one hundred Euros for each day, and after two days you can call the police and tell them the car was stolen and collect from your insurance company."

The woman appeared less astonished than Raymond had anticipated; she reached out and seized the bills with her right hand, examined them closely, and with her left rustled around inside a handbag until retrieving a ring of keys. Raymond waited while she removed a key from the ring and handed it to him with a smile. "You have the car" she gladly agreed; "I wait, in two days I call Policia, so for two days I ride the bus, you have fun with car."

"Gracias" exclaimed Raymond with an appreciative bow.

Ali found the registration in the glove box as they proceeded east along the busy main road, "The car belongs to Sebastian Orofante...this woman did not look like a Sebastian."

"Probably her husband, or a son" Raymond speculated; "It doesn't matter anyway. Nobody will report the car before two days, it would cause too many problems, remember, she has the money and we know where she works. Right now, we need petrol, the car is empty."

They drove the A-4 through Cordova and into Madrid; from there the A-2 to Saragossa and the E-90 to the coast and north to Barcelona. On the outskirts of the city, Raymond used a pay phone to call a friend with whom they later dined, drank Spanish beer, and spent the night. The next day Raymond and Ali departed early, following the main thoroughfare into France and traveling La Provincale until late that afternoon arriving in Nice. Raymond exited the bypass and after negotiating narrow passageways parked the Escort in the center of town; he and Ali wiped the interior with t-shirts soaked in gutter water and abandoned the car unlocked, windows down, key in the ignition.

After buying a local newspaper from a curbside vendor, Raymond led Ali to an outdoor café where they drank espresso and surveyed the classified list of available apartments. Six prospects met Raymond's preliminary criteria – monthly rent of less than four hundred Euros, a low deposit, pre-payment of no more than one-month's rent, centrally located, furnished, and an on-site owner or manager – and were circled in blue ink using a pen borrowed from their server. Once finished, Ali grabbed a free tourist map from an advertising kiosk and the two unemployed foreigners began shopping for an apartment.

The first building did not have a resident owner or manager despite advertisement to the contrary. The second building was next to the first; the manager showed them a small one-bedroom apartment on the second floor but when Raymond said they were interested the manager asked where they worked and suggested a credit record would be required. The third apartment was in a building three blocks away from the second; it was also on the second floor, with an outside entrance accessible by stairs, very close to curtained windows in an adjacent apartment building. This would not work. The fourth flat was down a flight of stairs and consisted of two bedrooms with small windows at the rear and a windowless sitting room with shabby furniture and a windowless kitchen at the front. When Ali tried to open one of the bedroom windows the owner of the property, a hobbling elderly woman with no teeth, explained in almost incoherent French that paint and nails sealed the window frames shut to prevent burglaries.

The fifth apartment was six blocks from the fourth on a tree-lined side street. The building owner, an Egyptian having resided in France for only two years, showed Raymond and Ali a furnished studio on the third floor with a window overlooking the street. Raymond declared almost immediately that he and Carlos – a name when heard causing the Egyptian's eyebrows to raise and lips to purse in obvious disbelief – would happily take the apartment and that he could pay in cash. The Egyptian's condescending reply in French was "Yes, of course you can;" as they descended the stairwell he added "I will rent to you, but will need three months' rent of six hundred Euros in advance."

Raymond tried negotiating to no avail and finally, succumbing to the likely reality this was he and Ali's best opportunity, handed over eighteen hundred Euros, telling Ali later "It really didn't matter because the money was to be Esteban's fee." The Egyptian for his part, while handing Raymond the key, issued in fluent English strong words of caution: "I will report you, as I would anyone, if I believe you are doing something illegal, or are *going to* do something illegal. Please don't let me see my building on CNN." With a wave and smile he bid Raymond and Ali good fortune as they entered the staircase.

Over the next three months Raymond and Ali hauled firearms and explosives into the apartment in small quantities usually hidden at the bottom of grocery bags. Most was purchased from local arms dealers; however, some was delivered from as far away as Paris. Ali asked Raymond on several occasions what they were going to do and when they were going to do it, but Raymond simply replied that Ali would know when the time was right, and the time was not right. By the end of April, their tiny apartment housed enough firepower to conduct a small war and the two spent most of their days at the beach or roaming around town and their nights in the apartment sleeping, if at all, very uneasily.

Raymond announced in early May that he was leaving for two weeks and would return "with fighters to complete our glorious mission"; Ali discreetly asked where he was going and Raymond replied "Mali."

"I see, so you must be flying" probed Ali to Raymond's oblivion.

"I will fly there and then we will drive back, the same as you and I."

"You will drive from Mali to Morocco?"

"Yes."

"Hmm, it will be hot through the desert; does your Jetta have air conditioning?"

"Yes."

"Fortunate for you...."

Raymond and Ali embraced; Raymond entered the security line and Ali bought a prepaid cell phone from a vendor in the terminal.

From the apartment bathroom, sitting on the edge of the tub, Ali dialed Hamidah's cell phone. After several rings, she answered and in response to Ali's voice joyfully cried "I had given up on you!"

Ali, having long since surmised – rightly or wrongly – his status was simply that of Hamidah's and Malik Said's pawn, wasted no time in explaining flatly that he was in Nice and did not yet know when or how he would return, but that within the next ten days was to "receive delivery of a white Jetta and one or more boxes of my clothes via the long desolate road through Western Sahara to Morocco. With these clothes, I will be able to complete my journey."

Hamidah responded tersely as does a woman inexplicably, at least to the woman, rebuffed; "I see, that is interesting Ali, please keep me updated on your plans and take good care of yourself."

Ali remained seated for several minutes after the call ended. "Maybe it was time to go home," he thought, back to his family and friends. Tears began to blur his vision. Head bowed, cradled in his hands, Ali tolerated a brief profound sorrow until wiping his cheeks with toilet paper and leaving the bathroom. There was no going home.

When Sandra answered the phone, Robert's rehearsed monologue suddenly seemed deplorable, asking his daughter not to vacation in Monaco with her boyfriend because of his entanglement with a dangerous criminal. The words simply would not materialize; instead, "Hi Sandy, how are you?" Excited to be off to Monaco and the Grand-Prix, of course, and basking in such joy that Robert could not bring himself to quell any moment of those rarest of emotions.

"I have good news!" proclaimed Robert; "You and Gilbert are invited to fly on a business associate of mine's private jet to Monte-Carlo!"

It was a surprising invitation and Sandra garbled her response: "When, how..., are you going?"

"Yes, of course, Sandy, we are all going...."

"When?" she suddenly pressed, "When do we leave? I haven't been to the store yet! Gilbert is going to buy me a dress, he said he would, I don't have anything here that's nice enough."

"Funny the things one worries about when everything appears

to be going right" thought Robert, hearing his daughter agonize over her fortunate dilemma. "Sandy, slow down. We leave tonight. You will need to meet me at my hotel at seven. There's plenty of time to buy a dress; but I also understand they sell them in Monaco."

Robert's faux-relaxed jovial bantering calmed Sandra as it always had; "Let me call Gilbert, I'll call you right back!"

In less than two minutes, Sandra confirmed that she and Gilbert would be in the lobby of the Hotel Internationale at seven, ready to go.

The smile on Robert's lips dissipated before the phone touched the nightstand. He sat at the edge of the bed first absorbed with self-pity, after enough of that, composing, harkened back to training as a Marine kindling the fighting spirit flickering within – a spirit igniting just when it seemed he could stand no more. There was nobody to turn to, no police, no army, nobody, besides him, was going to save his daughter. If they, he and Sandra, were to make it out of this quagmire of his creation, be it only by fight, his fight, one way or another.

While in the shower it occurred to Robert that there was a good chance one of the preeminent reasons Malik Said flew privately was the absence of a security screening. "The first thing to do" he decided aloud through a water dribble, "is buy a gun." Throwing on a pair of beige cotton dress pants, a dress shirt, and green cotton golf jacket, Robert embarked an expeditious search for a suitable weapon in a country without the slew of firearm purveyors as was common in the States.

Hailing a cab after meandering a few blocks on foot contemplating the best way to achieve his unlawful objective, Robert, not simply unlatching the door and getting in, leaned low and forward and through the passenger side window first analyzed the driver. Indian, he surmised, or maybe Pakistani, probably as good a prospect as any. He settled into the back seat. The driver stared in the rearview mirror at Robert while Robert stared in the rearview mirror at the driver.

"I am American" Robert finally announced in a measured

resonance of confidence, "Do you speak English or French?"

The driver responded in broken English laden with an Indian accent, "Either is okay. Where do you wish to go?"

Robert focused on the reflection of the driver's eyes, "I need to buy a gun, for protection; can you help me?"

The driver stared back into the reflection of Robert's determined and unwavering eyes and after several seconds replied "No, that is illegal, I can't help you, now get out."

Robert did not move; "Listen, I am not a cop, I will pay you well, I need to buy a gun, you just take me to the place and drop me off and then leave, it's just a fare, that's all I ask."

The driver looked ahead along the street, soon his head shook slowly side to side and concentrating on the rearview mirror he spoke, "I do not know where to buy a gun. I will take you to a place where people have guns. That's all I can do."

"Thank you, that's all I ask" agreed Robert.

After a fifteen-minute ride north, the cab slowed and pulled to the side of the road; "Here," the driver pointed up the street with his right index finger, "you may find a gun around here."

Robert shifted to the middle of the back seat and while leaning forward peered out the windscreen; "Okay," he handed the driver thirty Euros, "how do I get a cab back, do they come by?" The driver answered "Oui, of course."

Leaving the cab to make his way along the sidewalk with the other pedestrians, Robert was unsure of what, exactly, he was looking for. After walking anxiously for a block he stopped on a corner and gazed around at the buildings and people; very unlike the glitzy tourist brochures selling the world's most beautiful city, he decided with an imperceptible frown, poverty up close looks the same in any city.

"You lost man?" a ragged, obviously homeless, African man startled Robert from behind; "You lost? You got some money? I'll show you where to go. I need some food man." Robert pithily muttered "No" and began walking across a road, against the light and between cars; but the man followed, loudly pleading his plight, "Hey, man, I need some food, did you hear me, I'm hungry, don't walk away from me!"

Robert pretended not to hear. He also pretended not to be a hypocrite, giving every year at Christmas to the Washington, DC food bank while passing throngs of homeless men and women sleeping on the sidewalks of America's capitol. Always, he pretended not to see their squalor or hear their pleas. As he passed without acknowledging two African men talking in the foyer of a dilapidated building, Robert could not help but hear, as one of the men confronted Robert's vociferous pursuer to demand in a powerful French voice that the man desist. Robert paused to offer thanks, "Merci beaucoup," to the stocky man wearing blue jeans and an un-tucked blue button-down shirt.

"You're American" the man replied in clear English; "what are you doing here?"

His eyes first quickly surveying the surroundings, Robert declared firmly "I am looking for something."

The man took several steps until within an arm's length of Robert posed the question: "What are you looking for?"

"I want to buy a gun." Robert did not hesitate or blink.

The man's face resembled a solemn sculpture as eyebrows sank and the voice became low and serious; "Show me your passport." Robert wondered if perhaps he had carelessly solicited a police officer but, without a viable alternative, reached inside his jacket, unzipped a pocket, and held prominently for inspection a blue folder open to the first page identification. "How much will you spend?" asked the man.

"It depends; I have three hundred Euros, cash," Robert realized too late it was an extremely dangerous thing to say.

With the fingers of his right hand the man pinched the corners of his lips as one sometimes does during a moment of meditation; "I can get you one gun, a Python, but it is much more than three hundred Euros."

"How much?" was a very poor negotiation response also

appreciated too late by Robert.

The man shuffled his feet while appearing to study the concrete; "Fifteen hundred Euros, that is the best I can do, the gun is new, and I will throw in two hundred rounds of ammunition."

Time, without time, to shop or to haggle, Robert's options were nonexistent and so from under his left shirt sleeve he displayed the Breitling watch proudly presented as a gift by his wife on their second anniversary. "Here, it's worth a lot more than fifteen hundred Euros; it's real, take a look." The man leaned forward to examine the watch face and asked to hold the timepiece.

"No" answered Robert, "not until I'm holding the Colt."

They walked together along the sidewalk as Robert pondered his peril, one block, another, another, until the man pointed down an alley, "We will go to my flat, upstairs."

The apparent lunacy of his predicament was almost too much for Robert to bear; nevertheless, he acquiesced, "I'll follow you."

"Don't worry my Yankee friend, it is daylight, everyone has seen us together, all the cameras...." The man's casual words jarred Robert; how could he of all people not have remembered, considered, there was no hiding on the streets of any major Western European city.

They climbed the metal stairs of a fire escape to an exposed hallway, walked a short distance on dirty carpet, and entered a sparse one-room flat smelling strongly of urine. Robert waited just inside the threshold as the man opened a stubby refrigerator and removed what looked like a roast wrapped in brown paper. Suddenly, from under a brown couch darted a small weasel-appearing animal directly for Robert's feet. "Close the door!" yelled the man. Robert jumped and slammed the door.

"Charles," the man handed Robert the brown package and picked up the animal, "If he gets outside, forget it, I will be chasing him around the roof for an hour."

"What is it?" Robert asked in relief while calming his nerves and removing wrapper from the heavy revolver.

"Charles – named after our former esteemed leader who would never have let us in to this bungling Union – is a ferret." The man held the animal's nose toward the nose of an uncomfortable Robert, for just a second, and set it gently on the carpet to scurry back under the couch.

In his right hand Robert grasped the icy Colt Python and with both hands examined the cylinder, chamber, barrel, and trigger assembly; "This has never been fired?"

"Never;" the man went on to explain that a middle aged woman had purchased the gun legally when new but that, before ever firing it, became ill, ran into financial trouble, and had to offer the gun for sale, "I bought it four years ago from her son."

Robert placed the stainless steel revolver in the man's right hand, unhooked the watchband from around his left arm, and while handing over the watch asked "Do we have a deal?" After thoroughly examining the crystal, crown, and band, and reading the inscription on the case, the man nodded and solemnly replied "I'm sorry you have to make this trade." Following a brief silence he added, "Do you want the box, it is under the bed," and gestured to the couch, "I will get the ammo." Not willing to probe with his fingers under the couch, the second reason Robert did not want the box; the first, loosening his belt to insert the large weapon in the waist of his pants, zipping his golf jacket to cover the grip, and filling his pockets with 357 cartridges – it was a long public excursion back to the hotel.

Robert traversed interwoven squares and diagonal blocks of asphalt and concrete back to the main road trying not to think about the watch his wife had given him many years ago. She would understand he tried to rationalize. Witnessing the entire fiasco from beyond he was sure that she understood; the safety of their daughter came first. Of course, considering it was he creating the jeopardy in the first place, it was natural to consider how decisions made with general good intent could turn out results so corrupt. "I'm sorry Patty" he whispered, "I'm sorry."

Back on the road from which his illicit undertaking started, at almost the exact spot, Robert paused to gauge his course and after taking just a few steps along the sidewalk heard the repeated blare of a car horn across the traffic. Glancing over, he immediately recognized the face in the cab window, smiled, and sprinted across the road. "Boy, am I glad to see you!" he beamed; "What are you doing here?"

"I could see you may need a ride back" replied the driver with a grin, "so I waited."

"How long?" asked Robert sliding into the back seat.

"Maybe fifteen minutes, not long, I became worried, this is not a good part of Paris"; the driver's eyes lowered as the cab accelerated.

Robert relaxed, took a deep breath, and praised the driver's reflection, "You, my friend, are a lifesaver."

Once safely within the hotel room Robert placed the gun and ammunition in a zipped inner pouch of his carryon. He was briefly concerned Klaus might search his luggage, but after some deliberation concluded there would be no reason or precedent for such an act. The clock displayed 14:06; leaving just four hours to devise a strategy once and for all freeing him and his daughter from Malik Said.

The inception of any analytical challenge of this nature, Robert recalled, required an understanding of personalities and environment. On sheets of blank white paper retrieved from his carryon, began the planning, with circles, boxes, arrows, and stick figures. Three hours of sketching and writing, realizing he needed to shower and pack, the many pages were torn into narrow strips and dumped into a trashcan – the imperfect stratagem relegated only to memory.

Sandra and Gilbert were in the hotel lobby by the time Robert stepped out of the elevator; the three strolled and chatted through the seating area, past the lobby bar, and out the front door to request of the valet a taxi to Le Bourget. Soon they were crammed in the backseat of a Peugeot with Sandra in the middle, on their laps a variety of bags, suffering a thirty minute commute to the airport. An eternity later, Robert instructed the cabbie to pull in front of the executive terminal and the relieved yet excited travelers burst from the vehicle into plush surroundings. Their luggage soon followed.

Using an elbow to hold back a heavier than usual black computer case suspended from his left shoulder, Robert greeted and shook the hands of Malik Said and Klaus; thereafter, with somewhat more warmth, expressing great pleasure at again seeing Michelle and introducing his daughter and Gilbert all around. "What a beautiful daughter you have" declared Mr. Said with the look of a man observing fine art, "and you, Gilbert, may I call you that, have I not seen you somewhere before?"

Gilbert gave the matter some quick analysis and afterward replied "Perhaps so, yes, do you have an account at Worldwide Investment Bank here in Paris?" Robert tried to derail the exchange by asking an irrelevant question about flight logistics, but without success, as Gilbert continued, "That is where I work, as an account manager."

Mr. Said appeared unsure how to respond, "No, I'm sorry, perhaps it was someone else," and after a pause glared at Robert, "Shall we go?"

In a matter of minutes the group was outside following a red tarmac carpet up stairs into a waiting Citation CJ2 with three rows of individual leather reclining cushion seats separated by an aisle. Malik Said and Klaus were first on the plane and elected to sit across from one another in the furthermost seats. Robert encouraged Sandra and Gilbert to take the first two seats while he and Michelle settled into the middle seats. Unaccustomed to small jet flight, Robert, Michelle, Sandra, and Gilbert engaged in polite discourse tinged with composed anxiety; Mr. Said and Klaus, on the other hand, simply engaged in serious dialogue. After about ten minutes the pilot stepped out of the cockpit to introduce herself and the copilot, and to confirm the flight to Nice would last less than an hour. Soon they were climbing into air.

Once the jet leveled, faint voices could again be heard, most expressing exhilaration, others, pseudo-comic gratitude for withstanding takeoff. Robert and Michelle chatted unceasingly for the next forty minutes as if alone, talking about the trip, prior trips, food, recreation – nothing too personal or having to do with occupations other than Michelle asking Robert if he enjoyed being a professor. "Yes" answered Robert, "I did." Just as it seemed the jet had reached cruising altitude, it began a long descent into Nice, and from across the aisle Robert gently laid his hand over that of Michelle's firmly attached to an armrest.

The Citation taxied to the terminal at Aéroport de la Côte d'Azur and passengers deplaned into a brisk Mediterranean evening and from there a Bentley limousine. Gilbert was first to broach a question on the minds of two other Malik Said guests: "My understanding is we are to board Paul DuMorell's yacht in Monte-Carlo on Thursday morning; where will we be staying tonight and tomorrow night?"

Mr. Said promptly supplied the answer, "It was my understanding, Klaus, correct me if I am wrong, we were to go aboard the yacht for a party tomorrow night and you were going to stay at Villa Palmera tonight; but if you would rather stay elsewhere, we can of course take you."

Robert and Sandra and Sandra and Gilbert exchanged contemplative glances prompting Robert to issue a mutual reply, "This is the first we've heard, and I believe the concern is your convenience, we do not want to be a nuisance; certainly we can stay in a hotel."

At Robert's courtesy Klaus laughed loud, saying, "Do you have a reservation? As you know, this is the busiest weekend of the year here, where would you propose to stay?"

"Well" began Robert rather irritated, "I'm sure there are hotels, I could get online...."

"Don't be foolish" interrupted Mr. Said, "you will stay with me. It is no inconvenience, the place certainly has adequate room, and you will be free to come and go as you like."

"Well," the word lingered as filler again while Robert studied the faces of Sandra and Gilbert, "I suppose – and am certainly very grateful for your offer – if it is no problem, yes, we will accept your offer."

At considerable speed the Bentley glided along a motorway past Nice until exiting at a street marked by a sign Robert could not read and proceeding south through a series of side roads to Saint Jean Cap Ferrat. There, it maneuvered slowly through a dark maze bordered by the lights of opulent homes until arriving at a guardhouse. Mr. Said rolled down his window, produced a passport, and informed the guard he and his guests were staying at "Villa Palmera." An iron gate lifted and the limousine with its passengers proceeded down a dark road also bounded by distant lights, soon stopping in front of another iron gate.

Mr. Said removed a small paper from inside his coat, flipped on an overhead lamp, and addressed the driver through an intercom, "You need to enter a code on the keypad." The driver responded and Mr. Said recited a seven number code in French; the driver opened his door, walked to the keypad, entered the number, and jumped back in as the gate began moving. Past the dim glow of lamps recessed in the lawn and around a half-circle drive the Bentley crept, ultimately to rest in front of an exquisite covered marble entry. From between the grand double doors stepped a woman and a man graciously introduced as Genevieve and Marc, managers of the estate, who in welcoming Malik Said and his guests led everybody into the house and assisted the driver with luggage.

At that point Sandra could no longer contain her awe, "Wow!"

With a smile her father concurred, "Yes, wow!" and everyone, including Klaus, laughed.

Genevieve returned to the foyer to ask – ahead of luggage being carted into the main residence – if anybody would be staying in the guesthouse. "Yes, just one" answered Malik Said with a slight hand gesture identifying Klaus; "Mr. Adalbrecht will be staying in the guesthouse." Klaus and Genevieve promptly departed for the Bentley.

"Why don't we get settled and then meet back down here for a bite to eat and a nightcap" proposed Mr. Said on his way to the main sitting room, "My room is the end of the hall upstairs to my left. You are welcome to any of the many other rooms, most have private baths."

Robert and Gilbert met Marc in the foyer and carried their own luggage up the right half of the winding marble staircase, behind Sandra and Michelle engaged in a buoyant conversation about the Salvador Dali artwork adorning walls adjacent the stairs. Behind them, Marc, with some difficulty using both hands slowly wheeled two oversize soft-side suitcases over one precipice at a time. Clump, clump, they went. Peering down the lavish corridor in both directions at the top of the stairs, Sandra and Michelle deferred their discussion while waiting for a lead from Robert and Gilbert.

"I'm sure there are plenty of rooms on either side" assured Robert; "Why don't the ladies go to the right, and Gilbert and I will go to the left, where Mr. Said's room is."

Robert was first to return downstairs and discovered Malik Said seated alone at one end of an expansive dining table in a corner room with windows overlooking flickering lights along the Mediterranean coast. Mr. Said asked Robert if he had secured a suitable room, "Yes" replied Robert, "most suitable," and if he had any plans for the next day. To this Robert replied "No, not really, maybe spend some time with Sandy, is there something you would like to do?" Mr. Said responded in the negative…"but we do need to talk about your daughter's friend and his relationship to Worldwide Investment Bank in Dubai and DigiFouré."

Robert agreed, and proposed they break away in the afternoon.

"That would work fine," concurred Mr. Said.

"Am I interrupting something…?" Klaus asked from under a tiled arch between the dining room and kitchen.

"No, no, come in, we were just discussing our plans for tomorrow" responded Mr. Said; "Did you come in from the back?"

"No" answered Klaus while inspecting the room, "I tried, but the door was locked, so I had to walk around to the front."

"I see," Malik Said rose from his chair and looked out a wall of glass to the perfectly illuminated grounds of the estate, "I thought you could see the guest house from here, but I don't see it, it must be too far over"; turning to face Klaus, "What do you have planned for tomorrow?"

"I just wanted to make sure our equipment is in order and I want to meet with our friend here in Nice." Into a squat etched glass with silver trim Klaus poured cognac from a decanter shaped like a bowling pen that he found on a table in a corner of the room. "By the way, is Hamidah coming with Waters?"

Mr. Said glanced at Robert and replied "I don't know; I really am not sure who will be attending Mr. DuMorell's event."

Michelle was next to appear under the tile arch, wearing a black knit sweater over a flowery short dress, and, like Klaus, politely requested permission to enter the room. Mr. Said smiled and made an inviting arm gesture while Klaus inquired as to whether she would like a drink. "What are you offering?" Michelle bantered playfully. "All I seem to have is cognac and vermouth" glumly replied Klaus, lifting each bottle and skeptically examining the labels, "makings for a rather poor martini."

"I'm sure there is a better selection at the bar" offered Mr. Said, and the four promptly adjourned to the library where they were soon joined by Sandra and Gilbert dressed for an evening out, with Gilbert laughing that it took Sandra and he twenty minutes to find the others.

"Well, you have arrived," Klaus held up his glass of cognac, "now come join the festivities!" Gilbert approached the bar and Sandra took a seat next to her father. "Does anybody want wine?" asked Klaus, having assumed the role of bartender and nosing through the rack behind the bar; "I have a good looking red here, a California Cabernet actually, Silver Oak; may I?" he inquired of Mr. Said who replied "Of course." Klaus slid the bottle from the rack, rummaged through a drawer, pulled a small silver knife from a pant pocket, pushed a button, and with a flip of his wrist slit the cork wrapper.

After an hour, Mr. Said retired to his room and Klaus bid "bonne nuit" to the four remaining and left the library presumably for the guesthouse. Soon thereafter, Marc announced his presence from a doorway and asked if he and Genevieve could be excused. Robert answered "Yes, of course, thank you," realizing for the first time that Marc and Genevieve were a "couple."

It became a rather awkward affair at that point, with Robert and Michelle seated in a loveseat across a table from Sandra and Gilbert, seated in a loveseat. A very slight noise emanated from Robert's throat suggesting he and Michelle "go for a walk." "That would be nice" she encouraged, the last word a sultry-deep lingering note, and with a "Good evening" the two were soon strolling behind the villa taking in a cool Mediterranean night among broad-leafed palms lit by spots and a million stars. It was a setting much too romantic for caution.

Early the next morning, Klaus took a cab to La Promenade Des Anglais, sat on a bench overlooking the beach adjacent a café bakery, and waited for Ali. The young man arrived not long thereafter, wearing shorts, sandals, a yellow t-shirt, baseball cap, and sunglasses, and without acknowledging Klaus took a seat on the bench.

"My, it certainly is a beautiful morning, is it not?" proclaimed Klaus.

"Yes, all mornings in paradise are beautiful, are they not?" rejoined Ali.

"Yes, you are right, my young friend;" as Klaus continued talking each word became fainter than the previous, "do you know any more than you did a week ago?"

"No, Raymond did not come back, as expected, and I haven't heard anything from any others." Ali paused and ventured a delicate question, "Did you get all of them?"

Klaus spoke even more softly, "You don't have any idea of the plan? It could be tomorrow," intentionally disregarding Ali's question.

"No; I'm sitting on a pile of weapons and bombs and don't have any idea what to expect!" countered Ali in a voice of strained defense much too loud, "I will call as soon as I know something; I know how important this is to you and Mr. Said; I've already given you some information...."

"I understand, but it's not enough, we need more" snapped an exasperated Klaus caring less about decorum and turning his head to directly face Ali; "If something happens, if those weapons get used and we don't get a tip, it would be very unhealthy for all involved."

Ali understood – "all involved" meant him and Hamidah.

At a breakfast of eggs, potatoes, croissants, strawberries, banana, mango, pineapple, yogurt, ham, sausage, crêpes with various fillings, milk, juice, coffee and tea, laid out on the main dining table promptly at seven, Malik Said quietly informed Robert, as both scooped from saucers, they would be meeting at nine in the library instead of later that day. Robert acquiesced with a smile and carried his plate outside to join Michelle and Gilbert at a garden table, commenting while sitting, "I suppose Sandy will be down shortly."

"Yes, I saw her just a short while ago, on my way down, and she said she would be here after getting ready;" raising her eyes from a peach crêpe, Michelle briefly glanced at Gilbert to close in Sandra's defense, "She must have gotten up late."

Robert simply responded "Good, she won't want to miss this!" figuring the glass house built with Michelle only hours earlier certainly did not justify the throwing of stones.

The subject straightway changed to weather and scenery – and all at the table had much to say on these matters even as Sandra was with a free hand pulling on a chair-back previously touching the table. Gilbert jumped up and finished the task, offering also to retrieve any delicacies left to be desired. "No, thank you," replied Sandra with a grin; "I'm a croissant, yogurt, and tea kind of girl." For the next half hour everybody enjoyed light conversation and repeated trips to the dining table, relaxing and feasting in a tropical garden overlooking the deep blue ocean.

After breakfast, Michelle went to read a book she found in the library – *Once on a Moonless Night* by Dai Sijie – by the pool, while Sandra and Gilbert walked to the beach, and Robert prepared for his meeting with Mr. Said by adding topsiders and a navy sport coat to his preexisting attire of khaki pants and white polo shirt. Also, of course, Robert pondered appropriate responses to a list of hypothetical questions, those that Mr. Said may propound, until finally conceding futility he departed early for the library and stopped in the kitchen on his way for another cup of warm American coffee. Waiting alone in the peaceful room, Robert discovered a view between floral hedges to the pool and, on the other side, Michelle, reclining in a longue chair with a leg bent and knee up. Observing and sipping coffee, he wondered if a woman such as she could ever harbor any real interest in a man such as he – a college professor unlikely ever to provide the lifestyle she presently enjoyed.

"One wonders why one ever leaves;" Malik Said's voice caught Robert off guard and he felt a certain embarrassment, as might an adolescent school boy caught peering through a window into the girls' gym class, "but, then, there is the real world beyond, where we have to go about our business so that, on occasion, we may come to places such as this." Robert set his empty cup on the bar, "Or we find a job in a place such as this," and smiled. "It's not, I'm afraid, quite the same" was Mr. Said's assuredly truthful retort before shutting the library doors to pursue without further pleasantry a quite serious meeting.

"Robert, as you of all people know best, Walter Kragen has vowed some revenge for the biotech failure; I know that he has hired people to undertake some kind of act, and I believe it will be here, in Monaco, and it will, unless we can stop it, be quite serious. Do you understand?"

Robert's eyes alone communicated undivided attention to Malik Said but he answered "Yes, of course, please go on," fell into a cushion armchair, and crossed his legs.

Mr. Said paced slowly in front of the bar. "We know this because we have people on the inside, one of whom works for Worldwide Investment Bank. It seems the president of the Dubai branch, Stephen Waters, provided some assistance to Mr. Kragen. You know the bank had to settle with him; I don't know how much. I believe, actually have reason to believe, Waters connected Kragen with a terrorist, a man who is, who was, quite dangerous."

Robert uncrossed and re-crossed his legs; on his face a look of concerned attentiveness replaced a look of dissociated attentiveness.

"Now, we've dealt with that person, the terrorist, but the operation may still go forward. You can see why I am perplexed about Gilbert; why is he here and what is his involvement?" Robert started to say something but Mr. Said cut him short; "Obviously, he was involved with the DigiFouré offering, which in itself raises another series of questions. This Paul DuMorell, he has apparently been surrounding himself with luxury since closing the private placement; his boat, the one we are to enjoy, apparently cost upwards of one hundred million US dollars; he now has a house in Switzerland, perhaps also an account; I am told there is a Ferrari; God only knows what else."

Robert could not remain silent: "Aren't there laws? He can't just go spending the money the company raised; it's fraud!"

"Yes, well, he has us, the investors, shall we say, with our proverbial nuts in a vice; the company must succeed or we lose it all. I've spoken with our attorneys in the States and they tell me the stockholders can take action, maybe even have him removed, but, the offering memorandum appears to grant him considerable leeway. In other words, we would have very little chance of an injunction, either here or in the States, so that means a court case would take perhaps years and in the meantime the company will go belly-up."

"But I don't understand," Robert had moved to a standing position in front of the armchair, "what do you want from me?"

Mr. Said stopped pacing and looked directly into Robert's eyes; "If this Gilbert knows anything, anything at all, it could be useful. He may know something, or he may be able to find out something, in either case, we need every small advantage at our disposal."

Robert's head tilted and eyes narrowed. He could tolerate no more and addressing a man who could instantly cause his demise firmly – but politely – replied "This is a very delicate situation as I am sure you are aware, I cannot simply ask these questions of Gilbert..." when, suddenly, he understood what Mr. Said was telling him to do.

"It is not for you to ask these questions of Gilbert;" Malik Said's eyes training on Robert rendered an almost crushing glare, "these are questions for his beautiful lover."

Anger no longer controlled let loose in the face of Malik Said: "That beautiful lover is my daughter; I will not have her used as a tool! Why don't we all just leave, we don't have to attend this party, we will leave!" Robert's face, red, eyebrows, drawn close, heart, racing.

Mr. Said took a cautionary step back without unlocking his focus from Robert's eyes and considered for a moment his precise intent; sounding like a father apologizing to a reprimanded child he continued: "Apparently, you do not understand, and that is probably my fault." Robert turned away from the sound, rubbing his forehead as one might to alleviate a headache, but Mr. Said in an explanation for his behavior persisted. "These people aren't just after me. You, after all, signed the papers. Gilbert works for the bank. Your daughter, *your daughter*, is seeing Gilbert. It appears more than simple coincidence! Why do you think I asked you to fly down here with Klaus and me? They will never let you or those around you live. And please, do not attempt to place or transfer fault; you know as well as I, money, like sex, makes people do things they cannot later imagine having done."

Understanding the argument and accepting his failings, Robert issued a resolute sigh, slipped hands in pockets, took two steps, removed hands, placed them on the edge of the bar, leaned over, lowered his head, thought, and turned back around to Mr. Said; "Do you know any more at all about who is involved or what they are planning?"

"No" replied Mr. Said without emotion, "the leader was to be interrogated, however, a problem arose and he was eliminated before he and his people took the lives of most of my best crew."

It was a shocking thing to hear from somebody real, not like from a television actor, or in a theater, these were real people fighting to the death over money and loyalty without any consideration of involving police; it was a real world of which Robert knew very little and he simply stared at Malik Said until finally expressing awkward condolence.

VI DUPLICITY

"Sunspots!" yelled Swan descending the pilothouse stairs, "I thought there was a problem! The GPS was not working because of sunspots, flares on the sun, I just heard on the radio! We are lost! I told you so!" Swan's confirmation of a life-threatening emergency while at the same time boasting of his prowess as a seaman fell on unappreciative ears; Alwar's head shook and arms tossed up and down and from his mouth issued a deluge of inaudible French profanity.

"Do you know where we are?" asked Gatimu with an uncommon air of tranquility, perhaps the result of shock, gingerly touching his scalp.

"No" replied Swan, considerably less prideful, "it depends on how long the GPS was down, and that I do not know. It could have been minutes or it could have been hours."

Alwar resumed at least the appearance of self-control; "Your best guess, please, Swan, I know this isn't your fault. Based on the sun and the water, where to you estimate we are?"

Gatimu moved to sit on the gunwale, crossed his arms, and glared at Swan. Swan, the boat, rolled almost unnoticeably as long smooth swells passed under her hull.

Swan studied the vacuous sky and water horizon for several minutes in support of a theory: "I would say we have gone off course into the Atlantic, maybe fifty kilometers, maybe less, and based upon an average speed of maybe forty kilometers per hour, I would say we strayed off course a little over an hour ago. I also think we are maybe a hundred and fifty kilometers from Gibraltar and probably one hundred kilometers from Faro. I believe we are in the open ocean with very little fuel."

With his arms still crossed, Gatimu stayed silent so to permit Alwar undistracted pursuit of his more composed examination of the captain: "I take it from your answer that we do not have enough fuel to make it to Faro?" A quite perceptible frown contorted Swan's entire face and that, in combination with a single nod of his big head, confirmed the worst. "Then what, as captain, do you recommend?" continued Alwar.

The question dealt him again some authority – a single thread of control in a situation surely weaved from the uncontrollable – and Swan's frown dissipated, his proud head tilted back and his chest enlarged. "Let's see" began his oration, "there are two things that are of immediate concern. First, we do not want to drift farther out to sea; we are in the shipping lanes through the Strait, that is my belief, so I suggest we use just enough throttle to keep us where we are, point the bow toward Faro, and proceed very slowly, and hope that we get picked up by a passing vessel. There are many ships passing through the Strait. The second concern is water. We need to conserve what we have. There is not a problem now, but if we are here for days, well, you can see what I mean."

At his Gatimu finally exploded and bolting from the gunwale with arms flailing screamed "Days! We do not have days! We are supposed to be in Nice by the *one day* after tomorrow! If we are not there, it will not matter if we have survived being here lost at sea, we will not survive the punishment for having failed our mission!"

"There is another problem" Alwar calmly interjected, "most ships have to report passengers, they keep a log, and we most certainly would be reported."

"He's right" said Swan, "we would be fisherman, but they still would make a report."

"Who cares if they report?" interceded Gatimu; "Let them report; we are fishermen!"

Shaking his head, Alwar explained, "No, it is not that simple, they will tow our boat, the Swan, and take us to port, not the port we want, and there, we will be questioned and our boat searched. I know this. It happened to a friend; he spent a month in prison on Cape Verde."

Each person looked around, at the water, the sky, the deck, pacing or gripping the gunwale; Alwar, first to speak, affirmed the certain. "It is now too late to travel the planned route to Lagos and then Nice; we will never make it. So, as I see it, we have three options." He paused for a moment to consider exactly what they were. "If we can get to land quickly, maybe Faro or Gibraltar, we can still travel by car or train, if we are not detained. That is going to be a problem I am told. If we cannot travel by car or train, it will be necessary for us to go boat through the Strait and up the coast; and, if we can't do that, we will have to fly."

Swan glanced at Alwar and Gatimu, "All we need is fuel and water; I can take you to Nice. Of course, we would have to refuel and it is a long way, probably a thousand kilometers from here."

Alwar and Gatimu made quiet eye contact and in this very brief manner confirmed a mutual belief that any chance of arriving in Nice on schedule was minimal. Still, they must try. "Let's follow Swan's advice, motor toward Faro, slowly, and see what passes" suggested Alwar; "If it is a freighter, we show no trouble; if it is a yacht, we will have to decide. The goal is just to get fuel. Gatimu, do you agree?"

"Yes," he replied, "I better go make ready the weapons."

Swan fired the motor, applied a touch of throttle, and kept his eyes on the compass until the wooden hull pushed north through the water, moving very slowly and rocking side to side over the easterly current. Alwar and Gatimu took positions on either side of the deck, port and starboard along the transom, lookouts for any sign of voyagers. The late afternoon sun blazed white hot both from above and the water's surface. There was no escaping the heat. Alwar wrapped most of his head in a towel so that he appeared a pale ghost with sunglasses, while Gatimu pulled the back of his buttoned shirt over the top of his head, periodically removing the shirt entirely and letting it drift in the wake, adorning it thereafter as a makeshift parasol. The thought of thirst absorbed everyone's thoughts, yet no one said a word.

After an hour or so, Alwar shouted "Ship!" and quickly added, "It appears to be a freighter." Swan yelled back from the pilothouse, "Here, take the glasses, tell me if you can see a flag." Alwar hurried to the stairs and Swan handed down the binoculars. After studying the ship, Alwar announced his findings, "Liberian, I think, it's a long way off," lowered his arms and posed the question, "Why does it matter?"

"If they are Liberian registered," Swan again yelled from the pilothouse, "then they strictly follow the anti-piracy laws, which means, if we look suspicious, we will be reported."

"And if we just ask for fuel?" hollered Gatimu.

"They will mark our position and call the navy" responded Swan; "They will not lower a boat to bring us fuel."

They watched as the huge cargo carrier passed in the distance, and soon another, and after several hours, another, until the sun low on the horizon like a ball of fire immersed in water, eventually relinquished its radiance. "How much fuel is left?" Gatimu asked; "Very little" was Swan's reply. Alwar thought a silent prayer for which he felt some shame, for the prayer, if granted, would enable their voyage and their mission, allowing him to reap a ferocious vengeance for his sister's murder on some unsuspecting, possibly undeserving, victim.

More freighters and tankers passed in the gray until Swan from his high position captured the luminous silhouette of a sailboat with two masts and joyfully howled "Do either of you fishermen know how to sail!"

Alwar leaped to the stairs and partway up demanded, "What have you got?"

"A sailboat, a pretty good size one, probably from America," Swan gleefully replied, "and making a pretty good clip to pass in front of us."

"Can we intercept?" wondered Gatimu.

"Yes" assured Swan, "but to do so will take all our fuel."

"Can you reach them on the radio?" prodded Alwar.

"Maybe, maybe...."

"Go!" cried Gatimu; "Go, catch them, and also try to hail them!"

With his left hand Swan pushed forward on the throttle lever and the Swan's bow lifted from the sea as propellers churned and the stern dipped. "Mayday, mayday, mayday!" he called into the microphone in his right hand, the left firmly seized of the wheel, "Sailboat to our bow, this is the Swan, on your starboard, you are on course to pass and we are almost out of fuel, mayday, need assistance!" On he went until the two vessels were of one another, in easy view, yet no reply.

By this time, Alwar and Gatimu were also in the pilothouse, standing to the right of Swan, their hands tightly gripping a handhold positioned along the top frame of the windscreen. "Why isn't it slowing?" Gatimu demanded in anger. "It doesn't know we're in trouble" Swan answered with a guess; "They think we are just a fishing boat heading back to port with a large catch!"

"You will need to get their attention!" yelled Alwar.

"Go to the bow and wave your arms!" Swan roared; "But don't fall overboard!"

Alwar and Gatimu skittered down the stairs and trailed the railing and gunwale until standing at the pointed nose of the bow each held a line in one hand and with the other waved. Together, they yelled "Help!" Swan soon beheld a man onboard the schooner waving back with both arms as the yacht started to make a turn to port away from the Swan. Pulling back on the throttle, Swan lessened his boat's speed, the bow lowered, and the deck resumed a more level attitude. Three people could be seen standing on the schooner's deck.

"Ahoy, fishing boat to our starboard, do you read?" came a welcome sound from the Swan's marine radio; "This is the schooner *Enchantress*. You appear to be in some kind of trouble, please respond." Tight in his right fist the radio microphone; Swan squeezed and shouted. There was no reply. "Fishing boat to our starboard, are you receiving this message, awaiting your response." Swan cursed the radio and scrambled to find a square red cloth stowed for emergencies under his seat.

"Alwar, Gatimu, take this, quick!" he yelled while leaning over the side of the pilothouse and holding the cloth; "Go up front and hold this out so they can see!"

Gatimu dashed along the edge of the deck, grabbed the cloth, and in a few seconds he and Alwar were holding taught the red flag between them. In the distance they watched as one by one the schooner's sails dropped and, making a large loop, she motored to within twenty meters of the Swan. A man standing near the very back of the schooners' deck, wearing a baseball cap, jeans, and a white shirt with sleeves, bellowed "Hello there; do you have a radio?" "No!" yelled Swan from the pilothouse window; "I mean, we do, but it is broken; we are almost out of fuel; can you help?" The man shouted "We don't carry extra fuel. We can tow you to a port or call in your position; which do you prefer?" Alwar, Gatimu, and Swan exchanged furtive glances and in a low voice Alwar said to Swan, "Tow," a decision about which Gatimu nodded in agreement. "We think it best to be towed" replied Swan, "throw us a line!"

The Enchantress made another loop, motored closer alongside the Swan, and, as passing, a woman with yellow hair wearing shorts and a green bikini top tossed a line from the stern. Alwar caught the end of the rope, coiled it around a cleat, and shouted "Thank you!" Seeing the line rapidly losing slack the woman yelled back, "Is there anything else you require?" to which Alwar exclaimed "We may need water!" The woman held up her right hand to signal understanding by a circle of the index finger and thumb, turned, and walked along the edge of the deck until descending into a cabin.

The line snapped and, with a jolt, the Swan was in tow. Aboard the schooner three men worked to raise sails and after a short time the woman reappeared holding a bucket, hung it by a hook and pulley from the line, and gave a heave. The bucket rolled from light into dark and back into light until close enough that Alwar could lean over and snag the handle with a fishing gaff. Seeing the sparkling water, Alwar offered a loud "Thanks again!" with a smile and wave.

Gatimu discreetly motioned for Alwar to accompany him and the two moved to the stern where Swan waited, sitting on the deck under a lamp, legs spread, his grand belly like a bag half-filled with sand, resting against the gunwale content as if having completed a long day's work. "We need to talk" said Gatimu, with Alwar, seated on the other side of the deck facing Swan; "What port are they going to take us to, Swan?"

"We are going east to go through the Strait" answered Swan without hesitation, "they are not going to make a special trip to port this side of the Strait, so my guess is we are headed for Gibraltar, I don't think they would stop in Africa."

"What will happen to us in Gibraltar?" pressed Alwar.

"We will have to pass customs, the port authority will see us in tow, and we will need to be cleared to land and refuel." Swan shifted his weight to the left, his left hand planted against the deck for stability, his right stroking his scrubby black beard, "You have passports, no?"

"Yes..." answered Gatimu, "but they are African."

"And you are not on any lists are you?" Swan knew the delicacy of this question yet asked it in an almost condescending tone.

Alwar responded tartly, "We are fighters for the cause of good, for God, so of course, we are on lists!" for him, at least, a preemptory lie; "What of you, Swan, are you on any lists?"

Swan discontinued fiddling with the hair on his face and again sat upright to say "No, my friend, I am not on any lists as I do not have a passport, or for that matter, a name, or a number, or a document showing my birth." Alwar's and Gatimu's heads turned spontaneously to briefly evaluate the other's expression.

"What will you do in Gibraltar?" impatiently inquired Gatimu.

With his left hand Swan scratched the back of his sweaty neck. "I will not be in Gibraltar; I have not lived this long to be pulled to my finish by a boatful of Kens and Barbie's!" He roared with laughter. Alwar and Gatimu looked again at one another, neither knowing for sure the meaning behind Swan's reference to "Ken" and "Barbie," but knowing in Swan's other words some uncertain scheme certainly involving them.

As the big man's laughter subsided, Alwar and Gatimu pressed Swan for information, "How are you going to avoid the port authorities?"

"By taking the schooner" he replied matter-of-fact; "we will take the schooner as they sleep."

Alwar climbed to his feet and wordlessly peered for a time at Swan and Gatimu – both still seated on the deck into the other's eyes fixed in implicit agreement – until slowly turning to gaze into a black void above which a billion suns flickered. He knew this was coming. It was by design too easy; they would swim along the line to the schooner, go aboard, take the Americans hostage and force them to sail to a destination of their choosing. His prayer granted in greater perfection than he could have imagined, Alwar sighed, and in a few days the Enchantress will be located, adrift and lifeless. Those who had sown salvation would not also reap salvation.

"We need the crew" flimsily pleaded Alwar; "we can't sail the schooner."

"Of course!" belted Gatimu with a devious grin; "They will sail."

Swan suggested they ready weapons and rest until the moon's glow receded; they would seal the weapons in watertight bags and swim along the line to the schooner's stern, go aboard, and take the Americans hostage with such expediency as to prevent a distress call.

Gatimu enthusiastically agreed, adding that "if the cabin is locked, we will fire into the door until it opens; there will be no time to make demands."

"What if the door is steel?" Alwar maintained his plea; "Would not it make more sense to lure one of them out, we could loosen a sail, or do something, there has to be a better way than firing into the cabin."

Swan looked up, steadied his eyes on those of Alwar, and asserted in an agitated manner, "And while we are luring, if they hear footsteps, or get suspicious...do they have guns, are there other doors down below that could also be locked? If we are going to take the schooner, we do it as pirates, with force!"

Gatimu nodded in agreement and Alwar finally acquiesced,

"Yes, I see your point, I'm going to prepare my weapons and then go up front to lay down; I don't see that we will leave for another four hours or so."

In the cramped cabin below the pilothouse, Alwar removed the Beretta and ammunition from his duffel, worked the pistol's action, checked the nine-millimeter magazines, and placed both gun and ammunition in a gallon size plastic zippered bag retrieved from a cabinet. Next, from a side pocket inside the duffel he removed a large knife protected in a nylon sheath. He set the plastic bag and sheath on a table, reached back into the duffel, and pulled out a sleeve containing his passport, sixty-three francs and twenty Euros, which he also stuffed into the watertight bag. Last, he removed a Qu'ran from the duffel, held it for a moment in both hands, carefully replaced it and zipped the duffel.

Once ascended from the cabin, the plastic bag and knife hidden at his side, Alwar waved and bid a good night to Gatimu and Swan. Both simply nodded, however, in unfriendly reply. Sliding around the cabin by way of a narrow passage Alwar made his way to the tip of the bow, sat cross-legged, and stared meditatively beyond the dark where twenty meters ahead sailed the radiant Enchantress. About fifteen minutes passed; Alwar looked back over his shoulder at the cabin and lights beyond where, presumably, Gatimu and Swan remained.

Carefully slipping a beaded leather necklace over his head, pushing one end through a loop on the knife sheath, and pulling the other end through the necklace to secure the sheath, Alwar was able to slip the necklace back over his head so that the blade hung ready at his chest. He took several deep breaths, leaned toward the railing, grabbed the rope with his left hand and rolled over the side so that his body sank chest-high in the frigid water. Legs rubbed the Swan's hull. With a push and a kick Alwar was alone in the chilling black; it became then a matter of letting go of the line, grabbing the line, kicking, letting go, grabbing, kicking, over and over repeating the desperate process. A laborious and frightful effort it was indeed, one hand scarcely in grasp of the coiled fibers, another clenching the plastic bag as though life itself depended on it – and it did, at all times kicking furiously to maintain momentum.

When Alwar was five or six meters from the Swan he heard yelling from behind, stilled his legs, and turned his head; Gatimu and Swan were standing at the bow pointing and shouting. When Gatimu turned to run in the direction of the cabin even more adrenaline pumped through Alwar's arteries knowing what was to come. Kicking frantically, his body raised higher out of the water and he managed to fold his left arm over the line so that his weight focused at the elbow. Fingers of that hand reached the necklace, pulled, grasped the sheath, and seized the knife handle. Again by thrusting legs he was able to throw his right arm over the line so that the right shoulder supported his weight; in his right hand dangled a tightly-clutched bag, in his left, the knife, sawing desperately until twine frayed and split.

By himself, Alwar, in the vast dark Atlantic between two vessels, one sailing east, the other drifting west; two ropes floated into the emptiness; at the end of the faster rope, life, at the end of the slower, death. He felt a degree of terror that few people ever experience – as though suffocated by the sky itself; shock, hypothermia, unable to move, his face contorted with pain and despair. All but having given up, preparing for the end, in a flash through Alwar's body coursed an overwhelming peace and strength as though the angels were suddenly all around protecting and guiding him. Toward the vanishing lights of the schooner Alwar began to swim, a corner of the plastic bag clenched between his teeth, pulling through the water, long arm strides and steady deep leg kicks, remembering the swimming lessons as a boy, the races with friends in the ocean won.

Gatimu and Swan's recourse was limited to standing helpless at the Swan's stern, yelling and cursing, firing bullets only to have them splash somewhere far out of view. Their craft, no longer a boat, but a powerless timber adrift at the mercy of the sea; batteries soon to extinguish with the drinking water; the only hope another yacht to pirate before drifting into the Canary Current running south along West Africa. "I will kill him!" screamed Gatimu; "We will kill him!" assured Swan. Both could only wait in miserable dread as bolts of lightning east confirmed the distant threshold of ocean and sky.

Each breath of Alwar required considerable effort.   Teeth clenching the plastic bag he was able to breathe only through his nose, water flooded his lungs – coughing, heart racing straining to deliver oxygen to fatigued muscles, his thoughts were only of the frayed thin line floating somewhere ahead. Long arms reached and large hands pulled and Alwar's body moved steadily through the saltwater. Occasionally, he looked up, each time finding the lights closer, and so by faith endured.

Swimming hard for over a hundred meters Alwar could see the Enchantress within about ten meters; exhausted, he groped at the water searching for rope – kicking, flapping his arms, watching as the schooner seemed more and more the impossible end. It was just at stamina's end he saw arms and hands and water and, raising his eyes, a blinding light. Soon a life preserver splashed within arm's reach and following a few long minutes he was aboard the Enchantress, wrapped in a towel, sitting on a bench, shaking, gasping, choking, coughing, and between all, laughing.

"What were you doing out there?" excitedly asked the man who had hauled Alwar aboard; "What happened to your boat?"

Alwar raised his head and after wiping his mouth and nose with a corner of the towel, answered between deep breaths and coughs, "I left the boat...they were going to board you...kill you...I cut the rope...," given to a spasm of coughing Alwar's head bowed and he said no more.

"Why? Why were they going to do that?" the man demanded.

With his head still lowered, coughing and breathing hard, Alwar tried to explain, "They are terrorists; I am not one of them; I couldn't let them do it." Looking up at the man he said "Thank you, thank you for saving my life; now, who is in charge on this boat, is it you? I will need to talk with this man."

The man stepped back and for a moment his eyes narrowed, studying this stranger from the sea, until leaving for the cabin and taking with him the plastic bag. He soon returned, still carrying the bag, this time in the company of the yellow-haired woman wearing sweatpants and a sweatshirt. "Hi there, we meet again, my name is Silvia," she reached with her right hand and Alwar took hold with his right hand long enough to convey deep appreciation and, upon releasing, said that "It is nice to again see you; my name is Alwar, I am from Gabon, are you the captain?"

"I am him" answered Silvia with a smile; "You'll have to excuse me, I was asleep when Simon knocked on my door and said we have a problem, do we have a problem, Mr. Alwar?"

"I'm afraid so, madam captain" replied Alwar, "you see, the people with me in the fishing boat, they are criminals, terrorists actually, and they are going to France. Our boat, their boat, ran out of fuel. They were going to board your boat tonight, when you slept, and take you hostage. I went overboard and cut the line."

Silvia returned only a blank stare for what to Alwar seemed an uncomfortably long delay, in her own time saying "I of course, don't know what to think; I mean, you could be the criminal; after all, you are carrying a gun, and I see a knife."

Alwar's head shook repeatedly. "No, in the bag is my passport, you can radio in, check me out, see if I am wanted; I am working with British Intelligence."

Silvia gestured to Simon and he handed her the plastic bag; "You realize everything in here is soaked" she said while removing the leather sleeve and pouring saltwater onto the deck. "We will check you out in the morning; in the meantime, Simon and Tony will take shifts watching you. Simon, please take him below, to the empty cabin, give him some clothes and food, the head, a shower, then put him in the cabin and let him rest. I'll have Tony stand guard first with a Glock."

As Silvia was leaving Alwar gently stopped her, "There's something else...," her head turned to desperate eyes, "they will come after us if they can, they no longer trust me, and I must get to Nice before them."

"We are on our way to Cannes" Silvia countered in a tone certainly of suspicion; "Simon, try to reach the Spanish Navy and give them an alert; just tell them there is a fishing boat without power and give them our location." She looked at Alwar, "Isn't there somebody you want to call? Don't you people take care of one another?" paused for just a second, "We can drop you in Gibraltar" and turned again to leave.

"No!" Alwar quickly adjusted the tone from demanding to beseeching; "You don't understand, I am undercover, I know that sounds crazy...there may be one person I can reach, please, in the morning, for now, we must move quickly, and not stop in Gibraltar."

Silvia's appearance went from puzzled to skeptical leaving Alwar in the care of Simon; by that time, three other people were on deck, a man and two women, watching as Simon helped Alwar along the deck, past a dark wood dining table and eight chairs, to a steel cabin door, down stairs and through a sumptuous galley and dining area fitted in mahogany, teak, and brass. Alwar inquired as to the schooner's length and Simon replied "The Enchantress is about thirty-five meters – one hundred and five feet." After that, in a passageway approached another man carrying a handgun directed to the floor; he introduced himself as Tony, patted Alwar on the right arm with his free hand, and kindly said "You've had quite a night, sleep well."

Alwar smiled and nodded in appreciation, afterward thinking that "Pirating this vessel would have been no easy task."

Morning unfolded in a world of perfection for Alwar; first, being alive, and more, a ray of sunlight through a porthole on his face, then enjoying a shower followed by a breakfast of fried eggs and sourdough toast, and finally stepping on deck to hear the sound of the sails rippling taught in a firm breeze and above seeing the white billows confirm a brisk pace toward some other destination. Never had he been on such a vessel, crisp and clean, the crew jubilant and efficient, the captain a woman, and smiling; he wished that it were not a dream, that it was real, his life, exotic ports of call awaiting, the only dangers from above and below, not those inflicted by the deeds of man. For a long while, several minutes at least, Alwar stood on the bow of the Enchantress, out of the crew's way, giving silent thanks for the miracle that was his life.

"Quite a view isn't it?" Simon's voice from behind obviously caused Alwar surprise, "I'm sorry, Alwar, I shouldn't have snuck up on you." Alwar exercised restraint with a smile, "It's okay; I was just admiring the day." Simon understood. "I know, every day I'm out here, free, doing this instead of what I used to do, I'm thankful." Alwar was considering the meaning behind "instead of what I used to do" when Simon explained the reason for his visit, "Silvia wants to see you – she's waiting in the galley." They strolled together to the cabin entrance where Simon with a frown announced that he was off to clean the bilge.

Silvia was seated at the dining table drinking coffee and studying a map when Alwar entered the salon. She said "good morning," invited him to sit, which he did, and promptly got down to business: "We are just an hour or so from the Strait – Gibraltar right around the corner – and I need to know, why do you need to get to Nice, why don't you want let off in Spain, and why can't you call someone?"

Alwar, after a brief delay, decided to provide a truthful explanation, "Terrorists killed my sister in December. I agreed to help the British Intelligence Service find out about a terrorist mission. I infiltrated the cell, but I don't know what they are going to do, I don't know who is involved, and I won't be able to stop it. There is a meeting in Nice and I may be able to find something out, if, I get there, before the people I left behind."

Studying Alwar, staring across the room while sipping coffee, pretending to study the map, again studying Alwar, Silvia finally said "Okay; I'm going to take a chance. We have all of your passport information. We are going to go on to Nice, drop you off, and give you your papers and gun. I am going to give you eight hours in Nice before I call the authorities and tell them you are there." Without revealing emotion, Alwar observed Silvia as she talked, her eyes, her profile, and to him she spoke wisely. "If you are who you say you are you will have no problem; if you are in Nice for some other purpose, revenge for example, you will have eight hours. Now, we need to talk about your friends."

Admiration of Silvia's leadership impelled Alwar's respectful, yet cautionary, advice: "If you called the Spanish Navy" – "Which I did" interrupted Silvia – "then they, Gatimu and Swan, Swan does not have any documents, maybe they gave them fuel, unless Swan or Gatimu is wanted somewhere, I just don't know. They could be following us; they could be traveling by land. I just don't know. The important thing is, we keep a lookout, remain vigilant...they have many weapons."

Silvia focused on the map, "Maybe we should report them as criminals and try to have them picked up, if they aren't already locked up somewhere."

"I don't think we can" Alwar theorized; "they really haven't done anything, yet."

After removing a thin round tin of lip balm from her shirt pocket, dabbing it with the little finger of her right hand, spreading it on her lips and rubbing them together, Silvia considered asking Alwar if he wanted some but decided not, again studied the map, tapped the coffee cup with the index finger of her left hand, and finally said "We also are well-armed, as you may have guessed, I will post a lookout."

"If you don't mind my asking," Alwar tactfully inquired, "what are you doing out here?"

Silvia started to leave the table but stopped to explain that they were "going to Cannes, the film fest, to pick up the owner of this boat and his guests; I already cleared it with him to take you to Nice."

Alwar smiled. Waiting in the booth until after Silvia climbed the stairs he slowly slid from the leather cushion, poured water from the sink into a blue plastic drinking cup, and climbed to the deck with the intention of maintaining a constant watchful vigil at the stern. He had not wanted to frighten Silvia but, having spent time with Gatimu and Swan, Alwar believed their resourcefulness would eventually enable pursuit and, if he was right, very little time would pass until the Enchantress showered in grenades. In advance of taking up a position at the stern, Alwar made his way to the bow and, finding Tony trimming the foresails, asked if he could borrow a pair of binoculars; "Sure" obliged Tony, "take a look in the cabinets next to the aft wheel."

Alwar, stepping back around the aft cabin, found four waist-high teak cabinets on either side of the wheel. Bending over, kneeling, unlatching and opening the first door, he could see only the rolled edges of paper protruding from wooden squares which he assumed were charts. Among various other items scattered in the second cabinet – an old compass, twine, sunscreen, nautical books – Alwar could see a plastic bag and, examining closer, recognized his Beretta and the cartridge magazines.

He carefully withdrew the bag from the cabinet using both hands, noticed holes in the corner undoubtedly, he thought, in the pattern of his teeth, slid open the seal and removed the pistol. Squeezing the grip in his right hand, Alwar considered sticking the gun under his shirt, but upon a moment's reflection placed it back in the sealed bag and into the cabinet. From the third cabinet he retrieved a pair of Nikon marine binoculars, hung them from his neck, closed the door and relaxed into a swivel fishing chair with an unobstructed view off the stern.

A woman announced her presence, "Approaching from behind!" to the back of Alwar's head after he had spent several hours gazing at open water through dark glasses and telescopic lenses. He swiveled to find curly red hair wafting from a straw hat over rose-colored oval sunglasses with hands carrying a sandwich, pickle, potato chips, and plastic water glass on a pink plastic tray. "Lunch time, Mr. Mermaid!" announced the mouth under the sunglasses; Alwar started to stand but the woman insisted "No, sit, eat!" and handed him the tray.

"Thank you" returned Alwar modestly, "this looks wonderful."

"If you need anything else, give a holler, I'm Dee!" Alwar introduced himself and Dee quipped, "We call you Mr. Mermaid," with a giggle vanishing into the cabin. Alwar laughed also and with both hands lifted the sandwich, but not seeing anything between two slices of brown bread he peeled back a corner and spent some time puzzling over the mixture of brown sticky paste and red spotted jelly.

When the only objects remaining on the pink tray were an empty water glass and pickle, Alwar got out of his chair to return the tray, took a step, and rebounded to locate the source of a very faint murmur in the distance. He set the tray on the chair, lifted his binoculars, and studied the image of a large fast boat closing from the northwest, estimating her distance at five to ten kilometers. Remaining motionless, Alwar continued his visual examination of the approaching vessel in conjunction with an evaluation of several possible scenarios: no connection to Gatimu and Swan, the Swan in tow with Gatimu and Swan aboard the Swan, or Gatimu and Swan onboard the towing craft. The problem with all but the first scenario, he surmised, was that, that yacht would soon overtake the Enchantress.

Alwar lowered the binoculars, turned his head slightly to one side, and yelled "Boat, approaching fast from four o'clock!" Not immediately hearing an acknowledgment he formed a cone of hands around his lips, twisted his neck, and bellowed the warning.

Silvia jogged to the stern; "What do you have? Do you think there's a problem?"

"A yacht" Alwar replied, the large binoculars again covering his eyes, "a big one, and fast, heading in our direction."

Silvia reached out her right hand, "Let me see," and Alwar handed her the glasses; "I can't tell if anything is in tow, they're moving awfully fast, they wouldn't just leave your boat out there, it could be nothing, I mean, there are plenty of boats through the Strait every day, your guys could be in jail in Portugal for all we know...besides, what can we do?"

What *could* they do pondered Alwar; "Nothing, really, just keep watch and maybe get some weapons on deck." Silvia agreed, handed him the binoculars, and left to prepare the crew. In a minute, everyone was standing around the aft cabin, watching and waiting, not disappointed as the immense dark blue and white motor yacht passed within an eighth kilometer of the Enchantress.

Alwar strained to take in as much as possible through the lenses, as did Silvia with another pair, and also Tony; the yacht's name, *Splendeur*, probably about sixty to eighty meters overall, four decks visible, including an aft heliport deck supporting a four-person helicopter with folded wings draped in canvas. Alwar squinted. There were people on the bridge deck; not breathing he scrutinized each person when suddenly another person stepped into focus, a large man with black wavy hair and a black beard – Swan?

"Silvia, you need to call that captain and find out if they took on any passengers," Alwar dropped the binoculars to his chest and looked at Silvia, "I may see one from the fishing boat, be discreet though, we don't want them if they are onboard to get nervous."

Silvia asked somebody on deck, anybody, to raise the Splendeur's captain, and a man Alwar had never met accepted the task. The man darted for the forward cabin and swiftly reappeared to announce "The captain's on the radio." Enchantress protocol, per Silvia, prohibited the crew from ever referencing a captain by gender, a remnant of retained frustration from her days in the navy, but passing the man on the way to the cabin she asked anyway. "He's a man," the man replied. Alwar maintained watch with the binoculars as more and more distant became the yacht. Finally, Silvia returned.

"They didn't pick up any passengers" she said, "but they did hear over the radio that the Portuguese Navy found the fishing boat last night with no one aboard."

Letting the binoculars hang and assuming a more relaxed demeanor, Alwar began to speculate, "Did he say whether the boat was upright, had been damaged, maybe a freak wave?"

"You mean the captain?" said Sylvia with a teasing smile; answering Alwar's question, "It sounded to me like it was adrift, like they had abandoned her."

"I overheard your mate say a man...," Alwar felt childish offering a response to the jab but did so anyway; "it really looked like this man Swan on deck, on the bridge; did the captain sound right to you?"

Silvia thought about the question, and in so doing, her expression morphed from one of confidence, to one of vulnerability, experiencing the sinking feeling one has when understanding comes too late. "He sounded okay to me," she hesitated in what Alwar could tell was a retraction, "but, he did say something I thought was strange...." Alwar's neck tensed for the impending revelation. "He said he really liked our genoa; we're not running a genoa, it's a regular jib."

It took some time for Alwar to exhibit any reaction as the Jubilet did not have a genoa; "He probably just doesn't know the difference."

"He did;" Silvia looked down for just an instant, "he said he really admired the Enchantress, he said he used to own a small schooner and liked how they maneuvered in a high wind. He made a special point of mentioning the headsail; in fact, now that I think about it, he said he really liked to run a genoa."

She paused, but intentionally not long enough for Alwar to speak, turned to the man who raised the yacht on the radio, and said "Mo, please get the laptop for me; before going any further let's see what there is on this Splendeur." Alwar nodded; "Good idea."

The computer was set up on the aft deck dining table and within a few long minutes Silvia accessed the satellite internet system to finally read aloud information about the mysterious yacht: "Let's see...captain Henry 'Doc' Gibson, yep, he said his name was Henry but everyone called him Doc...one hundred ninety-five feet...crew of fifteen...passenger quarters for twenty...built by Searium Shipyards in two thousand eight...recently bought by Paul DuMorell...DigiFouré Telecom, never heard of 'em...ninety-eight million dollars, wow!"

Silvia looked up from the screen, "Do you really think your two terrorists could take a yacht with passengers and a crew of fifteen?"

"They just need to take one person, the person who is most important," replied Alwar solemnly, "the captain, or the owner."

"Shit" whispered Silvia to herself, and, for his part Alwar could only wonder "How did I get involved in a hostage mess again?"

Silvia perked as she regained confidence – captain of a magnificent schooner commanding "Mo, get me the Splendeur's captain again!"

To this directive, though, Alwar contested, "No! No! You mustn't call them, don't do anything; let's think about his for a minute. We don't know for sure they're on that boat, that's our first problem; two, if they are on there, these men will kill hostages, they will not be taken alive."

"Well, we can't just do nothing!" cried Silvia.

"Yes, we can" Alwar retorted, "this isn't your problem, it's mine, remember, we don't know for sure...."

"Your problem!" Silvia's temper ignited; "This isn't just your problem, this is basic seamanship, they could kill somebody, we do something, even if it's not perfect, we just don't go about our business and ignore it! We alert the navy – they can stop her, go on board, that's the least we can do."

Silvia had neither the experience to understand nor the disposition to absorb what Alwar long since had learned: desperate people with nothing to lose and everything to gain exercise no mercy. If Gatimu and Swan were on that yacht, reasoned Alwar, it meant there was some purpose, some advantage larger, more important than stopping him and the Enchantress. Cornered, heavily armed, Gatimu and Swan would sooner kill hostages trying to escape than surrender. Whether or not the hostages lived, the pirates would receive indefinite captivity, or death.

Alwar had been witness to this unwavering eventuality more than once as a member of the Nigerian Special Boat Service. The first time, negotiating for three days and finally delivering a ransom, only to load the decomposing corpses of slain oil workers into a flatbed truck while his commanding officer repeated the phrase "Hostages almost always die, there's nothing we could have done, it wasn't our fault." To Alwar, it was their fault, and the odor never left his memory.

"Listen to me, please," Alwar appealed to Silvia as Dee, Mo, Tony, and Simon silently looked on; "these are terrorists we are dealing with; they will kill everyone before being captured, I know this for a fact; and I don't know what they are doing, there's more to this, much more." He paused with head bowed as all on the aft deck observed; lifting his eyes to help underscore what he hoped was a very calm and rational request. "You are with me and that means you are dealing with the authorities; let me call someone, you may of course be present during the conversation."

Catching a quick glimpse of her tense crew, Silvia replied "Okay, we'll try your way first, I'll pull up Skype and get the headphone, the rest of you, back to work!" Alwar informed Silvia that he would need to retrieve the telephone number, went to the second cabinet next to the wheel and returned with the plastic bag. Silvia flashed a curious look and dashed below deck to find a headset. Upon returning she asked Alwar if he knew how to use a computer. "Yes, of course" he replied; "Have you used Skype?"; "Yes, yes, we have computers in Africa!"

Alwar slid the moist leather sleeve from the bag and with two fingers explored tight crannies until removing the business card: Freeland Export Company. Taking a chair, he positioned the headset, typed in the number, and clicked "call." After some delay a man with an English accent answered, very businesslike, and Alwar returned the greeting with "Hello, can you hear me?" The man replied that he could. "Good," continued Alwar, "Is Mr. Crane there?" "May I say who's calling?" replied Thomas; "Jubilet Fishing Company" answered Alwar, "tell him we've some good snapper from the Mediterranean." "Please hold" replied Thomas. The hold was not long at all; "This is Michael."

Alwar, somewhat nervous, spoke softly into the microphone, "Yes, hello, um, do you know who this is?"

"Yes, I believe so, didn't we meet somewhere, it's been quite a while, I can't remember where...," Michael wanted some confirmation the man on the line was indeed Alwar.

"We did meet, Mr. Crane, aboard the fishing boat, Jubilet, you came to buy some fish and I said that I was headed to the waters off Morocco, where we catch the big grouper."

Silvia maintained a half grin at being party to a spy monologue.

While Michael's grin, on the other hand, was quite broad; "Yes, now I recall, it must have been a long voyage, are you well?"

"Yes" answered Alwar, more relaxed, "but there is a problem. We have lost the school as it moves east through the

Mediterranean and the boat I am on is too slow...it is a nice boat, a good fishing boat, but we cannot catch the school, and I'm afraid they will get away."

Michael pondered for a moment the meaning behind Alwar's improvised yet clever code; was Alwar in some kind of present danger, using code for protection, or trying unnecessarily and ineffectively to protect him? "I see" responded Michael, "would you like a faster boat?"

Alwar shook his head, "No, that won't work, I will need flown to the fish" and sighed in some embarrassment at the sound of his request.

Michael understood, it would have to be arranged, "That's fine, give me your coordinates, we can be there in two hours."

Alwar glanced up at Silvia and whispered "I need our coordinates." She rushed to the wheel and back, and holding a yellow sticky note said "thirty-six point one two zero by minus two point two eight five." Alwar handed Silvia the headset, "Please tell him," and she repeated the coordinates into the microphone. "Did you get that?" Alwar asked Michael; "Yes," he replied, "what type of boat?" "It's a large schooner" replied Alwar, "and we are heading east." "What is the name, your radio handle?" Alwar asked Silvia and repeated for Michael her response, "svenchantressrifourtwoseven." "Be there shortly." With those words the call ended and Alwar removed the headset and stood from the chair.

Silvia, understandably impatient, probed Alwar for details: "So, what now? Are they coming?" Alwar explained that somebody he did not know would come by air, how, he did not know, but in some fashion he would soon be departing the Enchantress. "Should we drop the sails?" asked Silvia; "No, they will find us" assured Alwar. The two talked a while longer, to a point that Silvia declared a need to resume her duties as captain, and Alwar, to resume his duties at watch.

Settling back into the swivel chair, Alwar hoped to soon have his own toothbrush and clothes; he also thought about the Enchantress and her crew, especially Silvia, and how they would be missed, and how foreseeably hard would be the unforeseeable road ahead. After waiting restlessly for half an hour, in and out of the swivel chair staring through binoculars, Alwar heard footsteps and turned to see Dee a few feet away. "Well, Mr. Mermaid" she popped, "it looks like your spaceship is almost here! Silvia told me to tell you that a helicopter will be here in about fifteen minutes and she wants you to go up front for a 'debriefing,' as they say in your business." Snickering, Dee pivoted and strode around the cabin, leaving Alwar smiling and shaking his head.

In the forward galley Silvia leaned against a counter with arms crossed and a partially-full orange Fanta bottle in one hand, deep in thought, occasionally moving the bottle to her lips, staring at nothing.

Alwar stepped down the last stair and into the room – "You wanted to see me?"

Without moving Silvia answered "Yes" after a short pause; hesitating again as Alwar stood quietly at the bottom of the stairs. "Your people will be here in a few minutes. We're to put you in the dinghy and let it out a hundred feet or so; they're coming in a helicopter. I guess they're going to drop you a line...," she took a drink of soda and continued, "I think it's a crazy idea. The wind from the rotors will tear our sails so I'm having them taken down. How well do you know these people?"

Alwar's head jilted slightly, his chin lowered and eyes narrowed, "I do not know them, why?"

"Um, I mean," tact was not Silvia's strongest suit, "they are just going to fly out here, and you're going to be sitting all alone like a fish in a barrel...I would want to know them."

Alwar thought about what Silvia was saying and wished that she had never said it, "I see your point, but who else could it be?"

Silvia just looked his way, drank more soda, and shook her head, "I don't know, I guess that's the point."

With time running short, Alwar questioned Silvia about her radio conversation with the pilot – "All he said was he had orders to pick you up and take you wherever you wanted to go" – and decided to do as instructed rather than risk more delay trying to reach Michael.

Simon and Tony lowered a backup rowboat tender, threw down a ladder, and helped as Alwar climbed down. Slowly, Tony released line and the small wooden boat drifted and skimmed the surface as Alwar paddled long deep strokes. After some distance, Tony waved, Alwar stopped paddling, and the dinghy came to rest motionless but for the rolling movement of the sea. An eerie calm rattled Alwar's nerves. In the silence, alone, memories all too fresh of near drowning, he was glad to finally hear a faint buzz growing louder and deeper by the second and to see from the east a tiny airborne object continually enlarge.

Within three hundred meters of the rowboat a white helicopter came to hover and, when it did, Alwar cautiously edged close to one side of the tender and waved his arms. The helicopter dropped precipitously and gradually flew toward Alwar until not more than twenty meters away. The sea churned. Alwar and those aboard Enchantress squinted and those with hats held them tight. Alwar lowered his arms. He felt a tingle at the back of his neck and carefully moved his right hand to grasp the edge of the rowboat. Why wasn't the helicopter overhead, he puzzled, and why hadn't they dropped a rope?

Suddenly, the rotors tilted, and Alwar beheld for a split second eyes he recognized. When a blinding reflection took their place Alwar rolled to his right headfirst to the water; a deafening whistle, head submersing, a tremendous concussion, over the side – life's end. A painful blast of steam and he was quickly proved wrong however; Alwar burst into air clinging to the dinghy rocking violently in a sea of fire. "What happened – where is the helicopter?" Desperately searching for answers he focused on Enchantress and saw, at her stern, Simon, one arm waving, the other balancing a shoulder-fired missile launcher.

Tony and Simon tugged on the dinghy line, dragging Alwar to safety, and once again he was climbing aboard Enchantress having narrowly avoided certain death only through the efforts of her crew. Alwar offered more praise; perplexed, words jumbled and incoherent, the meaning nonetheless certain and clear to all around. Silvia ushered him to the aft deck dining table, asked somebody to bring a glass of water, and remarked with a mischievous wink "You really should avoid the water."

Alwar laughed loud and long, thanked Dee for the water, and questioned Silvia.

"I had Simon load the launcher with a rocket and stay down" Silvia nonchalantly answered; "then we saw the helicopter coming from the east, and through the glasses we could see it was small, so we figured it came from Splendeur. Your people would have come in from the north, maybe the south, but probably the north, and it would have taken them longer to arrive from land. When you dove into the water Simon knew there was a problem and fired. End of story; except now we know for sure that your terrorists are on the yacht!"

"One of them now" Alwar said glumly, "the other was inside the helicopter, the passenger. Why do you have a missile launcher? How did they know? What about my airlift?"

Silvia started off by saying "the pilot coming to get you probably confirmed or called the tower with a frequency available to Splendeur – they were probably listening," suggested there was no reason to believe the evacuation would not occur as planned, and finally talked about Enchantress and her crew. "The owner is Israeli. He lives part of the year in New York, part of the year in Israel. His main business is investing, and he produces films, which is why he's in Cannes, and because the world is the way it is, he tends to shall we say, exercise an abundance of caution. Most of us here are former members of the Israel Defense Force and most are former security services. Now, you need to get ready to leave again, this time hopefully with less fanfare!"

They both smiled. Alwar extended his right hand and Silvia took hold with her right hand. Words were no longer necessary.

A short while later, Tony yelled "Airplane from the north!" and within several minutes a white seaplane landed and taxied to within ten meters of the Enchantress. Alwar shook hands with Simon and Tony, and Mo, hugged Dee and Silvia, and climbed down a ladder back into the dinghy for a brisk row to the waiting transport. Circling overhead, Alwar waved what he believed to be a final goodbye on his way to Nice.

Knocking on the third floor apartment door for the sixth time that day, a tall white man with short dark hair wearing dingy jeans and a red pull-over shirt grew steadily angrier with each pound of his fist. Behind him, two men, one African and the other Arabian, surveyed a wide vista to assure they were not drawing attention; but as the knock became a pound, each thump accompanied by shouting, the Egyptian downstairs could take no more. He slipped on sandals, climbed the stairs, and cynically examined the three strangers; "He's not home."

"Do you know when he'll be back?" the white man's inquisition was really more of a demand.

"No; I am the owner and I have not seen him or heard him for several days" answered the Egyptian, "so, there is really no point standing here, trying to knock down the door."

The Arab interceded, "One of the men living here is my brother and I need to find him...," but the white man interrupted: "What do mean *him*, there are four people living here, right?"

The Egyptian took a deep breath and first answered the white man's question, "There were two – I would certainly not rent to four – and, of the two, I have not seen one for weeks"; directing his attention to the Arab, "Which one is your brother, what's his name?" The Arab answered "Ali," to which the Egyptian offered some hope, "He is the one that has been here, but, as I said, now he is gone."

Exchanging glances, mumbling appreciation, descending stairs, the three very unhappy travelers afterward paced the streets of Nice discussing a contingency plan. They were far from home and without much money. If Raymond, Ali, or the other two did not soon return to their apartment the white man and his accomplices would, they agreed, carry out the mission and keep all the reward. But first, they had to eat.

"We will break into the apartment" exclaimed the white man.

"What about the landlord?" asked the African; "And what if the apartment is wired?" asked the Arab.

It was therefore also agreed that they would not attempt a forced entry; they would instead try to find a sympathetic restaurateur.

The seaplane landed at the Port of Nice and taxied to a ramp late that afternoon. Alwar thanked the pilot for an interesting ride and pleasant conversation, the donation of five hundred Euros, and a French visa, and otherwise disembarked the plane empty-handed. The Beretta and ammunition were holstered at his chest under Simon's loose-fitting light blue Crew button-down shirt and the passport, visa, and money were tucked into a tight front pocket of Moshe's favorite worn Levi 501 jeans. A customs agent stopped him at the end of the pier. Alwar displayed his passport and visa without incident and ventured into the heart of the city with just the vague memory of an "X" penned on a map unfurled over a bonnet under the blazing Saharan sun.

Alwar knew that it would be almost impossible to find the apartment, so he focused on an alternative strategy, finding the people he and Gatimu were to meet, even perhaps finding Ali – before Gatimu arrived on the yacht. While such a task sounded, at best, daunting, especially in an unknown city, Alwar remained confident. He had known people that would kill for glory, or worse, and he understood their mentality. He pictured their faces, clothes, body types, demeanor, and needs; these were the type of people he was used to picking out of a crowd. If his first strategy did not quickly produce results it meant that his subjects were not in the city or remained sequestered in the apartment and, in that case, he would wait for Splendeur.

Middle Eastern restaurants and coffee houses were Alwar's first priority, and a tourist map led him on a tour of one such establishment after another and after another, until after two hours he had exhausted resources within the central business district of Nice. He considered for a moment mosques and churches but concluded the people he sought were not of faith, their god, instead, money. Strolling along the Rue de Congrés toward the beach, the air crisp and moist, Alwar decided to relax and get something to eat at a café along Promenade de Anglais.

The yacht would not arrive for at least several hours, so he found a quaint bistro with outdoor seating, ordered tea, and studied the menu.

With a server hovering over the table, pen in hand, and an order of greatly anticipated fried calamari on his lips, Alwar, by happenstance, glanced across the Promenade to the boardwalk and a young man very much resembling Ali. The man's hands were in his pockets, the head drooped, the gate a lethargic westerly shuffle seemingly to nowhere. Alwar looked up at the server and optimistically excused himself, "I'll be right back," jumped to his feet and ran across the sidewalk, waited for an opening in traffic, ran across three lanes, waited, ran across four more lanes to the boardwalk and assuming a steady pace strolled about thirty-meters behind the man. If this man was indeed Ali, identified too soon was the last thing Alwar desired.

The young man seemed to Alwar deep in thought, depressed actually, meandering around and through people without much heed until at a bench adjacent the Promenade apparently deciding to sit. Alwar froze and pivoted the opposite direction – the man was Ali. No way to get nearer without risking notice; all Alwar could do was continue walking as inconspicuously as possible and so he did.

It was not until Alwar was less than twenty meters from the bench that Ali glanced over and recognized one of the men he had set up for a violent demise in the desert. The young man sprung to his feet and ran headlong into traffic with Alwar close on his heels. Tires screeching, horns blaring, drivers yelling, Ali darted between cars, over hoods, stopping only when to do otherwise seemed suicidal; and the faster Alwar gave chase, sometimes having to wait as drivers not realizing he was in pursuit once again accelerated while others behind slammed on brakes.

Reaching the sidewalk, Ali paused, searching both directions for an exit he arbitrarily dashed west, but, seeing Alwar on the sidewalk, burst instead through the first available doors – the main entrance to the Museum of Modern and Contemporary Art. He plowed past screaming guards to the gallery where the attention of visitors all around drew from colorful and abstract spectacles to the fracas created by a frantic Arab man pushing his way through the crowd followed close at hand by frantic security guards followed in turn by a frantic African man.

The spectators did not have time to panic as Ali, realizing that to stay in the museum meant certain entrapment, turned and bolted past the guards. Thrashing arms to avoid seizure he passed also Alwar and the two charged through doors onto the sidewalk. Ali sprinted west to a corner and up the Rue Massenet. When he started to cut across a parking lot, however, a grappling force crippled his legs and he tumbled forward onto asphalt with Alwar sliding across his back.

From his own somewhat softer asphalt landing, Alwar pounced on the wounded Ali, grabbing his right arm and demanding "Get up! We have to get out of here! Come on, move!" Ali, in substantial pain nevertheless understood the exigency, lifted quickly to his feet, and, with Alwar tugging on his arm began running.

"Listen" Alwar yelled as they ran, "I'm not here to hurt you; we must get to the apartment – where is it!" Ali looked a pitiful sight with pants and shirt torn, knees and elbows bleeding, the left cheek scraped red, and running awkwardly with a limp in Alwar's firm grasp he knew not what to think. Alwar continued shouting: "Listen, Ali, if I would have wanted to kill you, you would be dead! We have to get to the apartment!"

Ali responded between heavy breaths: "It is the other way...but it is not safe...."

"Go! It is safer than out here!" Alwar broke in, "How far is it?"

Ali made a ninety degree turn. Alwar released his grip and the two ran down an alley, across a street, down another alley, up a hill and round a corner until ten minutes later stopping at the foot of a stairway. "Here!" Ali exclaimed while bent over, sweating, panting and coughing. Alwar grabbed Ali by the arm and hoisted him up one stair at a time, "Which one?" "Third floor" replied Ali, near collapse, making it only with considerable assistance to the top of the stairs. Once there he informed Alwar that several days earlier he hid the door key in a crack of a nearby tree limb. So bending and pushing branches and leaves, listening as Ali instructed "the other one" or "not that one," Alwar finally located the correct bough and after poking around in a tight fissure and receiving several splinters was able to grasp and withdraw the brass key.

Flipping a light switch as they entered the apartment, Alwar gazed in stunned disbelief at the weapons storeroom that once was a simple one-room apartment. Ali stopped gasping for a second to reiterate in a bated cadence "You see...it is not safe to stay here." Alwar, glancing Ali's way, placed hands on boxes filled with explosives, rifles, rocket launchers...; "Great mother of wonders, where did you get all this?"

"Everywhere" answered Ali after catching his breath, "some came from around here, some from Paris; I think some even came from Spain, maybe the Basques."

Alwar shook his head, went to a kitchen sink and drank from the faucet, wiped his mouth, and told Ali they needed to talk; "I know you gave Raymond and the rest of us away; I need to know who you are working for. I will not hurt you unless you do not tell me."

Ali stared blankly at Alwar and after a moment his head began rhythmically moving back and forth; "No, they will kill me" he replied.

Alwar considered pulling out the Beretta and threatening to shoot Ali, but decided wisely to pursue a different tact with this young Arab obviously on the verge of a complete emotional breakdown. "I, too, am working undercover, Ali, and I need your help. Now, you apparently aren't in agreement with what is going on here. We have very little time before someone else shows up at this apartment. Gatimu, do you remember Gatimu? He will be here very soon, and he is not nice, like me. I am working for British intelligence. Please...."

"Am I going to prison?" Ali interrupted.

"No" answered Alwar calmly, "I have no interest in you; I just want to stop what looks to me like certain carnage. If you help, you will not be in my report."

Ali paced a narrow stretch of carpet between crates and furniture; "How will you protect me, and it is not just me, how will you protect anybody who provides information or needs help?"

For his role in the dismal truth, Alwar apologized, "I don't know, I will do my best, but I don't know"; for Ali's part in the same truth, Alwar chastised, "Do you have a choice Ali? I know you, you cannot help them now, if you do, I will find you, and if not me, the people I work for; the only way for a long life is to see that the people here are stopped, the ones who are planning this evil act."

"I need some time to think" replied Ali; no longer pacing he sat on the floor, head in hands, leaning against a crate of assault rifles, "I just want to go home."

Alwar, exasperated and running out of time, rubbed his face and knelt in front of Ali. "We all want to go home, Ali," his words were forgiving and compassionate, "but now, we must be strong, we must be men, and do what is necessary; then, we go home proud, not as hyenas cowering in the shadows, but as men, worthy of respect."

Motionless, head down, ashamed to look at Alwar, Ali crouched in hiding as tears welled behind closed eyelids; but overcoming fear and doubt he mustered the fortitude to again lift his head and look into the eyes of one quite possibly his only earthly chance for salvation. "I never wanted this;" Ali's lips quivered with each barely audible word, "I wanted to do good things, I wanted to be a fighter for freedom." From a quiver, to a frown, tears trickled from Ali's eyes as Alwar reached out and with both hands grabbed the young man's hands. "They told me this was a holy cause, and stupid me, I believed them!"

At the juncture of despair and shame resides anger; each enraged syllable uttered next by Ali met Alwar's ears in a high and shaky pitch. "But *this*, these people fighting this cause, this is killing, just killing, there isn't anything else! We bring in guns and bombs, there aren't any books or food or medicine, it is all for money, no good purpose to make our people free!" Months of fear and loneliness surfaced, overcoming Ali, who, with head again low broke down as Alwar clenched both his hands; the older, more experienced warrior unable to wipe his own wet eyes in remembrance of Abeo and a life of joy so long ago.

Alwar, allowing only a brief emotional indulgence, arose, and in so doing pulled Ali upright; "Get up! The time for childish ways is over; we now must make things right! Go over to the sink and wash your face. Our story must be good. Go!" Ali wiped his face with a shirt sleeve, went to the kitchen sink and splashed cool water on his face, and had to wipe his face with the other sleeve.

"Who are you working for?" Alwar demanded.

"His name is Malik Said" replied Ali continuing with both arms to draw sleeves across his brow; "I have not met him. I work with a girl who works for him and her name is Hamidah...."

At that instant the first thump of an unrelenting series on the apartment door hushed Ali. Alwar placed his right index finger to his lips and in a whisper instructed Ali to remove his shirt and answer the door by cracking it open only slightly. Ali was to pretend to have been asleep and roused awake by the knocking; he was to tap the inside of the door one time if the visitor was someone he knew and twice if not. Ali hurriedly unbuttoned his shirt while from under his own shirt Alwar withdrew the Beretta and ducked into the bathroom.

Quietly the deadbolt receded and slowly the doorknob twisted; with his right hand and foot positioned against the wood panels Ali pulled the door only just slightly until recognizing the Egyptian. Ali's part played to no avail. "So, you're back" sarcastically pronounced the Egyptian, "what was all that noise, it sounded like you were screaming!" Ali maintained the groggy-eyed appearance of a young man startled from a deep slumber and in theatrics such as rubbing his eyes and clearing his throat rebuffed the landlord's inquisition. "I...don't know, maybe I had a bad dream...sometimes I do, people have said I sometimes talk loudly in my sleep." The Egyptian's head tilted and he seemed with undue consideration to scrutinize Ali; "I think I should take a look." Ali resisted, "For what purpose? I have been sleeping, now leave!"

The Egyptian placed his right hand near the front edge of the door, leaned in, and shoved, trying to catch a glimpse inside the dark apartment. But the chain and Ali restricted any view so he stepped back and leveled an extremely poorly-timed threat: "If you do not let me in, I will call the police!" For several seconds Ali considered the Egyptian's stern expression, the contracted eyelids, furled brow, pursed lips, but still unsure how to respond he tapped with a knuckle twice on the door.

From outside down the staircase, however, came the grim retort.

"You have no idea what a dumb thing that was to say" remarked the white man as he and the two other men ascended from the second floor landing. The Egyptian's stance changed from aggressive to meek; the three men with the white man in the lead neared the third floor landing; Alwar sprinted across the room to the door hinges, holding the Beretta near his head, the barrel pointed toward the ceiling; the white man peered into the narrow opening, saw Ali, and into the dark behind him yelled "Raymond, are you in there?"

Positioned in ready hiding behind the door, Alwar responded, "Yes, I'm here, who are you, who is with you?"

The Egyptian, hoping to disappear, started for the stairs but the white man thrust a strong hand to his chest and advised "Don't even *think* about screaming" and the Arab and African looked menacingly into the Egyptian's eyes and with their husky bodies blocked the exit.

"Raymond" said the white man, "my name is Ty, there are three of us; I've been sent by a mutual friend. Let us in."

Alwar remained motionless while considering mostly bad scenarios foreseeable perhaps only to him, signaled with his left hand for Ali to release the chain, and, still holding the Beretta high, stepped away from the door. "Come in Ty" he said, "just you."

As Ty stepped into the apartment Ali behind him closed and bolted the door. Ty's eyes had not yet adjusted to the dark when Alwar demanded "Tell me the name of your mission!" Ty squinted to perceive the source of such bluster and did not immediately answer, so Alwar issued an ultimatum, "The name of the mission, *now,* or I will act under the assumption you are an imposter!"

Ty's head tilted back defiantly: "Poisoned Paradise."

"That is wrong!" cried Alwar, playing a hunch, and stepping forward allowed Ty to view the outline of Alwar's facial features and the Beretta's iron muzzle mere centimeters from the left side of his head.

Upon seeing this Ty wasted no time in issuing a retraction: "'Illusion of splendor' – the mission is called illusion of splendor!"

Alwar lowered the Beretta; "That's better, now, what are we going to do with the landlord?" A question for which Alwar knew Ty's answer, and not disappointed, he proposed a milder solution; "He's already scared and he hasn't seen in here, have your men take him to his apartment and bind him well, he will not go anywhere." Ty failed to comprehend the logic, "Why not just take him to his apartment and slit his throat?" An answer sensible to people who routinely murder the innocent, there was not, so Alwar mustered the tone of an angry commandant and simply ordered the Egyptian bound and gagged. His life would be in the hands of the Almighty; that was the best he could do.

Ali flipped the light switch and Ty gazed around the apartment with an apparent astonishment that Alwar found of peculiar interest, prior to redirecting Ty's attention, "Let's get down to business, we need to go over the plan and make preparations."

"Where're the others?" asked Ty.

Alwar thought for a second and realized he must mean Gatimu and Izem; "Gatimu's aboard the Splendeur...," but with those words it hit Alwar like the rush of a cobra's venom – Illusion of splendor, Splendeur!

"He's already on board?" Ty sounded more than mildly perplexed.

"Yes," Alwar quickly improvised, "we were outside Gibraltar and they passed, fortuitous really, we claimed distress and Gatimu and Izem were able to board...." Upon telling the lie, however, Alwar foresaw the infinite follow-up queries so tried to dull their significance: "Swan also boarded, they took the yacht, I took the

Swan into Gibraltar, and the train here."

Meaningful dialogue failed Ty attempting to fathom how three men – even if professionals armed to the teeth – could overtake the crew and passengers of a super yacht on the high seas. The only sentence he was able to articulate, "Where are they?"

While explaining that Splendeur would be in port that evening and that they were all to board her and carry out the mission, Alwar's deception encountered interruption in the form of a tap on the apartment door that he politely request Ali to investigate. After peering through the narrow opening Ali shut the door, slid the security chain insert from its track, opened the door and with a slight bob of the head invited the two men to enter. After the door was again locked, Alwar questioned the men as he believed well might have Raymond, "Did you do as I asked?"

The African glanced at the Arab and responded sheepishly, "We tried, but he fought, hard."

"It was the Egyptian's day to die" thought Alwar sadly; "Alright then, sit down; we are discussing the mission ahead."

The two men did not sit, instead, remained awkwardly rigid and silent until the more talkative of the two, the African, again spoke: "He was Egyptian, from Cairo, in the end very brave and strong...." Alwar looked up at the talkative man, outwardly perplexed by the man's odd elucidation, inwardly concerned by his own waning authority. "He said Raymond had been gone for some time," Alwar began strategizing the fastest way to access the Beretta, "and he said that you," Alwar held the man's downward gaze without moving, "do not have a voice like Raymond."

Alwar jumped to his feet; "Imbeciles! You would listen to the ravings of a dying man! Do you know nothing; he would say anything! Now, sit!"

The talkative man and the quiet man were not, unfortunately, intimidated by Alwar's aggression and the talkative man looked straight into Ali's eyes as he stood very close and asked "Is this man Raymond?"

Ali did not shout "Of course!" but hesitated, for just a split second, a delay sufficient to drive Alwar desperately for his gun and the talkative man and the quiet man desperately for Alwar. To the carpet all three crashed. In a matter of only seconds the fates had changed: Alwar, face pinned flat against the filthy fibers with three large men applying their full weight to his back, Ali, standing by helplessly dumfounded.

Ty leaped and in Ali's face cast a slobbering rage: "How long have you known...why didn't you say anything, are you with him, who is he!"

In a voice shaking and soft Ali pleaded for his young life: "He held me hostage, his name is Alwar, that's all I know, there was nothing I could do, I was waiting for the right moment...."

Ty instructed the talkative man and the quiet man to lift Alwar and when they did, Ty beat him with fists, repeatedly striking his head and stomach until he hung limp in the abductors' arms; "Take him to the Egyptian's apartment and finish the job" Ty commanded.

"Wait!" Ali's voice resounded and the three men surprised to hear Ali speak, let alone intercede, paid him a curious momentary attention; "He traveled with Gatimu, he betrayed Gatimu, Gatimu will want that honor!"

The talkative man was first to respond by agreeing "He is right, I have heard of this Gatimu, if this man did that to him, he will want the privilege of killing him, and, knowing of Gatimu's reputation, it will be very unpleasant."

Ty looked at the floor and shook his head, "Okay" he acquiesced reluctantly, "find some rope, tie him well, over in the corner, we'll wait for Gatimu unless he gives us any trouble, if he does, I'll kill him"; to Ali he inquired further, "Do you know where Raymond and Gatimu, also the other one, are?"

"No" answered the deceiving Ali.

"We'll wait until tomorrow" Ty instructed his two accomplices, "and if they're not here by this time tomorrow, we'll go to Monte-Carlo and find the yacht; and tie this one too – Ali – I don't trust him. We'll give this Gatimu two for the price of one!"

VII RAPTURE

Hamidah basked in moonlight on the veranda overlooking Monte-Carlo and the Mediterranean Sea; an evening perfect for the gold-tone long sleeve sweater she put on early that morning in Dubai. From near and far lights sparkled and, below, a brilliant roadway turned racetrack with bleachers and concessions to accommodate international race fans and celebrities attending the Formula One Grand-Prix. She held her arms extended like the wings of a floating gull and inhaled a deep breath, smiled, took in the coast, and thought about Ali. It had been several weeks since his call warning of Walter Kragen's avengers traveling through the desert. The snake's head, Raymond, had been eliminated but the snake's body still held the capacity to inject deadly venom. She feared an impending storm and prayed for Ali's safety.

Occupying the four-room apartment adjacent Hamidah's suite, Stephen Waters, his wife, and their teenage son and daughter, making for a situation of some discomfort for Hamidah. She was, in reality, required to attend the event with Mr. Waters and his family, ostensibly for her benefit, or at least so represented, more so a result of Mr. Waters' growing infatuation with his exotically beautiful young assistant. Hamidah had for weeks rebuffed his advances though surely not as forcefully as she could; knowing she harbored no romantic interest but always leaving cunningly apparent the possibility as a form of leveraged job security. It was fear, fear that to curb her boss's romantic appetite might mean the end of her career at Worldwide Investment Bank.

The sudden music of unconstrained glee disrupted Hamidah's tangled train of thought – "It's beautiful!" and turning with a smile she saw Rebecca Waters standing alone against the outer wall of her apartment terrace. The young woman had not noticed Hamidah in the dark, observing with amazement how far life moves in a span of less than ten years, from innocence and untainted optimism to experience and manipulated compromise. After a few seconds Hamidah turned with the intention of stepping into her suite, to avoid disturbing Rebecca's moment, but heard "Hamidah? Hi! I didn't see you out here!"

The words caused her to pause at the threshold, look toward Rebecca, turn to face the ocean and react in her usual relaxing manner. "Yes, like you, I was admiring the view, beautiful, is it not?" Hamidah crossed her arms and peered motionless into the dark as Rebecca quickly shifted to the wall separating the terraces. "Are you excited for the race, and the yacht?" she asked.

Hamidah looked toward the voice but saw only the girl's shadowy features, "Yes, it will be nice, and you?"

Rebecca smiled and twice nodded her head; "I'm glad you're along. We're almost the same age, well, *almost* anyway!" The word "almost" sounded to Hamidah like a bird's chirp and she considered the irony of Rebecca's contemporaneous playful flip of long blonde hair while continuing with "and I hope we can be friends!"

"Of course we are friends, it will be fun!" Hamidah's enthusiasm was tempered by cognizance of the mildly mendacious relationship with Rebecca's father, making her unexpectedly uneasy, "Now, if you do not mind, I am going to go freshen up for dinner." Rebecca cheerfully concurred and each departed her own almost-private outdoors.

Stephen Waters had weeks earlier made dinner reservations for five at a charming family-owned Italian restaurant only several blocks from their accommodations. It was one of his favorites. The Waters family and Hamidah chatted while strolling along Monte-Carlo walkways dividing lawns and gardens, down narrow roads adjacent swanky stores, through an open door and into a cozy dining room where a man wearing a blue jacket and open collar white shirt bid the patriarch a patron's welcome. Guided were the diners to a round candlelit table in the back; the owner held a chair for Stephanie Waters and Stephen held a chair for Hamidah, which left for him only a chair between the two women. If Stephanie Waters harbored any reservations about the nature of her husband's interest in Hamidah, it was a concern well concealed, at least in public or the presence of her children.

The repast delicious, the wine splendid, the conversation pleasant, all too quickly their evening out concluded with the Waters family and Hamidah adjourning again to separate quarters.

Not very long afterward, however, a knock on the connecting door to Hamidah's suite interrupted a spat of titillating French television and, following a needless inquiry as to the visitor's identity, the door opened for Stephen Waters. "I just wanted to check in on you and make sure everything was okay" he said while stepping into the room uninvited.

"Thank you, everything is fine" Hamidah replied, "I was just about to get ready for bed."

Stephen stared at Hamidah a bit longer than was possible not to notice and she asked if he wanted anything; "No, no, I was just...wishing" but she disrupted his wine-enhanced advance, "It is late, Stephen...," and with a roguish smile he reluctantly withdrew to his apartment.

Sex, a vision of lustful passionate intimacy engulfed the flat screen, so much so, that Hamidah caught herself fixated on the images and breathing clearly harder than usual. She promptly turned off the tuner and engaged a hasty retreat to the closet where, slipping out of her dress, thoughts of Stephen Waters' desire mingled with stark images of a lover's seductive embrace. Hamidah longed for love; the right kind of love, vanquishing loneliness wrought by years devoted fleeing the trappings of ordinary poverty. In the floor-length mirrors lining the inside of both closet doors she studied her reflection, the smooth almond skin and solid round breasts under a translucent web of lace, the firm stomach, long toned legs; a waste, she thought, if not soon admired by one other than herself. She imagined only one man: Ali.

The birds of morning serenade for all regardless of station or circumstance. So it was that Wednesday. Robert, Sandra, and Gilbert awakened in a magnificent Riviera villa de facto prisoners of Malik Said and Walter Kragen; Hamidah awoke in a feather bed overlooking the harbor of Monte-Carlo in economic bondage to Stephen Waters; Alwar and Ali's eyes opened to armed guards in an unlit dingy one room munitions storehouse in Nice; and Paul DuMorell listened to a lone tern from the bridge deck of a magnificent yacht where his wife and children were captives of a madman named Gatimu. The song from above is one of joy rooted in simple freedom, resonating for many, much too late.

At almost seventy meters in length and over twelve meters in width, Splendeur was indeed an extraordinary vessel; six decks with four visible above the hull, an owner's stateroom over fifty meters square spanning the entire beam with a sitting area, his and her dressing rooms, and a private enclosed terrace overlooking the bow, seven guest staterooms, accommodations for a crew of fifteen, an exhaustive state of the art electronics and navigation system including night vision technology and an anchored stabilization system, two lifts servicing all decks, a custom nine-meter twin jet diesel main tender, three other tenders, a helideck, and, until quite recently, a new four-passenger single engine Eurocopter. As her name unabashedly implied, Splendeur was a sumptuous palace of luxuries and amenities unsurpassed on sea or land.

Two men with assault rifles subdued the crew and passengers in less than three minutes. Binding and taping explosive charges to Paul DuMorell's wife and twin eight-year-old sons effectively negated any subsequent thoughts of resistance. Splendeur was Gatimu's.

Hamidah stepped out to her terrace at just after seven to enjoy a cup of tea and immediately noticed a large blue and white boat near the horizon. Of the many ships, yachts, motorboats and sailboats dotting the Mediterranean, this vessel captured her attention, not only because of its size, because of its architecture. She continued to the outer terrace wall and spent some time admiring the design until the bustle below redirected her focus. After a couple of minutes, Stephanie Waters strolled out onto the adjacent terrace.

"Good morning," Hamidah tactfully announced her presence.

"Oh! Good morning Hamidah, I didn't see you!" Stephanie reacted with more zeal than Hamidah would have expected; "A beautiful morning, I see, how long have you been up?"

Hamidah moved to the white plaster waist-high wall of concrete separating the terraces; "Not long, actually, I just came out here to admire the view. How did you sleep?"

"Miserable" replied Stephanie with a laugh, "you?"

"Fine, that is, fine once I finally got to sleep," Hamidah smiled, "as is my usual routine."

Stephanie's brief silence in conjunction with a slight bob of the head and tilt of the eyebrows conveyed sufficient empathy from which to broach a new subject. "Anything interesting out here?" she asked while walking to the outer edge of the terrace. Placing her hands on top of the wall, she leaned over the edge just far enough to look straight down.

Hamidah from over the edge of her terrace did the same, "They are getting ready for tomorrow."

After admiring the meandering race course bordered by rows of seats and vendors, Stephanie gazed intently at the deep blue ocean, "Yes, it's going to be an interesting next few days; I guess we should be hearing from our host soon."

"I wonder if that's him out there;" Hamidah pointed with her right index finger to beyond the harbor and the slew of surrounding boats, "you see that big blue and white yacht?"

Stephanie visually identified the boat and studied it for just long enough to warrant an impromptu exclamation, "Wow! You could be right, that's some ship...," after which with a quick head pivot summoning her husband, "Honey; are you dressed? Come out here for a second and tell us if this ship belongs to that business friend of yours."

Stephen promptly strolled onto the terrace wearing red boxer shorts and a white t-shirt, in his right hand a small white porcelain cup, in his left a pair of binoculars. "These were on a shelf," noticing Hamidah, "Good morning, Hamidah, I didn't know you were out here," to which she responded congenially with a smile and deflecting glance.

After placing his cup on the wall, Stephen asked "Where is it," looked through the binocular viewfinder, and slowly moved his head until by adjusting a dial was focused on the yacht. "Wow!" He turned the dial another degree to better define the image; "Let's see...Splendeur, yep, that's her, damn, that thing is huge!"

Hamidah and Stephanie kept watch on the boat as Stephen continued his appraisal: "They must be waiting for a spot to open up; I don't think she's moving, and I can't tell who's on deck. I suppose we'll get a call." Lowering the binoculars he continued staring at the shape, muttered "Amazing what you can buy with other people's money," and dashed – in belated modesty – for the interior.

Malik Said from a high position on the back lawn of Villa Palmera also admired Splendeur; but staring through a pair of low power opera glasses, scarcely able to see passengers or crew, his face evidenced growing unease. "Why had there been no communication from the captain and why was the yacht at rest so far from port?" he wondered. Under these circumstances, he concluded, there needed to be some investigation starting with a call to the yacht. The sound of shoes brushing over new-mowed grass delayed implementation of Mr. Said's strategic vision, however, as from his right approached Klaus.

"The boat is out there" stated Malik Said in a voice devoid of surprise or emotion; "do you wish to see?"

Klaus took the glasses and after some difficulty finally located the yacht; "Yes, I'll bet that's her, what's she doing?"

"I don't know" answered Mr. Said, "and that's the problem. DuMorell should have called by now. We're supposed to go aboard this evening for a party. Why would they just sit out there?"

"They're probably waiting for a spot" proposed Klaus, still looking through the glasses, "I mean for God's sake, it's the bloody Queen Mary!"

Mr. Said shook his head – unseen yet nevertheless perceived by Klaus – in staunch dissent; "They would have made arrangements. Something's wrong. Let's try to get them on the radio or a cell phone." With that in mind, making hasty passage for the villa library Mr. Said left Klaus alone on the lawn peering through the lenses, also furtively confident to be witness of some malevolent force. He lowered the glasses and ran to catch up with Mr. Said. By the time they reached the library Klaus had time to remind the old warrior that, of all persons deceitful, the one with a gun to his head is most convincing.

Once seated comfortably in the library Mr. Said regained perspective, "We have a problem, Klaus, if there is a problem on Splendeur. We cannot let anything happen to DuMorell." Thinking for a brief moment longer he added "What did you find out from that kid, Ali?"

"He doesn't know anything" replied Klaus as though the lack of information was irrelevant common knowledge, "He's been kept in the dark, and I can see why, this isn't his game."

"Did you go to the apartment?" inquired Mr. Said.

"No" answered Klaus, "there was no need."

"You weren't curious?"

"No, not really, there would be guns and such, I mean, we could blow up the apartment but you and I both know there would be more."

Malik Said stood up and began pacing in front of the bar, one way, the other way, back, forth, eventually methodically working through his dilemma aloud; "I don't see any reason to go on board, other than to protect my investment, and the fact I do not intend to start or spend the rest of my life doing something I heretofore have not done – run. If they don't know we suspect...I believe we need to advise Robert and Gilbert of the problem, the potential problem, would you agree?"

Klaus mulled the suggestion as his left hand rubbed slowly across lips and came to rest supporting the chin; "I suppose if you want them on our side, if they are on our side, but then they are of course, useless."

At the slight upward motion of Mr. Said's head Klaus strolled to the dining room where he found Robert and Gilbert with forks picking food out of dishes on the table and discussing racehorses. "Secretariat" said one, "No doubt about it" concurred the other; nibbling betwixt on sausages and strawberries. Drawing their attention – but only after indulging a second hearty link from an embroidered white napkin – Klaus led the two men into the study and once there instructed Gilbert to close the door. Following several minutes of pleasantry and small talk, Mr. Said addressed the reason for their meeting; "Klaus and I believe there may be some trouble with Paul DuMorell," Klaus wiped grease from his lips and smiled, "so, if we go on board the yacht you will need to be prepared."

Robert and Gilbert looked to one another and evincing mutual concern stepped back in unintended unison to sit on a dark red sofa with gold rope fringe. Without either having a chance to say a word, Mr. Said continued, "That means you may need to defend yourselves, or someone else, and are going to need guns if you know how to use one...."

Gilbert lifted his right hand as though attending a sporting goods class on survival techniques and asked "Why are we not simply calling the authorities; I mean, there is a shore patrol."

"Good question!" Klaus exclaimed, running interference for Mr. Said from a roost alongside the bar; "That's a good question, and the answer is, first, we don't know for sure if there is a problem, and second, if there is a problem, it is a bad problem, and many people will be hurt if the marines storm the boat."

"But they have negotiators" responded Gilbert with some excitement, "and snipers, this is their job, this is what they do!"

Robert tapped Gilbert's left shoulder in anticipation of Klaus' or Mr. Said's hardened response to Gilbert's revelation, and looking calmly into the young man's eyes provided learned enlightenment, "Terrorist kidnappers, Gilbert, kill everyone if it appears they will not achieve their objective, and the French at least claim not to negotiate with terrorists."

"And" added Klaus, "neither do we."

Mr. Said abruptly preempted Gilbert's next anticipated diversion: "You do not have to do this, you may of course simply go home; this is not your fight."

Gilbert looked to Robert for guidance and he accommodated, "Take Sandy and leave; go back to Paris." "What will I tell her?" responded Gilbert; "Tell her it's not safe, but don't tell her anything else" countered Robert. Gilbert's nod signaled sad acquiescence for a man on his way to the top in the company of a beautiful woman and he assented with "Okay, than I will do that" in a most forlorn manner.

Upon rising from the couch, Gilbert requested permission to be excused and, once granted, departed for the dining room and prospect of an unpleasant letdown. As he was just about to turn the door handle, however, Malik Said called to him, "Why don't you and Sandra stay here, at Villa Palmera, and enjoy yourselves for a few days?"   Gilbert stopped, released the handle and turned around; assured the reaction of others in the room, foremost Robert, was positive, he responded as a man at the last minute delivered from a hangman's noose: "Yes that would be fine, there really isn't any reason to go back now and maybe we can be of some help here. Thank you. I'll tell Sandy."

As the library door latched behind Gilbert, Klaus tilted upright, having been propped against the bar, and in wanting to tidy loose ends declared "As I see it, we should be getting a call within the next several hours, and likely they will send a tender...."

"What about Michelle?" Robert interrupted; "She's not going is she?"

"That" rejoined Klaus with his eyebrows raised, "was what I was about to say. They will send a tender, and if it is just the three of us, just men, it's going to look a bit strange, don't you think?"

Robert lifted from the dark red sofa, slid hands into trouser pockets and walked to a window; "Why would it look strange?" he asked passively without really expecting an answer, "We can't take her, obviously."

Malik Said made his way to the same window and stood next to Robert; "She is in my employ Robert, she is not a guest; she understands the job has certain, shall we say, risks, and she is a very capable woman. If we need her, she will go, and we need her."

"And don't fall into the trap of worrying about her" Klaus added firmly; "you need to worry about you. Michelle can take care of herself, I know from experience...." The words dissipated in a smirk twisting Klaus' lips recalling a face plant on the tarmac in

Frankfurt a year earlier and a left cheek that remained red for three days.

"What if they don't call?" Robert's final and most thoughtless question prompted Mr. Said to cast a glare toward Klaus leaving no room for interpretation other than "What a stupid question."

At ten-fifteen that morning a faint tap on the apartment door prompted Ty to hold the muzzle of a newly-discovered Ruger semiautomatic forty-five caliber pistol against Ali's temple and insist "Not one word, either of you." The quiet man gently tiptoed to the door and asked "Who is it?" and, from outside, a voice sounding very much like that of a teenage boy answered "My name is Jerome, I'm from Splendeur, Gatimu sent me." The quiet man turned seeking direction from Ty, opened the door very slightly, reached, and pulled into the room a pale-faced blonde deck hand wearing white shorts and a damp, blue golf shirt.

To relatively innocent eyes emerged a terrifying scene.

"Well, don't just stand there" charged Ty; "What does he want?" Removing the gun from Ali's head he stepped toward Jerome with the barrel pointed to the floor. In a trembling voice the young man replied "He wants you to come with me." Ty stared at Jerome, evaluating his demeanor, and asked why Gatimu sent him instead of coming. "I don't know" he replied softly, "I mean, it's just him." Ty continued staring and after a moment asked "Why did you come, why didn't you run when you had the chance?"

It was soon apparent to all in the room that Jerome was shaking uncontrollably; "He's got Mrs. DuMorell and the kids tied, with bombs, he said if I'm not back by noon, with you, he'll blow up everyone, the yacht and everyone. He said if he saw any police, he would blow it up. You really need to come with me!"

Ty shook his head and sighed. First to the talkative man and the quiet man he instructed "Load as many guns and explosives as possible in bags, everybody will carry a bag and these two" – gestured toward Alwar and Ali – "will carry two bags with the kid in front." Finally glaring at Jerome he warned, "If there is any sign of trouble, we will kill you and them. Do you understand?"

Jerome's wide eyes bestowed a "Yes."

Over the next ten minutes, Ty, the talkative man, and the quiet man stuffed handguns, assault rifles, ammunition, trinitrotoluene – TNT, timers and caps into eight large canvas and nylon bags. "What about the rest of the stuff" asked the talkative man; "We're going to incinerate it" answered Ty, "it will also be a nice diversion as we walk through town."

At hearing this Alwar could no longer remain silent: "There are people living here in this building, children and women; if you're going to blow up the apartment, at least warn the other tenants!"

Ty zipped the last bag of weapons, examined the room, and advised Alwar not to worry as "any good diversion needs heroes."

When the quiet man finished removing rope and tape from around the captives' wrists and ankles, and hauling each man upright to wobbling legs, Ty instructed his men and Jerome to pick up a heavy bag and Alwar and Ali to each grab two. Then he got very close to Alwar and Ali and in a very menacing way advised that any sudden movement by either would mean certain death for them as well as Jerome. With that said, five men one by one stepped into the sunlight: Jerome in the lead down the stairs followed closely by Ali, Alwar, the talkative man and the quiet man.

Ty remained in the apartment with the door open long enough for the others to descend the stairs, and struck a match, lit the corner of a box and the corner of another box, struck another match and lit the corner of another box, struck another match and held it under fabric hanging from beneath the couch, and bolted through the door and down the stairs yelling "Fire!" Upon seeing this, Alwar, Ali, Jerome, and their captors began also screaming "Fire, feu!" so that when Ty reached the ground all six were running from the building yelling "Feu!" or "Fire!" as the first columns of smoke drifted out the doorway.

Along the side of a busy road in Nice marched an odd assortment of suspicious characters toting heavy duffels in a line formation, while in the distance men, women, children, some in the grasp of others, rushed down a fire escape as smoke billowed from a third floor apartment window. Alwar and Ali kept looking back.

Ty would say "Turn around," but every few seconds, one or both turned anyway, hoping to see the stairs vacant as a sign that all tenants made it safely to the ground.

There expectantly yet still shockingly came a thunderous explosion of such force that the ground shook under the men's feet almost a kilometer from the building. Everyone turned to see the top floor completely gone and flames erupting from every shattered orifice. "Don't worry" Ty counseled without emotion; "they had time." Alwar and Ali were by this vote of optimism of many things, including that, not so sure.

Traffic cops and passersby paid the men curious heed but toward them expended no further effort as smoke wafted in plumes from a hill above and sirens wailed in the background. Fifteen minutes later, the six were at the harbor with Jerome leading them along the docks to the sleek tender, *Lightning Dancer*, left in the care of a scraggy gray-mane fuel attendant. The old man rendered a quizzical expression as Jerome handed him a hundred Euro note while nervously uttering "merci" – sounding more like "mercy" – and climbing into a boat loaded with five unpleasant-looking men embracing eight large duffel bags. The fuel charge was only thirty-two Euros. Jerome turned a key and the twin three hundred horsepower jet engines growled, and purred, deep and mournful.

Lightning Dancer cruised nicely through the harbor until falling behind powerboats and sailboats at the mouth, making for a tense several minutes waiting as a large ketch hoisted sails. Finally, breaking into open sea, Jerome pushed on the throttle and the mournful purr became a shrill roar as passengers toppled like two rows of dominos to the deck. "Sorry!" he yelled above the jets, "But we need to hurry!" Alwar shuffled to his feet and peered over the side down an imaginary line from Lightning Dancer at one point to Splendeur at the far point; the mother ship loomed as a magnificent blue behemoth and, most assuredly under the control of Gatimu, his tomb.

Ty also leaned over the side to gauge Lightning Dancer's course and his hair flattened back – the laden hull still skipping over swells at almost sixty knots. Reeling, face and shirt soaked in saltwater, he exuberantly exclaimed "That looks like one hell of a ride!"

For the next six minutes five passengers sat quietly on cushioned benches and secured chairs thinking about what was inevitably to come. Ty wondered if he would like Gatimu or if Gatimu would like him, the talkative man thought about what he would do with the money, the quiet man thought about his wife and children back in Saudi Arabia, and Alwar, Ali, and Jerome simply prayed. All too soon, for some, the engines' pitch and the bow lowered; above the windscreen and Jerome's head could be seen the upper decks of the great yacht.

Jerome waved high into the air and a gray-haired man on the main deck waved back. Drawing the throttle lever, Lightning Dancer instantly decelerated; turning the wheel, the tender moved gingerly along the starboard side of the yacht. After careful maneuvering at the stern, lines were secured, and Ty stepped aboard Splendeur.

From the rear main deck the gray-haired man and another younger man solemnly observed the event. Ty first commanded the talkative man to disembark and the quiet man to pass to him the duffel bags. Once all eight bags were carefully stacked on the aft loading deck, and after instructing Jerome to come aboard and bring the keys, Ty ordered aboard Alwar, Ali, and last, the quiet man.

The gray-haired man loudly asked "Which one of you is Ali?" Ali looked at the others and softly replied "I am Ali," to which in a much warmer tone, clearly one of sympathy, the gray-haired man advised "You're to come with me; the rest of you, are to wait here."

Ali at that moment felt as though he was going to be sick and one of his legs buckled and Alwar standing next to the young man reached out with his left hand – unnoticed by the others – and squeezed Ali's right arm below the elbow, hard, as if to say "This is your moment, do yourself proud!" The legs regained rigidity and the back straightened and taking a deep breath Ali climbed each one of the loading deck stairs, so that behind the gray-haired man he soon vanished from Alwar's sight.

"I wonder what that's all about," Ty voiced curiosity; "they must be friends, this Gatimu and that Ali."

Alwar, saying nothing, flashed only a glance of despise.

Crossing an expanse of teak and stepping down a flight of white stairs with mahogany railing and traversing a long hallway with many doors, the gray-haired man with Ali at his back, reaching the end of the hall and an ornate double-door entry, paused, took a deep breath, and firmly pounded a brass knocker. From right behind the door Ali heard Gatimu gruffly ask "What?" The gray-haired man spoke into the door without emotion, "I have Ali." Bolts receded, a door handle twisted, and Gatimu peered through a crevice at Ali; "Send him in." With a look to Ali the gray-haired man expressed sorrow and regret, but into his eyes, Ali, no longer afraid, returned courage and forgiveness.

Passing the threshold into Gatimu's lair, Ali wished with all his heart for an opportunity to look into the eyes of young Izem whose merciless death he caused in the vast Atlantic, and beg forgiveness; but that, in this life, would never be. This life, this day, he faced a different man, a man alive in spite, a man without mercy whose forgiveness Ali would cast-off as surely would a dying man his wretched pain.

"Ali!" Gatimu cried out; "It is so nice to see you!" The gold teeth shimmered as Ali stood with his back to the closed door and his lips held tight trying not to inhale Gatimu's rotten breath. "Come in and join the party my young foolish traitor!" Gatimu stepped aside so Ali could see a woman and two children, their arms bound in yellow rope and gray tape, their abdomens strapped with bulky objects. On the floor around them lay wads of tissue and crusty spoiled food on white porcelain plates.

The stench of urine and feces jarred Ali; reflexively, he covered mouth and nose with his right hand but, realizing what he had done, quickly lowered the hand so as not to cause the suffering prisoners further humiliation. It was clear none had slept for days. The instinctive urge to attack Gatimu quickly subsided, however, as the barrel of a cocked Beretta pushed the base of Ali's skull and the woman pleaded "No! Please, no...not in front of the children."

"You think I'm going to kill you," Gatimu goaded Ali while

standing to his back, "don't you?" Ali said nothing. Gatimu broke into a peculiar hysteric laughter and exclaimed "You are to be praised, Ali, for doing what I was going to have to do anyway! Now the money is mine; *all* mine! So, now, you do not die, I need you, I will be watching you, when we are through with this mission, then you will die."

"Gatimu has gone mad" thought Ali, whereas, during the evaluations in January he was simply extremely dangerous.

"Now, tell me," Gatimu lowered the gun, "who is with you?"

Ali turned to face the architect of his fear and for the first time noticed a sharp pain in his right arm just below the elbow; remembering Alwar, his words rang strong, "There is a man named Ty, a white man, American, and two other men with him, one looks like he is from Arabia or Iraq, the other is African."

"That is all?" pressed Gatimu as if knowing the answer.

Ali hesitated, "Alwar."

"Ha!" shouted Gatimu with perverse glee; "another traitor has come aboard for the party! This is too good to be true!" He stared into Ali's eyes, leaned toward him, and softly said "Go, tell this Ty to come, get out of here before I slice off your head."

Ali approached the double doors and began fumbling with handles and knobs, turning and pulling, twisting and yanking, unable to budge a single door an exasperated Gatimu finally pushed him aside and within a couple of actions shoved Ali into the hall. Behind, the door slammed shut and Ali ran down the corridor, up the stairs, across the deck, until staring down at the aft loading deck, empty, he began screaming "Alwar, Ty, hey, where are you?" The gray-haired man appeared from above on another deck and in obvious relief shouted "They're up here!" Sweat seemed to ooze spontaneously from every pore of Ali's face. He wiped his cheeks and mouth with hands and sleeves, became confused, uncertain if it was sweat or tears or both, and why there would be tears, ran to get closer to the deck on which the gray-haired man stood and proclaimed loudly in a fractured rhythm, "Ty...is supposed to go to Gatimu...Gatimu wants to see Ty."

Ty emerged next to the gray-haired man, looked away, said something Ali presumed was meant for his two accomplices, and stepped casually down the stairs motioning with his right arm for Ali to lead the way. When they reached the end of the hall – not hurriedly as the result of compliance but slowly as the result of defiance – Gatimu again opened the door just a tiny bit. He stared silently through the sliver of space at Ty while Ty in silence stared back. Finally, Gatimu asked, "Who sent you?" to which Ty in response demanded, "Who sent you?"

Meanwhile Ali fidgeted, spinning, shuffling, rubbing his face with soggy shirt sleeves, smelling the awful odor of the room – the aroma of suffering. In a breaking panic behind Ty he pleaded "May I go?" but neither Gatimu nor Ty responded, not even a flinch, they just stared at one another. Ali took a step back, another, pivoted and walked fast. The end of the corridor, up the stairs, and another short return of stairs was a large salon and galley visible from the deck. Ali stopped at the top of the first flight of stairs and through the fog of muddled emotion considered his direction.

This, he knew, was perhaps the last time he would be alone and as such the last opportunity he would ever have. First looking around, making sure not to see Ty or the other men, Ali darted up the second flight of stairs into a magnificent open sitting area. Swiftly surveying the room through a prism of drying eyes, Ali determined to obtain a knife in the galley forward and to his left, and dashing in that direction realized only at the last moment there was someone seated at a counter.

"Are you lost?" slurred the man wearing a white captain's cap and obviously intoxicated, beside him on the counter a bottle of gin, in his right hand a stubby glass.

"Um, yes, yes, I was looking for the others" sputtered Ali, "the man with gray hair."

The man took a drink and in so doing his head bobbled like a dashboard doll; "Oh, you must mean Carl, I haven't seen him, he's not in here, last I saw, he was..." his words tapered in a swill of gin. The man seemed oblivious to Ali's untoward presence in the cabin.

After quickly evaluating his limited options, Ali decided to proceed with his plan, "I need to bring the man, Ty, a knife to cut some rope to tie the prisoners; are they in here, the knives?" and gestured with a look to the galley drawers and cupboards. The drunken man's head bobbed in what was unmistakably intended a nod and into the glass he garbled a disengaged reply, "Probably" – slurp – "I mean, that's the kitchen isn't it."

Ali smiled, moved in front of the man, and began rifling drawers until coming upon one containing a wood slab with knives of different shapes and sizes neatly inserted in rows of matching slots. He picked out a small bread knife with a razor-sharp serrated edge and stuck it handle-first in his left sock so the blade pointed up under his pant leg. "Don't cut yourself!" cautioned the man at the counter with a grin; Ali flashed an awkward smile and ran from the galley through the dining and sitting rooms down the stairs.

What to do with the knife was a question beyond the scope of Ali's makeshift strategy. He became concerned Ty's two accomplices would want to bind his legs, and when they did, discover the blade, and so bent over to transfer the knife inside the waist of his pants. Reaching under his pant leg, grabbing hold of the blade tip and carefully pulling straight up, he happened to glance to his side and through a row of low windows not more than three meters away a row of eyes stared back. Ali froze, irrationally believing for a second that to be motionless was to be invisible, but the faces in the windows started shaking, tipping and bouncing, women and men with eyes wide encouraging him, imploring him, and it quickly became apparent this was the crew locked in cabins.

Ali hastened to remove the knife from his sock; after examining a minor cut on his right index finger he tried to insert the blade down his pants before realizing it would not stay put or, if it did, would certainly cause painful bleeding lacerations. Knowing not what to do with the would-be weapon, he ran to the gunwale and propped it under a round white and red life preserver hanging from a brass hook under a coil of yellow rope. It was just in time. Ty breached the cabin entry and, seeing Ali jogging along the gunwale toward the bow, yelled "Hey, you, what are you still doing here?" Ali pretended not to hear but Ty shouted louder, "Ali! Stop!" in such a way that to not would have been calamitous.

"Yes?" answered Ali in a tone of surprising indignation after stopping and turning, "What do you want?"

Ty behaved in a much more agitated fashion than warranted by the circumstance, "I want to know why you're not up with the others!" and Ali accurately surmised it the result of an unpleasant interaction with Gatimu inside his ghastly improvised asylum.

"I had to use the toilet" answered Ali, "so I went upstairs."

Ty marched to Ali – quivering in full view of his clandestine audience – and the back of a large right hand flew against Ali's right cheek, almost knocking the weaker man to the deck. "You don't fucking breathe unless I say so, do you understand me! Now, get going; if I catch you lollygagging around again, I'll feed you in pieces to the sharks!" Ali slowly regained his posture and, glimpsing the white and red life preserver from the corner of his eye, wondered, if only the knife was still in the sock, knowing, a dash for the gunwale would almost certainly result in a bullet to his back.

On the aft upper deck lounged the talkative man and the quiet man in deep white leather cushion chairs like passengers on a cruise liner making small talk and gazing at the water, while Alwar and Jerome sat on hard fiberglass, shoulders and arms twisted back, hands and ankles bound tight with nylon rope. When Ali arrived the quiet man jumped up but hesitated upon seeing Ty in control. "Tie him with the others" the master ordered, "I've got to go find the owner of this boat, Paul DuMorell; it seems our friend Gatimu didn't realize he commandeered the boat we were supposed to steal! Go figure, out of all the boats floating around the Atlantic, this imbecile finds the right one by accident...." Ty chuckled in amusement at the same time shaking his head in bewilderment; "and you Raheem, don't just sit there, start placing explosives, go down below, rig the timers but don't set them yet, and *please*" he beseeched belittlingly, "write down where you put the bombs so we can find them when the time comes."

Starting at the bridge proved a correct strategy and so in the yacht's elaborate command center Ty found a man he believed to be Paul DuMorell, reclining in a captain's chair staring across twenty meters of bow to a limitless expanse of open water.

"Who are you?" the man inquired as Ty came around his right side.

"Don't worry about who I am" responded Ty bluntly, "just know that I am with that nut job in your room with your wife and your kids. You are DuMorell, aren't you?"

"Yes" replied the weary man; "yes, unfortunately, one and the same. Did you see my family; are they okay?"

With a scornful expression Ty shook his head, "Yes, I saw them, and no, of course not, they are not okay, they are alive, which means they someday may be okay, but that's about it. So, if they are ever going to have the chance to be okay, you need to do exactly as I say." Paul swiveled the captain's chair so that he faced Ty; his expression not one of compliance, but rather one of respite, how a man strategizing sweet revenge might react when confronted with an inevitable intervening responsibility.

Ty thoroughly laid out that responsibility: "There are now several of us aboard your boat. We are heavily armed and will kill if our demands are not met; is that clear?"

Having heard this repeatedly, from Swan and Gatimu, Paul simply nodded without displaying emotion.

Ty continued. "I know your plans. Tonight, there is a party here, on this boat, tomorrow, you and your guests are supposed to watch the race. I know who these guests are. Some are on board; some are not. You need to call the ones who are not, and tell them you were detained waiting for a suitable berth, tell them you are coming closer to the harbor, tell them you will send the small boat to pick them up, tell them you will pick them up at between five and five-thirty this evening at the harbor entrance, you will pick them all up in two trips. Use that kid, Jerome.

"Now, pay very careful attention. Gatimu and I will be listening to every word you say and watching every move you make. Gatimu will be watching on the closed circuit video you so conveniently wired in your room, and I will be standing here with you. If you so much as sneeze during this call, any of these calls, I will give a signal and your wife and children will be gone. Is that part clear?" Paul's lips tightened but the affirmation was unmistakable. "And they won't be the only ones" concluded Ty, "the crew, the guests, you...everyone. Splendeur is being rigged to go up like a roman candle on the Fourth of July."

Using his arms for leverage, Paul climbed from the large chair and calmly stated, "I'll need the crew if we are going in."

Ty considered the request and asked "Are you the captain?"

"No" replied Paul, "the last time I saw him he was engaged in a pity fest with a bottle of gin in the lounge, but I am capable of maneuvering Splendeur, with, of course, the crew's help."

"Alright, we need to make those calls, are you ready?" insisted Ty after giving the situation some consideration and concealing his resulting discomfort with the idea of Paul DuMorell at the helm.

Paul slipped an iPhone from his left pant pocket, touched the screen, and affirmed there was probably sufficient coverage to make cell phone calls. Ty thought for a moment, inherently suspicious of any proposal from a person in Paul's predicament, and asked "Is there another way to make the calls?" Paul answered "Sure, we could use the radio, but we have to go through an operator." The subject clearly beyond his knowledge, let alone expertise, Ty resorted to what he knew best, intimidation: "Listen, I don't care how you make the calls, but if I hear anything funny, or if any boats come near us, it's your family, got it!"

"I understand"; Paul wanted instead to quietly jab a knife into the heart of his tormentor. Focusing on the iPhone, scrolling and tapping, placing the phone to his ear brought a terse rebuff from Ty: "Put it on speaker!" Paul's expression evidenced clear displeasure to a response clearly anticipated; a tap to the screen, however, and soon the sound of ringing emanated from the device held chest level in Paul's right palm.

After four rings a woman answered "Hello" in English. Greetings were exchanged in a manner Ty found sincere, followed by small talk of family, the voyage, weather, and, after several long minutes as Ty paced the bridge, confirmation the woman with her husband, two children, and a guest would be waiting at the harbor at five. "We're looking very much forward to it!" exclaimed the woman joyfully. It was a sickening feeling Paul did not expect, risking the lives of innocent people, friends, even children, in exchange for the lives of he and his family.

"Good" Ty's voice resounded of callous resolution; "keep going."

Paul looked from the floor into Ty's eyes and asked somberly, "What are you going to do?" all the while knowing as meaningless the answer. It was a question really just designed to mitigate his shame. Time, time to extricate his family was all he asked, but Ty's terse reply shattered any justification for Paul's ruthless conduct.

"Don't look to me for your salvation."

Paul fell back disbelieving his ears and breathlessly announced he would not call Malik Said. In response, Ty simply smiled and pointed to a round smoked-glass object on the ceiling that Paul knew all too well – the digital video camera by which he used to monitor the crew while relaxing in the luxury of his stateroom. "A bargain with the devil offers no prize" thought Paul; the best hope was at that moment survival. He held the phone in his right hand and using the thumb carefully touched the screen. Ty pranced silently back and forth in the grand control room. The phone rang. Ty stopped.

"Yes?" answered the man in English.

"Hello, Mr. Said; it's Paul DuMorell, how are you?"

"I'm fine, Paul, nice to hear from you, and how are you?"

"Good, I'm good, and nice to talk with you as well" Paul responded while studying Ty, "I'm sorry about the late call, but we've been tied up here," it was a poor choice of words that seemed at least temporarily to go unnoticed by all but him, "with the harbor and all...."

"Yes Paul, of course" Mr. Said injected dryly; "you have a rather large vessel under your wing."

"Yes, that's true" responded Paul, "and we're looking forward to showing you around!"

"That would be nice." Malik Said's tone suddenly went from affable to dictatorial; "Tell me Paul, are you on a speaker phone, it's somewhat hard for me to understand you." Paul moved the phone closer to his face while awaiting Ty's hushed reaction; "Here, is this better, can you hear me now?" Mr. Said acknowledged an improvement but was still unsatisfied. "It's still pretty difficult...." Ty seemed uncertain how to react so Paul tapped the speaker button and moved the device to his right ear.

"There, hopefully this is better; I took you off speaker."

"Cough if you're in trouble." Malik Said's words were instant and firm; he gambled that any aggressor in the room with Paul would not yet have had time to position next to Paul's head and the phone's earpiece. He was right. Within a brief few seconds, Ty leaned toward the phone and Paul coughed, pretending to have inhaled some airborne menace swirling around Ty's head, coughed again, and again, moving the phone from his ear and coughing repeatedly into the coiled fingers of his left hand. Ty stepped away and conferred a very irritated countenance. When confident the act sufficient to surreptitiously convey the enormity of his troubles, Paul held the phone back to his right ear and apologized, "Excuse me, Mr. Said, I'm sorry, I must have inhaled something." Ty tilted his head and grabbed Paul's right hand, holding it, able to hear both sides of the communication.

Mr. Said delayed a strategic several seconds so as to recite his lines for a larger audience, "My, that's a bad cough; I hope you're not coming down with something. That would be a shame...."

"No, no," assured Paul, "I'm okay, and anxious for tonight's party! Speaking thereof, we're picking everyone up at the harbor entrance at five and five-fifteen; how many in your party?"

Mr. Said again hesitated and while doing so projected deliberation by means of a barely audible hum; "Now, let's see, four, yes, I believe four including myself; there were going to be two others, but the young lady came down with something, so four." Paul confirmed the Splendeur's tender would retrieve Mr. Said and his party at five-fifteen and thereafter Mr. Said abruptly ended the call with "That will be fine; goodbye."

Leaning back, but still very close to Paul, Ty stared into the narrow blue eyes darting uncomfortably up and down. Knowing it would be futile to inquire or make accusation about the strange sudden cough – that to do so would only make him in the uncertainty appear weak – by a forceful trance Ty nevertheless wanted Paul to understand his adversary was a man not easily played. Paul understood; that would be his last discreet success. Any future successes would be painfully indiscreet.

Malik Said slipped the cell phone back into an inside pocket of his blue blazer and, sounding more disappointed than worried, advised Klaus that "As we suspected, they've been taken hostage."

Klaus got up from a maroon overstuffed leather chair, strolled to the sink, opened a cupboard, removed a glass, filled it with water from the tap, and casually remarked "Such a pity, it was so easy" before taking a gulp. He set down the glass and confirmed "We're going aboard?"

Mr. Said nodded; "Yes, of course, we've been over this, what's our alternative?" Klaus leaned back against the sink and analyzed aloud, "If we want any survivors, none, really. We should assume there will be a search when we board; that means we either go in like raiders or..." the answer did not come, or if it did, offered such a multitude of harsh possibilities as to be unmentionable. Mr. Said stepped to the bar and gazed intently at Klaus – a silent communication making the utterance of words only redundant – and Klaus shook his head slowly side to side.

"I don't think we should take Michelle." Klaus had obviously given the matter some prior thought and despite plainly exposing a chink in his mental armor was willing to accept the consequences; "She will only get us killed." Mr. Said's focus transfixed the bar; he wanted to say "You have a fondness for her that will get *you* killed" but instead said "She is not weak." Thinking for a moment longer he decided "We will leave it to her. Go get her, and get Robert also, there isn't much time."

Once Michelle was apprised of the risks – partly through the efforts of Klaus prodding the beautiful woman in subtle but undeniable fashion to capitulate – she turned to Robert alone in the corner of the library and answered defiantly, "I will go." Robert took a step forward to heighten the impact of his pending plea in support of Klaus but Michelle turned away to address her employer: "I will carry the M9 between my legs and we will hope our enemy does not number more than fifteen." Robert stood motionless, in breathless, stunned adulation.

"Very well" responded Mr. Said, gliding casually alongside the bar to view a perfectly manicured emerald back lawn bounded by a perfectly manicured green hedge. He observed as date palm fronds bent toward the hills and, beyond them, the Mediterranean Sea a darker shade of blue than usual. "I want everyone back down here at four-thirty, and you better bring umbrellas, it looks like rain."

As Malik Said and Michelle passed from the library, leaving behind a closed door, Robert stepped to the bar and saw Klaus draining vodka from a Kettle One bottle into his water glass. "Would you like a shot?" Klaus asked Robert; "Yes, please," Robert replied. Klaus withdrew another tall glass from the cupboard and above it tipped the bottle until the swirling clear liquid measured four fingers. Passing Robert the glass he toasted, "May your worries be yesterday, your future long, and your dreams infinite," and with a clink into jittery stomachs poured an icy calm.

"And at this moment, especially, to a long future!" proclaimed Robert after the alcohol's initial sting subsided, following-up with a subject that had been on his mind for several minutes: "Are we going to warn the others? Gilbert, he could certainly alert his boss...."

Klaus set his glass with a noticeable "clank" in the sink and smiled, "And these people will go to the yacht if they are warned?"

"I don't know, no, probably not...," the sentence withered. Robert understood. Any obvious irregularity, such as an unusual or unexpected change of plans, would disrupt the element of surprise and of just as much or more importance: they needed the help. The more people on their side, or at least not on the other side, the better their odds.

"Klaus," Robert stepped away from the bar, "how do we have

any chance, just the few of us, mostly inexperienced with anything like this, going in blind?"

Klaus leaned with his back against the sink and arms crossed at his chest, willing, for Robert's sake, to divulge a confidence. "We have somebody on the inside; he helped us get the ringleader several weeks ago. There were only two others with him. Now, they may have joined up with some others, I don't know, but too many would attract attention. What's puzzling to me is how they got on board Splendeur...." He paused in reflection, as if some easy answer eluded him, allowing Robert time to assimilate the information and better understand the situation. "There probably are no more than five or six terrorists onboard" continued Klaus; "There are four of us, maybe another ten guests, a crew, at least ten, and, they will not take lives until their demands are met. We will need some luck, indeed, but I think we have a reasonable chance."

Robert nodded in appreciation of Klaus' candor – a considerable milestone given that Malik Said's enforcer had at one time threatened Robert's life or, at least, his health – and declared he was going to rest in his room. Nearing the top of the left staircase, Robert wondered if Michelle was asleep and so, at the top, paused, and glanced down the hall. Her door was closed. Robert considered knocking but, under the trying circumstances, thought it best to forego any intrusion.

Straight to his veranda went Robert, wondering about the growing bluster, but after a few minutes back inside with the sliding door open to feel and smell the circulating air while lying on the bed. The clock showed "13:30." Consumed by countless thoughts he fixated on the textured ceiling until eyelids lowered, very shortly thereafter again lifting to an almost unrecognizable sound of two light knocks on the door.

Michelle, as Robert fervently had hoped.

"Hi," Robert's pitch one of eagerness, "come in, I thought you'd be asleep, or resting, I almost came to your room."

Michelle stepped in; "I'm sorry, I hope I'm not disturbing you...."

"No, not at all, I was just lying down, thinking...you know."

"Yes, I know."

"There's quite a storm brewing." Robert, without any preconceived strategy yet desiring, needing, to lure Michelle into his domain, turned in earnest for the veranda and a better view of the enormous dark clouds overhead, but his remark about a developing storm was so apropos, on so many levels, that he and Michelle had to stop and laugh; "And now all I can say is, when it rains, it pours!"

Standing together at the terrace threshold smiles soon faded, unable to put aside the impending tempest in their lives. Robert lightly flexed his wrist to intertwine the fingers of his right hand with those of Michelle's left and over the next indelible minutes neither suffered worry or fear. She was there to make love with him, for the first and, perhaps, last time, and on her left heel pirouetted into his ready arms.

The dull rumble of thunder mimicked the exhilaration in Robert's chest as Michelle leveraged his shoulders so she could reach up and kiss his lips. Arms wrapped backs and necks and Robert's hands coursed Michelle's long dark hair. Their embrace, inseparable, heedless the swirling wind.

By a gentle nudge Robert started taking Michelle to bed but she pulled the other direction, to the tumultuous outdoors, and slowly on top of her and a brightly hued cushion longue he fell. His body engulfed hers. They tugged on clothing; he her black cotton blouse and flowery silk skirt, she, his striped button-down shirt and linen trousers. Tips of tongues touched, tickled, agape their mouths, each wanting desperately to bond with the other.

Kissing, not enough, in overpowering passion they spontaneously separated with Robert rising, back muscles quivering, lowering, touching his lips to each soft round button of Michelle's blouse starting at the neck, one button at a time, at the third pushing down against her sternum until between breasts, in his teeth, the button slipped through black cotton to expose a hint of red satin. Panting and pawing like wildcats they writhed and heaved. Robert with one hand carefully set loose the remaining buttons of Michelle's blouse as she with trembling fingers unfastened her bra to expose unblemished skin the color of ivory.

Straddling the longue with his feet on the veranda floor, Robert, not taking time to fiddle with buttons instead lifted the shirt over his head in breathless awe of the embodied perfection of Michelle. She, heart racing, breathing deeply, returned Robert's adulation, studying every bit of his physique, abdomen and chest, arms and shoulders firm and defined. On Robert's left bicep Michelle spotted a tattoo the shape of a shield; eyebrows raised and impulsively she asked "What's that?"

Robert glanced at his arm and answered, "It's the Shield of Achilles – the shield made for him by the god Hephaestus. Achilles used it in his battle with Hector."

"Yes, I sort of remember...the Iliad," Michelle's words came out soft, and smart, underscoring for Robert a riveting combination of strength and femininity and, as she lay beneath him in that instant, vulnerability; "he won that battle, didn't he, but, in the end, was killed."

Robert smiled; "In the end, Michelle, we all are killed."

In a lovers gaze they abandoned the future. Robert unbuttoned his jeans and gradually drew down the zipper, reached down, and using both hands carefully hitched Michelle's silk skirt; her black stockings stayed by the thin black straps of a sheer garter belt, which Robert carefully undid, all the while caressing and kissing until desire unleashed in a flurry of arms and clothes. Their intimacy subsumed the passion and intensity befitting two people on the brink of both love and war – bodies one a powerful machine, thrusting and drawing as over taught skin speckles of water and sweat coalesced to a thin film. She gasped, he tensed, and the veranda floor rippled with each tiny raindrop.

VIII ANGUISH

A drizzle ashore a driving rain over Splendeur, where Alwar, Ali, and Jerome sat bound and shivering in soaked clothing while Ty, Raheem, and the quiet man met under a canopy on the main deck strategizing a release of the crew. The gray-haired man and six other guests, including two children, lingered alone or with family in cabins. Women and men of the crew languished with sparse food in locked quarters; the captain slept on a chair in the grand salon with an overturned gin bottle at his feet; and Paul DuMorell reclined alone in the command center listening to storm advisories over the marine radio.

"Heavy rain overnight, dissipating Thursday afternoon means for a slick track on the first day of the Monte-Carlo Formula One Grand-Prix."

Gatimu, days without sleep, dozed in and out of consciousness on lavish bedding in the master stateroom; when partially conscious, polishing his Beretta and watching French television and closed circuit video monitors. In a semi-awake moment he slid from the feather bed, rubbed his eyes, surveyed the hostages laying apparently asleep in a corner of the room adjacent the dressing rooms, and assumed a slouched position in front of a bank of five monitors. After carefully scrutinizing the images on all five screens – three of which obscured by cascading water droplets – Gatimu studied the intercom panel until pushing a button and shouting "Ty, bring the other two and come down here!"

The words echoed from loudspeakers through every cranny of the yacht. Ty, Raheem and the quiet man searched in vain for the source of the intrusion until finally getting up and making their way under roof and awning toward the master stateroom. Paul, also hearing the announcement, jumped to his feet; concerned for the safety of his family he dashed down two flights of stairs toward the guest cabins to intercept the three interlopers entering the long hallway. He encountered Ty and his men on the soggy deck in front of the hall door.

"What does he want?" queried Paul even more agitated than

usual.

"How should I know?" responded Ty even more annoyed than usual; making no effort to otherwise answer he threw aside Paul to escape the rain and descend the stairs in front of Raheem and the quiet man.

Paul stayed a step behind, "I don't want...," but Ty in the lead cut short the plea with a gruff retort: "I don't care what you want, but, if you know what's best, you'll go back up on deck, now!"

Understanding that Ty was even more stressed than he had been and quite possibly in that condition, imminently dangerous, Paul stopped and let loose with an impassioned "Please don't hurt my family!" Ty sighed loudly; exasperated that Paul failed to give his directive due respect he also stopped and the other men stopped. After sliding past Raheem and the quiet man, in Paul's face Ty seethed, "I won't tell you again!" Paul took a step back but did not lower his gaze, instead, by a certain look promoted his plea until taking one step up the stairs heard "It would be pretty stupid, wouldn't it, to kill the hostages now." As though kicked in the stomach Paul felt the stab; catching his breath he turned and, mumbling disparaging profanities, reconciled to take action preventing someone, somehow, from meeting the kidnappers' demands.

Gatimu slammed the door shut after Ty passed behind Raheem and the quiet man, both of whom staunchly unwilling to look in the direction of the hostages huddled together like whelping dogs on a rug in a corner of the luxurious room. The tyrannical emperor of Splendeur ordered the three to sit on soft tan leather chairs around a round ornate glass table near the door. Once they had complied, Gatimu, looking more and more the lunatic with bloodshot eyes and greasy disheveled hair, announced calmly, the way one might if lacking the wherewithal to discern right from wrong, "We are going to have to kill some people today."

Even for those as hardened as Ty, Raheem, and the quiet man, it was in the hearing from this man a startling exposé of depravity.

"There are too many" continued Gatimu, "there was supposed to be at least six of us, but we are only four," pointing his left index finger Gatimu slowly counted each person around the table; "but there are at least ten crew, guests, more guests coming, we have no choice if we are to succeed!"

"Okay..." replied Ty with the syllables stretched as though playing a child's game, "and who would you have us kill today?"

Gatimu rubbed his grimy mouth to portray the appearance of wise deliberation and said, "I figure, five crew and five passengers," finishing with a vacuous expression witness to the complete collapse of sanity.

Raheem looked to the quiet man, looked to Gatimu, to Ty, and inquired of anyone at the table who may provide some enlightenment: "But what is our mission?   Is this part of our mission?"

The quiet man meantime stared intently at Gatimu waiting for him, the self-proclaimed leader of the group, to proffer a rational explanation, but it was Ty in his place responding "There is no mission, no noble cause...." Raheem's head popped back, his eyes grew wide, but the quiet man offered no discernible reaction. "Just money" concluded Ty.

Raheem, head low, wiped his left hand across his brow from one side to the other as the quiet man, having never released Gatimu from his glare, finally said in resolute disgust, "You will kill ten people for money?   Is there no purpose, nothing else, you believe in?"

"I will kill them *all* for enough money!" proclaimed the mad Gatimu with a hideous smile; as he defiantly stared back at the quiet man a treacherous unease enveloped the table.

Massaging his bottom lip between rows of gleaming white teeth Ty's thoughts splintered through anger's disassociating prism. Having endured all of Gatimu's previous transgressions in relative passivity, he solemnly studied the people at the table, and especially the crazed man with a Beretta concealed in his lap provoking the quiet man – a man who had done nothing but pose a rational question – to flinch. It was an easy decision really. In one smooth motion requiring in all no more than three seconds, Ty reached up, slid the Ruger from its holster, pointed it at Gatimu's forehead, and pulled the trigger. By the time anybody in the room comprehended the clasp of igniting gunpowder, Gatimu lay dead on the floor with most of his parietal cranium scattered behind an overturned soft tan leather chair.

Ty's anger stemmed not only from Gatimu's savagery, but from his reckless, yet unknowing, ambivalence and outright hindrance to the contracted and intended course of events. The taking of Splendeur, Paul and Marie DuMorell, and their guests, was not supposed to occur until late that night; while the revelers soundly slept a team of terrorists arriving by private boat from Mali would assume control of the yacht. Specialists, these men trained in seclusion over a period of almost a year for a sea approach originally targeting a British or Nigerian warship.

In January, however, Raymond learned of a different opportunity almost equally as polarizing but much less risky. He convinced the organization to revise their mission objective. In pursuing this objective, the divers would magnetically attach remote-detonated underwater explosives to the steel hull of Splendeur and soundlessly climb aboard using grappling hooks and rope ladders.

Raymond, Izem, and Ali were to assemble a cache of weapons in Nice, over which Ali and Izem were to stand guard while Raymond returned to the Wagadou Forest for Gatimu and Alwar. Ty and his team and Raymond and his team were to unite and, after transferring weapons to the Mali team on Splendeur, go aboard the yacht. By the next morning, Thursday, there were to be no fewer than ten heavily-armed terrorists on a yacht carefully rigged to explode at the touch of a button. Given this show of overwhelming force the passengers would likely remain unharmed, while official attention paid the massive Formula One crowd would help assure seclusion and secrecy.

The capricious wind of fate let loose during a solar storm, however, sparking a series of entirely comprehensible events unraveling a plan months in the making. With engines of the Swan sputtering on fumes, Gatimu and Swan spotted – whether fortuitously or by some malevolent predestined design – a colossal blue and white yacht voyaging toward the Strait of Gibraltar.

Betrayed by Alwar and drifting toward the southerly Atlantic currents, the two entrepreneurs packed their pockets with explosive, removed the bilge plug, and shot off an assortment of flares. The scuttled Swan not yet fully submersed under Splendeur's wake, Gatimu jammed the muzzle of his Beretta into the captain's ribs to underscore a list of demands, foremost, introduction to the attractive woman lounging with her two young children on the foredeck.

"Is he dead?" the woman excitedly asked. Marie DuMorell, a sophisticated socialite born to a respectable family, never could have dreamed that in just a few days' time – measured by thousands of individual seconds spent suffering and watching her children suffer – she would delight at the death of another human being.

Ty requested Raheem and the quiet man to unceremoniously "wrap the body in a blanket and throw it overboard" while he untied the hostages. From atop the bed, Raheem removed the white down comforter on which not more than an hour ago Gatimu lay polishing his gun, spread the large fluffy blanket on the floor, and, starting at one edge he and the quiet man reverently rolled the body until like a mummy it could be transported from the stateroom for a burial at sea. Meanwhile, Ty laboriously sliced through rope and tape, one thread at a time freeing Marie DuMorell from the last vestige of Gatimu. On the table Ty gently placed Mrs. DuMorell's bomb and, for each of the boys, carefully did the same until mother and sons sat speechless, rubbing their wrists and ankles, watching in bewilderment their deadly liberator.

"You may use the bathroom if you'd like" said Ty, not turning their way but instead with agile precision using his right index finger and thumb to unpack each of the bombs; "but nobody leaves this room." Pealing back tiny sections of brown butcher paper eventually revealed saran-wrapped globs of C-4 from which protruded metal blasting caps and pyrotechnic fuses. Ty studied the devices, at the same time frowning and shaking his head wondering how or if Gatimu intended upon igniting all three fuses simultaneously – to not do so could only mean the sadistic consecutive murders of mother and children. He pulled out the caps and laid them and the C-4 on the table.

A repetition of three and two knocks on the cabin door signaled Raheem and the quiet man returning from their service, soaked, still expectantly preoccupied with what Ty next intended. "The owner's full cooperation!" with a broad smile and crossed arms Ty confidently declared. Huddled near the door with Raheem and the quiet man, Ty elaborated as arms and hands flailed in animated reinforcement of a strategy the concoction of which obviously engendering profound pride.

"I'm going to explain to Mister Paul DuMorell that our insane African friend, Gatimu, is dead...that I, we, have taken control...that his family is now much safer, which he will see for himself...and all is to go as planned for tonight...that we are merely thieves, here to steal stuff from the passengers, like jewelry, watches, money, that kind of thing, and then will be escaping tomorrow when a boat arrives. I will also inform him that once we are gone he can have his wife and kids back."

Raheem and the quiet man eyed one another but quickly smiled in agreement that it was indeed a splendid strategy.

Upon further conference the three decided to restrain Alwar and Ali in the master stateroom until the other team arrived because, according to Ty, with Raheem's acquiescence, their elimination would not "look good"; the quiet man adding that he would not murder them without some divine cause and that they should be set free once their task was at an end. Paul DuMorell would be permitted a brief visit with his family; believing their safety conditionally guaranteed he would enthusiastically secure the full cooperation of crew and guests. Splendeur would proceed to Monte-Carlo. Jerome would transport the guests from the docks to the yacht. The evening's dinner and party would unfold as though nothing were out of the ordinary and Ty, Raheem, and the quiet man would remain in the master stateroom guarding hostages and monitoring events via intercom and closed circuit video until the other team arrived.

Raheem stood watch over Alwar, Ali, Marie DuMorell and her children – allowed to rest, watch television, shower, and move about their stateroom – while Ty and the quiet man went about implementing their plan. All was in accord until Paul freed the crew and four bolted from miserable confinement to the galley, where, wreaking havoc and despite Paul's stern warnings they plundered the stores and paid by either violently disgorging their feast or writhing in pain.

The remainder of cooks, deckhands, engineers, housekeepers, security, and stews arrived sporadically, some lethargic, some emotional, all weak. Not until almost an hour later was Paul able to communicate his dilemma to the entire staff and, by that time, anger had replaced hunger as the condition most in need of satisfaction.

"We can take them!" yelled the bulky executive chef; "There's more of us than them!"

A petite stewardess chimed in: "Yes! There are guns on board, I've seen them; we can break down the door!"

Chants of confidence arose from people not more than an hour earlier locked away in despair. Paul tried to subdue them; tried to explain that their enemies were professional killers and that his stateroom smelled of death where shards of bone and strands of brain strew mahogany walls and works of art. His pleas went unheard. The crew, men and women, were a mob – a lynch mob in an old west American town desperate to extract revenge.

Of particular curiosity to Paul was noticeable silence from his two security staff, a muscular man from New Zealand and a woman who used to serve as a uniformed police officer in Chicago. Finally, in a desperate attempt to rein in the crew before one of them suffered injury or death, Paul, gambling on support, loudly addressed the man and woman. "Bill and Linda," the room became less noisy, "Bill and Linda, can you hear me!" the room became almost silent, "You are the experts here, what is your recommendation?"

Bill's back straightened but Linda was first to respond. "This is a hostage situation and the people involved have nothing to lose; at the force, we sent in a negotiation team, storming the scene was an absolute last resort, for example, if they start killing people, or if the level of anxiety rises precipitously." With an unmistakable nod, Bill concurred.

"I agree" asserted a relieved Paul. "I don't want my family hurt, and I don't want you all hurt, we do as Linda said, and the decision is mine, with her and Bill's counsel, is that clear to everyone?" Without allowing any opportunity for objection he concluded: "Anybody who violates this directive will be terminated on the spot, and if somebody is injured, or worse, as a result, charges will be filed."

The petite stewardess suffered one last question; "Why can't we just call the police?"

Paul glanced at Linda, "Did you hear Linda – the key phrase was 'they have nothing to lose.' Well, I do have something to lose, my wife of ten years and my eight year old twins."

Following some introspection, grumbling, and overall tidying, the meeting adjourned. Almost four o'clock, Ty summoned Paul to his stateroom for an explanation as to why they were not yet underway. The account unfolded in whispers between door and doorframe; the crew proved more difficult than expected and the captain is drunk, but they should be underway in a matter of minutes and, besides, it would only take Lightning Dancer ten minutes from their current location to reach the harbor. While Ty was not pleased, recourse under the circumstances seemed limited to redundant threats.

"When are you going to tell the guests?" he asked.

"I'm going to do that right now" answered Paul; "they're being assembled in the bridge as you requested."

Ty closely observed by video cameras and microphones as Paul and the first mate conversed, flipped switches, turned knobs, worked levers, and studied gauges until Splendeur was underway. At that point, Paul swiveled in the captain's chair to address his guests, all of whom had been aboard since leaving Connecticut.

Sean McNeil founded a private equity firm; his wife, Helen, owned an art gallery in Stamford; their son, Sean, Jr., was a senior in high school and their daughter, Patricia, was a freshman at Yale.

Gretchen Steinberg-Huntington, in her seventies, was a produce heir who two years ago married her fifth husband, Thomas, a concert pianist in his late forties. The gray haired man traveled alone; Carl Demetrius was born in Greece, immigrated alone to the States when only eleven, and founded a chain of fine dining restaurants numbering in excess of fifty over two continents.

All of these people were good friends of Paul and Marie and none were accustomed to kowtowing to bullies; nevertheless, they understood the direness of their mutual dilemma and meaning behind the phrase "loose lips sink ships."

While Jerome in a bright yellow raincoat checked over Lightning Dancer and replenished the fuel tank, Paul attended to one final detail, reeling in the captain. "Doc, listen to me" Paul pleaded while slowly maneuvering half a bottle of vodka away from the befuddled seaman, "it wasn't your fault, for God's sake, they had a gun on you!"

The captain snatched the bottle from Paul's hand and topped his glass; "I'm not feeling sorry for myself, really Paul...I just feel bad for you and Marie...you've been so good to me, this job and all...."

"Doc, if you want to help...."

"I do want to help, but right now," his words slurred, "I just want to be left alone."

"I'm afraid I can't do that" Paul said with authority while once again, but with somewhat less finesse, negotiating the bottle; "We have a situation, I need you to...not be difficult...sober up!"

The captain tore the bottle from Paul's grasp; "I already resigned, you know that...what more do you want? Now go, leave me be." He took a long drink of vodka that would have gagged most professed drinkers.

Paul studied the face of his longtime friend in dismay. "At least, come with me, let me put you in a cabin, you need to stay out of sight until either you straighten up or the others leave."

The captain looked at Paul, looked at the bottle, and with some difficulty lifted from a stool so that Paul could lead him by the arm out the door, down the stairs, and down another flight of stairs. "If I run out of vodka, you'll bring me some...right?" "Yes, yes, I'll bring you some." It was a lie. Paul escorted the captain past cabin doors on the starboard, past cabin doors on the port, finally to the end of the hall and a set of double doors.

"You're putting me...in your cabin?" the captain belched.

"Yes" replied Paul.

"But, aren't they...in your cabin?"

"Yes."

The captain in faltering footsteps tried to back away but Paul grabbed his shirt and slammed him hard against the door, shouting "It's Paul, open up, I need some help!" Soon the door moved just enough to allow for the protrusion of a pistol barrel; "What *the hell* is going on?" demanded Ty. Paul pushed his friend against the doorframe while twisting the arm not appended to the neck of a vodka bottle behind his back. "This is the captain; he's very drunk; I need you to promise me you won't harm him; he needs to stay out of sight." Ty opened the door farther and lowered the Ruger. "That was a very smart move" he said to Paul. Grabbing the other arm Ty dragged Doc into stateroom and shoved him to the floor beside Ali.

Lightning Dancer chugged through the gush as Jerome – unable to make out anything beyond three meters – held back the engines. Navigating by sight was out, even catching a glimpse of the Maritime Alps over Monaco, so, he relied for direction on GPS and compass readings. Windscreen wipers flapped back and forth at about the same pace as Jerome's racing heartbeat; he squinted, pressed the throttle lever, pulled the lever, and strained in vain to capture any object or movement ahead. It seemed that after a while every pane of falling water revealed boats and buildings, derelicts and demons, and the young skipper's burgeoning fear of following Lightning Dancer to the sand far below.

Standing on the dock, partially covered by umbrellas, Stephen and Stephanie Waters tried to shelter their children from the blowing torrent. They were all excited and a little apprehensive, unlike Hamidah standing next to them, her eyes also concealed by an umbrella but instead of reflecting anticipation – anxiety. Not only was she aware the likelihood of traveling directly into peril, she strained under conflicting and demeaning loyalties owed Stephen Waters and Malik Said; and there was also, of course, concern for Ali. The scene was overall quiet except for an occasional "I wish this would stop" or "are we going to be okay" as water plunged in diagonal sheets.

A kilometer from the docks, Jerome finally shut down the twin jet engines propelling Lightning Dancer. Incapable of seeing more than two meters in the deluge, shivering though protected from the elements in a covered and heated wheelhouse, nearing mental collapse, the fulfillment of his responsibility became mentally and physically impossible. The boat adrift at the ocean's mercy rocked with swell and surge as the compass needle swiveled. Jerome began to panic and felt dizzy. "Need to call Splendeur" he thought aloud, "I need to tell Paul...." Around him the sights and sounds of a frenzied mind; blowing water cascaded onto the canvas top in irregular patterns and plumes of white leapt from the sea.

Jerome held the radio microphone to his lips, flipped a toggle and pressed a button, "Hello, this is Jerome on Lightning Dancer, do you read, Jerome, can you hear me?" but all he could hear in return was the deafening rumble of a kettledrum.

At the helm of Splendeur – pushing her way through the rainstorm at almost twenty knots – Paul did hear Jerome and frantically tried to communicate. "Jerome, this is Paul, I read you, where are you? Paul here, Jerome, do you read?" On he went with no reply. Finally, after several minutes, deeply concerned for the boy's safety Paul reduced speed and studied the radar. Just rain, he adjusted the controls, nothing. He turned on the spotlights and tried binoculars, nothing from any angle but water. He flipped the intercom switch, "All free hands to the bow, I need all free hands to the bow with flashlights; Jerome on Lightning Dancer is out there somewhere; if you see him, wave and hold your flashlight to show me what direction...." Different versions of the command echoed all through the yacht until Paul could see a trail of flashlight beacons bouncing on the deck. He turned on the horn and repeatedly blasted short bursts.

"I should never have sent him out in this" Paul admonished himself. Reluctantly, he picked up the intercom, depressed two buttons on the console, said "This is Paul; can you hear me down there?" and turned to face the video camera. "If you can hear me, go to the monitors, right below, you'll see a button with a light, press that and talk."

After a short delay Ty radioed back, "I hear you; I've also been watching and listening. How many other boats are on this tub?"

Paul speculated for a couple of seconds about the meaning of Ty's question, while watching points of light at the bow tip, and responded "Four others, but they're small, two are inflatable. Why?"

"'Cause you're not going to find the kid" answered Ty in a coarse and condescending fashion, "and we can't waste all night looking for him. You need to get in closer and then send two boats to pick up the people at the docks. The kid will show up tomorrow, probably in Spain."

Paul did not laugh; his head tipped and eyes gazed at the floor. "I'm not leaving him" he said calmly, the words ringing oddly familiar, "I won't start killing people, especially an innocent kid."

"Maybe I will," not in the least an unexpected retort from Ty. An eerie silence fell as the two commanders gambled like players in a poker tournament; the ante, a boy, the bet, a wife, a mother and children, the call, "I won't start killing people...."

A fold: "You've got ten minutes to find the kid."

Paul replaced the receiver and scanned out the windscreen while adjusting the spotlight angles; he looked at the clock; he transmitted over the marine radio; he sounded the horn. Two minutes passed. The six bright yellow raincoats on the outer edge of the deck remained motionless. Three minutes, lights, radio, horn...rain. "Where could he be?" Paul wondered; what could have happened?

Four minutes had passed when Carl Demetrius stepped just inside the bridge doorway, stalled, and asked if there was "any sign?"

"No" replied Paul "and we've only got six more minutes."

Carl waved his arms to draw Paul's attention and stepped out onto the bridge deck. Paul went to his side and Carl whispered, quickly and intensely, "I have a Luger in my cabin, it's an old gun, but it shoots well, a nine millimeter, I could get two of them, maybe that main guy, the white one, if they open the door." Without providing any indication of his receptiveness to such a brash scheme, Paul turned and walked back to the navigation console – five minutes – "He's got to be near, unless...." Carl waited by the door. Neither man said a word for fifty seconds.

"Four minutes left," this time it was Carl standing in view of the camera and as they both searched through the glass he mumbled "Listen Paul, either you leave the boy or I go down there it's that simple."

Paul took a step sideways, away from Carl, all the while staring out the windscreen and operating the radio, horn, lights. The raincoats did not move but there was no stopping the numbers on the digital clock; less than three minutes remained.

Carl studied Paul for a moment and declared nonchalantly, "Well, I'm going to my room...."

"No!" shouted Paul; immediately altering composure he sought to mitigate the adverse video and audio perception of this overly-dramatic reaction, "No, please, stay here with me, I could use the support."

Carl nodded and looked at the clock; two minutes.

With less than a minute remaining the intercom beeped and Ty's voice reverberated throughout the bridge, "Time to go." Paul glanced at the clock and pushed a button, "We still have thirty seconds." Ty laughed. Carl stood with his right elbow resting on his left forearm, his right hand rubbing his chin, and said to Paul, "Ask for another five minutes." Paul posed the question.

"I heard him" assured Ty, "and the answer is no."

Every fleeting second changed the numbers on the clock, forty,

forty-one, forty-two, forty-three. Paul, allotted ten minutes, otherwise lost, his family's welfare at stake, convinced himself that continuing the search would be futile because Jerome lay with Lightning Dancer at the bottom of the Mediterranean. "We're leaving." Paul faced the camera with eyes glistening like wet fiberglass in a flashlight's ray and after a moment, in some measure composed with Carl's help, broadcast for all to hear: "We're moving on. Stay out in front and keep a lookout; wave if you see anything, but we need to pick up some people. I'm sure Jerome will show up after the rain lets up. Say your prayers. Thanks."

Carl bid "so long" with a pat on Paul's shoulder and left the bridge.

Less than a quarter kilometer from the harbor without any sign of Lightning Dancer or Jerome, Splendeur's anchor dropped, and several of the crew uncovered and lowered one of the smaller tenders. The rain persisted with no sign of letting up, but the sea, though choppy with periodic larger breaks, maintained a relative calm. Paul sent two of the more experienced hands into the boat along with six extra raincoats in a watertight trunk, as the small open craft did not have a fixed or convertible enclosure. "Call in every five minutes!" he yelled as they pushed out to retrieve sodden party guests.

The Waters family was elated to see the vessel, though small, as it neared the dock, but considerably less so when alongside it became clear the fiberglass dinghy had no cover. One of the hands jumped out holding a line and announced there had been "an accident" involving the larger tender; "We don't think it was due to rough seas" he added as reassuringly as possible, "we didn't encounter any problems coming in." There was no mention of a possible fatality. The other hand helped each person aboard and distributed raingear. Hamidah was last in and had to squeeze onto a wet bench next to Stephen, who welcomed her with a smile inappropriately suggesting some mutual desire. Soon, sheathed in yellow Gore-Tex and orange life jackets, the passengers and crew were lugging through stormy weather toward Splendeur.

At the same time, Malik Said, Klaus, and Michelle in the back, and Robert in the front passenger seat, waited quietly in a Bentley parked on a side street two blocks from the harbor. The strident patter on the steel roof was more like that of a waterfall than rain; so loud in fact that no one in the car heard the ringing of Mr. Said's cell phone. It was purely by chance he noticed the backlit screen. "Hello Paul," there was brief silence, "Okay, thanks, bye." After hanging up, Mr. Said informed the others that "The first group just arrived at the yacht and Paul thinks the boat will be back at the harbor in twenty minutes."

Klaus, quite bored, and quite obviously admiring Michelle's stocking legs held tight together within a knee-length lavender dress between his and Malik Said's casually-positioned covered legs, could not resist inquiring with a playful smirk "Doesn't it hurt?" Robert turned his head wondering to what Klaus referred just in time to witness Michelle with an air of mystery reply, "It would, of course, and that is why I decided on a different location." Klaus frowned, his eyebrows raised, his mouth opened and Michelle, anticipating his next question, added "None of your business." The eyes of all four men engaged a cursory hem-to-neck inspection of the tight-fitting gown, after which Mr. Said and Klaus looked at one another and shook their heads, Robert and the driver looked at one another and grinned, and Michelle stared straight ahead with the sly look of a cat that swallowed four canaries.

Mr. Said's gritty voice brought them back to reality: "Let's go."

Despite only a short hike, made possible by maneuvering the bulky Bentley through narrow passageways – an especially arduous task given the maze of Formula One detours, and clinging to large umbrellas, Malik Said and the others were soaked from the knees down and suffering from varying degrees of chill by the time they arrived at the designated dock. It was therefore of no comfort to find their water taxi a small open craft from which almost twenty liters of rainwater needed pumped before they could embark.

"I'm sorry" said the young man handing out raincoats and life jackets, "we had a problem." Mr. Said and Klaus exchanged the subtly visible equivalent of "undoubtedly" as Robert asked, apprehensively, "What kind of problem?" The man handed him a raincoat and replied "Oh, nothing really, we lost Lightning

Dancer...but, I'm sure we'll find her tomorrow!" Robert thought it best under the circumstances not to inquire about the nature of Lightning Dancer, or where or how it became lost, as, by that point general edginess pervaded the group.

Hamidah and the Waters family, once unsafely aboard Splendeur, found themselves immediately shuffled to waiting staterooms; one for Hamidah and two for Stephen, Stephanie, Rebecca, and Logan. Stephen and Logan agreed to share one and Stephanie and Rebecca the other. Except for Logan, who wanted only to explore his fabulous and opulent surroundings, each of the damp, cold, and still somewhat nauseous guests was simply grateful for an opportunity to dry off, rest, change clothes, and freshen up. "You have one hour before drinks served promptly at five" advised a petite young stewardess displaying a rather tense and awkward demeanor; she would return to escort them to the salon and strongly implied they should until then wait in their quarters.

Hamidah stood watching rain out her window, lost in thought over the looming confrontation, until hearing familiar footsteps in the hallway. Walking briskly across the room she opened the door just in time to catch a glimpse of blue jeans over blue deck shoes disappearing from view up the stairs. "Logan" she thought, what could he be doing? Gently closing the door behind her, Hamidah sprinted down the hall, up a stairway, and out into pouring rain. With no sign of the boy on deck she jumped back inside to another set of stairs accessing a large unattended dining salon and galley. She whispered his name, "Logan!", and from the other side of a counter popped a full head of wet brown hair with wide eyes and swollen cheeks, both hands clutching a bag of cheddar popcorn.

"What are you doing?" probed Hamidah in a tone more resembling a maternal demand, having forgotten for a moment their surroundings.

"I was hungry" answered Logan as shards of popcorn shot from his mouth; "Do you want some?"

Hamidah shook her head; "Come on, we have to get out of here, we're supposed to stay in our cabins. Does your father know you left?"

"Naw" replied the boy still stuffing popcorn in his mouth, "he was taking a shower."

"Maybe we can get you back before he finds out."

Hamidah started for the stairway door after telling Logan to "put the popcorn back where you found it" and wincing at the thought of his hands going repeatedly from mouth to bag. Logan swung around to open a cupboard when with considerable noise at the salon doorway appeared a distinguished man in blue jeans and a button-down white cotton shirt with the sleeves rolled up. To Carl Demetrius, Hamidah and Logan – both frozen and speechless – appeared every bit guilty of something.

"Who are you?" the man posed intensely; but not allowing Hamidah a chance to respond he inquired, "Are you one of them?" Although unsure the meaning of "them," Hamidah started to sputter some kind of response when the man broke in with another question: "Are you with the kid?" After briefly studying Logan behind the counter the man again interrupted Hamidah to answer his own questions: "So you're not one of them, good, my name's Carl, I'm a guest on this tub as are I take it the two of you."

Stepping forward, Hamidah held out her right hand, introduced herself and Logan, and in a shallow voice – almost a whisper – went directly to the point: "How many are there?"

Carl hesitated, "Three or four I think; how'd you know?"

"I suspected" was all Hamidah would offer; "Is one of them a young Arab man?" The opportunity may not again exist for such a dialogue she had decided; deciding also to seize the advantage regardless of young Logan's perception or understanding.

Logan was indeed astutely listening from behind – puzzling over the mysterious questions and their somber tone.

"Yes, there are two possibly fitting that description, but one is also a hostage, Ali is his name, or maybe he's just a captive...;" Carl was curious about the question, "Why do you ask?"

Hamidah felt a guarded relief; "He's a friend – where are they?"

With ineffectual brevity Carl scrutinized the walls and ceiling of the lavish room, after which discreetly responding, "In a room down below, the master stateroom, the owner's cabin; but now we need to stop; there are cameras, not in here, but outside, you and the kid need to get out of here and go back to wherever it is you came from," he hesitated, "but perhaps tonight...." The remainder dangled for Hamidah's imagination.

After expressing gratitude, Hamidah motioned for Logan, and the two dashed back downstairs to the guest cabin hallway where, at Hamidah's door, Logan wanted to know "What's going on?" Acting upon instinct rather than analysis, Hamidah treated the seventeen-year-old as a man, "You need to keep this to yourself for now; do not tell anybody, even your family, can you do that?"

Logan's expression affirmed serious concern, "Yes, of course."

Hamidah peered deep into his eyes, "There are dangerous people on this yacht with us, not the guests or crew, just keep watch on your family, and a lookout, that's all you can do. There are those of us on board who are working to...fix the problem. Whatever you do, don't, under any circumstances, confront them if the opportunity arises."

"My parents don't know?" Logan asked in a voice clearly indicating he thought they should.

"No," Hamidah quickly shook her head, "Listen to me, there is nothing they can do, to tell them would only cause fear, especially for your mom and sister, understand?"

Logan nodded.

For Malik Said, Michelle, Klaus, and Robert, it was a worrisome quarter kilometer passage from the Monte-Carlo harbor to Splendeur. Though all in the tender would have a few minutes earlier believed it not possible, the rain intensified, so much so that one of the Splendeur hands spent the entire trip bailing water with a bucket. Fortunately, they were equipped with GPS and could hear the intermittent horn blast and, after a while, see the colored strobes. Within view of the yacht a seaman steering the dinghy made an ill-conceived spur of the moment remark, "Boy, if Jerome got caught alone in this...," that sent a shiver down more than one passenger's spine. Nobody asked who Jerome was; each just gazed off into her or his own watery imagination.

Paul met the tender as it pulled alongside the loading deck and along with members of the crew helped bring each of the guests and their luggage aboard. Two stews in raincoats assisted with removing life jackets, handing out large towels, and ushering the group across a short expanse of deck, up a brief flight of stairs, along more deck, and down a short flight of stairs to two staterooms. The makeup of the quartet made for awkward room assignments. After some discussion in the hallway – as at feet puddles formed – it was agreed the three men would bunk in the larger stateroom and Michelle could have the smaller to herself.

The four most recent Splendeur passengers did not have an opportunity to enter their cabins, however, before other guests emerged from nearby staterooms in perplexed – stunned really – disbelief to welcome the unfortunate newcomers. Within seconds the corridor filled with fifteen people engaged in a web of introductions and re-acquaintances. Malik Said knew Stephen but not Stephanie or their children, Rebecca and Logan; he did not know Sean and Helen or their children, Sean Jr. and Patricia; nor did he know Gretchen and Thomas although he had heard of Gretchen; or Carl; and pretended not to know Hamidah who pretended not to know him. Klaus knew Hamidah but neither acknowledged the acquaintanceship, Robert knew or at least had spoken with Stephen, and Michelle did not know any of the other guests.

As the cheer of new and renewed friendship and camaraderie wound down, some of the participants devolved to a state of anguished silence, unsure what to say, or to whom, about their universal plight. It was at that juncture Klaus, with his usual opportune timing, exclaimed during a wave and pivot that "If I don't get to the toilet these puddles are going to be yellow!" and a relieving laughter signaled an acceptable withdrawal.

"Excuse me everybody!" shouted the petite stewardess waiting impatiently by the stairs for the greetings to end; "I'll be back in thirty minutes to escort you to the lounge, at five-fifteen."

Upon entering the cabin, Malik Said set his overnight bag on a large bed next to the outer wall under a window, waited for the door to close, and remarked "It seems apparent that some of those people know there's a problem, I mean other than Hamidah, did anyone else get that sense?"

"Yes," Robert reacted first while tossing his bag on a top bunk, "I think that Gretchen and her husband knew, but I'm not sure about anyone else."

Klaus also threw his bag on a top bunk of the only remaining unoccupied bed, sat on the lower bunk, and started bouncing in an apparent attempt to evaluate the thin mattress' firmness; declaring at the end of his experiment that "The kid knows, the one with the long hair, not the junior, the other one, I could tell the way he looked at me when he shook my hand, like he was asking for help."

Mr. Said started to suggest they discreetly find out what they could while socializing that evening; however, his words were silenced by the rhythm of fingernails on the door that when opened by Klaus allowed Hamidah to dart into the room. "I'm sorry to barge in like this, but I thought you should know something before dinner."

"Yes, yes, go ahead Hamidah" replied Mr. Said, "please, tell us what you know."

"There are three or four down below in the owner's stateroom; they are holding Ali and, I believe, other hostages," she hesitated and looked at Mr. Said, "Nobody has seen Paul DuMorell's wife or children...."

"How did you find this out?" Klaus wondered.

"Most from a man named Carl" answered Hamidah, "you met him in the hall just now, gray hair, tall, Greek."

"Do you know anything else, what they are planning, anything at all that may be of more help?" probed Mr. Said.

"No," the word resounded as a certainly-unwarranted apology, "that was all I learned. There wasn't much time. Carl was concerned that we may be monitored by video cameras, maybe microphones. Oh, and I forgot to mention, Logan was with me when Carl said all of that."

"And Logan would be the long-haired kid" Klaus surmised.

"Yes; I better go." Hamidah started to turn for the door but stopped to ask one final question: "I assume the plan tonight is to find out what we can but not do anything, is that right?"

Malik Said looked to Klaus and Robert, "Yes, unless an opportunity arises which is too good to pass up, but we don't risk the lives of hostages," and hesitated, "at least not yet."

The three men had just enough time to change, splash faces and brush teeth, when the petite stewardess banged on theirs and the other guests' doors. Still wearing a look of discontent she nevertheless tried to play the giddy host, "Alright everyone, time to go and have some fun!" rounding up and commandeering the troupe with all the finesse of a girl-scout leader. Falling in line most of the guests were just anxious to soon be imbibing cocktails and nibbling hors d'oeuvre; the only single-minded exceptions being Malik Said and Hamidah. Certainly, Klaus, Robert and Michelle comprehended a duty of the utmost seriousness, but after the afternoon's preliminary ordeal, for them, the duty would need performed with wine glass and appetizer fork in hand.

In the lounge, Paul and a trio of handsome male stews in white jackets greeted the incoming partiers, handing out glasses of white wine and red wine and small morsels of meat wrapped in meat and meat rolled in dough, all held together by toothpicks, and directing any of those desiring a more potent beverage to the fully stocked bar. Jockeying for first position in front of a very lovely bartender adorned in a tight-fitting white sequin dress were Klaus and Carl, both holding half-drained glasses of white wine. "Excuse me" said one, "I'm sorry" replied the other; neither offering the slightest yield the young woman addressed them both, "Let's see, I'll bet...ouzo for you," she pointed to Carl, "and beer for you," she looked at Klaus. The men smiled; "Um, close, vodka martini, Gray Goose, dirty, but not too dirty, for me" said Klaus with a smile and wink, "And that sounds good, the same for me!" chimed Carl with a grin. The bartender produced a feigned pout while pouring vodka – an expression obviously on more than one occasion rehearsed – even more the titillating to two world travelers.

Mr. Said approached Paul and when the opportunity arose – albeit one lacking in privacy – asked the whereabouts of his wife. "I haven't seen Marie; will she be joining us tonight?"

Paul had anticipated the question, but not necessarily from Malik Said, "No, I'm afraid not, one of the kids came down with a bug so she is consumed with her duties as a mother."

The look in Paul's eyes told Mr. Said everything he needed to know; "I see, that's too bad, I hope he gets well soon, and I'd hate to have her delayed through the race."

"No, I think it's just a twenty-four hour bug" said Paul conveying a clear message: "by this time tomorrow everything should be okay."

Malik Said's face reflected a mixed reaction of surprise and doubt; the canny yet otherwise obtuse dialogue only served to aggravate curiosity and highlight the importance of quickly coming to terms with the situation. "Could you please show me where the bathroom – I guess you call it a head – is?" he asked Paul. Paul smiled and pressing his way politely around various size congregations of jubilant-appearing guests, led Mr. Said past the galley to a short hallway where he quietly and quickly presented the situation.

Mr. Said listened intently and asked in a manner beset by bewilderment, "They told you that they were going to steal yours and your guests' belongings and then leave? Do you believe them?"

Paul thought for a second, "Yes, I have no reason not to, the main guy, the ringleader, killed the crazy one and untied Marie and the kids. They had bombs," he started to choke up, cleared his throat, and continued, "bombs, tied to them, even the boys."

"Paul," Mr. Said altered the pitch and cadence of his dialect to convey genuine sympathy; "I just want to understand, they came aboard heavily armed, two of their own they hold has captives, they're waiting for a boat...," carefully, he weighed each noun, each verb, each chosen word, "is it possible they instead have another agenda?"

Rubbing eyes, somewhat embarrassed, Paul glanced at the floor and slowly redirected his attention to Mr. Said, "Certainly it's possible...but what can we do; they're still holding my family."

Mr. Said shook his head, "You're right, I don't know what we can do, if anything, while they have Marie and the kids; their safety is our highest concern. Let's get back." After first coaxing Paul to the head for a tissue, Mr. Said waited, and with contrived laughter and conversation the two rejoined the festivities.

In merry make-believe with the other guests Robert and Michelle mingled, chatting and laughing, drinking, winding their way eventually to a row of party trays on a counter where they sampled snacks made from unusual combinations of otherwise tasty ingredients. Behind the counter in a quiet corner of the galley stood a boy with brown shoulder-length hair, aloof, on what would otherwise be the outskirts of the party. He was obviously deep in thought, nibbling from a popcorn bag.

"Your name is Logan" Robert presumed with a casual flare, as though he and Michelle's proximity near the galley a mere coincidence, "isn't that right?" The boy nodded. "I'm Robert and this is Michelle; what are you doing over here by yourself?"

"Oh...," Logan reacted as one might when asked which tooth needed pulling, "I just don't feel like being social tonight."

It was Michelle's turn. "Well, perhaps you haven't noticed, but there are some lovely girls here!"

Logan's eyes narrowed and nose wrinkled; "Really, where?"

Robert looked around the room and with some confusion at Michelle, who promptly elaborated, "Why, Hamidah for one, don't you see her over there?"

The bridge of Logan's nose became a furrow; "Hamidah? She's, like, twenty-five or something, yea, she's hot...but my dad has a thing for her, and besides, she likes a guy named Ali."

"And then there's that server over in the corner" continued Michelle, pretending not to hear or perhaps comprehend Logan's candid revelation about his father, "the blonde girl, she's cute, right?" With an up and down motion of his head Logan confirmed agreement clearly the result of one or more earlier observations. "So how do you know Hamidah likes a guy named Ali" explored Michelle, "did she tell you that?"

"No;" Logan began to fidget, and the more he did, the more the empty popcorn bag crinkled and crumpled, "not really, I just heard her say something about Ali."

Robert inconspicuously touched Michelle on the arm and once the focus of her eyes, if not her thoughts, tried subtly, with a head vibration and squinty eyes, to dissuade her from persistent questioning. Not privy to Hamidah's earlier revelations and genuinely in the dark about Ali, however, Michelle did not comprehend the reason behind Robert's odd behavior. Nevertheless, she did not have time to cause further damage because Klaus, nimbly balancing a martini glass in his right hand, joined the assemblage with an offhand remark that hording appetizers was impolite followed by the disingenuous meddlesome question: "Who's Ali?"

Michelle snapped back that "He is no concern of yours, but, if you must know" – but, of course, Klaus knew – "he is apparently a friend of Hamidah's." Klaus nodded, "I see...," with a sip of martini; Robert took a sip of white wine; Michelle presented Klaus with a clear visual message of exasperation; and Logan set the popcorn bag in the sink and started to leave what was a few minutes earlier his sanctuary.

To this last act Klaus reacted in a manner surprising to all within earshot, "We may need your help, Logan." Klaus was not a practitioner of diplomacy, yet an astute judge of character, and his words held Logan's attention. "Stay alert, let us," the hand holding the nearly empty martini glass moved in the direction of Robert and Michelle, "but nobody else, know if you hear anything, and we'll let you know when we're ready to act." Logan stared at Klaus, "Okay, I've got a knife in my pocket, I got it over there," his face turned toward a row of drawers. Klaus flashed a look of admiration; "Knives are sometimes very helpful."

Robert, Michelle, and Klaus had been chatting for several minutes when suddenly interrupted by a booming "Hey, Paul,

when are you going to show us around!" It was Stephen Waters –
apparently with Stephanie the last adults on the yacht unaware
that they were hostages – well into his third glass of cabernet.
Malik Said, standing next to Paul, suggested he enlighten the
Waters family as to the understood "state of things, since everyone
else seems to know." Paul agreed, deciding to just make a general
announcement as he believed any unawares children in the room
were old enough and deserved to be apprised regardless of how
their parents felt.

"Please everyone" he began, "most of you already know this,
but some of you don't, and that wasn't intentional, it's just the way
the information came out. This vessel is under the control of four
men, three or four, holding us hostage. They say they are going to
take our possessions, valuables, and leave tomorrow. And, just so
you know, they are the ones holding Marie and the twins in our
stateroom; they...say they will harm them if we do not do as they
ask. They also say that nobody will be harmed if we do as they
ask. That's all I know."

There was a stir from behind several guests and Stephen,
unable yet to comprehend the shocking news, shouted from across
the room "So, when did they come aboard, when did they take your
wife and kids?"

Paul looked at Mr. Said and overwrought by a dozen emotions
declared "I can't do this right now...."

"When – when did you know?" again shouted Stephen, this
time in a tone rife with anger.

Mr. Said raised his hand, "Please...Paul had no choice, you will
understand later, but now...."

"No choice!" Stephen bellowed; "You mean he knew in time to
stop us from coming over? He knew in time...I could have
left...Stephanie and the kids; you didn't even warn us!" Stephen's
hostility seethed and pushing through other guests he moved
toward Malik Said and Paul until coming face to face with a guest
who did not budge.

"Hold it!" Klaus demanded, though nicely, placing his hands
lightly against Stephen's chest, "We're all in this together, we all

have family and friends to protect, we need to be calm and work together, not at one another's throats." Klaus stood ten or so centimeters taller than Stephen and his physique suggested that he was not a man to be taken lightly; but Stephen's anger was justified, and fueled by red wine, and so thrusting both arms he shoved Klaus back against Helen McNeil, nearly knocking her to the floor, and resumed his mindless advance.

However, not for long; grabbing Stephen by the collar, Klaus pulled, and over an extended right leg the tipsy banker flipped head first to the hardwood. Klaus turned as Stephen lay dazed on the floor with Marie at his side, repeating angrily "You didn't have to do that," and asked Helen McNeil if she was okay. Her demure response echoed a sentiment shared by all in attendance: "I really can't blame him for being mad."

Logan watched the events unfold in silence; he had liked Klaus, felt they connected, but the harsh treatment dealt his father altered this perspective. He too thought Klaus "didn't have to do that." With more compassion his father could have been subdued, a push to the floor instead of dropping him on his head, an arm twist, something, and no doubt existed in Logan's mind from the time they met that Klaus, the look, the confidence, was a professional at that sort of thing.

Logan's family was in danger, not only from unseen marauders but from trained thugs within. His father lying wounded on the floor, Logan willingly accepted the responsibility handed him by default as "man of the house." In reality, he had been planning for this eventuality since overhearing Hamidah and Carl, thinking about how to save his mother and sister, even his father. Logan's role as protagonist was revealed to him like a movie or videogame mirroring life. He, the reluctant hero, forced into action to lead his family from harm's grasp; the principal prop, an empty dinghy tethered behind Splendeur.

Kneeling around Stephen – sitting for the most part upright on the floor with his legs extended and holding his head complaining of nausea – Stephanie, Rebecca, Klaus, and Paul, who wondered aloud if Stephen could stand. Stephen shook his head slowly. Stephanie suggested they lift him by both arms but Stephen's head this time shook definitively from side to side; "I think I'm going to be sick" he mumbled. Klaus jumped up, ran to the counter and poured pink punch from a bowl but, within the few seconds that it took him to return, Stephen made good on his prediction.

"He's got a concussion" opined Robert standing to one side behind Klaus, "I don't suppose there's a doctor onboard?" He glanced around the room as if expecting to see a raised hand.

"I don't think so" answered Paul.

Patricia McNeil stepped between Robert and Gretchen to announce "I was a lifeguard in high school and know CPR and basic first aid; he needs to rest; you should get him to bed." Everyone agreed, and while the young men in white jackets worked with shallow breaths at mopping the burgundy muck with paper towels, Paul and Klaus lifted Stephen by his arms and helped him to the stairs, followed closely by Stephanie, Rebecca, and Logan.

"Alright everyone," Malik Said waved his arms to draw the crowd's attention, "let's all relax and get better acquainted. I'm sure Mr. Waters will be okay after a few hours' rest, and we need to get to know one another, especially under these most trying of circumstances." The hostages would need each other and a strong offensive strategy in order to have any realistic hope of survival was Mr. Said's conclusion, and it affronted his basic concepts of logic and sensibility to think that petty thieves operated as did their captors though considerable may be the take. More likely was it the pirates harbored a much more sinister scheme. "Please, come forward and let's talk."

Robert immediately made his way to Mr. Said for the purpose of delivering a sheet of paper towel on which in Michelle's red lipstick was printed "MAY BE MICROPHONES SUGGEST WE TALK IN A CABIN." Mr. Said nodded, "Of course, good point," held the message for everyone to see, and proclaimed loudly "My name, for those of you who don't know, or with memories for names like me, is Malik Said." Smiling and extending a right hand, Mr. Said strolled around the room until there developed among the fearful lot a kind of fraternal bond and by its own right a tenuous but very real sense of security.

As soon as Klaus and Paul very gradually lowered a sore and queasy Stephen onto his bed and Stephanie with difficulty smiled to bid the pair farewell, the cabin door closed, and Logan took charge. "You saw them; I think we were the only ones who didn't know this was a trap! It isn't right!" Stephanie tried to settle him down with no success. "We have to get off this boat and I know a way."

Rebecca studied her younger brother of thirteen months with theretofore undeserving pride but nevertheless offered scant support, "If we leave, won't the kidnappers kill that guy's family?"

"No" replied Logan firmly, "not if they don't know we left."

Stephanie held a damp cold washcloth against the upper back of Stephen's head while his posture in relation to the bed adjusted intermittently from sitting to lying depending upon perceived nausea. "They have cameras, Logan, looking around the boat" Stephanie advised without turning, "I saw one under the light when we came aboard."

Logan reacted with the coolness appropriate for one not capable of fully understanding the gravity of the situation: "Mom, we just need to get to the back of the boat, get on the boat we came in on, and leave. I'm sorry, but they could have told us not to come, it's us or them, and with the rain, they probably won't even see us."

Stephen, also incapable of grasping the danger, mustered a vote of support for Logan: "He's right...we should leave."

"Excuse me!" sounded Rebecca with a sarcastic inflection perfected over many previous occasions, "Can anybody drive a boat?"

Logan responded that it "isn't that hard, I watched the guy coming over, and, besides, dad had a boat."

Stephanie reminded Logan that it was a sailboat and the family discussion imperceptibly morphed from simply one of "if they should" try to escape to one of "how they could" try to escape. After several minutes, however, there remained no consensus as to the relative risk posed by either option. Stephanie and Rebecca theorized that it would be better to lose some jewelry and cash than drown; Stephen and Logan conjectured that it would be better to face a known obstacle than one completely out of their control. The only item of agreement was that nobody left, unless everybody left.

It was then that Rebecca made an offhand comment, "Well, I, for one, just in case, am going to hide some of my jewelry," which effectively cemented the family's resolve. Stephen and Stephanie considered one another in silence, their thoughts comingling, what kind of thief forewarns his mark? It could only mean one thing. "They've got another plan, they're probably waiting for help to arrive, that's why they stay in the cabin;" for Stephanie the realization a bittersweet epiphany, turning, studying the faces of her children, stepping into her role as protector, "so if we're going to do this, we better make sure it works."

While a parade of guests and crewmembers moved through the corridor outside their cabin, Stephen, Stephanie, Logan, and Rebecca debated about how and when to leave them and Splendeur behind. "We'll notify the authorities when we get to port" suggested Stephen in a gesture intended to clear the consciences of all. "Should we take any others?" Rebecca's conscience apparently needed more cleansing. "We could take some of the women and girls" proposed Logan, thinking really of only Patricia, but after brief debate the idea was abandoned as infeasible to Stephanie's singular summation that "They'll just try to stop us from going." It was eight-thirty; they would wait until midnight.

In Gretchen and Thomas' room – selected because of its size and location near the stairway furthest from the master stateroom – the crew and guests, all but the Waters who remained sequestered plotting escape, secretly convened at ten o'clock. Malik Said asked Michelle to take charge of the meeting with glum words of encouragement: "You know, of course, they are going to kill everyone if we don't kill them first." Monumental was her task, to mount an offensive against desperate terrorists holding a mother and her two young children, with just a band of spoiled socialites and the hands, cooks, and stews of a luxury yacht. Klaus flashed

Michelle a wink and lightheartedly offered to "carry the flag and blow the horn;" she just smiled and shook her head.

Twenty-one people stood tight and quiet as Michelle began speaking in a voice so low as to be nothing more than whisper. "First, are there any of you with any military or police training?" Three hands lifted: Linda, Bill, and Carl. "Please step forward" continued Michelle; "No others? Okay, I want women without military or police training, not you Hamidah, and those of you younger than eighteen to move to the back." Muted shuffles and footsteps ushered the transition and Michelle surveyed the result. "Now, I want everyone else with any kind of medical condition to stay put, the rest of you, not the women and kids, step forward and raise your hands." An index finger pointed at each hand, one, two, three, four, five, six, seven, eight, and..., as Michelle aloud made her assessment. "Okay, now, the rest of you, quietly, please, go back to your rooms, we will fill you in after we figure out what to do."

After all but fourteen had departed, Paul confronted Mr. Said and Michelle, "I thought we were going to talk, I didn't know you were going to do this, it sounds like you are going to try and take these guys on, you can't do that, Marie and the kids are in that room."

For Klaus it was well past time to set the record straight and his voice rang of hard compassion wrought from the worn shroud of gruesome experience. "These men are not thieves, you know they are not thieves, thieves steal, they don't take hostages, they are animals and they are going to kill your family," his left arm swayed above the group as he took note of each person, "and all of these people, and all of the people, the women and children, who left, if we don't get control of this situation before whatever they have planned happens. So, it's time to stop the illusion and the pretend wishing game. It's time to fight for survival."

Paul's expression conveyed the enormity of his dilemma: his family held hostage by pirates, their release uncertain, ineffective heroics could create or accelerate a tragedy. Untrained in battle tactics or execution – let alone guerilla warfare – it became clear that control of the situation was irrevocably slipping from his grasp. "I think it's time to call the police or navy, maybe coast guard, whatever they have here." The thought vented devoid of analysis; however, in saying the words Paul felt confident in the approach. "They're professionals and probably have hostage negotiators. We can reach them by cell from here."

"I believe, sincerely believe," Malik Said's low tone and slow cadence drew the respectful attention of all in the room, "that you are correct, that many lives may be saved...but certainly not those of Marie and your children. There will eventually be a gunfight, or perhaps gas blown through a porthole...well, you can imagine how it will play out."

"And if we're going to do that" Robert interjected, "we might as well get as many people off this boat as possible and as soon as possible."

"You see," Klaus addressed Paul by sight, "the only reason to take action is the hostages in your room, your wife and children, so," and by focusing on all of the people standing around him, "you should be the one to make the final decision."

Stillness descended on the stuffy cabin as occupants stared anxiously at Paul. Most hoped to be relieved of ultimate responsibility, cast away from Splendeur to spend the remainder of their lives pretending not to know what became of those less fortunate. Mr. Said, Robert, Klaus, Michelle, Hamidah, Linda and Carl hoped for the chance to once and for all eradicate the virus of terror infecting their world.

"Let's talk about a plan;" Paul needed time to think about the ramifications for everybody involved, "I'll make my decision based upon what I consider to be the viability of that plan." It was a rational approach, if not fatally flawed, considering his lack of experience.

Michelle passed responsibility for the next lesson on to Klaus. "How and when have you been delivering food to the stateroom?" – this simple question inspired even the most reluctant in attendance, reinvigorating lost hope and instilling courage, even for Paul, who suddenly realized the tools needed for success might just be closer at hand than he had previously thought.

Curiously present despite Michelle's instructions, to the surface only of non-crewmembers, the petite blonde stewardess from near the door spoke up. "I take it, or one of the guys takes it, twice a day and knocks and then leaves it at the door. They get the same thing every day, eggs and toast in the morning, oh, and coffee, and at night, actually late afternoon, they have some kind of meat and a vegetable, maybe potatoes."

Klaus asked how the food was presented.

"Nine plates, nine cups, they leave their dirty dishes by the door; it's kinda like room service, only no tip!" she laughed, and almost everyone else laughed.

"Okay" continued Klaus, "so the next feeding isn't until tomorrow morning." He paused; "We may not have that long. Let me tell you what has to happen so there is no confusion. We are going to storm the room. It is the only way, and it will be much easier if the door opens, because if we don't break down the door on the first try, and if we aren't close to at least one of them, there will be shooting."

Paul absorbed Klaus' recital with a heavy heart; "I wish I wouldn't have had that surveillance equipment installed...otherwise, we could have perhaps lured one out by telling them there was another boat approaching...and you can't just break down the door, there are steel plates laminated between sheets of mahogany." Klaus and Mr. Said exchanged expressions reflecting mild shock yet neither posed the question, "Why did you fortify your stateroom door?" Therefore, left for Robert was the obligation of announcing there was nothing they could do that night and the plan must evolve around the breakfast delivery.

"I don't think we have that much time" Klaus repeated dejectedly, looking at the floor and shaking his head; one of the deck hands asked Klaus what he thought was going to happen. "I don't know, but they're stalling, 'till tomorrow...."

"Then we need to be ready!" asserted Robert firmly; "We need to arm as many people as possible, be on the lookout, be prepared for an incursion, and have a communication network, a strategy...."

Without intending, Klaus and Linda jointly exclaimed "You're right!" and Carl announced "I have a gun," to which Michelle exclaimed, "I have a gun," next Robert, "I have a gun," followed by Malik Said, "I too have a gun." After that, Klaus confirmed he carried a gun and asked if anyone else in the room possessed a firearm. "I do;" it was the petite stewardess this time raising her hand, "a Smith and Wesson thirty-eight. You never know...." Klaus smiled, "No, you never know."

After an hour and a half strategizing, the clock radio displayed "10:37 PM" and the meeting adjourned. Guests crept to their respective cabins; Gretchen left the McNeil room when Sean arrived and returned to her and Thomas' room. A few minutes later, Robert, Klaus, Michelle, and Carl emerged from their quarters for a prearranged rendezvous at the top of the stairs. Each wore a bright yellow raincoat by consensus promptly removed for being too conspicuous, even in the dark rain, and each possessed a loaded handgun, two holstered, one pocketed, one held. Within just seconds all of their clothing was soaked through to the skin, but none seemed to notice the wet or feel the chill, consumed instead by the awesome importance of their calling.

The volunteer sentries conferred and decided that each would take visual responsibility for an expanse of one-hundred and eighty degrees at points centered midway on the bow, stern, starboard, and port. They also would remain away from the outer edge of decks to avoid camera angles from poles and the deck rooftops. That meant that, especially looking over the bow and stern, they would not have a view close to the hull. Their objectives were to watch, listen, and engage the enemy; darkness and heavy rain made these tasks difficult at best.

Michelle took a position next to a dinghy under the heliport deck, Klaus went to the bow and sat leaning against a deck chair, Carl took the starboard and crouched low under a row of windows, and Robert took the port on the bridge deck. Anybody perceiving anything believed to be out-of-place was to run and notify the person to his or her right, clockwise, who would notify the others. All would converge at the place of perception. The concept had multiple both deliberated and overlooked defects; the most glaring deliberated defect being a well-orchestrated incursion from more than one launch point and the most glaring overlooked defect being an out-of-place event from within.

A few minutes before midnight, the Waters family began their stealthy evacuation wearing bright yellow raincoats emblazoned with the Splendeur emblem. Logan took the lead and all except Stephen carried small bags. Creeping in close formation down the corridor they made the first set of stairs and, with slow deliberate steps, climbed to the top. Logan very quietly opened the outside door and stepped onto the deck. The others followed.

In driving rain the family huddled at the precipice of their gauntlet: four meters of open deck, another stairway, three meters of deck, and, hopefully, a waiting tender with the key in the ignition and sufficient fuel to make it ashore. They searched for any sign of trouble; the plan being that if it appeared safe, one by one they would dash to the loading deck stairs, descend the stairs, and run to the small boat. It fell to Logan as a self-appointed duty to go first, untie the boat, hold the line, and jump in once all others were aboard. They would surely be gone well before anyone monitoring deck cameras had time to react.

Of course, they did not foresee Michelle armed with a Beretta M9 hiding in the dark several meters from the loading deck stairs. Intense scrutiny over an infinite expanse of black water did not prevent an outside corner of her left eye capturing a moving object, what certainly appeared to be a person, disappearing down the stairs. Michelle had no time even to aim the Beretta. She instinctively moved to a crouching position with legs and feet in a running stance – perhaps for attack perhaps for retreat – when another person began sprinting from the door toward the stairs. Holding the powerful handgun with both hands and squinting as water washed over her face, Michelle peered down the barrel at an intruder and her right index finger came to rest on the trigger when, in a charcoal flash of raindrops under deck lights, there appeared a rather small bright yellow raincoat with a hood.

At that instant on the starboard side of the boat, Carl thought he heard something, squeezed the wet grip of his Lugar even tighter, and, disregarding the warning about cameras, leaned out close to the edge of the deck straining for a view of anything but the dim glitter of falling water on a black canvas. From his position were at least three meters of steel hull to the waterline and, looking over the edge, he could almost glimpse the ocean. Carl stared to his right down the hull and stared to his left down the hull – nothing, but the subtle fading glow from windows illuminating the night. Reeling back he wished for a flashlight and cradled the gun with both hands between his knees.

From his vantage point on the bridge deck, Robert also thought he heard something, a sound distinctive from the splatter of rain on wet fiberglass, or wood, or glass. This was a clanking noise, metal striking metal, and his first thought was of a scuba tank tapping a steel boat ladder. He jumped up and, similarly disregarding caution, extended over the side of the yacht searching for a source of the sound. The Colt ready, yet nothing, but the glow and unknown. "Clang" – again the noise – not that of a chain and flagpole, a singular note, very light but pronounced, unmistakably different from those of his ambient world. Robert leapt for the stairs, holding the gun, slipping and sliding with his left hand on the wet handrail, a sharp corner and down another flight of stairs he charged with the intention of alerting Klaus stationed at the bow.

Directly in his path, however, lay a black object that when slowly approached Robert recognized as a scuba cylinder. He fell back against the bulkhead of windows, the Colt barrel up near his chest while twice each second blood surged into swollen arteries, every muscle in his body flexing, a mental state for so long suppressed. In a flash, it was Christmas, 1992. Pressed flat against a mud wall in Mogadishu he pretended desperately to be invisible as AK-47 fire from around a corner pelted the dirt near his feet. Robert closed his eyes. No, just rain, raindrops, raindrops on the deck, on the yacht, in the Mediterranean Sea, and there are people, in danger, children, and women, Michelle! The skin on his face tightened as jaws clenched and eyelids opened – and the Shield of Achilles surged against soaked cotton.

Carl sprang to his feet; something was happening. The thumb of his right hand flipped the safety and he held the Lugar waist high; feet shuffling to the right, toward the back of the boat, the stern, facing toward the sea, his left hand touching fiberglass and glass, eyes and ears pursuing an ever-watchful vigil.   Another thump to his left – this time maybe four meters away, definitely not the rain, he stopped and pointed the gun. What to do? His orders, alert the person to his right, Michelle, his heart, confront and neutralize the threat.

Michelle held the Beretta with both hands, ready to fire, stepped out and yelled in a whisper, "Hey, who is that!"

Rebecca heard a woman's voice, paused at the top of the loading deck stairs, looked around and saw Michelle; for several seconds the two were linked in immovable disbelief.   With eyes wide in surprise and sounding either disappointed or relieved – Michelle never knew for sure which – Rebecca finally asked "What are you doing here?"

"What am I doing here!" cried Michelle, sad, angry, frustrated, and even the more so by glancing over her shoulder and seeing Stephen and Stephanie hovering in the light of the doorway.   She turned back to Rebecca; "What are you doing here? What are all of you doing?"

Rebecca sprinted down the stairs without answering and Michelle pivoted; directing the Beretta at Stephen and Stephanie she commanded "Go back, now! Go! I'll get them, go!"

When Stephen put his hand on the door handle, Michelle rushed toward the stairs in the hope of stopping Logan and Rebecca.   Her effort was in vain; the two teenagers lay face down on the deck while over them three men in hooded black wetsuits brandished assault rifles. Michelle's shoes slid on the wet deck as she tried without success to stop – not until dropping the Beretta and with a kick of her right heel skimming it toward the door did she raise her hands and plead in French for mercy. "They're just children!" she screamed two times not knowing if her words were too late.

Stephen and Stephanie partway down the stairs heard Michelle; Stephen, pushing Stephanie to one side, leaped and threw open the door.

"Stop!" bade Stephanie softly from behind, "Wait, what's going on?"

"I don't know" replied Stephen under his breath, "her hands are in the air, I don't know who's with the kids, I'm going out there."

"No, wait," on the verge of hysteria Stephanie sustained the appeal; "We didn't hear gunshots...the kids may still be okay, what's she doing?"

They watched through the rain as Michelle with her hands in the air stood motionless except for the backward thrust of her right lower leg.

"I think she's trying to tell us something" whispered Stephen.

"Where's her gun?" whispered Stephanie.

Stephen knelt and peering across the shimmering wood saw the Beretta almost half the distance to Michelle; "It's out there," he turned, "I'm going, wait here"; of course, Stephanie had no intention of doing anything to the contrary. Very discreetly Stephen lowered to the deck and like a salamander began crawling toward the gun.

Meanwhile, Robert, trapezius muscles molded to the bulkhead and clutching the Colt in both hands with the barrel pointing down, twisted his neck just enough to see around the corner. Michelle stood facing the loading deck near the stairs with her arms in the air and her lower leg moving up and down as somebody crawled toward her across the watery fiberglass and teak. He briefly studied the scene as gradually neck muscles contracted to present a view of endless liquid moving in every axis. Contemplating, crouching, waiting, turning, squinting; for what was the crawler searching? Stooping and swiveling, Robert watched as a hand reached and retracted and the crawler began a slow deliberate retreat. Another head appeared from the loading deck stairs.

Robert aimed the Colt...head...shoulders...chest; the muzzle of an assault rifle just centimeters from Michelle's waist...chest...face; the assailant talking furiously in a rapid French vocabulary Robert did not understand; Michelle no longer kicking but moving toward the stairs only to back away as the rifle nudged closer. Robert glanced to his left; the crawler knelt holding a handgun pointed in the direction of Michelle and the intruder. Another dark head appeared from the loading deck stairway and Robert thought he saw movement on the far side of the person kneeling and suddenly, three bullets split the rain.

Michelle fell backward as the assault rifle dropped to the deck and tumbling down the stairs went the two intruders. Robert ran to the stairway while from behind hearing the screams of a man and a woman, "No! Rebecca! Logan! No!", and peering over the railing edge beheld three bodies prone and two ready for war. All other options just dust floating in the wind of fate, Robert fired, and soon Carl, but the two below fired back with pointed steel easily piercing molded fiberglass.

Four in black wetsuits at the flank and three in black wetsuits at the front; "Run!" someone yelled; but where?

Never clear to Robert, when the firing stopped, or why; only that there were wounded, there were dead, and there would never again be any chance of escape. Michelle was not injured – Stephen's errant shot found lucky cover from Robert's Colt and Carl's old Lugar – and Robert suffered only a superficial leg wound and dislocated right shoulder. Carl, shot twice in the abdomen, died in a crimson pool and Rebecca died in Logan's arms from a gunshot wound to the femoral artery. Stephen, Stephanie, and Logan: physically unharmed.

IX ILLUSION

"What is he saying?" asked Ty of Raheem.

"He wants to know why we are here and not in town" answered Raheem.

"Tell him it's a long story, but we're here, so there's no point in telling it now" said Ty, "Tell him we have weapons and we put bombs around the boat."

Raheem looked at the man in a spongy black wetsuit and in French translated Ty's sentence; the man nodded and in French responded that "his people" would need to see the weapons. Raheem turned to Ty and said "He understands and asks if they could please see the weapons just so they know what is available." Ty nodded, and instructed Raheem to unzip the duffel bags neatly stacked near the bed and satisfy the man's curiosity, asking, "By the way, is he their leader? What's his name?"

In response to each question posed by Raheem, in French, the man provided a curt retort, in French, and Raheem subsequently informed Ty "Yes, he is their leader, his name is Jacque." In fact, the man told Raheem in French that "The stupid white American can't pronounce my name and will not know my name" – the wetsuit reminded Raheem of the famous ocean scientist, "Jacques Cousteau." Listening from the floor against a wall between Ali and Marie, Alwar smiled, but not only because he found the exchanges humorous.

When Raheem began repositioning and unsealing the duffel bags, the man he named Jacque motioned for two other men in wetsuits and between them there followed a brief conversation. After that, the two men handed Jacque an orange waterproof bag and began studying the contents of the duffels while Jacque went into the bathroom with the orange bag. After a few minutes, Jacque emerged wearing black sweatpants, a black t-shirt, and white Converse athletic shoes.

While this was going on, Ty waved for the quiet man to join him, and they left the stateroom for the first time in two days. It was almost two o'clock Thursday morning. They strolled down the hall without acknowledging a wetsuit-clad sentry carrying a Russian APS underwater assault rifle at the base of the stairs. Ascended through the hall door into heavy rain they found three terrorists standing guard over all of the drenched, shivering, and traumatized guests and crewmembers.

On deck lay the doubled-over body of Carl. Ty walked over, looked down, began biting his bottom lip, and loudly questioned the prisoners; "Who is this man – what happened?" Nobody answered. He approached one of the men wearing a black wetsuit and again asked what had happened. The man did not respond.

"They killed him" shouted Logan, clearly very distraught, standing at the front between his mother and father, "and they killed my sister!"

Ty left the man he was interrogating and asked the crowd, "Where's the girl? What were they doing out here? What happened?"

Stephanie wailed "She's down there!" and the crowd pointed to the loading deck. Ty's other questions went unanswered.

Ty stepped to the punctured fiberglass partition and looked over the edge to see a body covered by a coat and shirt; gnawing harder the lip began to bleed and the blood he spat into that draining from the lifeless body of Carl while mumbling "He's not gonna like this."

Standing above the corpse, facing the crowd, Ty demanded to know "Who belongs to him?"

When nobody else came forward, including Paul, Hamidah politely made her way through to the front and announced "I do." When Ty asked what she wanted to do with the body, Hamidah replied "I don't know what he would want, I know he was Greek, he may be Greek Orthodox, or maybe not, and I don't know what they do. We could take him to land for a burial I suppose...."

Ty shook his head, "No, I'm afraid not; we will have to do it here."

"What about Rebecca?" Stephanie sobbed; "You want her thrown out there?" and pointed to the emptiness all around.

"Listen lady," the tone was a mix of condolence and anger, "I didn't want any of this, but it's done, and we're not taking bodies to Monaco or France or Italy. If you want, we can see if there's a walk-in freezer...."

This idea not at all well received, a heated confrontation between the passengers and Ty as to a proper ceremony thereafter ensued with, of course, Ty prevailing; there would be a service right then and there and the bodies would be weighted and offered to the sea. The Waters family, Stephen, Stephanie, and Logan, were clearly in a state of shock and allowed to take shelter under the roof in the care of Hamidah, Gretchen, and Patricia. There they sat in tearful mourning as, forced by circumstance and an ancient duty as owner and itinerate captain of the yacht, Paul, the very man whose deceit had lured the Waters family into harm's way, reluctantly accepted responsibility for the eulogies.

He began to remember Carl as Ty on the rear decks in the rain and the quiet man in the main dining hall and galley searched for rope and objects of sufficient mass and of suitable shape to secure the bodies at seabed. "I'm sorry; I've never done this before." Paul's somber words could easily be heard by all of the guests and crew. "Carl was one of my best friends, we've known each other, we knew each other, for twenty or so years, he was a great man and a great friend, he has five children, and will be missed by all who knew him, I'm sorry, friend...," Paul's voice broke as he choked back tears, "may God guide your way back home." The scene one of terrible despair as black water poured from the sky over a dead friend's body, the mourners under guard by the killers, still, some in attendance managed to speak "Amen."

Ty and the quiet man finding nothing of practical use, walked instead from the stern to the bow along the main outermost deck, starboard and port, looking for scuba weight belts. Six in all were discovered and hauled back; three of which promptly strapped to Carl's neck and legs over the strong French objection of their previous owners. Robert, Paul, Thomas, and Malik Said volunteered to lift the arms and legs and to bear – if that meant no more than barely off the deck – Carl's weighted body, which they did, until with some difficulty shoving it over the side of the yacht.

As the body drifted through air and water Mr. Said described Carl as a "noble martyr who died a warrior's death."

Reflecting abysmal anguish the faces of guests and crew, knowing that next Rebecca, and after that?

"I," Paul's tears prevented more than one word; "I...."

Gretchen, seizing the initiative to relieve an appreciative Paul of his just burden, exclaimed that "The only perfect ones here among us are the children." The words sounded gentle in her low scratchy voice; "The rest of us who are any good at all, are riddled with flaws, flaws that prevent the sensible among us of any age from too readily casting blame or passing judgment." She deliberately stared straight ahead so as not to identify the several persons who could easily have been subjects of her discourse. "Rebecca was a beautiful child and she will certainly be missed by all who knew her or could have one day known her; her many good works will now, unfortunately for this world, never be known."

Gretchen took a deep breath. The serenity of the worldly woman's soothing intentions could no longer overcome a fuming hatred toward those directly responsible for Rebecca's senseless murder. "I didn't know this child, and I don't know why all of this happened, but I do know there will forever be an empty space here on earth. We have to remember that in heaven, though, there is a new angel it's God's will. Mistakes were made by flawed people, as good people sometimes make, especially when under pressure...but that is a far cry," her grandmotherly voice trembled with indignation, "from the evil committed here tonight by evil people and God willing these bastards will burn into eternity!"

This closing sentiment left many in attendance somewhat stunned as having prepared for grief and not anger, some wept, some wailed, others seethed; but the quiet man's face reflected the guilt of complicity, a persisting resistance deep inside to being a part of something so ignoble that, for money, alone, people would kill. This was service in the end not for the beleaguered, he believed, but for the oppressors who for a fraction of their immense wealth could acquire armies of evil people.

The quiet man found himself in the middle of what he

considered a purely capitalist conflict. Loyalties blurred. Among the oppressors, Paul DuMorell, wondering while standing in the rain how much money would be required to buy the freedom of his family, perhaps, even, guests and crew. Behind him, Malik Said, quite used to bargaining for evil and well aware that between black and white are many shades of gray – a world "riddled with flaws" as Gretchen so aptly noted – leaning toward Robert and whispering, "Have you seen Klaus?"

Philosophical and religious deliberation over the concepts of good and evil was never a luxury Ty could afford, and after biting the left side of his lower lip, glaring at Gretchen, he finally demanded without emotion that "Whoever is carrying the girl, get down there and take care of it." Stephen, Stephanie, and Logan slowly arose and as they did, every man, woman, and child, guest and crew, moved in a quiet procession toward the loading deck stairs. Those closest started the descent, each ready to take hold of some tiny part of the last earthly vestige of Rebecca. They were all in suffering and redemption, one, and when Robert and Mr. Said bent down to pick up weight belts, a guard lowering the barrel of his rifle found Ty and the quiet man reacting in a most unexpected manner – "Stay back!" To the amazement of all, except Gretchen, the service proceeded without further interference.

Raheem and the second team leader, "Jacque," stepped through the door and into the rain just in time to witness Rebecca tenderly handed over to the sea. Jacque conferred in French with his men and, after that, into the eyes of Ty warned in English, "Do not help yourself to what is ours again." Ty returned Jacque's stare, stopped chewing on his lower lip, smiled, and responded that he would "try to be more considerate in the future." Raheem and the quiet man observed their commander with learned apprehension; Raheem had once seen Ty pummel a bar bouncer in Lagos for telling him to take off his baseball cap and the quiet man's memory of Gatimu's final dying expression was all too fresh. Tomorrow, the mission would be over, they later discussed, but until, it would be wise to keep Ty and the belligerent second team leader apart.

All of the remaining guests and crew spent the next four hours confined to four staterooms and cabins under armed guard. Robert, Mr. Said, Paul, Stephen, Logan, Thomas, Sean, and Sean Jr. occupied one large stateroom; Michelle, Hamidah, Gretchen, Helen, Stephanie, and Patricia another; and members of the crew were arbitrarily driven into Gretchen and Thomas' stateroom and one of the cabins in which they were initially held. In the master stateroom meanwhile, Alwar, Ali, Marie and her two children, Antoine and Jean, and Captain Gibson, "Doc," sat or laid on the floor adjacent the portside wall. Alwar, Ali, and Doc were bound; their arms and legs held tight by nylon rope and strapping tape. Marie and the children, however, remained free to walk around and use the bathrooms. Of course, Ty and his men made certain that drawers and cabinets were empty of scissors or other sharp objects and the hostages remained under constant surveillance.

As such, the quiet man, having volunteered to keep an eye on the prisoners while Ty and Raheem slept in an empty cabin, reclined in a tan leather cushion chair behind a soiled glass table facing the portside wall with an automatic assault rifle in his lap and one eye shut. Alwar studied his adversary for some time and softly said, "You don't like this either"; the quiet man's right eye opened, "Are you talking to me?"

"I was only commenting" replied Alwar, "on what I observed."

The quiet man knew better than to encourage a discussion with hostages; however, frustrated by circumstance and curious to hear what the African had to say, he did not issue a reprimand. So Alwar's confidence grew and first apologizing to Marie, "I'm sorry for your children," he stated flatly to the quiet man that "You know as well as I the Africans are going to kill all of the passengers including the women and children." The quiet man still did not offer a reprimand so Alwar, ever bolder, persisted, "I can tell these are not your kind of people, these are not freedom fighters, they are after something else, probably money, and you are not one, not in your heart."

The quiet man leaned forward and set the assault rifle on the table; "You have a big mouth for a man sitting on the floor. What makes you think you know me?" It was at this juncture Ali, Doc, and Marie began to pay serious attention to events unfolding, for

Alwar appeared to have indeed struck a chord with their imprisoner.

"Because I am one of you" replied Alwar; "This too was my mission, until I saw the truth, and left the fortune hunters Gatimu and Swan to perish in the Atlantic."

The quiet man smiled, "Yes, I have heard, you ran, and left your brothers to die, you are nothing more than a coward!"

Alwar's back muscles tensed as a chill ran up his spine and burst forth at the base of the skull; to first ease his racing heart and erase a face of fury he remembered the woman and her young children, and after a moment responded calmly, cleverly, that "Cowards, run, I, continued on to warn the other freedom fighters, here, Ali, did I not warn you?"

Ali this time did not hesitate: "Yes, you tried, but I was stupid and afraid, and did not listen."

"You see," Alwar prodded the quiet man like a matador with his cape before a proud but wounded bull, "and now I warn you. These people are not like you and me. They have no heart, no God; their god is money, and for their god they will do anything, to anyone. How much are they paying you to kill women and children – *what is the going price for the death of an innocent young girl?*"

The quiet man became enraged and from his mouth words from his heart gushed forth: "I don't kill women or children for just money! I wouldn't even kill you for just money! I was told this was mission of freedom, to make us" – suddenly from the background were two loud knocks on the door – "taken seriously, feared and respected!"

As the once quiet man approached the door, Alwar let fly one last barb – "Nobody respects children killers!" in perfect accompaniment to a chorus of moans and sobs from Antoine and Jean. Marie held her children close, one on each side, pledging that nothing would happen, it was all just in jest, for fun, a play, and soon they would be home playing with their own friends. Alwar patted Jean gently on the back and rendered an explanation on the cusp of believability, "I'm sorry boys, your mom's right, we were just playing, everything, is going to be okay."

Rattled, confused, angry, the quiet man held the door for the second team leader and his next in command, but it was clear to them that something had happened, and Jacque inquired in English as to the cause of the quiet man's angst. "It is nothing" he replied with a shrug; "just some problems with one of the hostages, but now it is over."

Jacque's eyebrows sank and wrinkles formed across his brow, "Problems, what kind of problems, who was it?"

"I said it's over" answered the quiet man forcefully, "Please, have a seat, I've been making tea in the microwave – there's a microwave in the armoire – would you like some?"

Jacque said no and walked over to the row of hostages; slowly he passed by and to each, except Antoine and Jean, cast an imposing glare, looking for any sign of resistance. The quiet man observed the ritual with discomfort, believing the second team leader capable of atrocity against any victim including those inherently vulnerable; not like Ty, whose violence seemed to erupt only at men foolish enough to present a challenge. The last words from Ty to the quiet man before leaving for a nap: "Don't let anybody, *anybody*, hurt any more guests." Ty's purpose the quiet man respected. So, once again, the quiet man calmly requested Jacque to let the hostages be and, once again, his words went ignored.

It was the unfortunate captain unable to maintain composure when Jacque stopped to eye Marie: "What are you staring at you miserable cockroach; go find your stinking hole and crawl back into it!" Like a huge vacuum the words sucked all other sound from the room. Alwar, Ali, Marie, even the quiet man, each and all strained for a means to the captain's salvation but too soon the second team leader grabbed Doc's shirt collar and carted him across the floor like a sack of flour.

The quiet man stepped in his way; "I have orders," face to face in a relaxed voice he scolded Jacque, "so let him go."

Jacque pivoted and began beating both sides of the defenseless captain's head with his fists. The quiet man grabbed Jacque by a left arm poised to strike a hard blow; Jacque wheeled around, knocked the quiet man to the floor with a right fist to the left temple and began kicking his ribcage. This brought the second team second in command to the fray: from behind, wrapping arms, he dragged Jacque away from the quiet man and the captain and held on tight until Jacque cooled off.

The quiet man picked himself off the floor and wiped his nose with a shirtsleeve; he said nothing, just walked to the tan leather cushion chair, sat, and laid the assault rifle in his lap without displaying any emotion. Alwar and Ali meanwhile intensely scrutinized each participant in the fracas with breathless apprehension; certain that at any moment the quiet man would explode and perforate the second team leader. But he did not. After a minute, the second in command released his hold on the second team leader and, without glance or word to the quiet man, both departed the cabin. Alwar remained silent and made certain that Ali did the same for fear the quiet man may instead perforate them.

The captain with blood draining from his right ear and significantly more subdued, yet alive, thanks in large part to the injured quiet man, slouched back to the wall and slumped left of Marie.

In their congested cabin, Malik Said and Robert convened in a corner as far away from the others as possible, debating survival plans, speculating on the forthcoming ransom demand, mulling over the status and whereabouts of Klaus. Among the various hypothesis concerning Klaus were that he died in a battle with the terrorists, was wounded and died later, was wounded and hiding – perhaps incapacitated, or was simply hiding waiting for the right moment to strike. "Our strategy, I believe, should incorporate Klaus" decided Mr. Said; "Agreed" said Robert, "he's much too wily to be counted out without some proof."

Indeed, their decision was sound. At the pinnacle of Splendeur waited Klaus under a soaked canvas tarp, cold, wet, silent and unmoving with the Glock and silver knife, as a spider on its web waits in hunger patient for the ideal moment to seize an unsuspecting prey. He had been at his watch on the bow when the second team boarded the yacht from the stern and both sides. The realization of danger occurred with a flurry of gunshots from behind, far behind, and after sprinting across the bow deck, up a ladder over the bridge, another ladder to the pool and spa enclosure, and a third ladder to the gym roof, he passed under the radar and antennae arch just in time to witness Robert two decks below relinquish his Colt to the black sodden teak.

The next move for Klaus was either to start killing people or delay his assault in the hope of a more opportune occasion, when, the fates willing, there may be a chance to overwhelm the marauders. Where does one hide, though, on a yacht? Without time for analysis, and not in the least boat savvy, Klaus bolted back under the arch and down the ladder, ripped the wet canvas spa cover from its mooring, climbed back up the ladder to the gym roof and ascended the radar arch ladder dragging the tarp. There, among the electronics, he perched in waiting. It was an eerie yet invigorating roost in the company of albatross; strange noises accompanied the raindrops and, very occasionally, he even caught a glimpse of lights glittering in the Principality of Monaco.

At about six thirty, the sun began its journey across the western European sky and Klaus reveled in an unusual early morning rainbow that filled his heart with hopefulness. But not so in the cabins below, where a relentless gloom had descended upon the occupants. With the exceptions of Gretchen and Patricia, none of the guests or crew had managed any sleep and with the sunrise came the sound of Ty and Raheem tramping groggily down the hall to the master stateroom. Soon, the captives believed, would surface an explanation for their suffering.

The hands on Michelle's black and white-gold Chanel watch showed "7:37" when two of the second team guards, also wearing black sweatpants and t-shirts, opened the men's and women's guest cabins. From the hallway one forcefully announced "We are going to read a list of names, when your name is called, step into the hall and form a line." Looking at a sheet of paper, the other guard slowly pronounced and mispronounced each syllable: "Sean and Hel-en Mc-Neil"..."Gret-chen and Thom-as Stein-berg-Hunt-ing-ton"..."Carl Dem-et-ri-us"..."Ma-lik Sa-id"..."Ste-phen and Steph-an-ie Wat-ers"..."Paul Du-Mor-ell." This process had the foreseeable effect of creating a very unsettling ambience.

Several of those whose names were called considered the awful analogy of being released from a prison cell only to endure a final walk to the gallows. Sean, for example, had to help Helen, who had been throwing up over a toilet, to a sink and the hall. Robert, one of the fortunate or not so fortunate, for him too soon to tell, upon witnessing the pandemic of terror announced calmly for all to hear that "You are the ones with money, that is why you are leaving, you are not in danger!", almost inadvertently inserting the word "yet" after "not."

Upon entering the hallway Malik Said advised the guards, in French, that Carl Demetrius had perished a few hours earlier. "He was shot, no?" responded the first guard in English; "Yes," replied Mr. Said solemnly, "your people shot him."

The other guard counted each person in the hallway and took the lead, waving for the eight guests to follow, while last in the procession and toting an automatic assault rifle marched the English speaking guard. They walked down the corridor toward the stairs, up the stairs, and up the other flight of stairs into the formal dining and sitting salon. There, Ty instructed the guards to wait outside and the chosen guests to take seats around the great dining table.

"Each of you is receiving a sheet of paper with instructions"; as Ty addressed the apprehensive participants, Raheem walked around the table handing each person a sheet of white paper on which appeared black lettering generated by a computer and inkjet printer. "Now, I want to go through these instructions with you so there is no confusion...you are to wire from your bank the amount of five million dollars, that means each of you, and the wiring instructions, routing number, account number, and so forth, are printed on the paper. You will make the wire order in this room over the telephone I am holding." He held up an inexpensive flip cell phone. "Are there any questions so far?"

Sean McNeil lifted the fingers of his left hand from the table and as a grade school truant summoned to the principal's office, asked, "You don't mean both of us, Helen and I, you mean per family, right, I mean, we don't have ten million dollars in a bank account...."

Ty started to bite down on his bottom lip but noticed and stopped. "Whoever said there are no stupid questions was wrong; as I said, so clearly, *each* one of you, that mean you, and that means your wife – *each one of you* – and if you don't have the money, you can either borrow it from somebody else at this table, or be lunchmeat for the sharks, it's your call." Sean looked despondently at Helen and slinked into his chair.

Next, Paul looked at Stephen, sitting two chairs to his left on the other side of Stephanie, and seemingly in a state of panic blurted "Is this...?" Ty interrupted, "Hey! Talk to me, don't talk to somebody at the table, what's your problem?"

"This is my company!" exclaimed Paul in rather indignant and condescending fashion, "I mean, our company, that is, all of us at the table...we're supposed to wire money into the DigiFouré Telecom business operating account?"

At this question Ty did bite down on his lower lip; "Is that what it says?" Paul nodded. "Then that's what it means." Paul started to say "I don't get it," but abruptly froze as Ty put his hand to the grip of the Glock holstered under his left shoulder.

"Now" continued Ty, "some of you may not know the telephone number for your banker, or the bank may be closed, or your dog may have eaten the number, whatever; so let me just say, here and now, you can make up to three phone calls, and if the wire isn't placed during the last call, you will be dragged from this room, a bad thing will happen to you, and everybody left here will have to pick up your slack, meaning, make up the difference." He took a deep breath. "Which brings me to my next point: we are one short already, so, it isn't five million each it is six million each, comprendé?"

The people sitting around the table glanced at one other with stunned expressions; all except Malik Said, who sat rigid as a stone staring at the center of the table deliberating on the next dealt card. Wiring money into a company they owned; "But why?" he thought, for what purpose, and what next? Worse still, to access six million dollars in cash, quickly, he would have to call the bank in Iran and the money would have to wire from Iran. Whether the bank would even cooperate....

"My friend here is going to stand behind each of you during the call," Ty's left arm raised in the direction of Raheem, "and you are going to be on speaker, so, if you try to sneak in a warning, or say something cute, or yell 'help,' the call and your life will end and everybody left here at the table will pay your share."

He looked down at Sean, "Remember; it's only money," and handing him the phone quipped with a grin: "Do you want to phone a friend?"

Sean gazed around the table and glanced at his watch; "Does anybody know what time it is in New York?" Gretchen quickly replied "Six hours difference." Sean examined the face of his Rolex Cosmograph Daytona timepiece of sapphires and rubies costing more than the combined annual salaries of almost all of the Splendeur crewmembers, "So...it's about one in the morning in New York..." Sean looked up at Ty, "I don't understand, how can I place a wire at one in the morning?"

Pinching the bridge of his nose, eyes closed in exasperation, Ty slowly asked Sean for the name of his bank. "Bank of America" he replied. "Hmm, I see, well," Ty let go of his nose and, one foot on a chair, leaned toward Sean; with an almost comical sarcasm much to the disbelief of everyone in the room, except Raheem, Ty suggested "might they have a branch in the Emirates, Dubai perhaps, where the money just happens to be going, and where it is right now," flipping his left wrist Ty glimpsed the black face of his fifty-dollar Timex, "almost nine thirty on Thursday morning?"

Sean lowered his head; "I'll need to call my partner and see if I can take the money from the business account. He'll want to know why."

"And he mustn't know why" reacted Ty as if speaking to a child, "so you better try a different approach."

"I can't sign on my own for that much...."

"Oh, for crying out loud!" bellowed Gretchen, "I'll give you the damn money! You there," she firmly addressed Ty, "give that man a pen so he can make out his IOU." Ty smiled, waited for Raheem who eventually found a pen hanging from the side of an enormous refrigerator, and handed the pen to Sean. "You heard the lady" he managed to say as Gretchen began counseling Sean on how to word a note on the back of the wire instruction paper promising to repay twelve million dollars together with interest compounded at the rate of one half of one percent per day.

"No usury laws out here I'll bet" muttered Gretchen with a chuckle mirrored in earnest by Mr. Said. "Now, both of you...," she pointed with her crooked right index finger at Sean and at Helen, "sign it, date it, and hand it over."

Next with the phone, Stephen, looking as though he might collapse at any moment from the combination of a concussion, grief, and exhaustion; circles of dark around swollen eyes, face bright red, hair in all directions; with Stephanie appearing only slightly worse the two leaned together and pressed buttons until a perky female voice answered "Stephen Waters' office, this is Mariah, how may I help you?"

"Mariah, it's Stephen, I'm on...," unable to verbalize the word "speakerphone" was Stephen as the young woman on the other end chirped "Steve! I'm glad you called, I've...."

"Speakerphone!" shouted Stephen, "I'm on a speakerphone, here with Stephanie and some other people, actually, in a meeting."

"Oh, I see," the young woman's pitch dropped several octaves, "I'm sorry, I thought you were on vacation...hi Stephanie...now, how can I be of assistance?"

Stephen hesitated and after which delivered a very rapid response: "I forgot to transfer some money before I left so I need you to make the transfer, an intra-bank transfer, are you ready?" The woman opened and closed a drawer, "Um...yes, go ahead," and Stephen began the instructions with "This will be coming out of the orange account, twelve million dollars, going into the business account of DigiFouré Telecom, account number..." followed by twice reading numbers off the white paper.

"Is there any notation I should make on the ledger, a reason, or anything?" The question took Stephen by surprise as he never found Mariah to be particularly diligent. "No" he replied, "I'll take care of it when I get back in the office, but be sure to make the transfer right away, alright?" She said "certainly" and after a friendly "Enjoy the rest of your vacation" followed by a melancholy "Thanks, I will," the call ended.

Raheem took the phone from Stephen while Ty considered the devastated man with apparent suspicion as a prelude to "You bankers, you're so clever, orange account, ledgers, my, my...;" his hand moved to the holstered Glock in an excessive demonstration of control, "Now enlighten all of us here at the table, what is the orange account?"

Stephen cleared his throat and spoke as though forced to reveal a secret, embarrassed, maybe even ashamed; "It's just a discretionary account at the bank controlled by a few top executives." The men and women around the table paid keen attention as all had some connection to Worldwide Investment Bank.

"I see" said Ty, "So, just so I'm clear, you weren't giving little Candy there some kind of code, were you, with orange, like in terror alert?"

Stephen shook his head vigorously, "No, no...that's not it at all!"

"And," Ty walked around the table to stand behind Stephen as a way of emphasizing the next point, even though all in attendance knew what it would be, "it wasn't your money you just gave away, was it, it was the banks, meaning, it was your depositor's money, right?"

Malik Said marveled at Ty's questioning; "A rather enigmatic fellow" he thought, too clever for simply a hired gun.

Stephen fidgeted and out of a habit evolved over many conferences scooted back in the chair to assume a more dignified posture, "Well...technically that's right, but, I would have to pay it back."

Ty could not help but dig the blade deeper before resuming his place at head of the table: "You just took money from the other DigiFouré Telecom owners to pay DigiFouré Telecom...and, by the way, if you did give any kind of signal, of course, you will be the first casualty." Stephen started to garble something in rebuttal but Ty cut him short by telling Raheem to "Hand the phone to our next contestant!"

Raheem walked behind Paul and placed the cell phone in Thomas' hand, where it remained for only a couple of seconds until Gretchen snatched it away to quickly dial a series of twelve numbers. "Raul, it's Gretchen, I need you to do me a favor, well, actually two favors...." "Yes, of course, hello Gretchen, what do you need?" The man had a noticeable accent of some uncertain derivation, Spanish or Indian perhaps, or Israeli, maybe Pakistani, and many at the table pondered his nationality.

"I need twenty four million dollars US wired to this account" ordered Gretchen; "Are you ready?" "Yes, go on." Gretchen read the numbers – "Did you catch that?" The man on the line read the same numbers back. "Good, now, do that at once, and also, close all of our accounts at Worldwide Investment Bank, understand?" "Yes, I believe so...*all* of the accounts?" "All of the accounts; disburse the funds to several of our other accounts offshore." Gretchen pressed the end key and handed the phone over her right shoulder to Raheem.

"I would have told him to sell our interest in DigiFouré," Gretchen leaned forward and glared at Paul, "but the units are restricted," and after leaning back mumbled, "Damn."

Ty laughed. "It should all go that easy; see everyone, that's how it's done!" He nodded to Raheem, who walked around the table and handed the cell phone to Malik Said, who, in turn, studied the keypad and also quickly pressed a series of twelve numbers. After several seconds, ringing, and, after four rings, an answer – a man, and in a language nobody sitting at the table understood, the man and Mr. Said carried on a conversation which included near conclusion the recital of numbers from the white paper.

"Persian, I presume?" Ty queried when the call was over; "Yes,

Farsi," replied Mr. Said without any sign of discomfort; while around the table, there were no eyes focused anywhere, except on Mr. Said.

"Good, two in a row!" exclaimed Ty, allowing everyone some time for reflection despite the eagerness of turning his attention to Paul; "One more to go...the envelope please!" he hollered with a hoot, but clearly, none of the participants found Ty's cocky humor as amusing as did he.

Raheem received the cell phone from Mr. Said, walked back around the table, and handed it to Paul, certain for good reason that he was the morning's main attraction. "I don't have six million dollars" he started off by saying; "Whoa" belted Ty, "Who said anything about six million? It's twelve million, you and your wife." Paul sighed. "Well, if I don't have six million, I certainly don't have twelve million."

Ty removed his left foot from the arm of a chair, walked around the table toward Paul, and once behind him calmly advised "You can ask somebody here for a loan or you can make up to three calls – what do you wish to do?"

Paul gazed around the table for some indication of support. Certainly, Gretchen and Thomas, out of the question, neither so much as returned his glance; Sean and Helen did not have the money and offered apologies; that left only Stephen and Stephanie, and Malik Said. Stephen made eye contact with Paul; for some reason that neither Paul nor Stephanie ever understood, however, he thereafter looked at Mr. Said whose facial expression and head turn clearly communicated "No."

"I'm sorry Paul" responded Stephen with considerable sincerity, "I'd like to help you, but I can't, I'm sorry."

The room was dead quiet, with everyone, including Ty, captivated by the unfolding drama. Paul, speechless, could only gaze back and forth at Stephen and Malik Said sitting there in his hundred million dollar yacht, investors, bankers...friends, so he thought. "Why are they doing this to me?" he agonized. Stephanie too was speechless, unbelieving of the entire episode, the murder of her only daughter, her family held hostage, extramarital affairs, questionable finances, like a terrible nightmare that might if she thought too hard turn out to be real.

Ty looked somewhat confusingly at Malik Said and down at the top of Paul's bowed head; "Who will you be telephoning?" After a moment, almost too long, Paul replied "I don't have the number; it's on my laptop, in my room." Ty asked him where to find the laptop; "In a drawer under the video monitors." With a jerk of his head Ty directed Raheem to the master stateroom, slid the Glock from its holster, and took a position standing by the door. In very short order Raheem returned, set the Mac in front of Paul, and Ty slipped his gun back into the holster and went to stand behind Paul.

Paul booted the computer and everybody – other than Ty, Raheem, and Malik Said – waited in perplexed silence as he typed on the keyboard, scrolled down the screen, and finally pressed a series of cell phone buttons. "Speaker!" demanded Ty. After several rings, a woman speaking English with a French accent greeted with "Thank you for calling Investors Bank of Zurich, how may I direct your call?"

"Hello...I have an account and need to arrange a transfer...can you connect me with the proper department?" It was apparent Paul did not want to be placing the call with an audience and especially with an audience of his investors. Mr. Said reached his right arm over the table and motioned for Sean or Helen to slide him the pen, which Helen did. Ty observed the interaction without any sign of displeasure. Mr. Said flipped over the wire instructions and wrote "How much money is in account?" turned, and handed the note to Raheem, who walked around the table and handed it to Ty, who, without any expression quietly read and held onto the note.

Following a delay, Paul connected with the account management department and a woman named Helene. "I would like to make a transfer" Paul told her, "from my personal account to my business account at a different bank." The woman asked for Paul's account number and personal identification number and retrieved the account information at her desktop. "How much will you be transferring?" she asked. "Twelve million US dollars" answered Paul. The woman asked for the transferee information, which Paul read from the white paper, and quoted a rather steep transfer fee which Paul grudgingly approved. After that, Ty tapped Paul on the shoulder, showed him the note from Malik Said, and advised him in a whisper to "Ask her this." Paul's hesitation caused Ty reflexively to slap the back of his head and, when Paul reacted with a snort, the woman asked if everything was "okay."

"Yes," Paul lied in a voice portending the fact everything was definitely not okay but quickly containing his anger, explained, "Oh...I just poked my finger with my pen, an accident, sorry, and, hey, I need to find out my current account balance."

There was a brief period of silence followed by "After the transfer you have forty-two million dollars, US of course, will there be anything else?"

Paul replied "No, thank you," they politely closed the conversation, and Paul pushed the "end" button. His eyes, however, did not leave the phone. Stephen looked at Malik Said with his jaw agape. Mr. Said only shook his head as if to say "Shame on all." Sean cast a disparaging look Paul's way. Gretchen directed her attention to Stephen and, pointing with her crooked right index finger, loudly exclaimed "You're the one that got me into this, just remember that!"

"He, or she as the case may be, who is without sin" bantered Ty lightheartedly, "cast the first stone...good thing we won't need any stones! All right, everyone, you're free to do as you please, without leaving of course; remember, there are bombs, and armed guards everywhere with itchy trigger fingers, and Paul, there is a ray of sunshine, your wife and children will be released from your cabin. We will all meet back here in this room, that means your wife too," his eyes met Paul's, "at two o'clock for the finale. Don't be late!"

It was almost nine-thirty and the rain showed signs of letting up. Gretchen and Thomas returned to their cabin and the McNeil and Waters families to theirs. As promised, Ty released Marie and the twins; Raheem escorted them down the hall and into the waiting arms of Paul for a tearful yet unsettled reunion. Michelle offered her cabin to the DuMorell family and after moving her belongings to the men's cabin, for at least temporarily, they gratefully made themselves comfortable to an extent feasible under the appalling conditions.

Ty also released the captain. Doc went straight to his cabin for a shower and change of clothes, returning then to the master stateroom. "What do you want?" asked Ty more than a little bewildered; "I'd like to stay here with the others" answered Doc. Rather than elicit what would likely be a nonsensical explanation for this most unusual request, Ty studied the captain, especially his eyes, and, after the quiet man patted for weapons, let him sit next to Alwar and Ali.

Almost as soon as Michelle settled in the stateroom with Malik Said and Robert, Hamidah stopped by, like Robert and Michelle wanting to hear from Mr. Said what had happened. He provided an overview of the morning's events – money wired into a business account and some activity to take place that afternoon – noting in conclusion that "Ty, who, by the way, is not as obtuse as you might expect, referred to it as a 'finale'; one thing's for sure, though, everyone's dirty laundry, and, believe me, it is dirty, is now in plain view."

"In plain view" – Robert lay on the bunk underneath where he had planned to sleep and thought about the significance of those words. It was not so long ago that he lectured roomfuls of eager young minds on the concept of privacy; the easiest and most basic of all self-preservation mechanisms, he had instructed, the last bulwark against government intrusion. Considering those words a world away from the classroom, in actual practice albeit under a cloud of physical and mental exhaustion, he felt confident in the correctness of his lesson. Privacy acts just as another tool in the arsenal necessary for survival. "Like prehistoric peoples stashing food and water" he thought, those in society better able to administer privacy conferred on their families a higher quality of life than others not so adept or equipped to maintain secrecy.

"But what a pile of 'dirty laundry'," he lamented, dirty, laundered, money. Privacy enabled deception and Robert by then rightly viewed himself a willing participant with Malik Said and every bit as guilty. Well compensated for privately handling Mr.

Said's illicit affairs, Robert pursued elaborate measures to conceal that ill-gotten reward. In reality, he knew, whether a fortress of stone or a house of cards, a foundation of deceit provides little support. He lay pondering the relationship between deception and privacy; realizing people maintained the privacy of many things for many reasons. Not always, or even often, was the reason illegitimate. As eyes closed he thought of the irony, fretting over cameras and computers while the wealthy amassed entire fortunes in secret.

Hamidah meanwhile, sitting with her feet over the edge of Mr. Said's large bed, meditated on the unspeakable damage caused by her breach of secrecy at his behest. Rebecca was such a beautiful girl, so full of life, so much appreciation for beauty; watching her joy on the veranda, talking with her, so much to live for, so much to offer, so young to die, why? "Why didn't I stop them?" she grieved, tell them it was dangerous, too dangerous, especially for a family. The Waters family need not have been on that yacht – Hamidah punished herself with blame – but Mr. Said wanted every possible soldier. These were not warriors; they were children, mothers, husbands and fathers. Not trained mercenaries, like Klaus, this family was simply cannon fodder, that was all, sacrificial people in a senseless private war. Hamidah lowered her head and wiped tears from under her eyes. Guilt, anger, sadness; pawns, easily manipulated, easily discarded. Good intentions always open the door, she remembered, but the paths from there lead in many directions.

Malik Said stepped to the other side of the bed, sat for a moment, and laid with his head on a pillow. "I'm just going to do as Robert there, close my eyes for a little while, you can rest too if you'd like Hamidah." She knew that he sensed her sorrow, smiled, and replied "Thank you; I'll go take a short nap in my room." As she neared the door Hamidah asked Michelle, whose posture in a cushiony cream-color reclining chair also on the other side of the bed appeared something between a sit and a lay, if she wanted to share her room. "That would be great!" Michelle managed to sound chipper and appear alert but was not so inclined while rising from the chair and gathering personal items.

Two doors down, Paul, having built his entire grandiose persona atop a foundation of lies, was forced to reveal to Marie that he was the root cause of her and their children's unimaginable suffering over the past several days. "There's something I need to tell you" he said quietly after Antoine and Jean fell asleep, "come over here and let's talk."

"Honey," Marie softly spoke, "can it wait; I am awfully tired myself."

Paul shook his head, "Unfortunately, no, we need to talk while the kids are asleep, I'm sorry." He led her by the hand to two chairs, helped her down into one, and sat in the other. "At two this afternoon there will be another meeting and you and I will have to attend. This morning, I transferred twelve million dollars from an account in Switzerland to the DigiFouré business account." Marie's tired face took on a look only of mild surprise; over the previous three days she had been under the constant cloud of death, watched helplessly as her children suffered, endured the most humiliating of conditions, witnessed with relief the violent execution of a human being, and was by that point far beyond ready susceptibility to shock. "I have a Swiss bank account and before the transfer there was fifty four million dollars in it...."

At least perplexed, Marie shook her head and asked Paul, "Where did you get fifty four million dollars?"

Paul's head hung; "I took it from the companies."

Marie's eyes closed. Pushing back deep into the chair she said nothing for several minutes, holding her hand up when Paul would try to say something, until finally, she opened her eyes and wanted to know "What are they going to do at two?"

"I don't know" answered Paul.

"Wake me and the kids at one-thirty" and, upon saying that, Marie instantly fell to sleep.

In a cabin across the hall, Stephen, Stephanie, and Logan were also trying to sleep; of course, heartache consumed their very existence. Stephen's head still hurt and bouts of dizziness only seemed worse when lying down, so he sat on the bed, a pillow between his head and the wooden slat headboard. Stephanie reclined with her eyes closed in a cushion chair and Logan lay on sofa that he did not bother to convert into a queen bed. In his hands, the kitchen knife flipped and twirled, as he imagined stabbing the man who murdered his sister.

A dreary silence ended when Logan burst out with "I wonder what happened to Klaus."

Stephen's head jilted forward so the pillow slipped down to his back, "That's a good question; I haven't seen him since...."

"I wonder if he's dead," Logan – in his own realm – deliberated aloud, "maybe they killed him."

In response his father speculated, "I don't know, maybe they did, maybe he's being held in the stateroom, or hiding," in a manner accurately portraying at best disinterested curiosity.

Logan flipped the knife in his right hand and caught it with his left. Stephanie, eyelids barely wide enough to see through, told her son "Don't do that, you'll cut yourself"; but Logan, pretending not to hear or not to care, flipped the knife again and this time missing the catch it landed handle-first on his stomach.

His mother reacted with a very noticeable sigh of disapproval.

"Do you believe in an eye for an eye?" Logan probed his parents; "Doesn't it say that in the Bible?"

Stephen and Stephanie exchanged fleeting displays of concern. Stephen thoughtfully replied, "Those were different times, Logan, with fewer people, a frontier, without law and order, not like today with police and judges, and laws to deal with criminals."

Logan, sill fiddling with the knife, retorted "There aren't any laws or police or judges out here, are there, so, would it be right for me to kill the man who killed Becca?"

Stephen and Stephanie's eyes again met, this time culminating with Stephanie's impassioned plea, "Whether or not it's right, which, it isn't, more important is the fact I do not want to lose another child," followed by Stephen buttressing the warning with "That's right Logan, these are terrorists, murderers by profession, once we are back on land, we'll do everything we can to make sure they are punished, severely punished."

Logan set the knife on a sofa table and after a minute pronounced, with an unsettling serenity, "Yea, everybody who is responsible...needs to be very severely punished."

The black diver's chronograph on his left wrist displayed "10:52:48," the rain had finally stopped, the sun's rays were beginning to highlight the blue between white puffs, and Klaus, in the early stages of hypothermia, slowly unbuttoned his wet shirt, rolled it into a ball, and heaved it toward the sea. The improving weather meant a change of hiding places; his nest on the radar tower becoming much too evident. Below him strolling and standing on the decks, people, not just those carrying assault rifles, but crewpersons and guests. He stuck the Glock down the front of his pants, pivoted, and slid – icy muscles unable to contract or expand with sufficient rapidity to climb – down the ladder and, correctly anticipating a great deal of pain, leaped onto the sundeck.

It was not a graceful landing. There was no roll; simply the loud thud of cold skin, bone, and muscle impacting hard rough fiberglass. Slowly raising, crawling, limping, Klaus made it to a reclining longue and lay on his stomach. The handgun in a most uncomfortable position, he pulled it from his trousers, left it on the cushion, and rolled over. He had a good view into the gym: no movement and no people. "What a relief!" Next, he scanned for cameras and a place to hide the bulky weapon: no cameras in view and nearby deck chairs with blue and white stripe seat cushions. He shoved the Glock down the back of his pants, dashed to a chair, sat, and maneuvered the weapon under a cushion.

Initially taking a few minutes to revel in the warmth of the sun, Klaus, shirtless, skinned and bleeding knees and elbows, every bit the castaway he stepped gingerly down the stairs and once more unto the treacherous breach. His first encounter was a deckhand polishing brass lighting fixtures mounted to the side of a stairway door. "Good day!" Klaus pleasantly bid the young man; "And a good day to you!" the crewman's cheery reply. "Undoubtedly the most optimistic of greetings imaginable" thought

Klaus, considering their horrid predicament.

Through the doorway and down the stairs Klaus speedily advanced, on through the corridor – nodding at oddly unresponsive sentries – to the stateroom.   After a couple taps on the door it opened to Robert's look of mild surprise and a muted "Welcome back to hell!"

"Glad to be back" rejoined Klaus as behind him the door closed, "I haven't missed all the fun have I?"

Robert's face grew exceedingly sullen; "Not much fun, I'm afraid, two dead – including a young girl – and one missing, presumed drowned."

"That's too bad...," Klaus' tone implied the need for a harsh reprisal, "I heard the gunfire but by then it was too late, I went and hid up top, my gun's still up there."   He sat on the bed next to Malik Said, who quietly with his right hand took hold of Klaus's extended right hand in a warm unspoken "Glad to see you're alive."

Robert also sat on the bed, next to Klaus, "They are suggesting this all may be over today"; Klaus flashed him a perturbed glance, "Really? Are they going to kill everyone?"

Robert proposed Mr. Said enlighten Klaus on the morning's events and so, after rubbing his tired eyes, clearing his throat, and sitting up, Mr. Said provided a very concise summary ending with "finale, that's what he said." Upon hearing that, Klaus, by way of a stiff incline, left the bed and asked if he could borrow one of Robert's shirts.   "Of course" replied Robert.   Limping to the armoire, Klaus pulled out Robert's favorite casual button-down shirt, linen, beige with blue stripes, but suddenly exclaiming that a toilet and hot shower took priority threw the shirt on a chair and hurried to the bathroom.

Just when Mr. Said and Robert had again begun to doze, the bathroom door swung open and Klaus announced while buttoning Robert's shirt that he "did some thinking in the bathroom." Robert's eyes popped open despite his best effort otherwise. "What if the finale is bad?" continued Klaus; "Maybe they will have you move money into their account and then, well, what do they need you for?"

Mr. Said rubbed his eyes again but without otherwise moving informed Klaus that "Robert and I talked about what to do," his voice rough and deep, "We have only two guns, mine, and a second, a little derringer that Michelle brought, and well, yours too, if you can get to it. I was going to carry Michelle's derringer into the meeting, concealed of course, and Robert was going to take my gun, if it looks like we're in danger than...."

"I see" interrupted Klaus, "so, really, you don't have a plan at all...."

"It's pretty hard to make a plan under the circumstances" interrupted Robert.

Klaus again lowered onto the large bed. "That's precisely what I was thinking about, we can't be defensive because we don't have the slightest idea what they're up to, I mean, usually by now it's pretty clear, they say, here's the ransom demand, if it isn't paid we'll kill you, if it is paid, you can go free. Of course, you may not go free, but at least you know how much time you have, something...."

Malik Said sat up, "Agreed, what than do you propose?"

Upon hearing the question, Robert also took a more attentive position, sitting on the edge of the top bunk with his feet dangling.

"We take the offense!" Back on his feet Klaus enhanced his oratory with hand gestures, "We get everybody organized now and take the bridge, barricade ourselves in, and get this thing moving toward the harbor. They'll probably jump ship if we can get close enough." He walked over to a window, slid it open, and took a deep breath; "You can hear the race, listen." In the distance powerful machines accelerated down straightaways and decelerated into curves.

Sliding the window again, this time until it latched, Klaus continued, "I know they have placed bombs and will threaten to blow up the yacht, but, I don't think they will, because they haven't got anything, at least not yet, the money was all put in the business account."

Malik Said stood up to consider the idea and went to look out the window; after a moment turning to ask Robert his opinion. The professor deliberated Klaus' suggestion aware the outcome meant no less than life or death for him and many others. After what seemed a long half-minute as Mr. Said and Klaus gazed impatiently out the window, Robert submitted the verdict: "Ordinarily, I would agree with Klaus, but, in this instance, no, and my reason is, Ty. From what you have described, he does not sound like a cold-blooded killer, a killer perhaps, but not the type who would simply take life for no purpose. I think there is something else going on here."

Klaus seized on Robert's analysis and invited Mr. Said to tell him "a bit more about this Ty." In response, Mr. Said described Ty as apparently smart, educated, not just a contractor but somebody higher up in an organization, a vice president perhaps, concluding with "I think Robert's right, he doesn't strike me as a terrorist or murderer."

"You realize of course that if you are wrong about this man...."

When Klaus hesitated, Robert took the opportunity to say "The other thing is, I do think they will blow up this boat, the Africans that is, I don't get the feeling they and Ty are totally on the same page."

Malik Said agreed and the three decided to remain quasi-prepared for any eventuality. Mr. Said would not carry a gun into the meeting and Robert, Michelle, and Klaus, but not Hamidah as there was not a fourth gun even if she did know how to shoot, would try to find separate places to linger without drawing attention – the considered opinion of Robert and Klaus being that a locked cabin was not where they wanted to die.

By twelve thirty, very few clouds disrupted the bright blue sky over Mediterranean seas southwest of Monte-Carlo. Jerome held the back of his head with one hand and the edge of a bucket with the other; the bilge pump had fortunately extracted most of the water so his task was not as daunting as might otherwise have been the case. After about ten buckets he made it to his feet and once again surveyed the horizon; "Thank goodness for GPS" he thought, treading several centimeters of remaining saltwater to start the engines.

"Yes!" he screamed upon hearing and feeling the engines. Only a quarter tank of gas but based on GPS location enough to return to Splendeur, if it is still in Monaco, surmised Jerome, plotting a course to the harbor. He spun the wheel, pushed the throttle lever, and picked up the radio microphone, "Splendeur, come in, Splendeur, this is Lightning Dancer, Paul, do you read, it's Jerome, come in please." He leaned deeper into the throttle and repeated the hail.

After Jerome's second appeal, Ty pushed from the couch on which he had been laying in the master stateroom, shuffled to the radio, flipped switches, pushed buttons, and repeatedly spoke into the microphone. It was clear from the lack of a response, however, that his voice was not transmitting. "Next time" he mumbled to nobody, "I work on land."

"Either of you know how to operate this thing?" he inquired of Raheem and the quiet man. They just shrugged and replied with "No" and "Sorry." Alwar did not have time to volunteer assistance as Ty simply flipped the intercom switch and broadcast a yacht-wide advisement: "Hey Paul DuMorell or somebody, your boy Jerome's trying to call you on the radio, probably from Barcelona...," he chuckled into the intercom, "better get to the cockpit."

Paul and all of the crewmembers – especially the petite stewardess, and all of the guests, erupted in a spasm of jubilation with hugs and handshakes and hand-slaps all of which served to confound and irritate the second team and especially their leader. The sun is shining and Jerome's alive, beamed the captives, goodness and hope persevere! Paul rushed down the hall and up the stairs, across decks and more stairs, into the bridge he scrambled to grab the microphone. "Jerome! Are you there? Jerome! Come in...."

"Yes, it's me, I'm here, I'm sorry...."

"It's okay, it's okay, where are you?"

"About thirty kilometers southwest, quarter tank," answered Jerome, "she'll make it if you are still in Monte-Carlo."

Paul confirmed Splendeur's coordinates but instructed Jerome to go back to Port de plaisance for fuel. "The fuel card's in the dash compartment; we don't want you drifting away again and I'll certainly understand if for any reason at all you can't make it back." Jerome acknowledged the directive and Lightning Dancer ripped through a curve toward Boulogne-Sur-Mer. Paul replaced the radio microphone, hoping the young man also understood his meaning.

"Jerome is alright!" announced Paul over the loudspeakers, followed by a "Thank God!"

Sitting with Mr. Said and Robert in their cabin – the dream of sleep for each fatigued man all but abandoned – Klaus took a sip of American microbrew lager from his blue highball glass and remarked, "That was awfully unusual, for a kidnapper-terrorist-pirate to alert the hostages that one of theirs is alive, and allow communication, not just allow, but encourage, like this former hostage, who is now free and safe, may actually not alert the authorities and may instead return to being a hostage. Very, very strange...." He took another sip.

The warm sunshine drew many people from their cabins, including Logan, who wandered out onto the main deck to absorb the ocean and mountains and eventually without really intending was standing at the railing overlooking the loading deck and swim platform. Staring down, he could see himself kneeling with Rebecca's head in his lap, telling her she was going to fine all the while watching as dark red life drained from a hole in her leg like soda pours from an overturned bottle. He was there when she screamed in pain, when she cried in fear, when her eyelids closed, when her last breath left – unable to protect her, unable to stop her pain, unable to ease her fear, unable to make her live.

"Hey," the word, though sensitively spoken, startled Logan, "I'm sorry" continued Patricia, "do you want to be alone?"

Logan turned his head away, "Yea...um, no, it's just...," he sniffled; Patricia knew he had been crying and said softly "You must be hurting really, really, bad, I'm sorry, I can't even begin to understand, but I think I would want a friend." She stayed next to him at the railing.

After a while, Logan's head moved just slightly so that he stared off the stern at a horizon of blue water, still unable to look in Patricia's direction, but at least talking; "She was my best friend...." Patricia remained quiet, listening, waiting, until Logan was composed enough to say "and there was nothing I could do."

Patricia thought hard for a moment trying to find the right thing to say, unable, she finally placed her left arm around Logan's back and laid her head gently on his shoulder. Both gazed off into a world still spinning, still alive, still beautiful, and Logan said "I'm gonna miss her."

A few minutes before two, Splendeur's main dining salon doors swung open and harried hostages began passing to take their places around the grand table. Ty, Raheem, and the quiet man stood on the far side of the dining table, near a wall, with Raheem and the quiet man squeezing the plastic and steel grips of nine-millimeter pistols. Once the guests all were seated, the quiet man closed and took up a position in front of the salon doors, Ty stepped around to the end of the table, and Raheem stayed on the far side of the table near the wall.

"I have a sheet of paper here for one person at this table" began Ty handing the paper to Raheem, who, in preconceived theatrics, strolled almost all the way around the table to stand behind Paul. "Mr. DuMorell, this afternoon is your show!" Raheem placed the paper on the table in front of Paul and went back to his station on the far side of the table. Paul made sure that his head did not move, that he not appear interested, but his eyes judiciously scrutinized the writing.

"This morning...," Ty also walked the long way around the table, for dramatic effect, to take a stance behind Paul, "you all transferred a total of fifty-four million dollars into the DigiFouré business account. Now, Mr. DuMorell here, as CEO of the company, is going to transfer one million dollars to each of twelve organizations; these organizations are listed on this sheet of paper, together with wiring information. Mr. DuMorell, I would like you to read the names of these organizations aloud for all to hear before I hand you the phone and, Mr. Waters, since you're his banker, you may want to pay close attention. Go ahead."

Paul lifted the paper from the table, swallowed noticeably, and began reading down the list, starting with "East-West Business Development Foundation...."

"Louder!" yelled Ty.

"East-West Business Development Foundation...."

"Mr. Said's nonprofit organization if I'm not mistaken" exclaimed Ty, "Would that be correct sir?" Malik Said tried not to show any reaction but it was clear to everyone that he was stunned, that a deep nerve had been struck, "Well, I mean, it's, I'm, a board member...."

"I see" said Ty, "and I believe this organization is on the international terrorism watch list as a promoter of or as having links to terrorist organizations, isn't that also correct Mr. Said?"

"I don't know about that!" the flimsiest of all retorts and Mr. Said, normally a man of considerable self-control and discipline, had to swipe a bead of sweat from his left cheek that had rolled all the way down from above the temple.

"Now, now, Mr. Said...." Ty delighted in his role as a real-life game show host; "Anyway, today is certainly your lucky day! You've won one million dollars! That is, your terrorist organization has won a million dollars, or should I say, sponsor of terrorist organizations? Paul DuMorell, please continue reading the names."

It felt as though he were in a tightening vice and Malik Said's mind raced through the many possible adverse scenarios resulting from the day's banking transactions. Not the least of which: the cross-border deposit into his foundation would draw considerable scrutiny from international bank regulators and intelligence and law enforcement agencies. The deposit, ostensibly from DigiFouré Telecom, would also involve the company in countless securities and terrorism investigations, undoubtedly negating its contracts, ruining its business, and wiping out any share value. Because the shares were restricted from resale, nobody could sell, everybody at the table would forfeit all of the money they had invested, and Ty had made sure they all knew Mr. Said was the person responsible. Mr. Said leaned back in his chair, avoiding eye contact with anyone, especially Gretchen, and thought "What a beautiful scheme of vengeance Walter Kragen concocted!"

The beauty became even more apparent as Paul read aloud the other benefactors of his company's generosity; all publicly suspected by the United States, the United Kingdom, and other Western nations as being terrorist organizations or direct sponsors of terrorist organizations. Each of the twelve would receive one million dollars from DigiFouré Telecom upon the orders of a CEO who embezzled from the company with help from a bank president who privately placed the company's securities and used shareholder deposits as a slush fund. Blaming the transfers on duress would not be sufficient to exculpate the dirty players.

"I may have been made ill by Walter Kragen's wicked potion" thought Malik Said; but for some others the concoction may be terminal.

Once Paul finished reading the names, Ty walked back around to the end of the table and announced "Mr. DuMorell, it's time for you to call Mr. Waters' bank and make the transfers, and let me remind both of you," he glared at Paul and Stephen, "if you do anything, I mean *anything*, that appears in the least bit fishy, these two men," his arms stretched and index fingers pointed to Raheem and the quiet man on either side of the table, "they will not hesitate on my instruction to shoot the one you love the most, sitting next to you, do you fathom?"

Paul and Stephen nodded.

Ty handed the cell phone to Raheem, who handed it to Paul, who asked Stephen for the telephone number and with each word punched a number on the keypad until communicating with Worldwide Investment Bank Dubai. Following some initial confusion and resistance from the account manager, overruled by a staunch directive from Stephen, the transfer orders placed so that in a matter of not much more than ten minutes, DigiFouré Telecom became the world's most aggressive corporate funder of international terrorism.

Unable to utter a sarcastic word was Ty as Sean promptly quipped "So, do we get our money back, less, of course, the money just transferred?" This was enough to send Gretchen over the edge. "You idiot!" she yelled, "You didn't have any money and I certainly don't want that money, after all this, transferred back into my account! Don't you see what they've done? Didn't your mother ever tell you the tangled web story?" Ty snickered, as did Malik Said, though trying hard not to, and Helen, for whom the snicker quickly turned to a despondent laugh.

"And it's worse than that Mr. McNeil; it is McNeil, isn't it?" Ty felt more than a rush of devious exhilaration; "All of your calls have been recorded and those recordings and this cell phone," he nodded to Raheem who snatched the device from Paul, "will be provided to US and UK law enforcement agencies, anonymously, of course."

Sean, accustomed to the front of the class, could not help but blurt out "We'll turn you guys in when we get back!"

With a moan Gretchen's head dropped to her forearms on the table; Thomas, Stephen, Stephanie, Paul and Marie shook their heads in wide-eyed disbelief; Helen's giggle became even more disconcerting; Mr. Said, wishing in earnest he had brought the derringer, just glared at Sean; and Ty smiled and shook his head.

"You are all free to leave" Ty announced calmly following Sean's senseless threat; "You however," Ty's attention turned to Malik Said, "I need to have stay."

Mr. Said remained seated while the others left the table and passed as couples quietly through the doorway, down the stairs, and into the sunshine. Stephen and Stephanie decided to take a walk around the yacht for some badly needed exercise, Gretchen and Thomas returned to their cabin, and Sean escorted Helen – in tears – to the sundeck for some open-air lounge relaxation. Paul and Marie continued down the stairs to what had become Hamidah and Michelle's cabin, where they thanked Hamidah for watching Antoine and Jean before going back on deck to also walk and allow the boys some time to run and play. Such was the fantastical atmosphere aboard Splendeur; hostages mulling about having lost loved ones and fortunes, pirates brandishing assault rifles around every corner, and what next, who only knew.

Back in the sumptuous dining salon, Ty took a seat at the table across from Malik Said, instructed Raheem to crack open the door and make sure nobody came close, "especially Jacque and his gang," leaned across the table, folded his hands, looked into Mr. Said's eyes, and bluntly said "We have a problem." Mr. Said's forehead wrinkled and eyebrows curved downward toward the nose; he was perplexed, not to learn there was a problem, clearly this he knew, but because Ty actually admitted to having a problem. "Nobody was supposed to be hurt, let alone killed" explained Ty, unfolding his hands and leaning backward. "At this juncture, we, meaning my team and the team that boarded later, the Africans, were to leave; however, that is not now looking to be likely, I don't believe these Africans will just leave."

Malik Said shifted forward in his chair, arms resting on the table, hands folded as were Ty's just a moment ago, and without feigning naiveté responded that "You had to know this might happen when you hired these guys, they look like real terrorists, the kind who blow themselves up to kill scores of innocent people. Frankly, I'm surprised there aren't more dead."

Ty did not look away from the eyes of Mr. Said; "Yes, they do look like terrorists and I believe they are, but these are certainly not the type of men that we hired, I don't know any of these operatives." With those words the face of the old warlord began to reflect newfound satisfaction in the possibility of a mutual enemy; divide and conquer the most basic of battle precepts. "I suspect" continued Ty, much more serious than Mr. Said had previously observed, "that the one who was supposed to organize their side, Raymond, went into business for himself.

"My theory is also backed up by Alwar, the African we held, who, by the way, I have released, along with your man Ali. Alwar travelled with Raymond and this crazy guy you never met, Gat-mu-something. Alwar told us that Raymond was trying to cut people out, telling them different stories, offering different money. He was never supposed to have this many operatives or as many weapons or explosives; the apartment in Nice was a stockpile that me and my team destroyed.

"The original discussion involved three, maybe four people.

Alwar and I are pretty sure he secretly assembled a group to take Splendeur and the passengers, figuring he could get more than what we were offering, or.... Anyway, something happened to Raymond, though, and it looks as though his people came here on their own, or maybe that was always the plan, I don't know. But, it is interesting that their leader never asked me about Raymond."

Eyes witness to countless unthinkable transgressions trained on Ty as Malik Said casually stated "I had Raymond eliminated and tried to have the others also eliminated before they got here, but that Alwar and Gat-mu got away, killing many of my men. Alwar and Gat-mu showed up here separately, Gat-mu on this vessel with another guy and Alwar in Nice with Ali."

"Well, I eliminated Gat-mu here" proclaimed Ty, equally as detached, "because he was a liability. Did anybody ever go back to Africa, go back and maybe tell the others...?"

"Not that I know of," Mr. Said believed he was fully in sync with Ty's train of thought, "My man, Klaus, stayed in touch with Ali for a while, he was, is, our informant, but I wonder who Alwar is working for?"

Ty shook his head, "I don't know, but I do know that Gat-mu was going to kill him, him and Ali, so, the enemy of my enemy...."

Mr. Said nodded.

Then he asked what Ty proposed and heard far too meaningless a response; "We need to see if we can either get them, the Africans, off this boat, by giving them the money; or see if we can get the other guests and crew off. But, if we can't...."

"How much were they supposed to be paid?"

"One million US dollars upon completion of the assignment" declared Ty rather proudly for a reason theretofore lost on Mr. Said; "Raymond was to make a call to find out if the money was deposited into a certain Nigerian bank account by a certain nonprofit organization having just received the money from a certain global telecommunications company. He would make the call and find out the money was there and then all of us would leave on the boat they came in on."

"How did the Africans get here?"

Ty shook his head, "That, I don't know, and I've been wondering...."

"If you are correct, and these are terrorists, martyrs, they will want to make a statement for their people" assured Mr. Said, "and the money will not matter."

"I think it mattered to Raymond and Gat-mu, maybe Alwar too," suggested Ty, "but, you're right, it may not matter to the others. Raymond probably figured to take all the money and then leave the yacht and passengers in care of the guys out there. These guys may not even know how much they were supposed to be paid or, as you say, it may not matter, but I don't think we should give them any reasons to...."

Mr. Said suddenly bestowed a look and tone of utter skepticism, "Why would terrorists with nothing to lose, on a mission, leave a luxury yacht full of rich people for a million dollars?"

"They may not...alright, you're right, they won't," Ty leaned back again, his bulky arms concealing the wooden arms of a large chair, "and that's the point, that's why I'm talking to you, we are at an impasse. These are not the men we hired to detain everyone until the bank transactions could be finalized, these are opportunistic terrorists and there is nothing standing between them and kidnapping, extortion, murder, not only are there rich people aboard, but the yacht itself would offer significant potential to a terrorist organization for any number of unsavory reasons of which I'm sure you can imagine."

"Which of the organizations on your list was going to pay the Africans?" Mr. Said inquired after a thoughtful silence.

Ty smiled, "East-West Business Development Foundation of course – I was wondering when you'd ask; are you ready to place the call?"

"You must be kidding!" Malik Said exclaimed gruffly.

Ty, a slight one-sided grin, shook his head slowly and holding the cell phone reached across the table, "Do you need the bank's number?"

"I'm curious, Ty," with the look of a man hopelessly ensnared Mr. Said reached and grabbed the phone, "what is your relationship to...."

"Just a well-paid handyman."

"I see; you'll get along with Klaus." While pressing the keys Malik Said acknowledged dryly his dual roles in the tragic comedy: "Hold me up and then have me buy the getaway car. It's brilliant."

X SPLENDOR

Splendeur floated like a lazy seesaw over long ocean swells from North Africa passing under her stern in route to glamorous beaches along the Côte d'Azur. To be a passenger on the yacht that day in late May was to be in an intoxicatingly blue world of water and sky; the weather perfect, sunny, warm, a few voluminous clouds drifting far overhead as underneath sea gulls floated concentric rings. From beyond her contours one would never suspect the grand vessel of anything other than a posh haven of tranquility; splendor, magnificence incarnate, ownership of the thing itself a crowning financial achievement.

For Paul, a dream fulfilled at an awesome cost: twenty-five million dollars cash and almost seventy-five million dollars financed. Every month required an investment of almost five hundred thousand dollars just to pay the interest and expenses to keep her afloat. As a seagoing mansion the yacht's fittings and amenities included fine art, custom hand-crafted furniture, crystal chandeliers each worth more than a luxury automobile, a climate-controlled cellar stocked with over a thousand bottles of premium wine, a swimming pool, spa, gym, bowling alley, steam rooms, saunas, pool tables, and the list went on. Splendeur was indeed, super, the absolute epitome of extravagance that for the same money could have bought ninety-eight million-dollar homes. Paul leased Splendeur to DigiFouré Telecom for one million dollars each month – reward for hard work and a well-connected investment banker.

The view from over the bow of Splendeur that Thursday afternoon was for many on deck equally as awe-inspiring. Monaco, white and peach on a dark green floral billboard screaming splendor are the beautiful, the rich, the famous; all deservingly untouched by the mundane of commonality or worse yet the despair of poverty. Charles Darwin believed the fittest became so through a process of gene selection conferring the highest chance of reproduction – a self-perpetuating cycle of concentric rings ever narrowing to splendorous perfection. Paul had learned that with money he could buy things that brought happiness, but only in spurts, a vanilla peach ice cream cone of momentary ecstasy. Happiness is in this universe of temporality found not in the center, but in the rings, bounded on one side by chaos and the other by agony.

2:43 PM – In a large swivel captain's chair at the helm of Splendeur sits Paul facing the open door with his back to the controls when, without warning, the second team leader enters the bridge flanked by two stout terrorist guards and their black automatic rifles. The leader approaches Paul alone while the guards wait on each side of the doorway. Staring into Paul's eyes the daunting man asks softly, "Did you know Raymond?"

Concerned about the threatening inquisitor's odd behavior, Paul's response is docile, "No, I don't think so, I mean, I've heard his name...."

"He was a genius!" decrees the second team leader, his voice louder, his face more intense; "He," a right fist raises and shakes in Paul's face, "...had vision, vision way beyond what you and I possess!" The dark commander lowers his arm and steps to the side, relaxing somewhat, fixating on inanimate objects and pastoral scenes through the windscreen while eloquently elaborating: "The rich American came to Raymond with a simple idea, take hostages, extract revenge, be handsomely paid...but Raymond, seeing outside, saw opportunity, opportunity for his, for my, our, suffering and oppressed people, a once in a lifetime chance to get close to the extractors and oppressors."

At a loss, yet mesmerized, Paul studies the leader's profile and watches as his head turns and the pupils of the man's eyes meet his.

"Raymond worked day and night to create something worthy of the opportunity. He called in all his debts, and those who owed him came to pay; one of those, a British intelligence officer working in Gabon, a Nigerian, a man born in a Nigerian oil camp run by the imperialist oil company, this man owed a young man, also from Nigeria, peddling bananas and papayas on the streets, a debt from long ago, and he paid with information: a ship from Saudi Arabia carrying the oil minister and many of the world's highest ranking oil company executives, from America, Great Britain, Russia, from

China – the very men and women who rape the resources of my country! Raymond, in his genius, had a vision, and made it come true."

"I don't...understand," Paul timidly confesses, "what does this have to do with me?"

The second team leader smiles. "You, are a very fortunate man, you have a purpose, a special purpose, and soon you will know your purpose, to be a part of history; this ship, your ship, you are part of Raymond's dream, it is you, Paul DuMorell, who deliver us to glory!"

2:53 PM – At the port in Boulogne-Sur-Mer, Jerome, pondering his options, waits on the dock as high-octane fuel gushes into the Lighting Dancer tank; he could walk into town, call his parents, and fly back to Minneapolis, tell the fuel attendant what was going on and hope that the authorities rescued the hostages before the terrorists blew up Splendeur, or, go back, to his friends, to Paul, to Laurie, to captivity, and possibly death. The more he thinks, the more he realizes that walking away in silence is not for him a viable option, which means his only real choices are to tell the authorities, or return, alone, to Splendeur.

Almost overwhelming the consequences of a wrong move, so, Jerome thinks some more, about Paul, who could have called the authorities at any time, but didn't, about all the others aboard the yacht who could have called for help, but didn't. Finally, he concludes with a whisper, "Then I guess it would be a mistake for me to call the authorities...." In the end a combination of youthful naïve nobility, accidental deductive reasoning, and a burgeoning romantic interest in Laurie, a petite spunky yacht stewardess, leads but to one answer – return alone to Splendeur and face the danger with those left behind.

Jerome keeps one eye on the fuel pump as it zips through numbers and the other on a man a few meters away carefully studying Lightning Dancer. The attendant replaces the nozzle at the pump and Jerome hands him a credit card and starts to untie the bow dock line when the curious man says "Excuse me, I couldn't help but notice, it says Splendeur on the transom; is this its tender?" Jerome is unable to respond before the attendant returns the credit card along with two receipts; Jerome holds one receipt against a wooden pylon, signs and holds it for the attendant, and shoves the other along with the credit card into his right pants pocket. "Um, yea, why, do you know of Splendeur?" he asks the man while nervously clenching the bowline.

"Yes" replies the man, "sort of...how are things, what brings you here, is she laying here, at this port, oh, by the way, my name's Moshe, Mo," he holds out his right hand and Jerome with his right hand tensely tosses it about; "Jerome, nice to meet you, no, she's in...Monaco, actually, for the race, how do you know...?"

Mo does not immediately respond. It is a delicate situation and he is unsure how much to say or ask; but Jerome certainly does not seem like an aggressor – more like a possible victim. "I'm with the schooner Enchantress, we're in Cannes, were in Cannes, she's over there," he points to a long beautiful sailboat alongside an end dock, "We saw you just this side of the Strait, you passed by."

He pauses, "So...how are things on Splendeur?"

Although obvious to Jerome that Mo knows something beyond what his words are actually communicating, he is not comfortable engaging in a dialogue, simply replies "Good, they're fine, well, gotta be going, nice meeting you," and turns to untie the stern line. When he does, Mo sees the dried blood in Jerome's blonde hair and the dark red stain running down the back of Jerome's shirt.

"Whoa...what happened to you, it looks like you got hit with an oar!"

Jerome had forgotten about his head, "Oh, that, it's nothing, I fell down, that's all, and hit my head on a tackle box." Mo asks if Jerome is sure that he is okay, and Jerome replies "Yea, I'm fine, I've gotta get back though, or I'll be in trouble, see you later."

Mo waits as Jerome unhitches the stern line, jumps in, waves, and floats away in rumble and fume.

3:17 PM – Malik Said walks out of the dining salon and his meeting with Ty, climbs two sets of stairs, and finds Klaus on the sundeck relaxing in a blue and white cushion armchair with his face tilting toward the heavens.

"There's been a development" advises Mr. Said in very low voice after reclining into an adjacent chair; "it seems the tables are turning. Ty and his team are now with us. He fears the Africans have a rather unpleasant design in store."

Klaus' head tilts forward; "Is there a plan?" he asks.

"No, we are supposed to develop some kind of an idea," Mr. Said shuffles forward in the soft chair, "and we haven't much time I'm afraid, Ty thinks they will act as soon as they receive confirmation the money was wired." Klaus inquires about the money and Mr. Said explains, as best he can, "...and so it seems I paid them one million dollars."

Klaus' head again tilts back; "Hmm, they seem to be much better negotiators than me!" he jokes.

Mr. Said laughs; "They had an agent."

This time more slowly Klaus' head tilts forward; "Unless you can catch them all together – and that implies knowing how many there are – you risk a very large explosion. I'm sorry Malik, but in the instance I don't see how we can do it without considerable risk of life."

Mr. Said nods, "Yes, I agree, but, it sounds to me like it will be a considerable risk to not do anything. We are, I'm afraid, caught between that rock and that hard place."

Klaus sits upright and repositions the bulky Glock under the rear waistline of his pants. "Unfortunately," weary the word rife with experience, "that's a very hard place." His other words pass to Mr. Said's ears with equal solemnity: "We will have to send the non-combatants overboard in anything that floats while those of us remaining onboard confront the pirates, keeping them too busy, hopefully, to quickly detonate the explosives. It is of course, suicide."

Malik Said regains his feet, Klaus too, and they stroll across the sundeck to the stairs and down three flights to the main deck. There, they find Michelle gazing out over the side and explain to her the task at hand. "Of course, I will remain with you, here, on

Splendeur." Mr. Said smiles and cradles her right hand in both his hands for a few seconds until asking Robert's whereabouts. Michelle thinks perhaps the bow, and Mr. Said asks that she bring him to their cabin.

"Ty and his people will be meeting us there," he glances at his watch, "in five minutes, at three-thirty."

3:27 PM – Michelle finds Robert sitting on the bow contemplating Monaco. "So close but yet...." Robert always appreciated Michelle's lighthearted humor; "I could almost swim there" he counters, "I used to be a pretty good swimmer, freestyle, on the swim team in high school." Michelle sits down next to him on the deck; "Well, if you're going, you better go now, because if not..." she glimpses a seagull floating on the breeze and wishes for a moment herself to fly away. Robert watches her go, her eyes, to the side of the rainbow where troubles melt like lemon drops.

"Come on," she springs from the fiberglass, "time to pay the piper."

3:30 PM – Luck, the most important of all battle tactics, cast her passing smile through the guest cabins precisely at that moment. Ty, Raheem, the quiet man, Alwar, and Ali slip into the Said cabin during a brief guard hiatus while Doc keeps watch at the stairs. In the room are Mr. Said, Klaus, Michelle, and Robert. Niceties dispense; everyone says "Hello" or "Hi" and Ty asks what the Said team has in mind.

Klaus takes the initiative of edifying in his usual flip and therefore tactless fashion, "Diversion, non-combatants over the side in preservers or boats, whatever there is, then full attack by our teams...most likely a standoff until the yacht blows up."

Ty's lips form a half grin; he does indeed like this Klaus or at least the way he operates. "Don't try to sugarcoat it...." Everybody laughs and for those four seconds it is okay. "Actually, that was our conclusion also" resumes Ty in a manner more befitting the occasion, "there really isn't any other option that we could think of; but, I will also add, the captain is going to try and send a distress call when the fighting begins and if it looks like the civilians are safely away, we all, need to jump."

In support of that idea there is unanimity.

3:35 PM – A loud "thump" interrupts the battle and escape planning. The quiet man standing closest to the door starts to twist the deadbolt when a very scared man from the hallway shouts "They're coming!" Guns spout from pants and holsters. "I hate plans" mutters Klaus with the fingers of his left hand tight around the door handle; "I'll try to draw them away to give you time to get back to your room. It's been fun...." He hurls through the doorway. Robert yells "Shit!" and takes up the rear, or so he thinks, his Colt gleaming in the corridor lights, but Alwar without a word flashes by and falls in close behind with a Beretta.

3:36 PM – The six approaching pirates are not prepared for three armed insurgents charging from the cabin corridor. They fumble with assault rifles and Berettas as the three disappear up the stairs and Ty, Raheem, and the quiet man dash unseen to their stateroom.

3:37 PM – "Leave them" directs the second team leader in French to his second in command; "they just try to waste our time. They will surrender to save the lives of their friends. It is as old as warfare itself."

3:38 PM – Returning to Enchantress with two bags of groceries, soda and beer, Moshe passes Silvia in the dining salon and mentions his encounter with Jerome. "He looked pretty beat up and acted pretty nervous" recounts Mo. Silvia leans back in her chair and asks if there was any mention of Alwar. "No" replies Mo, "I didn't want to say too much, it was a touchy encounter, but there's no doubt something's not right."

"I wonder what's going on" contemplates Silvia aloud, "Why is the yacht tender out running around with a kid...." She stands, walks down the hall, and knocks on a door, "Sam, it's me, you got a second?" After several seconds the door opens and a short bald man with a gray beard and no shirt invites Silvia into his cabin; "What's up?" Silvia explains that the yacht she had previously told him about was in Monaco and relates what Moshe told her.

Samuel Baer offers Silvia one of a pair of well-worn light blue fabric cushion chairs and sits in the other, "I know the boat's in

Monte-Carlo because Gretchen Steinberg's on board. You know, I've been trying to catch up with her for weeks, she's a real pain, then I read in the Times that she's attending a party on this yacht, the same one you were talking about, imagine that."

"Small world" replies Silvia without really appreciating Sam's irony, "anyway, sounds like they've got a problem, but, Alwar, the guy we had on board, made me promise not to call in the army."

Sam leans forward, places elbows on knees, and says with a puzzling fusion of sympathy and indifference which Silvia has grown accustom, "Well, I can see why, if they're being held, I mean, as hostages, from what you told me, these sound like bad characters; but we have to take a pass by just so I can try to get a chance to talk with Gretchen, we really need her investment in the film, and opportunity, you have to take it when it comes. Get us underway and tell the crew what's going on; I'll call over there when we're closer."

When Silvia returns to the deck she finds most of the crew at the starboard rail; "What's the fuss?" she asks. "Out there," Dee points to the horizon, "we thought it was a cruise ship, but Tony looked it up, it's one of the Saudi royal yachts." Simon hands Silvia a pair of binoculars and she surmises after studying the enormous craft that it "must be going to Monte-Carlo for the race." "They are," confirms Mo, "I read online that the oil minister's on board together with the top executives from several oil companies. Looks to be quite a shindig."

Silvia lowers the glasses and with a look of uncertain revelation declares "Well now, that's interesting."

3:45 PM – Splendeur guests and crewmembers were rounded up by the second team and herded into the grand salon, where they now wait in terrifying silence. Inside the door stands the second team second in command; to each side of him, two terrorist guards, and at the front of the salon, six guards. Loudspeakers positioned around the yacht crackle and hum. After several seconds a deep voice in English announces: "I have been told there are three people not accounted for. You three have five minutes to come to the large room on the second level. For every minute after that, that you delay, we will kill one of your people."

3:46 PM – A man with a handgun enters the grand salon and whispers to a man holding an automatic rifle, who whispers to the terrorist who speaks English, who in turn abruptly points to Malik Said, Sean McNeil, and Hamidah. "Come with me" the man orders. Patricia wails and Helen screams "No!" Sean's legs turn to mush. Two terrorists drag him across the room and out the front door. From the upper deck three terrorists and three hostages climb to the bridge deck and from there to the sundeck. In the background loudspeakers pulsate: "You three, look to the sun and see your comrades, your first sacrifices to the god of war!"

3:47 PM – Ty and Raheem are prevented from accessing the bridge by two terrorists; with precious time remaining they start for the sundeck stairs but are stopped by two other terrorists, who also take their weapons and lead them downstairs to the grand salon.

3:48 PM – A terrorist on the sundeck places the muzzle of a nine-millimeter Beretta against Hamidah's forehead and with his thumb pulls back the hammer. His finger lightly touches the trigger. Malik Said yells "Klaus, Robert, if you can hear me, they're going to kill Hamidah, come out and give up your weapons, and there are more of them...." At least ten meters away can be heard the thud of rifle butt against bone and, not having to wait long, the thump of limp flesh on fiberglass.

3:49 PM – Klaus, Robert, and Alwar – hiding in the pool and spa enclosure on the other side of the gym – pitch their guns behind chairs; Robert pulls open the door and all three sprint across the gym.

3:50 PM – Alwar pushes open the door to the sundeck and Klaus, Robert, and he emerge just in time to see a darkly clad terrorist pivot toward Sean McNeil. "Boom!" a sound wave ripples across an eternity of air and water. The new prisoners watch in shock as Sean's head flies back and his body flips backward over the sundeck railing. On the deck lays Malik Said face down in a growing puddle of blood with Hamidah at his side.

3:52 PM – Two terrorists heave Malik Said's limp body over the sundeck railing and into the ocean; Alwar, Klaus, Robert and

Hamidah observe in silence until being led to the grand salon.

3:53 PM – The second team leader speaks in English to the frightened audience in the grand salon. "What you should be asking yourselves right now is why you are still alive. The reason you are alive is that your purpose in life has not yet been served, that is why you are alive, and your purpose in life will be served very soon. Everybody has a purpose in life, but very few ever find it, only a very fortunate few are given the chance to know their real purpose, so you should all be very thankful that you will soon know your purpose."

Addressing the captives like a preacher to his a congregation, the second team leader, pacing back and forth while peering through the triangle created by his touching fingertips. Quite clearly, he is a delusional egomaniac. The level of fear created by this spectacle is such that a pin drop would cause a stampede; but not a pin drops.

The second team leader studies the frightened faces until setting his gaze upon the captain, Doc, the man who earlier had dared to challenge his assertion of absolute power. "You sir, are a fortunate man" the madman exclaims, and using his gun blows a huge orifice into Doc's left lung. Doc gasps and hurls back into the chef as the room erupts in unbearable noise ending only when the other captives realize they are alive and will only, if only temporarily, remain alive by being silent.

"You see," the second team leader looks around the room, "that man's purpose was to show all of you how easy it is for me and my team to take a worthless human life." Beyond the salon threshold passes the second team leader like an executioner departing a dungeon, leaving behind minions brandishing assault rifles and pistols. Prayer is heard, sobbing is heard, what cannot be heard are the frantic unspoken efforts of Klaus, Ty, Michelle, and Robert to find a way of defeating the undefeatable. Clearly, the question of horror is not if, but when.

3:54 PM – Malik Said is under Splendeur's swim platform, peeking around a corner, waiting, remembering earlier times behind boulders in the hot sun, waiting, ever so patient for nightfall to ambush an enemy superior only in weaponry. The old warrior held his breath while lying on the deck in excruciating pain as blood trickled from above his right ear. He held his breath while dragged by his arms across several meters of coarse fiberglass and wood, while contorted, lifted, dropped, and while sailing through almost ten meters of air until slamming and sinking into the frigid Mediterranean Sea. He held his breath while swimming underwater to the hull, surfaced, gasping, and swam to the stern where he hung precariously by fingertips from under the swim platform. There, his head remained mostly submersed under the very edge, tilting sideways to take advantage of a thin expanse of air.

4:16 PM – Malik Said hears a powerboat approaching from the port side, releases his finger hold, and remaining underneath the platform treads water to the platform end. There, again dangling from the edge of the platform and tilting his head with one eye out of the water, he sees what appears to be Lightning Dancer perhaps a quarter kilometer distant and quickly approaching. Floating out from under the platform he looks around the stern and gazes up the side of the hull at least three meters to the main deck. Leaning out he studies the edge of the upper deck, and still farther, the edge of the bridge deck. The speedboat is within a hundred meters and slowing precipitously, turning to the right, and Mr. Said recognizes Lightning Dancer coming in at Splendeur's stern to moor at the loading deck near the swim platform.

"That stupid kid" thinks Malik Said, what is he doing coming back here – they'll shoot him on sight!

Treading water until just around the stern, Mr. Said hugs the portside hull, turns, kicks his feet, throws his arms in the air and waves side-to-side over his head. "Come on Jerome, look!" he whispers. Lightning Dancer is now about fifteen meters from the loading deck; Jerome glances over to get his bearings, sees a head bobbing next to the swim platform with arms waiving wildly in the air, pulls back on the throttle lever, and nudges Lightning Dancer to the left, port, to take a closer look and assist the drowning man.

Fearing the worst Malik Said kicks harder, thrusting with his arms, as if to say "Back, get back, go, away!" but Lightning Dancer floats ever closer. With the tender not more than ten meters from the yacht, Jerome realizes what the man he now knows to be Malik Said is trying to communicate and twists the wheel hard to right, but not a split second before Mr. Said yells "Get out of here, go, go, run!" and a shot rings out from the sundeck.

The windscreen shatters and Jerome ducks, reaching up with his right hand he jams the throttle lever forward and Lightning Dancer springs. The bow careens airborne as jets blow saltwater high into the sky, within seconds transporting Jerome well out of harm's way. Malik Said slides back under the platform not knowing whether the terrorists also heard his warning or, if they did, whether they knew from where it came. He waits, barely breathing, listening as water laps the hull for footsteps, voices, or the unmistakable clatter of a chambered bullet.

5:22 PM – Leaning against the sundeck starboard railing the second team leader admires the Saudi royal yacht through binocular lenses – lowering them, lifting them, trying to assess the distance. "It will not come too close to the harbor or the other yachts" he tells one of his men standing next to him; "I think it will be over there," he points in the direction of Nice, "probably about as far out as are we." He returns the binoculars, climbs down the stairs and across to the bridge.

6:00 PM – In the Splendeur grand salon, nothing grand, simply the despondent faces of traumatized people all walks of life, old and young, rich and poor, caught up in the rings, huddling together helpless as the day they were born. Helen, Sean Jr., and Patricia have joined the mournful ranks of Stephen, Stephanie, and Logan; Robert and Klaus, Ty also, sit quietly remembering Malik Said; Paul, his two best friends in life, Carl and Doc, gone forever. All except Logan wondering: "How do I go on?" The mood so heavy as to be a dense fog; when Ty stands to stretch and a guard orders him to sit, Ty just raises his middle finger.

6:12 PM – Two knocks on the grand salon door. A very tall muscular guard holding a machine gun flips the bolt, conferences with someone on the other side, turns, and pronounces the words "Paul...DuMorell." Paul rises. Marie squeezes his hand; though a look of dread she remains silent. Paul smiles, kisses her forehead, hugs Antoine and Jean, and steps forward. The man waves him over and through the doorway.

6:48 PM – From the grand salon to waning sunlight on the sundeck now appear the hostages, all but Paul DuMorell, aligned into two rows along the starboard railing as though posing for a class picture. The first row is made to kneel, the second, to stand. Nobody smiles. Robert, shoved into the first row, refuses to kneel and so a guard swinging an AK-47 strikes his left shin with such force that bone splinters and the once defiant man drops wincing in excruciating pain. Another guard with a small digital video camera begins filming, turning his head very carefully to capture each of the hostages' forlorn faces, stepping back, stepping forward, until the second team leader appears in front of the lens to recite in English a prepared monologue.

"My name is Imoh. I am one of the leaders in the organized movement to assure that African natural resources benefit Africans. My team has taken the yacht Splendeur and her passengers and we have unfortunately had to kill some who resisted. Our cause is simple, to bring attention to the atrocities committed by foreign oil companies in Nigeria and especially the Niger Delta and to stop these atrocities. To serve our cause, we are going to execute the Saudi oil minister and the responsible oil company executives if the foreign oil companies do not agree to leave Nigeria and return the land and resources to the people."

The man with the camera pans from Imoh and the hostages to the Saudi royal yacht, zooming in, zooming out, finally pushing the power button and looking to Imoh for guidance. Imoh tips his head portside, towards Monaco, confirming a previously delivered instruction and causing the man to sprint down the stairs and within minutes pilot a small tender toward the harbor. Klaus watches the boat jettison from below, thinking, "Imoh and his men know the oil companies will never agree to leave Nigeria, there isn't to be any demand, any condition. What form of execution have the terrorists devised?"

7:00 PM – In Washington, DC, Glenda's monitor displays "13:00" so she logs on and lays the remains of her grilled eggplant sandwich on the desk next to a Redskins coffee mug. Sixteen unread messages – about usual for a thirty minute lunch break –

she methodically reviews the email subject lines and either tags for follow-up, deletes, or scrolls to the next message. Clicking on the eighth email she reads aloud, "East-West Business Development Foundation...What the heck is the east west business development foundation?" and clicks "open." The email is from the U.S. Department of the Treasury:

"Per your pending request for information, the sum of $1,000,000 USD has this date been deposited via electronic bank transfer into the account of East-West Business Development Foundation; Transferor Bank: Worldwide Investment Bank Dubai/London (HMRC); Transferor: DigiFouré Telecom France; Transaction ID: 4922kffa33441la; Transferee Bank: International Bank of Turkey; Pending Transaction: $1,000,000 USD; Transferor Bank: International Bank of Turkey; Transferor: East-West Business Development Foundation; Transaction ID: asffi344932jllc; Transferee: 27 Ltd Nigeria; Transferee Bank: Nigeria Savings Bank."

Glenda grabs her coffee mug and stands. "Heidi," she looks at the photograph pinned to the acrylic divider, "there's just too much to do and I can't keep track of everything!" Returning to her cubical after a quick trip to the coffee maker, Glenda still cannot recall the significance of East-West Business Development Foundation and consequently initiates a hard-drive search. "Bingo!" she smiles; Robert Downing, professor, lectured at a Paris conference sponsored by East-West, invitation presented by Malik Said. Pieces of the puzzle fall together as Glenda reviews her case notes, revealing a very bizarre picture culminating with payment to an unknown Nigerian company.

"Suspected, my foot!" She looks back at the Treasury Department email; "A million in, a million out, London, Dubai, Lagos, geez, could they be more obvious?" Glenda reactivates the matter and updates her task list: recheck Downing, recheck Said, recheck EWBDF, contact DigiFouré accountant/controller – who sent wire, research 27 Ltd – who sent wire. She thinks for a moment and erases "recheck Downing" to instead type "talk with Downing." Nice day for a trip to Georgetown; she winks at the photograph and grabs her purse and bus pass.

7:24 PM – Paul is standing, staring out the windscreen. "I can't do it alone, I'll need help." Imoh thinks about Paul's statement, lowers the binoculars, and replies "I will help you." "No, I need my own person," Paul is playing his last card, "and I have someone in mind." Imoh takes a step toward Paul and asks quite seriously, "Are they experienced?" Paul turns toward him and replies "No, not in the least, but, I trust him, he'll do what I say, besides, you and that gorilla with the machine gun will be watching." Imoh rubs his chin, "I don't understand why you would want someone not experienced...." "Because" bellows Paul angrily, "you murdered the captain, there is nobody left with any experience!"

It was a lie, the part about experience, but it rang true and Imoh agrees, "Alright, what is his name?"

"Ty" answers Paul, "his name is Ty."

7:27 PM – Ty appears at the bridge under two-man armed escort. "Search him" orders Imoh, and the huge man guarding the door steps in front of Ty; they glare at one another like two wolves sizing up the opposition and afterward Ty holds out his arms and the man pats his shirt and trousers. "You are wondering why you are here – what is your purpose," speculates Imoh, "as am I." Ty's eyes move from Imoh to Paul for some kind of indication.

"I need you to help me pilot Splendeur" Paul says, as if the information obvious, and sits in one of the swivel captain's chairs.

Ty chews his lower lip and continues his focus on Paul; "How did you know I was in the navy?" as if reading from a script.

Paul smiles, "I didn't, but I could tell you know your way around boats, so I figured you were as good a candidate as any."

Ty stops chewing his lip and asks "Where are we going?"

"Not far actually" replies Paul, "just a short jaunt to another yacht, the Saudi royal yacht as a matter of fact."

"Well," Ty retorts, "let's get started!"

Imoh observes the conversation with curious interest and shakes his head, "Not yet, in a few minutes, first," he moves toward the console, "I want you to tell me what this gauge is," and points to an analog dial.

Paul sits breathless.

Ty gives a look of indignation, walks over, and glances at the instrument, "Well, let's see now, it's a voltmeter," points to another gauge, "and this is an oil pressure gauge," another, "and this is a temperature gauge," and another, "an hour counter...."

"Okay, okay" Imoh concedes, "that's enough; it seems you do have a purpose."

Paul exhales, through a Cheshire grin.

7:46 PM – With the sun low on the horizon Malik Said decides the time has come to leave the relative safety of the water, glances quickly over the swim platform, removes his pants and shirt leaving only a pair of black briefs, pulls his body up, crouches low and darts to the wall. There he lies motionless for several minutes; no plan, not even an idea, understanding as did Klaus that plans are in a volatile environment simply prescriptions for failure. Klaus bolted past the guards to draw their attention, took action, in hindsight possibly a mistake, but hindsight is for historians, not for those living in the rings.

7:49 PM – Malik Said is back on the move, slithering on his belly up the stairs from the loading deck until able to raise his head just slightly and view the main deck extending to the guest staterooms. The expanse appears vacant. He lowers his head and gazes up, finding nothing out of the ordinary at the rim of the upper deck or the bridge deck, but what looks like a rifle barrel protruding from the sundeck. "Where is everybody?" he wonders; cabins, dining salon, grand salon, sundeck?

Slowly, Mr. Said lifts his head again to peer across the main deck and, as he does, a small object slides to within arms' reach. He ducks and waits a second before quickly popping up, grabbing a Beretta, and ducking back down. "A miracle!" softly proclaims Mr. Said after finding the magazine full.

Somebody is on his side, somebody also free, and there is now – though still certainly slim – a fighting chance. Malik Said sticks his head up again, looks around, and scurries on hands and knees to take cover behind a chair. Next, he carefully makes his way behind another chair, and another, until slipping under a tablecloth comes face to face with the quiet man holding his right index finger across his lips.

Slowly moving his finger the quiet man whispers "They are all on the top deck."

"What do you propose?" Mr. Said asks the quiet man.

A thoughtful and courageous reply the quiet man offers: "We are going to die so we must do something to save as many as possible. I have my gun and you have a gun, the extra that I brought. We will just fight until we can fight no more."

7:50 PM – Aboard Enchantress, Sam wanders pensively the length of the deck until reaching Silvia at the wheel, "I tried calling but they didn't answer"; he sounds to Silvia as though genuinely concerned; "How long before we're there?" Silvia examines the GPS monitor and replies "maybe ten minutes." Sam glances at his feet and the starboard horizon. "Don't get too close, just go in slow and easy, like we're going to the race, take down the sails and motor in, study them with binoculars, but don't let them see you." Silvia nods, "Will do...don't worry."

Running with a good wind the schooner dances under the setting sun and several minutes pass when Moshe at the bowsprit notices a boat directly on their course. Into a handheld radio he warns "Silvia, there's a small boat ahead about a thousand meters, appears to be stationary, do you read?" Silvia acknowledges and Enchantress starts a graceful turn to starboard. Mo studies the boat through binoculars and advises Silvia, "I think it's the Splendeur tender," laughs for a second, "I think it's the kid I was telling you about."

"Lower the sails" replies Silvia; "we'll go on fossil fuel for a while."

Jerome watches the big schooner drop sails and cruise toward Lightning Dancer with his right hand firmly atop the throttle lever. He observes Mo waving enthusiastically from the bowsprit and waves back hesitantly, much less enthusiastically, considering whether to gun the engines, break away, and find another place to meditate. "Maybe I'll just see what they want" he mumbles as the yacht slows, but that's all; don't get Splendeur in any more trouble.

"Ahoy Jerome!" yells Mo; "Are you in distress?"

"No!" Jerome yells back.

Enchantress, some twenty meters from Lightning Dancer, moves gracefully by and as she does other crewmembers wave and Jerome waves back until finally a blonde woman standing at the very end of the sailboat yells "Jerome, we know about Splendeur, pull in back here, come on, we all need to work together!" In the graying dusk he watches as the two towering masts and long sleek hull obscure like a train caboose into fog. "She was right" he admits; it will take more than him to save Laurie. Within seconds Lightning Dancer is close enough for Jerome to toss a line to Silvia who, first wrapping the rope tight around two cleats, slows Enchantress enough for Jerome to jump aboard.

8:15 PM – Now two-fifteen in Georgetown, Glenda steps off the bus, studies her cell phone GPS, and begins a short hike to Robert Downing's townhome. "Two hundred feet, turn left, one hundred twenty feet, your destination is on the right...." Glenda smiles at her phone, "What did I do before you came along?" The brownstone resembles every other townhome on the block except, she observes from the street, odd bits of trash strewn on the porch and a mailbox overflowing with junk mail.

She continues along a short concrete sidewalk, steps up three stairs, and knocks on the door; of no surprise, no answer. She bends down and picks up an envelope. Two weeks earlier reads the postmark. Downing did have a lecture in Paris and probably took an extended vacation, she speculates while examining the other envelopes, all junk mail – no personal mail, no bills, no magazines, just junk mail.

Glenda returns to the street and calls her office, "I need a telephone number...," and after waiting several minutes, "Thanks Sharon."

Keying in the number – disconnected – "Bingo!"

8:22 PM – Malik Said and the quiet man dart from under the table to the stairway; the quiet man in the lead sprints up three stairs at a time holding a Beretta with both hands. He performs a cursory inspection of the upper deck and motions for Mr. Said who falls in behind with a Beretta. They pivot and more cautiously ascend another flight of stairs to the bridge deck. The quiet man stops. He surveys the area. The two bolt to a windowless wall and stand with backs against the fiberglass; around the corner, windows and the bridge door; across the deck, stairs to the sundeck. The men have no idea what they will find or what they will do; all they know is that time is their enemy. With night descending and hostages corralled, anything is possible.

8:23 PM – Malik Said and the quiet man hear the bridge door open, and close, followed by footsteps of two maybe three across wood and fiberglass onto the stairs. They strain to hear, waiting, until a voice from the sundeck: "In a few minutes we are going to go for a little cruise and I want you to enjoy yourselves. The bar is now open. Please, relax, have fun." Mr. Said's and the quiet man's eyes meet. Mr. Said kneels, shuffles around the corner and quickly back, "Locked." There is nowhere to hide on the upper deck. "We'll never make it up the stairs, we have to crawl to the front, under the windows, and then up" whispers the quiet man. Mr. Said's return glance conveys the unsaid fear of both men – guards on and overlooking the bow deck. "Go!"

8:24 PM – The quiet man drops to the deck and expertly slinks back and forth like a lizard moving across hot sand; behind, Malik Said, his face confronting the tattered leather soles of the quiet man's old shoes while maneuvering equally as quick across the warm fiberglass. Their prone figures slide in and out of windows' glow, sometimes precariously hanging partially over the edge, looking down to the black water below, fingernails digging into the smallest crevices, pulling, sliding, until the narrow passageway begins to open up at the front deck sitting lounge.

8:26 PM – Stopping, searching, and studying, the quiet man challenges the intermittent dark for any sign of life. Malik Said breathing deep breaths around the plastic Beretta grip between his teeth clings to a narrow stretch of fiberglass. The leather soles creep forward, stopping, moving again, very slowly the quiet man enters the open bow, gazing up, at the ready in an instant to unleash the Beretta's firepower. Into the recessed seating his body eventually pours and Mr. Said crawls in behind, ducking low on the floor behind soft cushions, still visible from the spa railing above they lay silently catching their breath.

8:29 PM – A sudden loud metallic rumble from behind startles Malik Said and the quiet man who instantly flip to their backs ready to shoot – but there is no one. The rumble persists. Finally, Mr. Said nudges the quiet man and whispers, "It's the anchor going up." They roll back over and peer up at the vacant railing and the quiet man in a hushed voice confesses a mutual dilemma, "We'll never make it over the window without being seen." Mr. Said counters, "It won't matter."

"If they're raising the anchor, it means we're going somewhere, and, to my knowledge, there're only two people on board who can pilot this thing, the captain and Paul, and both are on our side. Now, unless somebody else is looking out the windscreen, we'll be okay; but, the other problem is, we can't raise the ladder, it will take too long, so you're going to have to stand on my shoulders."

"How will you get up?" whispers the quiet man.

Mr. Said hesitates. The answer comes in a low voice, "I'm going back to the stairs." The quiet man starts to say it is suicide but Mr. Said cuts him off: "It's the only way. I knew it before we left the back deck. They'll hear me coming and that will hopefully give you a chance with your Beretta to take out several of the guards. Maybe I can get one." The quiet man pays a somber respect, "I wish I would have gotten to know you better." Mr. Said smiles; turning his head to reexamine the obstacle he replies softly, "Don't give up on me yet."

8:31 PM – The quiet man waits below while Malik Said crawls a short distance to the windscreen, holds his breath, raises his head and peeks into the bridge. Under the fluorescent lights it is easy for him to see Paul in a captain's chair almost directly at the center and, to his surprise, Ty, standing to Paul's right. Behind them two pirates – one extremely large – conversing by the door. Mr. Said taps the windscreen.

Paul reflexively glances to the sound and, seeing a ghost, bounces back in his chair, causing Ty to look over and he too seeing Mr. Said act as if nothing were out of the ordinary. After Ty observes an index finger point upward from outside the windscreen, he nods, turns, walks to the door, bellows "Hey, I need to use the head...now!" and grabs the door handle. Imoh and the large guard grab Ty's arm, resulting in a brief scuffle, during which the quiet man leaps onto Mr. Said's shoulders and scales the glass until his old shoes disappear from view. "Alright, I won't use the head" agrees Ty while straightening his shirt.

8:32 PM – Malik Said's first thought upon slipping back into the lounge area is "Thank goodness Ty was there"; quickly checking the bridge roof he responds to the quiet man's short wave with a nod and a smile. One, two, three – Mr. Said counts silently to ten. No crawling this time, no pistol grip in his mouth, just running, along the ledge, past windows, until on the upper deck behind the bridge sprinting to stairs accessing the sundeck. His heart thumping, lungs expanding and contracting, one step, another, index finger on the trigger....

Neither Malik Said nor the quiet man were given to second guessing, for had they been, might have considered a rescue with less potential for collateral damage. The fear of reacting too slowly trumped the fear of accidental harm. They were convinced the terrorists would kill all of the hostages – it was only a matter of time, and neither could bear the thought of having been helpless to prevent the slaughter.

8:33 PM – The sundeck is illuminated in fine fashion for a party. Traumatized captives gulp drinks and nibble wafers as pirates in flowery Hawaiian shirts – barely disguising pistol holsters – wander among them. Imoh is adhering to Raymond's well-conceived plan: Splendeur should appear the harmless toy of a pampered tycoon as it drifts closer and closer to the Saudi yacht, so harmless, in fact, that the Saudis will neglect to take evasive or defensive action until it is too late and the glorious five thousand ton floating bomb is at the royal yacht's flank.

8:34 PM – It is Hamidah first glimpsing Malik Said on the stairs with the Beretta; startled, elated, anxious, she somehow manages simply an inconspicuous smile and shake of her head to make clear any gunplay would have a very bad outcome. The determined Mr. Said at first heeds the warning and takes a step backward and down, but options nil, has to finally shake his head "No" in reply; no place to hide on the upper deck, no way to blend in on the sundeck, no chance to stop the quiet man approaching from the gym roof. Hamidah understands Mr. Said is in difficult predicament – though unaware the extent – and motions for him to toss her the Beretta. Initially, he resists, but her persistence finally wins over and crouching low on the stairs, he reaches up, hands her the gun, and proclaims very softly, "There's another coming over the roof."

8:35 PM – With a smile and nod, Hamidah turns, glances at the roof, slides her right hand and the Beretta into the right pocket of her cream chiffon skirt, meanders whimsically through the many glum faces, finds the terrorist who murdered Sean McNeil and placed a gun to her forehead, strolls toward him with a seductive smile, gets very close, looks into his eyes, slowly pulls the Beretta from her pocket, very lightly touches his Hawaiian shirt with the muzzle, carefully draws back the hammer, whispers "You have no purpose" and squeezes the trigger.

Hamidah bends down and rips open the killer's bloodied flower shirt as he lies dying on the fiberglass, yanks a Ruger nine-millimeter semi-automatic from its holster, and screams "Get down, everybody, get down!" The quiet man with his Beretta has picked off two terrorists like a sharpshooter at a turkey shoot and Malik Said, clad only in black briefs, has his arms wrapped around the neck of another. Within seconds only Hamidah, Malik Said, Michelle, Klaus, Robert, Alwar, Raheem, Ali, Gretchen, Logan, and twelve terrorists armed with semiautomatic handguns, are standing under glimmering party lights.

8:36 PM – Hearing gunfire from the sundeck, Imoh decides to pursue a backup plan and orders Paul to accelerate toward the Saudi royal yacht not more than five kilometers distant. "Faster!" yells he and diesel fuel surges into the two huge Caterpillar engines. Splendeur howls and her prow parts the sea in waves. Ty looks at Paul but sees only the profile of a man determining the future. "He must know they want him to ram the Saudi yacht" believes Ty, plunge Splendeur deep into the giant's side and detonate the explosives wired throughout her hull!

"So you're going to kill us all?" Ty prods Imoh but Imoh prods back:

"No, *you're* going to kill us all!"

All the while Paul stares ahead, wondering if his family is still alive, watching as Splendeur bears down on its unsuspecting target.

8:37 PM – On the sundeck, Hamidah points the Beretta at a man raising a Beretta at Klaus and fires; the man leans forward in pain and turns his weapon on Hamidah; Klaus swivels and leaps, but not in time, from the side flies Ali directly into the path of glory. Hamidah kneels at Ali's side and in a scene of chaotic cataclysm presses her right palm just below his right armpit to stem the bleeding.

"Are you alright?" asks Ali with considerable difficulty.

"Yes Ali, you saved my life," softly assures Hamidah.

Klaus meanwhile takes up a kneeling defensive position on the other side of Ali; touching the young man on the shoulder, Klaus nods and winks "Well done," while with his left hand motioning for the Ruger. Once in possession of the weapon Klaus bursts to his feet and begins surveying the area, feet shoulder width apart, knees slightly bent, twisting, turning; the consummate professional protecting two young people having to express untold love in the merciless words of goodbye.

Ali manages a slight smile through unbearable pain and Hamidah smiles in return the look of sorrow, bends down, and kisses his mouth. Ali's eyelids began to quiver and he coughs; a trickle of blood drains from the corner of his mouth and Hamidah wipes it with her skirt. She takes both of his hands into her own and again bends down, this time, lying gently on his stomach she covers his upper body with hers and positions her head carefully next to his. Ali can feel Hamidah's heartbeat and she his, and she whispers her love for him, and he coughs and his heart beats rapidly and slowly and skips. He coughs again, and the beat is no more. Hamidah's eyes close – "I'm sorry Ali."

8:38 PM – The quiet man from the rooftop picks off another. Robert runs, reaches down, and grabs the dead man's Beretta just as a bullet tears through his right shoulder. The gun drops. Robert drops, to his knees, desperately he grapples with his left hand for the firearm. Another bullet whizzes past and lodges deep in the fiberglass. Michelle slides across the deck; seizing the Beretta she twists and discharges three bullets, shredding a Hawaiian shirt and sending its occupant wobbling backward into oblivion.

Logan removes the kitchen knife from his pocket and runs toward a Hawaiian shirt; the man turns his gun on Logan but a timely clasp from the quiet man's Beretta brings the man down. The knife slips through Logan's fingers as he stands paralyzed. Malik Said leaps from crushing his opponent's windpipe, onto Logan, slamming the boy to the deck and shielding as three tiny spears impale thin skin and aged muscle.

Alwar, a man tortured, physically and mentally, pushed to the brink no longer of fear with such ferocity charges a terrorist that the man freezes, cannot work the trigger, allowing Alwar to rain horror upon his trembling life. A bullet from out of nowhere skims Alwar's left arm, he turns, just in time to see a Beretta tumble and eyes bulge as wet crimson saturates the front of a blue and yellow Hawaiian shirt. A small silver handle protrudes from the man's jugular.

Having spent all of his ammunition the quiet man stands erect on the gym roof, identifies his target, sprints, and catapults almost three meters onto the terrorist who just killed Malik Said. The big man crashes face first to the fiberglass, on his back rides the angel of death, a bullet from his own gun flushing the killer into eternal night.

Gretchen a short time earlier thought herself a pillar of strength, and rightly so, not one to cower in the face of challenge she refused to take cover on the deck; now, front row witness to unimaginable bloodshed she possesses neither the physical fortitude nor the mental capacity for escape. The last surviving terrorist on the sundeck steps from the gym with a high caliber automatic rifle and selects the stationary upright old woman as his first victim. Gretchen stares silently into the face of her executioner, but, as a finger comes to rest on blue steel, a pauper, the uneducated son of poultry farm workers in the Central African Republic, from across the sundeck lets fly a soft seat cushion with such velocity that it jars the terrorist and allows Alwar the time necessary to leap and knock the aggressor to the deck.

Raheem soon is at Alwar's side subduing the fanatical psychopath as Klaus scours the deck for rope, twine, electrical wire, anything to bind the man's legs and arms. He can find nothing. "We can't just kill him and we can't let him go!" yells Raheem and Klaus yells back "And we can't send him over the side – he'll just return!" Several meters away sits Gretchen wrapped in Thomas' blazer; observing the fracas she finally stands up, walks over and says, "Give me a gun and I'll watch him." Klaus asks her if she knows how to use a handgun and she answers, "Yes, of course, I grew up in New York, and it wasn't Fifth Avenue!"

8:39 PM – Enchantress and Lightning Dancer hover motionless in the dark water. Jerome aboard the tender jiggles the key and flips the ignition. The two power plants purr. He lowers the canvas top and flashes the "okay" signal to Silvia. A woman and two men dressed completely in black and shouldering Tavor assault rifles emerge from the aft cabin door and silently assemble around Silvia and Sam. Silvia instructs them to follow her and as they pass Sam takes a hand, smiles, and wishes each "mazel tov." Silvia pauses at the railing, looks over the side into the small boat and its young captain softly illuminated by mast lights overhead, and gently lets him know "Jerome, we're ready."

Jerome jumps to Lightning Dancer's starboard side, grabs the rope and wood ladder dangling from Enchantress, and tugs until the bumpers touch the schooner. "Okay!" First down, Dee, introducing herself and politely requesting permission to board; "Um, yea, sure" responds Jerome, unaccustomed to such formality, "Sit anywhere, oh, and life jackets...." Next, Moshe, offering the same greeting, this time Jerome more prepared replies "Permission granted, please, sit anywhere, and put on a life jacket." Finally,

Simon receives permission to board, "Granted," well in advance of making the request.

Once all are securely seated, lines are released and stowed, except one, and Jerome pushes the throttle lever just slightly and rotates the wheel. Soon he can see Splendeur and applies more force to the lever, guesses the yacht's speed and distance, rotates, pushes, guesses a conservative triangular intercept course, rotates, flips off all the lights, jams the lever all the way forward, grabs the wheel with both hands and says a prayer.

At over sixty knots, one tiny slip of the wheel could send Lightning Dancer and all of her precious cargo into the abyss. Jerome clenches the wheel using all of his strength while choreographing the nine-meter bolt to an intercept point midway between a careening super yacht and a lethargic royal yacht. The formidable task at that point, bring Lightning Dancer alongside Splendeur – cruising at about twenty-five knots – and keep her there long enough for the Enchantress team to somehow board. They would first try the loading deck and swim platform at the stern; if that proved impossible, they would have to go in over the side.

8:40 PM – There was only one person aboard Splendeur, Paul had deduced by careful observation, capable of singlehandedly neutralizing Imoh and his enormous accomplice. Ty, the man who had killed the maniac threatening his wife and children, a brute, but more, street smart; as far as Paul was concerned, Ty was their only hope. Now, with a lull in the terrible gunfire, pounding, crashing, and screaming from above, and not knowing whether his wife and children were injured or even still alive, the time had come to implement his plan.

Imoh stands at the console between Paul and Ty, confident his troop of expert combatants has neutralized any minor uprising on the sundeck, watching with glee an ever-closer Saudi royal yacht. Paul clears his throat and, sounding of authority, instructs Ty to "turn the azimuth counter to ninety degrees, I think the port engine's getting a little warm." Imoh glances down at the gauges surrounding Paul and back to the horizon. Ty hesitates but soon fumbles with a couple of switches, rotating them one way, waiting a second, rotating them back, thereafter advising "Okay, ninety degrees, done" while silently worrying the instruction may have been legitimate.

Paul deliberately waits a few seconds and casually explains "You probably already know this, Ty, but sometimes one or two big pieces of sea crud get stuck in the azimuth and it makes it hard to turn," and after briefly hesitating, leans forward, turns his head, and declares with more force "and you have to remove that crud to make the turn."

Ty ponders Paul's words and, understanding, responds with a grin, "Hmm, so how do you get the crud out?"

"That" answers Paul awash in adrenalin, "is up to you."

Dark eyelids lower and using the back of his left hand Imoh slaps the right side of Paul's face and, when he does, Ty jams his left elbow into Imoh's right temple. Clutching Imoh's slouching body, Ty flips around, and pushes toward the imposing sentry. Using the body as a shield, Ty advances, all the while patting frantically to find Imoh's pistol holster. Paul begins to spin the wheel to the left and continues until it will go no farther; Splendeur lets out a shrill whine and the hull creaks and the super yacht lists far to starboard.

The guard tilts; bullets from his automatic rifle rake Imoh and the windscreen. Ty drives his wounded blockade into the guard, destabilizing the big man long enough to grab the rifle barrel with his left hand, and reaching with his right hand clenches the terrorist's broad neck at the trachea. The towering man lets loose with his right fist, catching Ty on the left side of his head, dislodging the rifle and windpipe. The guard tries to regain control of the rifle but Ty charges, pushing the man back into the door; the rifle drops to the floor, Ty strikes under the guard's chin with an upward thrust of his right palm and the guard's head slams the door. The guard wraps his left arm around Ty's neck and squeezes and Ty, with his head pressing against the man's chest, tries to push free but the guard reaches his right arm around and Ty's face turns red and Paul makes a dive for the rifle.

Seeing Paul advance, the guard tries to abruptly twist Ty's

head and break his neck, but Ty is too strong and continues pounding his fists against the big man's ribs until he finally releases his hold and reaches for the rifle. The three men embrace the weapon; Ty and the guard on opposite sides of the barrel, Paul at the stock, like a strange slow motion ballet they grapple when suddenly Ty lets go and the barrel jolts and Paul's right hand slips down the stock so he can pull on the trigger and, when he does, a flurry of rounds splatters the guard.

To the floor drop the guard and the rifle, and Paul and Ty wheezing, coughing, Paul crawling back to the captain's chair in dazed disbelief asks "Are they both dead?" and Ty nods, raises from the floor, and stumbles toward the windscreen.

"We're going in circles."

"Yea," replies Paul.

Ty turns to Paul, "Nice going by the way, now...," a deep breath, "I'm going out there and see what happened, maybe try to exterminate some more rodents, what are you going to do?"

Paul glances at Ty, "Take her out to sea, I suppose, it won't be long now before...," he stares through the windscreen and spins the wheel gradually to the right. Ty knows. What he does not know, whether they will first hear the sound or feel the infernal concussion.

8:43 PM – Jerome draws back the throttle lever. "They turned!" he yells; "They made a complete circle and are heading away from the ship!" His passengers jump up and peer over the windscreen. Mo asks Dee what she wants to do and she replies "Follow them, no, actually, intercept...let's stick to the mission parameters, I don't know what's going on, but something's still not right."

8:44 PM – "Sam, wait!" hollers Silvia; "Don't call the Saudi's yet, Splendeur turned, she's heading away from their boat, seems to be leaving Monaco...." Sam pauses at the door; "That's strange...what's the dancer boat doing?" "Still pursuing" answers Silvia with the binoculars at her face.

8:47 PM – The other guests and crewmembers quickly

transferred to the gym now sit quietly along the walls as those versed in firearms ready for an anticipated defense of the sundeck and an assault on the bridge. Klaus studies the steel magazine, "...four rounds, you?" "Two in this Beretta" replies Robert reclining against the railing, shirt bloodied, leg battered; "Six" answers Michelle, "and, I found my derringer"; Alwar pushes a magazine back into the AK-47 that almost killed Gretchen, "This thing's almost full;" "Six in here" says Raheem; "Three" the quiet man declares; "Two in this one" answers Hamidah; "Four, but this one's got three," Laurie accomplishes a slight smile while holding up two pistols. Around them a gruesome setting is made all the more shocking under a dazzling array of colorful party lights.

8:48 PM – Stars twinkle and a crescent moon glows in an otherwise black night sky over the Mediterranean Sea. The air, calm and cool, the ocean's surface, tranquil, just an occasional whitecap glistening under the lamps of passing vessels. From far above, gazing down, one could see four points of light: the brightest, a huge stationary yacht, its royal passengers peacefully unaware the surrounding turmoil; farther out to sea, the next brightest point, Splendeur, a glamorous moving stage on which courageous actors confront their destiny; the third brightest point of an equilateral triangle, Enchantress, also stationary, but unlike the royal yacht a cauldron of tension; and finally, the terminus of a wavy line from Enchantress and the least bright of the four points, only in terms of luminosity, soon succumbing to Splendeur's radiance.

Lightning Dancer trails a hundred meters behind Splendeur while Simon, Dee, and Moshe try to figure out where and how to climb aboard. "I can probably push us right up against the swim platform" Jerome confirms, "but it will be really, really rough with the wash." Simon asks about getting up close to the side; "Yea" replies Jerome with about the same degree of optimism, "not as rough, but how are you going to get the rope up?" Dee agrees, adding that, "if they spot us we'll be sitting ducks on a rope," from which she cannot help but follow up with "actually hanging ducks, we'll be sitting ducks in the boat, and we'll be standing ducks on the back deck!"

8:49 PM – Ty hovers in a shadowy corner of the bridge deck with a black AK-47 assault rifle most recently fired at its former owner. The bridge door is closed and locked. It is eerily calm.

8:50 PM – Kneeling on the sundeck by the stairs, Klaus listens, after less than a minute elevating only slightly and running hunched-over to the captured terrorist. He cocks the Ruger and places the muzzle on the man's forehead. Raheem, guarding the terrorist, takes a step forward but Klaus holds up his left hand in an unmistakable sign – "Don't!" Raheem stands still. Klaus confronts the terrorist in an intonation calm but firm: "I know you speak English; tell me, now, how many of your team came aboard." The man's head shakes furiously back and forth, "Je ne parle pas anglais, s'il vous plaît!" Alwar hears the man's plea and crawls forward; "Let me…" he says, and softly asks the man in French how many terrorists came aboard Splendeur. The man replies in French and Alwar slaps his face with the back of his left hand and yells something in French. The man says nothing. Alwar turns to Klaus expressing regret. Klaus grabs the terrorist and pushes him back against the railing. Others on the sundeck turn away. Klaus raises his right hand high to cave the man's left temple with the Ruger grip and the man screams out "Fourteen, there are fourteen, twelve here, two below!" Klaus lowers the gun and the man slumps to the deck.

8:51 PM – Ty heard the terrorist's desperate capitulation from above and considers various scenarios including that it could be the cheese in a most unpleasant trap; nevertheless, not willing to wait in the shadows all night, he jumps to the base of the stairway leading to the sundeck and judiciously takes two steps. The situation, a very difficult conundrum, he reexamines the bridge deck, listens again, and shouts "It's Ty, I'm alone; who's up there?" After a few seconds, "Ty, it's Klaus, clear up here, I'm coming down, meet me halfway." Ty perceives footsteps on the sundeck and stairs. He sees the dark silhouette of a man's legs and takes two more steps. Klaus takes one more step and Ty takes one step; soon the barrel of an assault rifle meets the muzzle of a Ruger. Both smile, and leap up the stairs.

8:53 PM – Klaus and Michelle follow Ty down the sundeck

stairs; he moves quickly at first, slowly while surveying the bridge deck, quickly across the fiberglass and wood to the bridge door. Klaus and Michelle are soon at his side, their backs to the wall, keenly observant of the many dark expanses. Once reasonably assured of no movement or sound, Ty presses the intercom button and asks Paul to unlock the door. Paul checks the monitor, captures Ty's wave, and opens the door to the rush of three anxious messengers; "What's going on, how are...?"

Michelle flashes a brief smile as her head shakes back and forth. "Your family is okay," she takes a breath, "most everyone else is alive. The terrorists may be eliminated...you took two here and we took twelve up there; our prisoner says there were a total of fourteen that came aboard."

Paul has the look of someone for whom there has been so much bad that good news is disturbing; "And you...?"

"Yes" interjects Klaus, "because the numbers match, twelve up there, two here, fourteen all together, besides, he seems to want to live."

8:55 PM – Paul, Ty, Klaus, and Michelle hastily discuss a prudent course under the extremely volatile circumstances and decide it would be best to anchor the yacht far away from other traffic, report the pirates and explosives, and promptly disembark in any way safely possible. They believe that with all of the terrorists incapacitated there is little danger of a triggered explosion and that, given the terrorists' objective, none of the bombs are on timed detonators.

9:00 PM – Paul and Ty – now priding himself an experienced first mate despite the lack of naval experience – begin to reduce Splendeur's speed as a general sense of relief settles in on the guests and crew. Paul calls out a mayday, "Yacht in distress, explosives on board, need quick passenger extraction by professional shore patrol or navy only," concluding with Splendeur's description and location. The message repeats three times. After the third transmission a woman's voice resonates from the speaker: "Motor yacht Splendeur, this is the schooner Enchantress, we're very close and can be there in about four minutes, we will send three boats to your stern loading deck, be ready to board." Silvia also notifies Jerome that Enchantress is going in with runabouts and suggests Lightning Dancer participate in the extraction.

9:01 PM – Simon notices something on the water moving toward Splendeur from the west. Whatever it is, it is not running lights. Jerome grabs a pair of binoculars and describes "a boat, with a cabin, going about ten knots, no lights...." Dee instantly screams "Go, go, go, go, intercept, go!" Jerome jumps, startled, grabs the throttle lever and leans in. Dee orders Simon and Mo to brace for a fight; "If I'm right" she yells over the engines with her left hand clenching the windscreen handhold, "it's a backup team, the terrorists on the yacht have been neutralized, these guys are going in for the kill!"

Robert rises to catch a view off the dreary sundeck and sees the dark cabin cruiser motoring toward Splendeur from less than a quarter kilometer away. "Klaus!" he shouts. Just stepping over the last sundeck stair Klaus jogs over to Robert, "What is it?" "Look," Robert points to the vessel. "Damn" exclaims Klaus, "more bad news, Alwar!" Alwar is in the gym with Sean, Jr. assisting people across the sundeck to the stairs and lifts; he pops out the door and asks loudly "What is it?" "Trouble, big trouble" Klaus yells back, "Bring your AK quick!" Robert advises that he can see what looks like a person holding a rocket launcher and even more excitedly "Wait, look, is that Jerome, that thing is flying!" The seven people now at the sundeck railing begin to cheer and scream and some even jump up and down.

Occupants of the dark boat have no time to react other than by discharging a few sacrificial rounds – Lightning Dancer passes directly across their bow at over sixty-five knots. Spray deluges and wake rattles. Jerome swivels the wheel without releasing the throttle; Simon almost goes overboard but Mo grabs him; Lightning Dancer straightens but hits a wave off-center and careens thirty meters through the air sideways; Jerome tries to spin the wheel back and the boat twists and bounces and within seconds is through the very center of the dark boat's hull. A cumulative gasp from the breathless spectators turns to mumbles of distress staring into the black. A flash of lightning brilliant is gone.

9:02 PM – Very faint the cries for help. At the sundeck railing a Beretta that Laurie's been clenching drops to the fiberglass. She asks if Logan can "drive a jet-ski" and when he starts to mutter something about Mexico she grabs his arm and yells "Follow me!" They race across the sundeck and down the stairs. The Enchantress is now clearly visible as are the three points of light leaving the schooner in their wash.

9:03 PM – Splendeur comes to a complete stop and Paul and Ty hurry to the sundeck. There, at the railing, Klaus is first to notice the two jet-skis speeding from around Splendeur's stern in a dead heat for the crash site. As they approach, one veers slowly toward the dark boat's fiery stern and the other slowly toward its bow. About fifty meters from the front of the severed hull, floats Lightning Dancer, upside down.

From the sundeck can be heard Logan combing the invisible for survivors; "Is anybody out there?" he pleads as arms reach out. "Here, I've got you" he tells a man, "hang onto the side." He steers cautiously around in the darkness hoping that his headlamp shines on survivors and not casualties. An arm waves and Jerome applies a slight throttle and the man clings to the foot rail. Another, a woman, "Can you hang on?" he asks; "Yes, I'm okay" she answers, "What about Jerome?" Logan shakes his head, "I don't know. Laurie's at the boat."

Laurie swerves, using the jet-ski's headlamp to search for Jerome around Lightning Dancer, until pulling alongside the overturned tender and diving into the black water. Spectators on Splendeur hold their breath as they know must she, all alone, swimming underwater into a cave of horrendous possibility. Laurie's arms reach out, fingers spread, feeling her way as bubbles float from her nose. Under the gunwale, up inside, walls all around, she floats into an air chamber gasping in pitch blackness. "Jerome" she pleads; "Are you here? Jerome...?"

Laurie's feet kick and her hands thrash and her left hand touches hair and a head; "Oh God" she cries and kicking harder lifts the head into the air chamber. She feels for a mouth and moves her mouth over a mouth and pinches a nose and exhales and pulls away and inhales and repeats the process over and over all the while having to keep them both afloat. But panic sets in. Blind in a constricting pocket of oxygen Laurie is afraid – maybe Jerome has drowned and she too will drown. The fear becomes so great that she panics and hyperventilates; it feels like she is underwater unable to exhale.

9:04 PM – "Breathe normal" the voice calmly says; "easy, relax, it's just an air tank regulator, just breathe normal, slow down, easy…." There are arms around Laurie, holding her up, she wants to get away, the panic, but the voice returns: "It's okay, we've got the other one, just be still and breathe, you're okay, and when you tell me you're ready, then we'll swim out of here, okay?" Laurie gives a little unseen nod and wraps her arms around the voice, breathes for a minute, and moves her head up and down. "Okay" the voice says, "I want you to just relax, don't try to swim, hold onto the regulator and let me do the swimming, this will only take a few seconds." Laurie nods again, takes hold of the regulator with her right hand, and keeps her left arm around the voice. In a matter of seconds she buoys to the surface and a world of lights.

9:05 PM – "I will just be a minute" Raheem tells Ty; "Please, let us be alone for just a minute, it will take you that long to get everybody else into the boats." Ty studies them both, tips his head, and descends the stairs. The arms and legs of the captured terrorist are bound tight with nylon rope wrapped around a steel support. "I am from the Central African Republic and I understand your cause" begins Raheem, "I know what is happening. Our people starve while the foreign companies and their shareholders grow rich from our oil and gold and diamonds. They destroy our land and pollute our land and water and use our people."

Raheem lowers his eyes; "I believe in your cause, but I don't believe in your methods, I don't believe killing is helping to fix the problem."

The terrorist is angry. "And how would you fix the problem my brother? Here, now, what have you done? We do not have the money to fight them in court or buy a leader who will fight them; it is all about money! We are poor people and we fight with what we have and what we have is our lives. That is all! On that big ship over there, rich people eat caviar while my sister sleeps on the dirt floor of a shack in Nigeria! Her babies go hungry and from their shack the stink of gas flares day and night – you tell me my way is wrong? There is no right and wrong in this world any more my brother. There are those who have and those who take. And the rest just give until there is no more to give."

Raheem draws a nine-millimeter Beretta from the holster under his left arm and with tears in his eyes says, "They will cage you like an animal when they come and you will spend the rest of your life locked in a small room. I don't think you want that."

The terrorist looks long into Raheem's eyes, "Thank you brother."

9:06 PM – Ty is not surprised by the sound; he finishes helping Gretchen into a boat, lowers his head, and smiles.

9:12 PM – Splendeur is alone and lifeless but from Enchantress the tremendous yacht appears to rule the waves. Her passengers huddle quietly together in the schooner's aft outdoor seating area; some on soft chairs, others on mats and towels. Silvia introduces herself and tells Enchantress' weary new guests that food is being prepared and cabins readied. Laurie asks about Jerome and is told he was taken below breathing on his own and that somebody is trying to find a hospital, but that in a few minutes emergency medical teams should be on hand. Certainly, Silvia concludes, "law enforcement people will scour Splendeur and want to talk with all of her passengers as soon as possible."

Paul approaches Silvia when she has finished and asks to speak with her alone. Passing through a door they descend into a dining and galley area and stop near a large table with booths where Silvia asks Paul if he wants something to drink. "No, thank you, um, I have a delicate situation..." – Silvia's eyebrows lower – "I need to get three people off this boat before the authorities arrive." Silvia's eyebrows raise; "A...okay, do you want to tell me why?" "No" answers Paul, "I would rather not. Let's just say, they are not...without some guilt...but none of us would be here now, alive, if it weren't for them. I ask this as a personal favor."

Silvia ponders the situation for a moment, "None of us is without some guilt...there is a small yellow boat at our stern that should have just enough gas left to make it ashore. The key might be in the ignition and I don't think it would be missed for several days. And then, well, it's just a small boat, hardly worth the effort."

9:13 PM – Robert uses his cell phone to call Sandy at Villa Palmera; he assures her that everything is fine, that he is okay, and explains there will be news coverage and she should defer any requests from reporters to him. Lastly, they make arrangements for Gilbert and her to spend the next day with Michelle, Klaus, and him in Monte-Carlo.

9:14 PM – Ty, Raheem, and the quiet man stand near the swim platform getting ready to board the small yellow boat. In a peculiar procession, Klaus, Alwar, Paul, Michelle, Hamidah, Robert, and Gretchen pass by three of their former captors, clasping hands offering gratitude and best wishes. After Paul bids Ty farewell he finds an inexpensive flip cell phone and a miniature digital audio recorder in his right palm.

Paul responds with a smile and "Good luck captain."

"God Speed!" shouts Klaus as the boat pulls away.

"Look for me in Belize!" yells Ty back.

From the Enchantress main deck almost all Splendeur guests and crewmembers wave until the small yellow boat vanishes in the distance.

12:16 AM Friday – Flipping remotely through the six o'clock news channels with the audio on mute, Glenda hesitates at the photograph of a beautiful blue and white yacht over the caption "Terrorism on High Seas." She presses the mute button and listens: "...owned by Paul DuMorell, chief executive officer of DigiFouré Telecom, a French company that recently raised two hundred and fifty million dollars through an international private placement. Sources in Monaco close to the investigation tell us that fourteen terrorists boarded the yacht on Wednesday and that the passengers and crew were able to overcome them by late Thursday. There are reports of multiple casualties including several of the passengers and all fourteen of the terrorists. The terrorists' motives appear to have included a ransom, but exactly how the passengers and crew were able to overpower fourteen heavily-armed terrorists is still unclear. We'll keep you updated as events unfold." Glenda presses the mute button and stares in astonishment at the television screen. After several seconds the caption changes to "Business News" followed by "Kragen Industries buys British telecommunications company." Glenda flips the channel; "Aw, who cares about that Heidi."

Morning unfolded in a world of perfection for Alwar; first, being alive, and more, a ray of sunlight through a porthole on his face, then enjoying a shower followed by a breakfast of fried eggs and sourdough toast, and finally stepping on deck, this time not to the sound of sails rippling taught in a firm breeze, but to the faces of men, women and children free from the bonds of tyranny.

Klaus approached Alwar as he stood by the railing enjoying deep breaths of cool fresh air; "I hear you're staying on!"

"Yes" Alwar confirmed with a grin; "Silvia and Mr. Baer asked if I could, would like to, as long as I want since...." He seemed for several seconds to forget what he was saying. "Um, after Israel we go back to New York and then in several weeks down the east coast of America and through the Panama Canal; they said we would travel along Mexico to Los Angeles, California. I've never been any of these places. I can't wait!"

"Well," Klaus smiled, "Robert, Michelle and I are going to a race and then home..." he hesitated and reached out his right hand, "I just wanted to say it's been an honor, and I hope we get the chance to meet again, preferably over a cold drink on a warm sailboat."

Alwar laughed, "And for me also! I owe you this day and all to come – be well, and remember you've got a friend."

Logan, Patricia, and Sean, Jr. were seated around an outdoor dining table behind the wheel when Klaus, Robert and Michelle strolled by on their way to the tender; they all talked for a minute until Michelle caught a glimpse of Hamidah downstairs in the main dining salon. "I'll just be a minute" she alerted Robert and dashed down the stairs.

Michelle and Hamidah hugged and cried and exchanged business cards, but Hamidah's façade of serenity eventually could not overcome her sorrow and shame. "Ali's father will be here today to get the body" she told Michelle, "I don't think I can face him after what I...."

Michelle stopped Hamidah: "You face him and stand tall Hamidah. Ali died bravely fighting terror to save your life, he didn't die for money or fame or something you did, he died for you, that's how much he believed in and cared for you. Live your life affirming him and his belief, and remember what that woman said, *all good people* are riddled with flaws."

As soon as Michelle, Robert, and Klaus arrived in Monaco they went to the Centre Hospitalier Princesse Grace and found Jerome's room. There sat Laurie at his side, laughing, as was Jerome. "Excuse us!" Robert announced with a tap to the open door; "Are you accepting any other, just regular, visitors?" he quipped with a smile. Jerome yelled "Sure!" and waved them in as Robert continued, "We just wanted to come by and say hi and tell you that if we ever need a speedboat captain...." "It will be anybody but you!" Klaus teasingly concluded. The three stayed for about five minutes, chatting and laughing, leaving with a warm "so long" to convey their gratitude to Moshe and Dee on the same floor.

Afterward, just beyond the hospital main entrance, Michelle asked Robert and Klaus if they were attending any of the services. Klaus confirmed he would be going to Malik Said's service in Turkey but that was all; "I can only take one funeral a month." Robert offered that he would be attending the service for Mr. Said and also wanted to express his gratitude to Simon's family in Tel Aviv but was not sure if that would be possible; "I may just send flowers and a note."

"I wonder if Jerome knows...," Michelle knew the answer but said the words as way of expressing grief.

The three looked toward the concrete.

"He's awfully young for that much reality" said Klaus.

"He'll need support...Laurie" added Robert.

They walked in silence for two blocks until surrounded by joyful people only a little less raucous than the Formula One cars speeding by a short distance beyond. "Man, do I need a drink!" bellowed Klaus; "Me too!" shouted Michelle; "Where do we buy tickets?" hollered Robert. Soon, the three friends were back in a ring of happiness – eating, drinking, laughing and frolicking within a vanilla peach playground bounded by dark green hills and the deep blue sea.

CPSIA information can be obtained
at www.ICGtesting.com
Printed in the USA
FSOW04n2348040615
7678FS